TRAVEL THE MANY DIMENSIONS OF WONDER

Journey beyond the limits of your imagination with master storyteller Charles Beaumont as your guide. Inside you'll find

> —an infernal bouillabaisse
> —a world where plainness is forbidden
> —a graveyard's revenge
> —a strange *thing* found by the riverbank
> —a deadly dream and a foolproof murder

PLUS more than a dozen more voyages into the mind including two tales "Insomnia Vobiscum" and "Three Thirds of a Ghost," published here for the first time in any form.

"Charles Beaumont was a writer of ideas, notions, fancies. . . . There he is, out in the middle of the play yard, yelling with delight, chuckling at ideas, building his castle of metaphors, and all too obviously enjoying what he does. . . . What he would have done with his talent had he lived another ten or twenty years, one can only guess."

RAY BRADBURY, from his *Introduction*

D1287905

Bantam Science Fiction and Fantasy
Ask your bookseller for the books you have missed

BABEL-17 by Samuel R. Delany
THE BALLAD OF BETA-2 by Samuel R. Delany
THE BEGINNING PLACE by Ursula K. Le Guin
DARKWORLD DETECTIVE by J. Michael Reaves
DRAGONDRUMS by Anne McCaffrey
DHALGREN by Samuel R. Delany
THE EINSTEIN INTERSECTION by Samuel R. Delany
EYAS by Crawford Killian
THE FALL OF THE TOWERS by Samuel R. Delany
THE GLASS OF DYSKORNIS by Randall Garrett and
   Vicki Ann Heydron
THE GREY MANE OF MORNING by Joy Chant
HELLSTROM'S HIVE by Frank Herbert
HOMEWORLD by Harry Harrison
THE HUMANOID TOUCH by Jack Williamson
THE JEWELS OF APTOR by Samuel R. Delany
JEM by Frederik Pohl
THE KALEVIDE by Lou Goble
LORD VALENTINE'S CASTLE by Robert Silverberg
MAN PLUS by Frederik Pohl
MOCKINGBIRD by Walter Tevis
NEVERYONA by Samuel R. Delany
NOVA by Samuel R. Delany
SONG OF SORCERY by Elizabeth Scarborough
THE STAINLESS STEEL RAT FOR PRESIDENT by
   Harry Harrison
STARWORLD by Harry Harrison
SUNDIVER by David Brin
TALES OF NEVERYON by Samuel R. Delany
TIME STORM by Gordon Dickson
TRITON by Samuel R. Delany
VOYAGERS by Ben Bova
WHEELWORLD by Harry Harrison
THE WINDHOVER TAPES by Warren Norwood

BEST OF BEAUMONT
by Charles Beaumont

With an Introduction by
Ray Bradbury

MIDDLEBURY COLLEGE LIBRARY

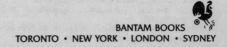
BANTAM BOOKS
TORONTO • NEW YORK • LONDON • SYDNEY

PS
3552
.E2
A6
1982

4/1983
gen-l

BEST OF BEAUMONT
A Bantam Book / December 1982

All rights reserved
Copyright © 1982 by Charles Beaumont.
Cover art copyright © 1982 by Dave Passalacqua, Jr.

COPYRIGHT NOTICES AND ACKNOWLEDGMENTS

The copyright notices are listed below and on the next page, which constitutes an extension of this copyright page.

"The Infernal Bouillabaisse", copyright © 1957 by Charles Beaumont (never appeared in magazine form—originally appeared in "The Hunger & Other Stories," published by G.P. Putnam's).

"The Beautiful People", copyright 1952 by Charles Beaumont. Originally appeared in *IF Magazine*.

"Free Dirt", copyright © 1955 by Fantasy House, Inc. Originally appeared in *Fantasy and Science Fiction*.

"Fritzchen", copyright 1953 by Charles Beaumont. Originally appeared in *Orbit Magazine*.

"You Can't Have Them All", copyright © 1956 by Charles Beaumont. Originally appeared in *Playboy*.

"Mother's Day", copyright © 1958 by Charles Beaumont.

"Last Rites", copyright © 1955 by Charles Beaumont. Originally appeared in *IF Magazine*.

"Blood Brother", copyright © 1961 by Charles Beaumont. Originally appeared in *Playboy*.

"The New People", copyright © 1958 by Charles Beaumont. Originally appeared in *Rogue Magazine*.

"Father, Dear Father", copyright © 1956 by Charles Beaumont. Originally appeared in *Venture Science Fiction* as "Oh Father of Mine".

"A Classic Affair", copyright © 1955 by Charles Beaumont. Originally appeared in *Playboy*.

"Perchance to Dream", copyright © 1958 by Charles Beaumont. Originally appeared in *Playboy*.

"The Customers", copyright © 1957 by Charles Beaumont (never appeared in magazine form—originally appeared in "The Hunger & Other Stories", published by G.P. Putnam's).

"Hair of the Dog", copyright © 1954 by Charles Beaumont. Originally appeared in *Orbit Magazine*.

"Insomnia Vobiscum", copyright © 1982 (never published previously).

"The Crooked Man", copyright © 1955 by Charles Beaumont. Originally appeared in *Playboy*.

"The Jungle", copyright © 1954 by Charles Beaumont. Originally appeared in *IF Magazine*.

"Sorcerer's Moon", copyright © 1959 by Charles Beaumont. Originally appeared in *Playboy*.

"The Trigger", copyright © 1958 by Charles Beaumont. Originally appeared in *Mystery Digest Magazine*.

"The Love-Master", copyright © 1956 by Charles Beaumont. Originally appeared in *Rogue Magazine*.

"Three Thirds of a Ghost", copyright © 1982 (never published previously).

"Place of Meeting," copyright © 1953 by Charles Beaumont. Originally appeared in *Orbit Magazine*.

This book may not be reproduced in whole or in part, by mimeograph or any other means, without permission. For information address: Bantam Books, Inc.

ISBN 0-553-22760-2

Published simultaneously in the United States and Canada

Bantam Books are published by Bantam Books, Inc. Its trademark, consisting of the words "Bantam Books" and the portrayal of a rooster, is Registered in U.S. Patent and Trademark Office and in other countries. Marca Registrada. Bantam Books, Inc., 666 Fifth Avenue, New York, New York 10103.

PRINTED IN THE UNITED STATES OF AMERICA

O   0 9 8 7 6 5 4 3 2 1

Contents

Beaumont Remembered
Ray Bradbury

The facts have been written before. In the summer of 1946, when I was 26, a sixteen-year-old boy bumped into me in Fowler Brothers Book Store in downtown Los Angeles, and began babbling about his *Terry and the Pirates* comic collection, plus *Tarzan*, plus *Prince Valiant*, plus who-can-remember-now how many other truly amazing and life-enhancing subjects.

It could only follow, out of such a passionate encounter, that a friendship developed like those stop-motion films of flowers speeded up from seed to stem to full blossom in ten seconds flat. I invited Charles Beaumont, for that was the young man's name, over to gaze at my *Buck Rogers* Sunday color panels. He trotted along his somewhat dog-eared copies of *Terry* and his irresistible *Pirates*. We made some trades, and moved on into a friendship that would last until his untimely death twenty years later.

What followed over the years was joy in the sandbox, or, if you prefer, tomorrow is New Year's so what does that make *today*?—a celebration! For Chuck there were no cries of *"Thank God, It's Friday."* It was always the long weekend, as it was with me, when some new love occupied, hell, preoccupied the senses and delivered us forth to worlds where nothing else existed except our creatures and our architectures. Our friendship leaned half in and half out of cinema long shots, comic-strip surrealistic closeups, carnival magicians, old radio shows, and longlegging it to ancient bookstores for a hyperventilating snuff of book dust. If I had allowed them, dogs might have followed me down the street. I didn't know where I was going, but it was sure great going there. Which is what dogs and budding writers are all about. Chuck was the same, save the dogs *did* dance about him, and friends...too many, perhaps. They used up his air. In the end, it might be true, he dispensed so much creative and conversational energy that there was none left over to fight any disease that chanced to dart in. But, all that comes later.

First, after a series of jobs, working for United Parcel delivery services, and finally in the music-copying department at Universal Studios, Chuck showed up at my house one night in the early fifties with his first short story. He handed it over, his face flushed with excitement, and cried, "It's good! Or—I *think* it is!"

I read the story, cried:

"Good, hell; it's fine!"

I sent the story out to an editor. It sold.

Bombed into super-activity by the sale, Chuck wrote dozens more, hundreds more, over the years. I often use him as an example to other young writers. It *does* work. Writing, that is, a story a week for a year, three years, ten years! You can't help but get better every single week of every single year. Chuck got better.

Better at what?

He was, and remains in his work today, a writer of ideas, notions, fancies. You can tell his ideas to your friends in a few crisp lines. He is a story-teller who weaves his stories out of those ideas, some large, or, you may claim, predominantly small.

No matter. At least the seeds are there, as they have rarely been since Poe got lost in the snow, Melville sank from view, shipwrecked on land, or Nathaniel Hawthorne invented a mechanical butterfly to be promptly destroyed. For, remember, those American writers of the 19th century were, one and all, idea folks. Slap their backs and they spat cosmic seeds.

The years between 1830 and 1900 were brimful of metaphor, chock full of nuts, fruits, and, if not sublime Holy Ghosts, at least headless horsemen ruining your midnight sleep, but delighting your tranquil noons.

Charles Beaumont, if not equal, is at least heir to these, even as most of us in the science fantasy field have felt ourselves to be their lost sons.

You can, in sum, remember Beaumont's ideas long after the stories slide away into yesterday. Compare this with trying to *tell* the ideas of Hemingway, Faulkner, or Steinbeck. In Faulkner's case, the metaphor, while present, is lost in place, time, and character, if not completely sunk in an endless timbercut of words.

You cannot remember or describe Steinbeck's *Grapes of Wrath* or his *The Long Valley* in terms of metaphor. What you warmly recall is well-rendered scene, blooded people. The Joads may well be, and are indeed, symbols for us on our way somewhere, toward a future, every dawn, settling at dusk to dream it better than it happened three hours ago. But we rarely deep-think Steinbeck. We deep-feel him, and arrive at our thoughts later.

So it is with Hemingway, and the mob of imitators who have flooded his wake since 1929. His metaphors are obvious, but the bullfight is too easily symbolic, as is the running of the Pamplona bulls, or the shooting of the white hunter in lost Africa. Again, we remember places, people, but none of Hemingway's characters go anywhere, even though they move. They do little to change time, or the architecture of anyone's future, even their own. They stand still while traveling, and die dumb, not knowing where they've been or how it all happened. Paco, who gets a kitchen knife in his belly, in Hemingway's masterful "The Capital of the World," represents them all. He sees his blood on the floor and wonders how it got there. Why *him*?

Jules Verne's characters, more primitive, of course, nevertheless deliver idea-talk. They live metaphor more grandly and uniquely. It is boy-chat yes, but Verne's metaphors span the globe and land us on the Moon. Listen to Verne; he really moves your mind, heart, soul, body, and blood. Listen to Papa and you fire your gun at a sky where you think there are birds, but none exist.

Verne's characters *make* things happen. If their blood falls on the ship's planking or the rocket's hull, they know the reason why, and are not afraid to say it. Nemo is out to sink the world's armadas, and thus sink War. He is the metaphor of Peace, dreadfully personified.

Beaumont, it follows, is closer kin to Verne and Hawthorne than he is to Hemingway or most of the writers who have come up through the Forties, Fifties, and Sixties of our time.

Am I claiming that Charles Beaumont is the equal of or superior to those giants? No, I only say that while those large talents strode deeply, Beaumont gives better companionship. He's more fun because he is the neglected thing in our present society: the idea-writer.

Now consider this. America is *the* Idea culture of all time. Our fancies have fulfilled an Industrial Revolution, split the atom, delivered us to the Moon, and promised us incredible futures stored and delivered forth by computers. Yet how ironic it is to prowl your local bookstore only to find the average novel hip-deep in dishwater and dull as soapsuds. Among one hundred best sellers, hardly one with a ghost of a fancy, or half the spirit of a notion. Ideas, stillborn, everywhere.

Here is where Beaumont, and many another science fiction writer today, takes over, even if at a minor level. Offer his stories to school kids, then watch them toss his notions, at play. His metaphors are fresh, vivid, irresistible.

Hand Hemingway's Spanish toreros or African cowards to most students, and they will be hard put to do their own variations. Same with the Joads in their rickety Ford, heading out of the dust into the sunset. Same with Faulkner's Hound. Their stuff, great and beautiful as it is, cannot be hurled at students, hot after literature, seeking the right corn to drop in their heads to make the Ideas pop.

Idea is everything. So say most modern science-fiction and fantasy writers, who stand as true avant-garde forces at the center of writing today. So says Beaumont. Ricochet one of his ideas around a classroom, and crack a dozen variations within minutes. If you want children to read, Beaumont cries, for God's sake bomb them with Revelations! Give them a chance to join the author's game, feel smart, guess themselves into creation.

The stories gathered here prove my point.

Beaumont plays a game for himself, but invites *you* in. His stories are four-man basketball teams; you are the fifth player. Often, you feel that you've won the game yourself, because you write your own version of Beaumont's metaphor. Which is what makes him, finally, such fun.

How can you resist a story like his "The Beautiful People," in which we find a world where everyone has been made over to beauty, where all bodies are perfect, all faces cookie-stamped to handsome-lovely? Then, what happens? One revolutionary girl, one soul, stands up and refuses to be operated on, cookie-stamped, changed!

Okay, class, in the next hour, write your *own* variation on *that*!

Haven't we all, at one time or another, been more in love with a car than any girl who rode in the car with us? Read

"The Classic Affair," then remember yourselves. Write your own endings, happy or sad.

Or how about a vampire complaining to his psychiatrist about the high cost of being a night-stalker, financing a coffin, keeping his shirts clean, hating blood, being afraid of bats?

Ready, class? Begin!

Quickly, now, idea after idea, story after story, a summation of metaphors.

Write me a tale about when Mr. Death comes to visit, obviously in the guise of a cemetery-plot salesman.

Write me another about a man who invents a Time Machine so he can shuttle back and shoot his own father, thus causing his own suicide or—what?

Imagine the most unusual and the most frightening baby monster you can possibly imagine, make it grow, call it "Fritzchen," scare the hell out of yourself and thus—scare the hell out of me.

Every single one of these stories is the fox in the hen yard, stirring up a cackle and flurry of ideas among those students fortunate enough to read and react to them.

An aside here. Chuck and I lived in the same Los Angeles territory, where we both passed a cemetery which sported a hand-painted sign: "Free Dirt." This intrigued me so much over the years that I jotted notes in a file folder and commenced a story based on the idea of cemetery earth. What would happen if you bought and *used* it? For *what*?

Then Chuck showed up at the house one night with a story titled—you've guessed it—"Free Dirt."

I read it and threw up my hands. "Okay, it's *yours*! You did it first! Someday I may revise my "Free Dirt" yarn, but, for now—mail this out!"

Chuck laughed, sent out his story, sold it. My story remains in the file. Chuck's earned the right to no competition in the stretch. Why? Because he was having fun.

I realize what a risk I take by daring to use the truly operative word Fun here. It could well label Charles Beaumont and damn him to hell amongst the agonizers and intellectual duck-pressers of the world. For, as you have noticed, you simply *must* agonize for them. If you do not sweat blood by the pint or the jeroboam, if you do not think loud and long or silent and heavy, and show traces of the sunken pit and the glorious masochism of the *litterateur* on your faces, you, sir, you, madam, are *not* a writer. Your novel took twenty years of

nailing yourself to the cross over your typewriter? Splendid!
You say that you revised your short story eighty-nine times,
and are *still* not happy with it? Superb! Your three-act drama
was in and out of your eyeballs and down on paper through
ten thousand revisions! The Croix de Guerre is yours. But
don't be surprised if you trip over copies of your boring books
as you leave the house. Literature? No. Doorprops is more
like it.

I don't know when the masochistic, brooding, oh God it's
torture, O Jesus will it never end, kind of writing, or inter-
pretation of writing, got its start. It smacks of Byron, but I'm
sure he had more schnapps. Joyce's *"Ulysses"* inspired a run
on tedium as life-style. Katherine Anne Porter's "Ship of Fools"
poured concrete around tens of thousands of hopefuls' novels
and sank them without a sound.

So Charles Beaumont is terribly suspect. There he is, out
in the middle of the play yard, yelling with delight, chuckling
at ideas, building his castle metaphors, and all too obviously
enjoying what he does.

Unforgivable.

Let's have no laughter here, no smiles. No roars of welcome as an end-of-the-line caboose-idea changes to a locomotive-
front-running metaphor and knocks the happy author flying,
glad to be hurled, knocked into creativity.

For that's the grandest memory I have of Chuck. He would
call to shout over the phone: Listen to *this*! Or he'd sit in our
front parlor with mobs of friends, and read a story, or quote
the framework, and beam and flash his thick glasses, "Okay,
gang?" Then we'd all pitch in.

Sometimes, of an evening, Richard Matheson would toss
up the merest dustfleck of notion, which would bounce off
William F. Nolan, knock against George Clayton Johnson,
glance off me, and land in Chuck's lap. Before anyone could
grab or knock it again, Chuck would outline the rest of the
tale, sketch in the characters, butter and cut the sandwich,
beginning, meat-middle, and end. *Voila!* Applause.

Sometimes we all loved an idea so much we had to assign it
to that writer present who showed the widest grin, the
brightest cheeks, the most fiery eyes. More often than not,
that was Chuck.

What Charles Beaumont would have done with his talent
had he lived another ten or twenty years, one can only guess.
And that is a cruel and sad business, for I would imagine that,

with his sensational curiosity, he would have grown into a half-dozen new fields.

His life revolved around a special desk which he had designed and had built by one of the finest cabinetmakers in the West. His files were beautifully stashed, labeled, and stuffed with a half-million notions, idle fancies, half-grown or full-blown dreams, most of it the result of our first encounters when I had urged, no, goaded him to write one short story a week for the rest of his life. And he had promptly, by God, done so!

We have often wondered, his friends and I, if his very frenzy, his fire, didn't take a final great breath and blow that same fire out. It must remain idle conjecture. I have no easy answers. I admired and envied him while he lived, and suffered his absence when he moved away into illness and death.

Where Charles Beaumont's reputation will be by the end of the century, I cannot say. I am too fiercely involved with his life, too immersed in his travails as a beginner, too proud of his successes in the brief years before he was stopped. I would certainly place many of his stories in the good company of John Collier and Roald Dahl. Which may or may not be a downer to certain critics who have never been able to enjoy those two authors as I have. No matter. Collier, on at least three occasions, told me of the pleasure he took in reading much of Beaumont. That's good enough for me.

Now, on to the end.

Funerals are always ironic, no matter what the weather. If it's raining, that's too much: the sky weeps. If the sun is bright, that's worse. It kills the heart when you stand there in the blaze. Whoever is in the grave, you imagine, hates your living soul for being up and about. Or so you imagine, anyway. The friends of Charles Beaumont, at graveside, felt all the above, and more. We felt, above all, that a time was over, and things would never be the same. Our old group would meet less often, and then fall away. What was central to it, the binding force, the conversational fire, the great runner, jumper, and yeller, was gone. None of us felt up to taking his place. We wouldn't have dared. And, trying, we would have failed.

It was, indeed, never the same after that.

We all went our separate ways from the burial ground, stayed in touch, made new liaisons, occasionally dined together, and watched as Charles Beaumont's books and stories began to move toward the edge of that damned pit and fall in. It wasn't right.

Now all that has stopped. No more vanishing books, no more burials. Here are his stories, back in the light on, I hope, some permanent basis.

This selection is, of course, incomplete. I am dissatisfied, because there are at least a dozen stories I would have liked to have included. Others among you will protest, no, there are *three* dozen stories left out; how come?

That will have to wait.

If this collection is popular, there can be another, and another, in years to come. And I will be happy to preface the lot.

For now, here's Charles Beaumont. *My* cup of tea. Is he *yours*?

Ray Bradbury
Los Angeles, California
July 28th, 1981

BEST OF BEAUMONT

The Infernal Bouillabaisse

"I like to think of our stomachs," Mr. Frenchaboy said, in conclusion, "as small but select museums, to which a new treasure should be added at least once a day. We are all curators, gentlemen; and I believe that we ought to be careful to maintain our gastronomic establishments in the best possible taste. No cheap reproductions! No penny-a-lot artifacts of dubious origin! But, instead, only the finest, the *crème de la crème: shared one with all*." He sent a sharp look in the direction of Mr. Edmund Peskin, and adjusted his bifocals. "The exhibits themselves," he said, "may not linger long in our museums. But the memory of them is a lasting pleasure. Thank you."

Mr. Frenchaboy nodded to gloved and spiritless applause and made his way to the dinner table. Once he had seated himself, a hundred napkins flew listlessly into a hundred laps and seven expressionless men in velvet jackets entered the hall bearing trays.

The meal, if it mattered, which it didn't, was a masterpiece. Mr. Frenchaboy had begun preparations five weeks previous and worked himself into a nervous tic over the selection. Why? He could not say. Force of habit, perhaps, a blind refusal to admit that there was no point to the Gourmet's Club any more. Honeycomb Tripe à la Creole had been the first thought. It might have been a good thought, too, except that Peskin had written a monograph on the subject—damn and damn him! Braised Pigeons on Croutons followed, but this was a rather pedestrian choice, and where could one get the right sort of mushrooms these days? Rapidly, he'd hit upon and rejected Roasted Saddle of Young Boar, Steamed Chicken Mère Fillioux, Sweetbreads à la Napolitaine, Cock

3

in Vintage Wine, Chicken in Half Mourning, and Escargots à la Frenchaboy; all unworthy. As time had grown shorter, he'd become desperate—almost as in the old, pre-Peskin days! —wandering the house in a half-daze, muttering recipes aloud: Sauté of Baby Armadillo, Gizzards of Lizards in Sauce Bearnaise, Pie of Bull's Cojones, minced, Brain of Veal à la Mustafa, Suckling Pig with Eels—but when he would hit upon something pleasant, he would remember Peskin's Bouillabaisse, and then he would turn the color of a broiled lobster.

At last, ill with weakness—for in preparing the feast he had neglected to eat—he sent a cable to a friend in South America, requesting immediate delivery of two healthy young llamas. The llamas arrived, and were carefully slaughtered by Mr. Frenchaboy himself and put on ice. On the day of the semi-annual meeting of the Gourmet's Club, of which he was president, he placed the animals in a Mexican pot of hard wattle and allowed them to simmer for five hours.

Fricasee of Llama; Truffles de Chambéry; Gazpacho of Malaga: a chef d'oeuvre, indeed, to the most exacting! Mr. Frenchaboy had blended the tastes, the sharp and the mellow, as a fine artist blends colors; and the result was an addling mixture of dark and light, overwhelming as a late Goya, exotic as Gauguin, humbling as Tintoretto. But Mr. Frenchaboy did it all automatically, with less than half a heart. The spirit was not in him. It was not in any of them.

Even as he sat discreetly spooning the last traces of Sorbet de Champagne, he knew; and the knowledge made him sadder than if he had been ordered onto a lifetime diet of enchiladas and bottled pop.

"Magnificent, Frenchaboy," they said, when the meal was over; and, "Frenchaboy, really, you know, you have outdone yourself!" but he knew what they were thinking.

They were thinking, it was all very excellent, old man, but how can we be genuinely enthusiastic over anything after having tasted Peskin's Bouillabaisse? Don't fret, though: he has reduced all of our best efforts to second rate. One must, after all, go on, mustn't one?

No, Mr. Frenchaboy thought, suddenly: one mustn't. Because one can't. For two years, ever since the blasted meal was first served up, I've been at him. I've made every appeal to the man's sense of good sportsmanship, even going to the length of *asking* him, in so many words, for the recipe. And how he strutted then! Miserable peacock, how he smirked and danced and made it clear to us all that we would get the Bouillabaisse only when he might deign to let us; when and if... Disgusting! Mr. Frenchaboy glared at the large man at the end of the table and fumed, quietly. Peskin. A rank amateur, and not a very gifted one at that, before the trip to Africa or wherever the devil it was that he went; then, magically, with that one dish, shooting to the very forefront of the Club, holding them all in thrall, enchanting and tantaliz-ing them, and destroying their morale—

Of course, it had occurred instantly to Mr. Frenchaboy that Peskin had resorted to some sort of jiggery-pokery with human flesh; and so—at considerable risk, and with little real hope—he had tried fillets of deceased chauffeur; but it was patently not the answer. No: The secret did not wholly lie in the ingredients, however rare some of them might be: breast of condor, he detected, Alsatian rat tails, et cetera; it lay also in the mixture. And finding this through trial and error was an impossible task. Mr. Frenchaboy knew. He had tried. Simple enough! Peskin had found the *perfect* combination, probably by accident, and had every intention of holding it over their heads indefinitely. And so they would go on being second-raters, for it was true: Nothing could rival (and his mouth began to water as he thought of it) the Bouillabaisse à la Peskin. . . .

"Delicious," a last voice said, insincerely. "My compliments."

The members filed out the door, a disconsolate cortège all but the red-faced fellow, and soon Mr. Frenchaboy was left as alone as a stick of dynamite in an empty warehouse.

He sat down and put his head on his arms.

Dying, he thought: We are dying, thanks to that insuffer-able ass of a Peskin. Oh—I would do anything to bring back the enthusiasm, the éclat, the downright fizz that were the hallmarks of the club!

He looked up. "Anything?" a small, silent voice inquired.

And Mr. Frenchaboy answered, silently: "Anything."

"Then," inquired the voice, "what are you waiting for?"

Mr. Frenchaboy sighed. "He's too well known. I'd be caught. They'd hang me."

"Not," said the voice, "necessarily."

Mr. Frenchaboy listened. Then he went home and got his wallet and his small .32 revolver, and drove to the home of Edmund Peskin.

He knocked.

"Yes?"

"Peskin," Mr. Frenchaboy said, stepping inside, "I will be candid. The Club is not pleased with you."

"Ah?"

"The Club," Mr. Frenchaboy said, more strongly, "is, in fact, not pleased at all."

"I can't imagine what you're talking about."

"Simply this. It has been an unspoken rule with us for twenty years that all recipes are to be shared. Yet you have insisted upon withholding the secret to your Bouillabaisse. Why?"

"That," Edmund Peskin said, "is, I think, my affair. I suggest that you tend to your pots and pans, and I'll tend to mine."

Mr. Frenchaboy turned red. "You refuse to share the secret?"

"Exactly."

"Very well. In that case, I have little choice." Mr. Frenchaboy withdrew a large wallet from his breast pocket. "What is your price?"

The large man looked at the wallet, and drew himself to his full stature. "I am not remotely interested in your crass offer," he said. "There is only one copy of the recipe for Bouillabaisse à la Peskin in existence, and it reposes in my wall safe—where it shall remain. You are wasting your time and mine. Good night."

Peskin turned on his heel and started for the library.

He never reached it.

The report of the revolver sent Mr. Frenchaboy stone deaf for a moment; he trembled; then, ears ringing, he walked over to the still form on the rug, aimed carefully, and pulled the trigger twice more.

The safe proved to be a flimsy affair: relatively little gunpowder was required to blow it apart.

Within, there was a single sheet of paper, folded and tied with a blue ribbon. Mr. Frenchaboy had barely enough time to memorize the contents and burn the paper when the knocking began at the door.

"Come in, gentlemen," he called.

They took him to jail at once, on suspicion of murder. But, for all the brutality of his crime, Mr. Frenchaboy was a model prisoner, polite to the guards and uncomplaining of his gray situation. It is true that he fasted, but he made no fuss over it.

Slow days plodded upon slow days. The trial was conducted in a peremptory manner, and Mr. Frenchaboy was found guilty as charged and sentenced to hang; yet he bore up with a stolidity and good humor unmatched in the history of the great stone pile. Of him they said: "He's a cool one, all right. Headed for the rope and he still makes jokes. It's eerie!"

Eerie or not, there seemed nothing that could destroy the little man's imperturbability. He whistled loudly, read an astonishing number of cookbooks, and slept like a lamb before the slaughter.

To the members of the Gourmet's Club who visited him, he said only: "Eat well, my friends; the menace is gone!" and "Don't worry. They'll not hang me."

And so it went, for two months, during which time Mr. Frenchaboy ate only fresh bread and drank pure water.

On the third month, third Tuesday night, a group of somber men came into his cell. "Frenchaboy," they said, "it is almost time."

"Quite so," Mr. Frenchaboy said, with a twinkle in his eyes.

"Are you ready?"

"Doesn't that seem a rather pointless question?"

The somber men looked at one another. One of them came forward. "Have you nothing to say?" he asked.

"Nothing," Mr. Frenchaboy said. "And you?"

The man shook his head. "Although it is doubtful that you can have much of an appetite," he intoned, "you are, of course, entitled to your choice of menu for this evening's meal."

Mr. Frenchaboy sat forward. "Indeed?" he said, a sudden glitter to his voice. "Is that quite true? Anything I wish to eat, no matter what?"

"Yes, yes," the man said, as though pained by the discussion. "No matter what."

"Well, then!" Mr. Frenchaboy crossed his legs and leaned backward on his elbows. "For my last meal," he said, "I should like—Bouillabaisse à la Peskin."

There was a moment of silence.

"What was that?"

"Bouillabaisse," Mr. Frenchaboy repeated, "a la Peskin."

"Very well," the man said, and exited.

In a short time he was back.

"The prison chef informs me that there is no such dish," he said.

"The prison chef," Mr. Frenchaboy said, "is mistaken. For verification, I suggest you telephone any member of the Gourmet's Club. They have all had Bouillabaisse à la Peskin at least once."

"In that case," said the man, "perhaps you would care to give me the recipe, which I shall pass along to the chef."

"If only I could!" Mr. Frenchaboy sighed. "I'm afraid it's out of the question, though. I haven't the slightest idea of what goes into it, or in what quantities, you see."

The man paused, opened his mouth, closed it, and went away.

An hour later he returned, looking trapped.

"Mr. Frenchaboy," he said, "it is impossible for us to serve you this Bouillabaisse à la Peskin. The recipe does not exist."

"What a pity," Mr. Frenchaboy said, with deep regret. "I'd so looked forward to it. However, there is a bright side to the picture."

"Eh?"

"I allude to the fact that now the sentence cannot be carried out."

The man blinked. "How is that, sir?"

"Well," Mr. Frenchaboy said, rubbing his thin hands together, "my understanding of the law is—and you have verified it—that a man is entitled to the meal of his choice before he is executed. I have made my request but it has not been granted. Therefore," he smiled, "you can't hang me."

The man looked a trifle panicky for a moment. Then he said, "I'll have to find out about this."

"By all means," Mr. Frenchaboy said. "But I think you'll find that I'm correct."

He listened to the disappearing footsteps, and chuckled.

Unfortunately, they did not find that Mr. Frenchaboy was correct.

They decided to feed him hamburgers and malted milks, and hang him anyway.

But when they came to get him just before sunrise the following day, they discovered that the sentence could not be carried out after all. Mr. Frenchaboy was in no condition to be hanged.

He had passed away in the night.

Of acute indigestion.

The Beautiful People

Mary sat quietly, and watched the handsome man's legs blown off, watched on further as the great ship began to crumple and break into small pieces in the middle of the blazing night. She fidgeted slightly as the men and the parts of the men came floating dreamily through the wreckage, out into the awful silence. And when the meteorite shower came upon the men, flying in, gouging holes through everything, tearing flesh, and ripping bones, Mary closed her eyes.

"Mother."

Mrs. Cuberle glanced up from her magazine.

"Do we have to wait much longer?"

"I don't think so; why?"

Mary said nothing, but looked at the moving wall.

"Oh, that." Mrs. Cuberle laughed and shook her head. "That tired old thing. Read a magazine, Mary, like I'm doing. We've all seen *that* a million times."

"Does it have to be on, Mother?"

"Well, nobody seems to be watching. I don't think the doctor would mind if I switched it off."

Mrs. Cuberle rose from the couch and walked to the wall. She depressed a little button and the life went from the wall, flickering and glowing.

Mary opened her eyes.

"Honestly," Mrs. Cuberle said to the woman, beside her, "you'd think they'd try to get something else. We might all as well go to the museum and watch the first landing on Mars. The Mayorka Disaster—really!"

The woman replied without distracting her eyes from the magazine page. "It's the doctor's idea. Psychological."

Mrs. Cuberle opened her mouth and moved her head up

and down, knowingly. "I should have known there was *some* reason. Still, who watches it?"

"The children do. Makes them think, makes them grateful or something."

"Oh. Of course, yes."

"Psychological."

Mary picked up a magazine and leafed through the pages. All photographs, of women and men. Women like Mother and like the others in the room; slender, tanned, shapely, beautiful women; and men with large muscles and shiny hair. Women and men, all looking alike, all perfect and beautiful. She folded the magazine and wondered how to answer the questions that would be asked.

"Mother—"

"Gracious, what is it now! Can't you sit still for a minute?"

"But we've been here three hours."

Mrs. Cuberle sniffed.

"Do I really have to?"

"Now, don't be silly, Mary. After those terrible things you told me, of *course* you do."

An olive-skinned woman in a transparent white uniform came into the reception room.

"Cuberle. Mrs. Zena Cuberle?"

"Yes."

"Doctor will see you now."

Mrs. Cuberle took Mary's hand, and they walked behind the nurse down a long corridor.

A man who seemed in his middle twenties looked up from a desk. He smiled and gestured towards two adjoining chairs.

"Well, well."

"Doctor Hortel, I—"

The doctor snapped his fingers.

"Of course, I know. Your daughter. Well, I know your trouble. Get so many of them nowadays, takes up most of my time."

"You do?" asked Mrs. Cuberle. "Frankly, it had begun to upset me."

"Upset? Hmm. Not good at all. But then—if people did not get upset, then we psychiatrists would be out of a job, eh? Go the way of the M.D. But I assure you, I need hear no more."

He turned his handsome face to Mary. "Little girl, how old are you?"

"Eighteen, sir."

"Oh, a real bit of impatience. It's just about time, of course. What might your name be?"

"Mary."

"Charming! and so unusual. Well, now, Mary, may I say that I understand your problem—understand it thoroughly."

Mrs. Cuberle smiled and smoothed the metalwork on her jerkin.

"Madam, you have no idea how many there are these days. Sometimes it preys on their minds so that it affects them physically, even mentally. Makes them act strange, say peculiar, unexpected things. One little girl I recall was so distraught she did nothing but brood all day long. Can you imagine!"

"That's what Mary does. When she finally told me, Doctor, I thought she had gone—you know."

"That bad, eh? Afraid we'll have to start a re-education program, very soon, or they'll all be like this. I believe I'll suggest it to the Senator day after tomorrow."

"I don't quite understand, doctor."

"Simply, Mrs. Cuberle, that the children have got to be thoroughly instructed. Thoroughly. Too much is taken for granted, and childish minds somehow refuse to accept things without definite reason. Children have become far too intellectual, which, as I trust I needn't remind you, is a dangerous thing."

"Yes, but what has this to do with—"

"Mary, like half the sixteen-, seventeen-, and eighteen-year-olds today, has begun to feel acutely self-conscious. She feels that her body has developed sufficiently for the Transformation—which of course it has not, not quite yet—and she cannot understand the complex reasons which compel her to wait until some vague, though specific, date. Mary looks at you, at the women all about her, at the pictures, and then she looks into a mirror. From pure perfection of body, face, limbs, pigmentation, carriage, stance, she sees herself and is horrified. Isn't that so? Of course. She asks herself, 'Why must I be hideous, unbalanced, oversize, undersize, full of revolting skin eruption, badly schemed organic arrangements?'—in short, Mary is tired of being a monster and is overly anxious to achieve what almost everyone else has already achieved."

"But—" said Mrs. Cuberle.

"This much you understand, doubtless. Now, Mary, what you object to is that our society offers you, and the others like you, no convincing logic on the side of waiting until nineteen. It is all taken for granted, and you want to know why! It is that simple. A non-technical explanation will not suffice. The modern child wants facts, solid technical data, to satisfy her every question. And that, as you can both see, will take a good deal of reorganizing."

"But—" said Mary.

"The child is upset, nervous, tense; she acts strange, peculiar, odd, worries you and makes herself ill because it is beyond our meager powers to put it across. I tell you, what we need is a whole new basis for learning. And, that will take doing. It will take *doing*, Mrs. Cuberle. Now, don't you worry about Mary, and don't you worry, child. I'll prescribe some pills and—"

"No, no, doctor! You're all mixed up," cried Mrs. Cuberle.

"I *beg* your pardon, Madam?"

"What I mean is, you've got it wrong. Tell him, Mary, tell the doctor what you told me."

Mary shifted uneasily in the chair.

"It's that—I don't want it."

The doctor's well-proportioned jaw dropped.

"Would you please repeat that?"

"I said, I don't want the Transformation."

"But that's impossible. I have never heard of such a thing. Little girl, you are playing a joke."

Mary nodded negatively.

"See, doctor. What can it be?" Mrs. Cuberle rose and began to pace.

The doctor clucked his tongue and took from a small cupboard a black box covered with buttons and dials and wire. He affixed black clamps to Mary's head.

"Oh no, you don't think—I mean, could it?"

"We shall soon see." The doctor revolved a number of dials and studied the single bulb in the centre of the box. It did not flicker. He removed the clamps.

"Dear me," the doctor said. "Your daughter is perfectly sane, Mrs. Cuberle."

"Well, then what is it?"

"Perhaps she is lying. We haven't completely eliminated that factor as yet; it slips into certain organisms."

More tests. More machines, and more negative results.

Mary pushed her foot in a circle on the floor. When the doctor put his hands to her shoulders, she looked up pleasantly.

"Little girl," said the handsome man, "do you actually mean to tell us that you *prefer* that body?"

"I like it. It's—hard to explain, but it's me, and that's what I like. Not the looks, maybe, but the *me*."

"You can look in the mirror and see yourself, then look at—well, at your mother and be content?"

"Yes, sir." Mary thought of her reasons; fuzzy, vague, but very definitely there. Maybe she had said the reason. No. Only a part of it.

"Mrs. Cuberle," the doctor said, "I suggest that your husband have a long talk with Mary."

"My husband is dead. The Ganymede incident."

"Oh, splendid. Rocket man, eh? Very interesting organisms. Something always seems to happen to rocket men, in one way or another." The doctor scratched his cheek. "When did she first start talking this way?" he asked.

"Oh, for quite some time. I used to think it was because she was such a baby. But lately, the time getting so close and all, I thought I'd better see you."

"Of course, yes, very wise, uh—does she also do odd things?"

"Well, I found her on the second level one night. She was lying on the floor, and when I asked her what she was doing, she said she was trying to sleep."

Mary flinched. She was sorry, in a way, that Mother had found that out.

"Did you say 'sleep'?"

"That's right."

"Now where could she have picked that up?"

"No idea."

"Mary, don't you know nobody sleeps anymore. That we have an infinitely greater life-span than our poor ancestors, now that that wasteful state of unconsciousness has been conquered? Child, have you actually *slept*? No one knows how anymore."

"No, sir, but I almost did."

The doctor breathed a long stream of air from his mouth.

"But, how could you begin to try to do something people have forgotten entirely about?"

"The way it was described in the book, it sounded nice, that's all."

"Book, book? Are there *books* at your Unit, Madam?"

"There could be. I haven't cleaned up in a while."

"That is certainly peculiar. I haven't seen a book for years. Not since '17."

Mary began to fidget and stare nervously.

"But with the Tapes, why should you try to read books ... Where did you get them?"

"Daddy did. He got them from his father, and so did Grandpa. He said they're better than the Tapes, and he was right."

Mrs. Cuberle flushed.

"My husband was a little strange, Doctor Hortel. He kept these things despite anything I said. Finally hid them, as I see."

The muscular black-haired doctor walked to another cabinet, and selected from the shelf a bottle. From the bottle he took two large pills and swallowed these.

"Sleep...books...doesn't want the Transformation...Mrs. Cuberle, my *dear* good woman, this is grave. I would appreciate it if you would change psychiatrists. I am very busy and, ah, this is somewhat specialized. I suggest Centraldome. Many fine doctors there. Goodbye."

The doctor turned and sat in a large chair and folded his hands. Mary watched him and wondered why the simple statements should have so changed things. But the doctor did not move from the chair.

"Well!" said Mrs. Cuberle and walked quickly from the room.

Mary considered the reflection in the mirrored wall. She sat on the floor and looked at different angles of herself: profile, full-face, full-length, naked, clothed. Then she took up the magazine and studied it. She sighed.

"Mirror, Mirror on the wall..." The words came haltingly to her mind and from her lips. She hadn't read these, she recalled. Daddy had said them, "quoted" them, as he put it. But they, too, were lines from a book..."who is the fairest of—"

A picture of Mother sat upon the dresser, and Mary considered this now. She looked for a long time at the slender, feminine neck, knotted in just the right places. The golden skin, smooth and without blemish, without wrinkles and without age. The dark brown eyes and the thin tapers of eyebrows, the long black lashes. Set evenly, so that the halves of the face corresponded precisely. The half-hearted mouth, a violet tint against the gold, the white teeth, even, sparkling.

Mother, Beautiful, Transformed Mother. And back again to the mirror.

"—of them all . . ."

The image of a rather chubby young woman, without lines of rhythm or grace, without perfection. Splotchy skin full of little holes, puffs in the cheeks, red eruptions on the forehead. Perspiration, shapeless hair flowing onto shapeless shoulders down a shapeless body. Like all of them, before the Transformation.

Did they *all* look like this, before? Did Mother, even?

Mary thought hard, trying to sort out exactly what Daddy and Grandpa had said, why they said the Transformation was a bad thing, and why she believed and agreed with them so strongly. It made little sense, but they were right. They *were* right! And one day, she would understand completely.

Mrs. Cuberle slammed the door angrily, and Mary jumped to her feet.

"Honestly, expenses aren't so high that you have to leave all the windows off. I went through the whole level, and there isn't a single window left on. Don't you even want to see the people?"

"No. I was thinking."

"Well, it's got to stop. It's simply got to stop. Mary, what in the world has gotten into you lately?"

"I—"

"The way you upset Doctor Hortel. He won't even see me anymore, and these traumas are getting horrible—*not* to mention the migraines. I'll have to get that awful Doctor Wagoner."

Mrs. Cuberle sat on the couch and crossed her legs carefully.

"And what in the world were you doing on the floor?"

"Trying to sleep."

"You've got to stop talking that way! Why should you want to do such a silly thing?"

"The books—"

"And you mustn't read those terrible things."

"Mother—"

"The Unit is full of Tapes, full! Anything you want!"

Mary stuck out her lower lip. "But I don't want to hear all about wars and colonizations and politics!"

"Now I know where you got this idiotic notion that you don't want the Transformation. Of *course*."

Mrs. Cuberle rose quickly and took the books from the corner and from the closet, and piled her arms with them. She looked everywhere in the room, and gathered the old, brittle volumes.

These she carried from the room and threw into the elevator. A button guided the doors shut.

"I thought you'd do that," Mary said, slowly, "that's why I hid most of the good ones. Where you'll never find them!" She breathed heavily, and her heart thumped.

Mrs. Cuberle put a satin handkerchief to her eyes.

"I don't know what I ever did to deserve this!"

"Deserve *what*, Mother? What am I doing that's so wrong?" Mary's mind rippled in a little confused stream now.

"What?" Mrs. Cuberle wailed, "*What?* Do you think I want people to point at you and say I'm the mother of a mutant?" Her voice softened abruptly into a plea. "Or have you changed your mind, dear?"

"No." *The vague reasons, longing to be put into words.*

"It really doesn't hurt, you know. They just take off a little skin, and put some on, and give you pills and electronic treatment, and things like that. It doesn't take more than a week."

"No." *The reasons.*

"Look at your friend Shala, she's getting her Transformation next month. And *she's* almost pretty now."

"Mother, I don't care—"

"If it's the bones you're worried about, well, that doesn't hurt. They give you a shot, and when you wake up, everything's moulded right. Everything, to suit the personality."

"I don't care, I don't care."

"But *why?*"

"I like me the way I am." *Almost, almost exactly. But not quite. Part of it, though; part of what Daddy and Grandpa must have meant.*

Mrs. Cuberle switched on a window, and then switched it off again. She sobbed. "But you're so ugly, dear! Like Doctor Hortel said. And Mr. Willmes, at the factory. He told some people he thought you were the ugliest girl he'd ever seen. He says he'll be thankful when you have your Transformation."

"Daddy said I was beautiful."

"Well, really, dear. You *do* have eyes."

"Daddy said that real beauty is more than skin deep. He said a lot of things like that, and when I read the books I felt the same way. I guess I don't want to look like everybody else, that's all."

"You'll notice that your father had *his* Transformation, though!"

Mary stamped her foot angrily. "He told me that if he had to do it again he just wouldn't. He said I should be stronger than he was."

"You're not going to get away with this, young lady. After all, I *am* your mother."

A bulb flickered in the bathroom and Mrs. Cuberle walked uncertainly to the cabinet. She took out a little cardboard box.

"It's time for lunch."

Mary nodded. That was another thing the books talked about, which the Tapes did not. Lunch seemed to be something special long ago, or at least different... The books talked of strange ways of putting a load of things into the mouth and chewing these things. Enjoying them, somehow. Strange and wonderful....

"And you'd better get ready for work."

Mary let the greenish capsule slide down her throat.

"Yes, Mother."

The office was quiet and without shadows. The walls gave off a steady luminescence, distributing the light evenly upon all the desks and tables. It was neither hot nor cold.

Mary held the ruler firmly and allowed the pen to travel down the metal edge effortlessly. The new black lines were small and accurate. She tipped her head, compared the notes beside her to the plan she was working on. She noticed the beautiful people looking at her more furtively than before, and she wondered about this as she made her lines.

A tall man rose from his desk in the rear of the office, and walked down the aisle to Mary's table. He surveyed her work, allowing his eyes to travel cautiously from her face to the draft.

Mary looked around.

"Nice job," said the man.

"Thank you, Mr. Willmes."

"Dralich shouldn't have anything to complain about. That crane should hold the whole damn city."

"It's very good alloy, sir."

"Yeah. Say, kid, you got a minute?"

"Yes, sir."

"Let's go into Mullinson's office."

The big, handsome man led the way into a small cubbyhole of a room. He motioned to a chair, and sat on the edge of one desk.

"Kid, I never was one to beat around the bush. Somebody called in a little while ago, gave me some crazy story about you not wanting your Transformation."

Mary looked away, then quickly back into the man's eyes. "It's not a crazy story, Mr. Willmes," she said. "It's true. I want to stay this way."

The man stared, then coughed embarrassedly.

"What the hell—excuse me, kid, but—I don't exactly get it. You ain't a mutant, I know that. And you ain't—"

"Insane? No; Doctor Hortel can tell you."

The man laughed, nervously. "Well . . . Look, you're still a cub, but you do swell work. Lots of good results, lots of comments from the stations. But Mr. Poole won't like it."

"I know. I know what you mean, Mr. Willmes. But nothing can change my mind."

"You'll get old before you're half through life!"

Yes, she would. Old, like the Elders, wrinkled and brittle, unable to move correctly. Old.

"It's hard to make you understand. But I don't see why it should make any difference, as long as I do my work."

"Now don't go getting me wrong, kid. It ain't me. But you know, I don't run Interplan. I just work here. Mr. Poole, he likes things running smooth, and it's my job to carry it out. And as soon as everybody finds out, things wouldn't run smooth. There'll be a big to-do, y'understand? The dames will start asking questions, and talk. Be the same as a mutant in the office—no offense."

"Will you accept my resignation, then, Mr. Willmes?"

"Sure you won't change your mind?"

"No, sir. I decided that a long time ago."

"Well, then, I'm sorry, Mary. Couple, ten, twenty years ago you could be centraled on one of the asteroids, the way you been working out. But . . . if you should change your mind, there'll always be a job for you here. Otherwise, you got till March. And between you and me, I hope by then you've decided the other way."

Mary walked back down the aisle, past the rows of desks. Past the men and women. The handsome model men and the beautiful, perfect women, perfect, all perfect, all looking alike. Looking exactly alike.

She sat down again and took up her ruler and pen.

Mary stepped into the elevator and descended several hundred feet. At the Second Level she pressed a button and the elevator stopped. The doors opened with another button and the doors to her Unit with still another.

Mrs. Cuberle sat on the floor by the TV, disconsolate and red-eyed. Her blonde hair had come slightly askew, and a few strands hung over her forehead.

"You don't need to tell me. No one will hire you."

Mary sat down beside her mother.

"If only you hadn't told Mr. Willmes in the first place—"

"Well, I thought *he* could beat a little sense into you."

The sounds from the TV grew louder. Mrs. Cuberle changed channels a number of times, and finally turned it off.

"What did you do today, Mother?" Mary smiled, hopefully.

"What *can* I do now? Nobody will even come over! Everyone thinks you're a mutant."

"*Mother!*"

"They say you should be in the Circuses."

Mary went into another room. Mrs. Cuberle followed, wringing her hands, and crying: "Mutant, mutant! How are we going to live? Where does the money come from now? Next thing they'll be firing *me!*"

"No one would do that."

"Nobody else on this planet has ever refused the Transformation. The mutants all wish they could have it. And you, given everything, you turn it down. You *want* to be ugly!"

Mary put her arms about her mother's shoulders.

"I wish I could explain; I've tried so hard to. It isn't that I want to bother anyone, or that Daddy or Grandpa wanted me to."

Mrs. Cuberle reached into the pocket of her jerkin and retrieved a purple pill. She swallowed the pill.

When the letter dropped from the chute, Mrs. Cuberle ran to snatch it up. She read it once silently, then smiled.

"Oh," she said, "I was so afraid they wouldn't answer. But we'll see about this *now!*"

She gave the letter to Mary, who read:

> Mrs. Zena Cuberle
> Unit 451-D
> Levels II & III
> City

Dear Madam:

In re your letter of Dec. 3 36. We have carefully examined your complaint and consider that it requires stringent measures of some sort. Quite frankly, the possibility of such a complaint has never occurred to this Dept., and we therefore cannot issue positive directives at this present moment.

However, due to the unusual qualities of the matter, we have arranged an audience at Centraldome 8th Level 16th Unit, Jan. 3 37, 23 sharp. Dr. Hortel has been instructed to attend. You will bring the subject in question.

> Yrs.
> DEPT. F

Mary let the paper flutter to the floor. She walked quietly to the elevator and set it for Level III. When the elevator stopped, she ran from it, crying, into her room.

She thought and remembered and tried to sort out and put together. Daddy had said it, Grandpa had, the books did. Yes. The books did.

She read until her eyes burned, and her eyes burned until she could read no more. Then Mary went to sleep, softly and without realizing it.

But the sleep was not a peaceful one.

"Ladies and gentlemen," said the young-looking, classic-featured man, "this problem does not resolve easily. Doctor Hortel here, testifies that Mary Cuberle is definitely not insane, Doctors Monagh, Prynn, and Fedders all verify this judgement. Doctor Prynn asserts that the human organism is no longer so constructed as to create and sustain such an attitude as deliberate falsehood. Further, there is positively nothing in the structure of Mary Cuberle which might suggest difficulties in Transformation. There is qualified evidence for all these statements. And yet—" the man sighed "—while the Newstapes, the Foto services, while every news-carrying agency has circulated this problem throughout the universe, we are faced with this refusal. Further, the notoriety has become excessive to the point of vulgarity, and has resultantly caused numerous persons, among them Mrs. Zena Cuberle, the child's mother, grievous emotional stress. What, may I ask, is to be done therefore?"

Mary looked at a metal table.

"We have been in session far too long, holding up far too many other pressing contingencies of a serious nature."

Throughout the rows of beautiful people, the mumbling increased. Mrs. Cuberle sat nervously tapping her foot and running a comb through her hair.

"The world waits," continued the man. "Mary Cuberle, you have been given innumerable chances to reconsider, you know."

Mary said, "I know. But I don't want to."

The beautiful people looked at Mary and laughed. Some shook their heads.

The man in the robes threw up his hands.

"Little girl, can you realize what an issue you have caused? The unrest, the wasted time? Do you fully understand what you have done? We could send you to a Mutant Colony, I suppose you know . . ."

"How could you do that?" inquired Mary.

"Well, I'm sure we could—it's a pretty point. Intergalactic questions hang fire while you sit there saying the same thing over and over. And in judicial procedure I dare say there is some clause which forbids that. Come now, doesn't the happiness of your dear mother mean anything to you? Or your duty to the State, to the entire Solar System?"

A slender, supple woman in a back row stood and cried, loudly: "*Do* something!"

The man on the high stool raised his arm.

"None of that, now. We must conform, even though the problem is out of the ordinary."

The woman sat down, snorted; the man turned again to Mary.

"Child, I have here a petition, signed by two thousand individuals and representing all the Stations of the Earth. They have been made aware of all the facts and have submitted the petition voluntarily. It's all so unusual and I'd hoped we wouldn't have to—but, well, the petition urges drastic measures."

The mumbling rose.

"The petition urges that you shall, upon final refusal, be forced by law to accept the Transformation. And that an act of legislature shall make this universal and binding in the future."

Mary's eyes were open, wide; she stood and paused before speaking.

"*Why?*" she asked.

The man in the robes passed a hand through his hair.

Another voice from the crowd: "Sign the petition, Senator!"

All the voices: "Sign it! Sign it!"

"But *why?*" Mary began to cry. The voices stilled for a moment.

"Because—Because—What if others should get the same idea? What would happen to us then, little girl? We'd be right back to the ugly, thin, fat, unhealthy-looking race we were ages ago! There can't be any exceptions."

"Maybe they didn't consider themselves so ugly!"

The mumbling began anew and broke into a wild clamor.

"That isn't the point," cried the man in the robes, "you *must* conform!"

And the voices cried: "Yes!" loudly until the man took up a pen and signed the papers on his desk.

Cheers; applause, shouts.

Mrs. Cuberle patted Mary on the top of her head.

"There now!" she said happily, "everything will be all right now. You'll see, Mary, dear."

The Transformation Parlor covered the entire Level, sprawling with its departments. It was always filled, and there was nothing to sign and no money to pay, and people were always waiting in line.

But today the people stood aside. And there were still more, looking in through doors, TV cameras placed throughout, and Tape machines in every corner. It was filled, but not bustling as usual.

The Transformation Parlor was terribly quiet.

Mary walked past the people, Mother and the men in back of her, following. She looked at the people, too, as she did in her room through turned-on windows. It was no different. The people were beautiful, perfect, without a single flaw. Except the young ones, young like herself, seated on couches, looking embarrassed and ashamed and eager.

But, of course, the young ones did not count.

All the beautiful people. All the ugly people, staring out

from bodies that were not theirs. Walking on legs that had been made for them, laughing with manufactured voices, gesturing with shaped and fashioned arms.

Mary walked slowly despite the prodding. In her eyes, in *her* eyes, was a mounting confusion; a wide, wide wonderment.

She looked down at her own body, then at the walls which reflected it. Flesh of her flesh, bone of her bone, all hers, made by no person, built by herself or Someone she did not know... Uneven kneecaps making two grinning cherubs when they straightened, and the old familiar rubbing together of fat inner thighs. Fat, unshapely, unsystematic Mary. But *Mary*.

Of course. Of course! This *was* what Daddy meant, what Grandpa and the books meant. What *they* would know if they would read the books or hear the words, the good, unreasonable words, the words that signified more, so much more, than any of this...

"Where *are* these people?" Mary said, half to herself. "What has happened to *them*, and don't they miss *themselves*, these manufactured things?"

She stopped, suddenly.

"Yes! That *is* the reason. They have all forgotten themselves!"

A curvaceous woman stepped forward and took Mary's hand. The woman's skin was tinted dark. Chipped and sculptured bone into slender rhythmic lines, electrically created carriage, made, turned out...

"All right, young lady. Shall we begin?"

They guided Mary to a large, curved leather seat.

From the top of a long silver pole a machine lowered itself. Tiny bulbs glowed to life and cells began to click. The people stared. Slowly a picture formed upon the screen in the machine. Bulbs directed at Mary, then re-directed into themselves. Wheels turning, buttons ticking.

The picture was completed.

"Would you like to see it?"

Mary closed her eyes, tight.

"It's really very nice." The woman turned to the crowd. "Oh yes, there's a great deal to be salvaged; you'd be surprised. A great deal. We'll keep the nose, and I don't believe the elbows will have to be altered at all."

Mrs. Cuberle looked at Mary and grinned.

"Now, it isn't so bad as you thought, is it?" she said.

The beautiful people looked. Cameras turned, Tapes wound.

"You'll have to excuse us now. Only the machines allowed."

Only the machines.

The people filed out, grumbling.

Mary saw the rooms in the mirror. Saw things in the rooms, the faces and bodies that had left, the woman and the machines and the old young men standing about, adjusting, readying.

Then she looked at the picture in the screen.

A woman of medium height stared back at her. A woman with a curved body and thin legs; silver hair, pompadoured, cut short; full, sensuous lips, small breasts, flat stomach, unblemished skin.

A strange woman no one had ever seen before.

The nurse began to take off Mary's clothes.

"Geoff," the woman said, "come look at this, will you. Not one so bad in years. Amazing that we can keep anything at all."

The handsome man put his hands into his pockets, and clucked his tongue.

"Pretty bad, all right."

"Be still, child, stop, stop making those noises. You know perfectly well nothing is going to hurt."

"But what will you do with me?"

"That was all explained to you."

"No, no—with *me, me!*"

"You mean the cast-offs? The usual. I don't know, exactly. Somebody takes care of it."

"I want me!" Mary cried. "Not that!" She pointed at the image in the screen.

Her chair was wheeled into a semi-dark room. She was naked now, and the men lifted her to a table. The surface was like glass, black filmed. A big machine hung above in shadows.

Straps. Clamps pulling, stretching limbs apart. The screen with the picture brought in. The men and the women, more women now. Doctor Hortel in a corner, sitting with his legs crossed, shaking his head.

Mary began to cry loudly, as hard as she could, above the hum of the mechanical things.

"Shhh. My gracious, such a racket! Just think about your job waiting for you, and all the friends you'll have, and how lovely everything will be. No more troubles now."

The big machine groaned and descended from the darkness.

"Where will I find me?" Mary screamed. "What will happen to *me*?"

A long needle slid into rough flesh, and the beautiful people gathered around the table.

And then they turned on the big machine.

Free Dirt

No fowl had ever looked so posthumous. Its bones lay stacked to one side of the plate like kindling: white, dry, and naked in the soft light of the restaurant. Bones only, with every shard and filament of meat stripped methodically off. Otherwise, the plate was a vast glistening plain.

The other, smaller, dishes and bowls were equally virginal. They shone fiercely against one another. And all a pale cream color fixed upon the snowy white of a tablecloth unstained by gravies and unspotted by coffee and free from the stigmata of breadcrumbs, cigarette ash, and fingernail lint.

Only the dead fowl's bones and the stippled traceries of hardened red gelatine clinging timidly to the bottom of a dessert cup gave evidence that these ruins had once been a dinner.

Mr. Aorta, not a small man, permitted a mild belch, folded the newspaper he had found on the chair, inspected his vest for food leavings, and then made his way briskly to the cashier.

The old woman glanced at his check.

"Yes, sir," she said.

"All righty," Mr. Aorta said and removed from his hip pocket a large black wallet. He opened it casually, whistling *The Seven Joys of Mary* through the space provided by his two front teeth.

The melody stopped, abruptly. Mr. Aorta looked concerned. He peered into his wallet, then began removing things; presently its entire contents was spread out.

He frowned.

"What seems to be the difficulty, sir?"

"Oh, no difficulty," the fat man said, "exactly." Though the wallet was manifestly empty, he flapped its sides apart, held it

26

upside down and continued to shake it, suggesting the picture of a hydrophobic bat suddenly seized in mid-air.

Mr. Aorta smiled a weak, harassed smile and proceeded to empty all of his fourteen separate pockets. In a time the counter was piled high with miscellany.

"Well!" he said impatiently. "What nonsense! What bother! Do you know what's happened? My wife's gone off and forgotten to leave me any change! Heigh-ho, well—my name is James Brockelhurst: I'm with the Pliofilm Corporation. I generally don't eat out, and—here, no, I insist. This is embarrassing for you as well as for myself. I *insist* upon leaving my card. If you will retain it, I shall return tomorrow evening at this time and reimburse you."

Mr. Aorta shoved the pasteboard into the cashier's hands, shook his head, shoveled the residue back into his pockets and, plucking a toothpick from a box, left the restaurant.

He was quite pleased with himself—an invariable reaction to the acquisition of something for nothing in return. It had all gone smoothly, and what a delightful meal!

He strolled in the direction of the streetcar stop, casting occasional licentious glances at undressed mannequins in department store windows.

The prolonged fumbling for his car token worked as efficiently as ever. (Get in the middle of the crowd, look bewildered, inconspicuous, search your pockets earnestly, the while edging from the vision of the conductor—then, take a far seat and read a newspaper.) In four years' traveling time, Mr. Aorta computed he had saved a total of $211.20.

The electric's ancient list did not jar his warm feeling of serenity. He studied the amusements briefly, then went to work on the current puzzle, whose prize ran into the thousands. Thousands of dollars, actually for nothing. Something for nothing. Mr. Aorta loved puzzles.

But the fine print made reading impossible.

Mr. Aorta glanced at the elderly woman standing near his seat; then, because the woman's eyes were full of tired pleading and insinuation, he refocused out the wire cross-hatch windows.

What he saw caused his heart to throb. The section of town was one he passed every day, so it was a wonder he'd not noticed it before—though generally there was little provocation to sightsee on what was irreverently called "Death

Row"—a dreary round of mortuaries, columbariums, crematories, and the like, all crowded into a five-block area.

He yanked the stop-signal, hurried to the rear of the streetcar and depressed the exit plate. In a few moments he had walked to what he'd seen.

It was a sign, artlessly lettered, though spelled correctly enough. It was not new, for the white paint had swollen and cracked and the rusted nails had dripped trails of dirty orange over the face of it.

The sign read:

FREE DIRT
APPLY WITHIN
Lilyvale
Cemetery

and was posted upon the moldering green of a woodboard wall.

Now Mr. Aorta felt a familiar sensation come over him. It happened whenever he encountered the word FREE—a magic word that did strange and wonderful things to his metabolism.

Free. What was the meaning, the *essence* of free? Why, something for nothing. And to get something for nothing was Mr. Aorta's chiefest pleasure in this mortal life.

The fact that it was dirt which was being offered Free did not oppress him. He seldom gave more than a fleeting thought to these things; for, he reasoned, nothing is without its use.

The other, subtler circumstances surrounding the sign scarcely occurred to him: why the dirt was being offered, where free dirt from a cemetery would logically come from; et cetera. In this connection he considered only the probable richness of the soil, for reasons he did not care to speculate upon.

Mr. Aorta's solitary hesitation encircled such problems as: Was this an offer an honest one, without strings where he would have to buy something? Was there a limit on how much he could take home? If not, what would be the best method of transporting it?

Petty problems: all solvable.

Mr. Aorta did something inwardly which resembled a smile, looked about and finally located the entrance to the Lilyvale Cemetery.

*   *   *

These desolate grounds, which had once accommodated a twine factory, an upholstering firm, and an outlet for ladies' shoes, now lay swathed in a miasmic vapor—accreditable, in the absence of nearby bogs, to a profusion of windward smokestacks. The blistered hummocks, peaked with crosses, slabs, and stones, loomed gray and sad in the gloaming: withal, a place purely delightful to describe, and a pity it cannot be—for how it looked there that evening has little to do with the fat man and what was to become of him.

Important only that it was a place full of dead people on their backs under ground, moldering and moldered.

Mr. Aorta hurried because he despised to waste, along with everything else, time. It was not long before he had encountered the proper party and had this sort of conversation:

"I understand you're offering free dirt."

"That's right."

"How much may one have?"

"Much as one wants."

"On what days?"

"Any days; most likely there'll always be some fresh."

Mr. Aorta sighed in the manner of one who has just acquired a lifetime inheritance or a measured checking account. He then made an appointment for the following Saturday and went home to ruminate agreeable ruminations.

At a quarter past nine that night he hit upon an excellent use to which the dirt might be put.

His back yard, an ochre waste, lay chunked and dry, a barren stretch repulsive to all but the grossest weeds. A tree had once flourished there, in better days, a haven for suburbanite birds, but then the birds disappeared for no good reason except that this was when Mr. Aorta moved into the house, and the tree became an ugly naked thing.

No children played in this yard.

Mr. Aorta was intrigued. Who could say? Perhaps something might be made to grow! He had long ago written an enterprising firm for free samples of seeds, and received enough to feed an army. But the first experiments had shriveled into hard, useless pips and, seized by lassitude, Mr. Aorta had shelved the project. Now...

A neighbor named Joseph William Santucci permitted himself to be intimidated. He lent his old Reo truck, and after a few hours the first load of dirt had arrived and been shoveled into a tidy mound. It looked beautiful to Mr. Aorta, whose passion overcompensated for his weariness with the task. The second load followed, and the third, and the fourth, and it was dark as a coalbin out when the very last was dumped.

Mr. Aorta returned the truck and fell into an exhausted, though not unpleasant, sleep.

The next day was heralded by the distant clangor of church bells and the *chink-chink* of Mr. Aorta's spade, leveling the displaced graveyard soil, distributing it and grinding it in with the crusty earth. It had a continental look, this new dirt: swarthy, it seemed, black and saturnine: not at all dry, though the sun was already quite hot.

Soon the greater portion of the yard was covered, and Mr. Aorta returned to his sitting room.

He turned on the radio in time to identify a popular song, marked his discovery on a post card and mailed this away, confident that he would receive either a toaster or a set of nylon hose for his trouble.

Then he wrapped four bundles containing, respectively: a can of vitamin capsules, half of them gone; a half-tin of coffee; a half-full bottle of spot remover; and a box of soap flakes with most of the soap flakes missing. These he mailed, each with a note curtly expressing his total dissatisfaction, to the companies that had offered them to him on a money-back guarantee.

Now it was dinnertime, and Mr. Aorta beamed in anticipation. He sat down to a meal of sundry delicacies such as anchovies, sardines, mushrooms, caviar, olives and pearl onions. It was not, however, that he enjoyed this type of food for any aesthetic reasons: only that it had all come in packages small enough to be slipped into one's pocket without attracting the attention of busy grocers.

Mr. Aorta cleaned his plates so thoroughly no cat would care to lick them; the empty tins also looked new and bright: even their lids gleamed iridescently.

Mr. Aorta glanced at his checkbook balance, grinned indecently, and went to look out the back window.

The moon was cold upon the yard. Its rays passed over the high fence Mr. Aorta had constructed from free rocks, and splashed moodily onto the now black earth.

Mr. Aorta thought a bit, put away his checkbook and got out the boxes containing the garden seeds.

They were good as new.

Joseph William Santucci's truck was in use every Saturday thereafter for five weeks. This good man watched curiously as his neighbor returned each time with more dirt and yet more, and he made several remarks to his wife about the oddness of it all, but she could not bear even to talk about Mr. Aorta.

"He's robbed us blind," she said. "Look! He wears your old clothes, he uses my sugar and spices, and borrows everything else he can think of! Borrows, did I say? I mean *steals*. For years! I have not seen the man pay for a thing yet! Where does he work he makes so little money?"

Neither Mr. nor Mrs. Santucci knew that Mr. Aorta's daily labors involved sitting on the sidewalk downtown, with dark glasses on and a battered tin cup in front of him. They'd both passed him several times, though, and given him pennies, both unable to penetrate the clever disguise. It was all kept, the disguise, in a free locker at the railroad terminal.

"Here he comes again, that loony!" Mrs. Santucci wailed.

Soon it was time to plant the seeds, and Mr. Aorta went about this with ponderous precision, after having consulted numerous books at the library. Neat rows of summer squash were sown in the richly dark soil; and peas, corn, beans, onions, beets, rhubarb, asparagus, watercress, and much more, actually. When the rows were filled and Mr. Aorta was stuck with extra packs, he smiled and dispersed strawberry seeds and watermelon seeds and seeds without clear description. Shortly the paper packages were all empty.

A few days passed and it was getting time to go to the cemetery again for a fresh load, when Mr. Aorta noticed an odd thing.

The dark ground had begun to yield to tiny eruptions. Closer inspection revealed that things had begun to grow. In the soil.

Now Mr. Aorta knew very little about gardening, when you got right down to it. He thought it strange, of course, but he was not alarmed. He saw things growing, that was the important point. Things that would become food.

Praising his fortune, he hurried to Lilyvale and there received a singular disappointment: Not many people had died lately. There was scant little dirt to be had: hardly one truckful.

Ah well, he thought, things are bound to pick up over the holidays; and he took home what there was.

Its addition marked the improvement of the garden's growth. Shoots and buds came higher, and the expanse was far less bleak.

He could not contain himself until the next Saturday, for obviously this dirt was acting as some sort of fertilizer on his plants—the free food called out for more.

But the next Saturday came a cropper. Not even a shovel's load. And the garden was beginning to desiccate. . . .

Mr. Aorta's startling decision came as a result of trying all kinds of new dirt and fertilizers of every imaginable description (all charged under the name of Uriah Gringsby). Nothing worked. His garden, which had promised a full bounty of edibles, had sunk to new lows: it was almost back to its original state. And this Mr. Aorta could not abide, for he had put in considerable labor on the project, and this labor must not be wasted. It had deeply affected his other enterprises.

So—with the caution born of desperateness, he entered the gray quiet place with the tombstones one night, located freshly dug but unoccupied graves and added to their six-foot depth yet another foot. It was not noticeable to anyone who was not looking for such a discrepancy.

No need to mention the many trips involved: it is enough to say that in time Mr. Santucci's truck, parked a block away, was a quarter filled.

The following morning saw a rebirth in the garden.

And so it went. When dirt was to be had, Mr. Aorta was obliged; when it was not—well, it wasn't missed. And the garden kept growing and growing, until—

As if overnight, everything opened up! Where so short a time past had been a parched little prairie, was now a multifloral, multivegetable paradise. Corn bulged yellow from its spiny green husks; peas were brilliant green in their half-split pods, and all the other wonderful foodstuffs glowed full rich with life and showcase vigor. Rows and rows of them, and cross rows!

Mr. Aorta was almost felled by enthusiasm.

A liver for the moment and an idiot in the art of canning, he knew what he had to do.

It took a while to systematically gather up the morsels, but with patience, he at last had the garden stripped clean of all but weeds and leaves and other unedibles.

He cleaned. He peeled. He stringed. He cooked. He boiled. He took all the good free food and piled it geometrically on tables and chairs, and continued with this until it was all ready to be eaten.

Then he began. Starting with the asparagus—he decided to do it in alphabetical order—he ate and ate clear through beets and celery and parsley and rhubarb, paused there for a drink of water, and went on eating, being careful not to waste a jot, until he came to watercress. By this time his stomach was twisting painfully, but it was a sweet pain, so he took a deep breath and, by chewing slowly, did away with the final vestigial bit of food.

The plates sparkled white, like a series of bloated snowflakes. It was all gone.

Mr. Aorta felt an almost sexual satisfaction—by which is meant, he had had enough . . . for now. He couldn't even belch.

Happy thoughts assailed his mind, as follows: His two greatest passions had been fulfilled; life's meaning acted out symbolically, like a condensed *Everyman*. These two things only are what this man thought of.

He chanced to look out the window.

What he saw was a bright speck in the middle of blackness. Small, somewhere at the end of the garden—faint yet distinct.

With the effort of a brontosaurus emerging from a tar pit Mr. Aorta rose from his chair, walked to the door, and went out into his emasculated garden. He lumbered past dangling grotesqueries formed by shucks and husks and vines.

The speck seemed to have disappeared, and he looked carefully in all directions, slitting his eyes, trying to get accustomed to the moonlight.

Then he saw it. A white fronded thing, a plant, perhaps only a flower; but there, certainly, and all that was left.

Mr. Aorta was surprised to see that it was located at the bottom of a shallow declivity in the ground, very near the dead tree. He couldn't remember how a hole could have got

dug in his garden, but there were always neighborhood kids
and their pranks. A lucky thing he'd grabbed the food when
he did!

Mr. Aorta leaned over the edge of the small pit and
reached down his hand toward the shining plant. It resisted
his touch, somehow. He leaned farther over and still a little
farther, and still he couldn't lay fingers on the thing.

Mr. Aorta was not an agile man. However, with the intensity of a painter trying to cover one last tiny spot awkwardly
placed, he leaned just a mite farther, and plosh! he'd toppled
over the edge and landed with a peculiarly wet thud. A
ridiculous damned bother, too: now he'd have to make a fool
of himself, clambering out again. But the plant: He searched
the floor of the pit, and searched it, and no plant could be
found. Then he looked up and was appalled by two things:
Number One, the pit had been deeper than he'd thought;
Number Two, the plant was wavering in the wind above him,
on the rim he had so recently occupied.

The pains in Mr. Aorta's stomach got progressively worse.
Movement increased the pains. He began to feel an overwhelming pressure in his ribs and chest.

It was at this moment of his discovery that the top of the
hole was up beyond his reach that he saw the white plant in
full moonglow. It looked rather like a hand, a big human
hand, waxy and stiff and attached to the earth. The wind hit it
and it moved slightly, causing a rain of dirt pellets to fall upon
Mr. Aorta's face.

He thought a moment, judged the whole situation, and
began to climb. But the pains were too much and he fell,
writhing.

The wind came again, and more dirt was scattered down
into the hole: soon the strange plant was being pushed to and
fro against the soil, and the dirt fell more and more heavily.
More and more, more heavily and more heavily.

Mr. Aorta, who had never up to this point found occasion
to scream, screamed. It was quite successful, despite the fact
that no one heard it.

The dirt came down, and presently Mr. Aorta was to his
knees in damp soil. He tried rising, and could not.

And the dirt came down from that big white plant flip-
flopping in the moonlight and the wind.

After a while Mr. Aorta's screams took on a muffled quality.
For a very good reason.

Then, some time later, the garden was just as still and quiet as it could be.

Mr. and Mrs. Joseph William Santucci found Mr. Aorta. He was lying on the floor in front of several tables. On the tables were many plates. The plates on the tables were clean and shining.

Mr. Aorta's stomach was distended past burst belt buckle, popped buttons, and forced zipper. It was not unlike the image of a great white whale rising curiously from placid, forlorn waters.

"Ate hisself to death," Mrs. Santucci said in the fashion of the concluding line of a complex joke.

Mr. Santucci reached down and plucked a tiny ball of soil from the fat man's dead lips. He studied it. And an idea came to him. . . .

He tried to get rid of the idea, but when the doctors found Mr. Aorta's stomach to contain many pounds of dirt—and nothing else, to speak of—Mr. Santucci slept badly, for almost a week.

They carried Mr. Aorta's body through the weeded but otherwise empty and desolate back yard, past the mournful dead tree and the rock fence.

They gave him a decent funeral, out of the goodness of their hearts, since no provision had been made.

And then they laid him to rest in a place with a moldering green woodboard wall: the wall had a little sign nailed to it.

And the wind blew absolutely Free.

Fritzchen

It had once been a place for dreaming. For lying on your back in the warm sand and listening to the silence and making faraway things seem real. The finest place in all the world, for all the reasons that ever were.

But it had stopped being this long ago. Now, he supposed, it wasn't much more than a fairly isolated cove, really: a stretch of land bleeding into the river at one of its wide points, cut off like a tiny peninsula; a gray, dull place, damp and unnatural from its nights beneath the tidewaters—decaying, sinking slowly, glad to be eaten by the river. As Edna had put it: Just a lot of dirty wet sand. Not a place for dreaming any more.

Mr. Peldo shifted his position and sighed as he remembered. He took from his mouth the eviscerated end of a lifeless cigar, flipped it away distastefully, watched as the mud whitened and oozed where it landed, and the spiders lumbered clumsily away in fright.

The spiders made him think of his snakes. And soon he was thinking, too, of rabbits and goldfish and ooo wow-wow puppy dogs, all flop-eared and soft, common as a blade of grass—and his bread-and-butter. His living.

He was almost relieved to hear Edna's coarse voice beside him.

"Jake."

She would now make some complaint about the foolishness of this whole trip, adding that it made her sinuses runny.

"Yes, Chicken, what is it?"

"Go and see to Luther."

Go-and-see-to-Luther. Eight-year-old kid ought to be able to see to himself, by God.

"All right. Where'd he go?"

36

"Somewhere over in that direction, there by the trees. I'm worried he might think of going in the water, or get lost."

Mr. Peldo grunted softly as he pulled his weight erect. Exertion. Oh well, that was all right. Soon he would have started with the frustration, thinking about the lousy pet shop and his lousy life. Better to hunt in the trees for spoiled brats.

It was hard going. Had to end in a few yards, of course, but still, it *was* . . . exciting, in a small, tired, remembering way. He pushed aside a drenched fern, and another, needles of wet hitting him.

"Luther."

Mr. Peldo continued for a few feet, until he could distinctly hear the current. A wall of leaves rose at the curve, so he stopped there, let the last of the thrill fall loose from him, then listened.

"Luther. Hustle, boy."

Only the water. The vibrant, treacherous river water, hurrying to join the Sound and to go with it to the ocean.

"Hey, *Luu-therr.*"

Mr. Peldo stabbed his hands into the foliage and parted it. From the window, by peering close, he could see his son's back.

"Boy, when your father calls you, *answer* him, hear!"

Luther looked around disinterestedly, frowned, and turned his head. He was sitting in the mud, playing.

Mr. Peldo felt the anger course spastically through him. He pushed forward and stopped, glared.

"Well?"

Then he glimpsed what his son had been playing with. Only a glimpse, though.

"Fritzchen!" Luther pronounced defiantly, shielding something in his hands. "Fritzchen—like I wanted to call Sol's birdie."

Mr. Peldo felt his eyes smart and rubbed them. "What have you got there?"

"Fritzchen, Fritzchen," the boy wailed. There was another sound then. A sound like none Mr. Peldo had ever heard: high-pitched, whiny, discordant. The sound an animal makes when it is in pain.

Mr. Peldo reached down and slapped at his son's mouth, which had fastened like a python's about the calf of his left leg. Then, by holding his thumb and forefinger tightly on

Luther's nose, he forced him to drop the thing he had been hiding.

It fell onto the slime and began to thrash.

Mr. Peldo gasped. He stared for a moment, like an idiot at a lampshade, his mouth quite open and his eyes bulged.

A thin voice from across the trees called: *"Jake, is there anything wrong? Answer me!"*

He pulled off his sport coat and threw it about the squirmy thing. "No, no, everything's okay. Kid's just acting up is all. Hold your horses!"

"Well, hurry! It's getting dark!"

Mr. Peldo blocked Luther's charge with his foot. "Where did you get that!"

Luther did not answer. He glowered sullenly at the ground, mumbling. "He's mine. I found him. You can't have him."

"Where did it come from?" Mr. Peldo demanded.

Luther's lower lip resembled a bloated sausage. Finally he jerked his thumb in the direction of the river bank.

"You can talk!"

Luther whimpered, tried once again to get at the wriggling bundle on the sand, sat down, and said, "I found him in the water. I snuck up on him and grabbed him when he wasn't looking. Now he's mine and you can't have—"

But Mr. Peldo, having recovered himself, had plucked off the coat and was staring.

A place for dreaming.

Roadsters that would go over two hundred miles per hour. Promontoried chateaus with ten bathrooms. Coveys of lithe young temptresses, vacant-minded, full-bodied, infinitely imaginative, infinitely accessible . . .

"JAAAAke! Are you trying to scare me to death? It's cold and my sinuses are beginning to run!"

Luther looked at his father, snorted loudly and started for the trees.

"He's Fritzchen and he's *mine!*" he called back as he ran. "All right—I'll get even! You'll see!"

Mr. Peldo watched the small creature, fascinated, as all its legs commenced to move together, dwarfed, undeveloped legs, burrowing into the viscous ground. Shuddering slightly, he replaced the coat, gathered it into the form of a sack and started through the shrubbery.

Edna's nose had turned red. He decided not to show Fritzchen to her, for a while.

* * *

"Got no empties," Sol said slowly, eying the bundle Mr. Peldo held at arms' length. Sol didn't care for animals. He was old; his mind had fallen into a ravine; it paced the ravine; turned and paced, like a contented baboon. He was old.

Mr. Peldo waited for Edna and Luther to go around to the living quarters in the back. "Put the capuchin in with Bess," he said, then. "Ought to have a stout one. Hop to it, Sol, I can't stand here holding this all day."

"'nother stray?"

"You—might say."

Sol shrugged and transferred the raucous little monkey from his carved wood cage to the parrot dome.

Then he looked back. Mr. Peldo was holding the jacket-bundle down on a table with both hands. Whatever was inside was moving in violent spasms, not the way a dog moves or a rabbit. There were tiny sounds.

"Give me a hand," Mr. Peldo said, and Sol helped him put the bundle, jacket and all, into the cage. They locked it.

"This'll do for a while," Mr. Peldo said, "until I can build a proper one. Now mind, Sol, you keep your mouth strictly shut about this. Shut."

Sol didn't answer. His nose had snapped upward and he held a conched hand behind his ear.

"Listen, you," Sol said.

Mr. Peldo took his fingers off the sport coat, which had begun to show a purplish stain through.

"First time it ever happened in sixteen years," Sol said.

The silence roared. The silent pet shop roared and burst and pulsed with tension, quiet electric tension. The animals didn't move anywhere in the room. Mr. Peldo's eyes darted from cage to cage, seeing the second strangest thing he had ever seen: unmoving snakes, coiled or supine, but still as though listening; monkeys hidden in far corners, haunched; rabbits—even their noses quiet and frozen—; white mice huddled at the bottom of mills that turned in cautious, diminishing arcs, frightened, staring creatures.

The phlegm in Mr. Peldo's throat racked loose.

Then it was quiet again. Though not exactly quiet.

Sol quit his survey of the animals and turned back to the occupant of the capuchin's cage. The sport jacket glistened with stain now, and from within the dark folds there was a scrabbling and a small gurgling sound.

Then the jacket fell away.

"Tom-hell, Jake!" Sol said.

The animals had begun to scream, all of them, all at once.

"Not a word to anyone now, Sol! Promise."

Mr. Peldo feasted. He stared and stared, feeling satisfaction.

"What in glory is it?" Sol inquired above the din.

"A pet," Mr. Peldo answered, simply.

"Pet, hey?"

"We'll have to build a special cage for it," Mr. Peldo beamed. "Say, bet there ain't many like this one! No, sir. We'll have to read up on it so's we can get the feeding right and all . . ."

"*You* read up." Sol's eyes were large. The air was filled with the wild beating of birds' wings.

Mr. Peldo was musing. "By the way, Sol, what you suppose it could be?"

The old man cocked his head to one side, peered from slitted eyes, picked out the crumpled sport jacket quickly and let it fall to the floor. It dropped heavily and exuded a sick water smell. Sol shrugged.

"Cross between a whale," he said, "and a horsefly, near's I can see."

"Maybe it's valuable—you think?" Mr. Peldo's ideas were growing.

"Couldn't say. Most likely not, in the face of it."

The chittering sound rose into a sort of staccato wail, piercing, clear over the frantic pets.

"Where in thunder you get it?"

"*He* didn't. *I* did." It was Luther, scowling, in his nightclothes.

"Go to bed. Go away."

"I found Fritzchen in the water. He likes me."

"*Out!*"

"Dirty stinking rotten lousy rotten stealer!"

Sol put his fingers into his ears and shut his eyes.

Luther made a pout and advanced towards Fritzchen's cage. The sobbing noises ceased.

"He hadda lock you up. Yeah. *I* was gonna let you loose again." The boy glared at his father. "See how he loves me." Luther put his face up to the cage, and as he did so the small animal came forward, ponderously, with suctionlike noises from its many legs.

Mr. Peldo looked disinterested. He inspected his watchstem. Neither he nor Sol saw what happened.

Luther stamped his foot and yelled. The right side of his face was covered with something that gathered and dripped down.

"Luther!" It was Mr. Peldo's wife. She ran into the room and looked at the cage. "Oh, that nasty thing!" She stormed out, clutching her son's pink ear.

"Damn woman will drive me crazy," Mr. Peldo said. Then he noticed that the shop was quiet again. Sol had thrown the damp jacket over Fritzchen's cage. There was only the sobbing.

"Funny!"

Mr. Peldo bent down, lifted the end of the coat and put his face close. He jerked back with abnormal speed, swabbing at his cheek.

There was a sound like a drowning kitten's purr.

Luther stood in the back doorway. Hate and astonishment contorted his features. "That's all he cares about me when I only wanted to be good to him! Now he loves *you*, dirty rotten—"

"Look, boy, your father's getting might tired of—"

"Yeah, well, he'll be sorry."

Fritzchen began to chitter again.

When Mr. Peldo returned to the shop after dinner, he found a curious thing. Bess, the parrot, lay on her side, dead.

Everything else was normal. The animals were wakeful or somnolent but normal. Fritzchen's cage was covered with a canvas, and there was silence from within.

Mr. Peldo inspected Bess and was horrified to discover the bird's condition. She lay inundated in an odd miasmic jelly, which had hardened and was now spongey to the touch. It covered her completely. What was more, extended prodding revealed that something had happened to Bess's insides.

They were gone.

And without a trace. Even the bones. Bess was little more than skin and feathers.

Mr. Peldo recalled the substance that had struck his face when he examined Fritzchen's cage the last time. In a frenzy he pulled off the tarpaulin. But Fritzchen was there, and the cage was as securely locked as ever.

And easily twenty feet from the parrot dome.

He went back and found the capuchin staring at him out of quizzical eyes.

Luther, of course. Monster boy. Spoiled bug of a child. He had an active imagination. Probably rigged the whole thing, like the time he emasculated the parakeet in an attempt to turn it inside out.

Mr. Peldo was ungratified that the animals had not yet gotten used to Fritzchen. They began their harangue, so he switched off the light and waited for his eyes to accustom themselves to the moonlight. Moonlight comes fast to small towns near rivers.

Fritzchen must be sleeping. Curled like a baby anaconda, legs slender filaments adhering to the cage floor, the tender tiny tail tucked around so that the tip rested just inside the immense mouth.

Mr. Peldo studied the animal. He watched the mouth especially, noting its outsized relationship to the rest of the body.

But—Mr. Peldo peered—could it actually be that Fritzchen was *larger*? Surely not. The stomach did seem fatter, yet the finely ground hamburger, the dish of milk, the oysters, sat to one side, untouched. Nor had the accommodating bathing and drinking pool been disturbed.

Then he noticed, for the first time, that the mouth had no teeth. There did not appear to be a gullet! And the spiny snout, with its florid green cup, was not a nose after all, for the nose was elsewhere.

But most curious of all, Fritzchen had grown. Oh, yes, grown. No doubt about it.

Mr. Peldo retired hours later with sparkling visions of wealth. He would contact—somebody appropriate—and sell his find for many hundreds of thousands of dollars. Then he would run away to Europe and play with a different woman every night until he died of his excesses.

He was awakened a short time later by Sol, who informed him that the bird of paradise and one dalmatian pup had died during the night. He knew because he'd heard the racket from clean across the street.

"Oh, not the ooo wow-wow," said Edna. "Not the liddle puppy!"

Luther sat up in bed, interested.

"How'd it happen?" Mr. Peldo said.

"Don't know. No good way for definite sure." Sol's eyelids almost closed. "Their innards is gone."

Edna put her head beneath the covers.

"Fritzchen?"

"Guess. Y'ough't'a do somethin' with that crittur. Bad actor."

"He got out—that it?"

"Hey-up. Or somebody let him out. Cage is all locked up tight as wax, 'n it wailin' like a banshee."

Mr. Peldo whirled to face his son, who stuck out his tongue.

"See here, young fellow, we're going to get to the bottom of this. If I find out that you—"

"Don't think t'was the lad," Sol said.

"Why not?"

"Wa'l . . . that there thing is thrice the size t'was yesterday when you brung'er in."

"No."

"No nothin'. Stomach's pooched out like it's fit to bust."

Mr. Peldo got up and rubbed his hand over his bald head.

"But look, Sol, if it didn't get out, and—Luther, you didn't let it out, did you?"

"No, sir."

"—then how we going to blame it? Maybe there's a disease going around."

"*I* know, *I* know," Luther sang, swinging his feet in the air. "His nose can go longer."

"Be still, boy."

"Well, it *can*! I saw it. Fritzchen did it on the beach—hit a bird 'way out over the water and he didn't move out of my hands."

"What happened to the bird, Luther?"

"Well, it got stuck up with this stuff Fritzchen has inside him, so it couldn't do anything. Then when it was all glued, Fritzchen pulled it back closer to him and shot out his nose and put his nose inside the bird's mou—"

Mr. Peldo felt his cheek, where the molasses had gathered that time. Both he and Luther had thought of it as an affectionate gesture, no worse than a St. Bernard leaping and pawing over you, raking your face, covering you with friendly, doggy slobber.

That's why Luther had gotten angry.

But Fritzchen wasn't being affectionate. It didn't work only because Fritzchen was too small, or they had been too big.

Mr. Peldo remembered Bess.

Edna poked her head out of the covers and said, "You listen to that! The neighbors will kill us!"

The sounds from the shop were growing stronger and louder and more chaotic.

Mr. Peldo dashed to the hall and returned with a telephone book. "Here," he said, tossing it to his wife, "get the numbers of all the zoos and museums."

"He's mine, he's mine!" Luther screeched.

Sol, who was old, said, "Jake, you never you mind about that. You just fished up something quaar, is all, and the best thing you can do is chuck 'er back where she come from."

"Edna—Get those numbers, do you hear me? All the museums in the state. I'll be back."

The wailing had reached a crescendo now.

And Luther had disappeared.

Mr. Peldo put on a robe and hurried across the frosty lawn to the back door of the shop.

"Luther!"

The small boy had a box of kitchen matches, holding a cluster of these in his hands, lighting them and hurling them into Fritzchen's cage. The fiery sticks landed; there was a cry of pain and then the matches spluttered out against moist skin.

"Luther!"

"I wanted to be good to you," Luther was saying, "but then you hadda take up with *him*! Yeah, well, now you'll see!"

Mr. Peldo threw his son out the door.

The painful wail became an intermittent cry: a strange cry, not unmelodious.

Mr. Peldo looked into the great jeweled milk-white eyes of the creature and dodged as the snout unrolled like a party favor, spraying a fine crystal glaze of puce jam.

Fritzchen stood erect. He—it—had changed. There were antennae where no antennae had been; many of the legs had developed claws; the mouth, which had been toothless the day before, was now filled with sharp brown needles. Fritzchen had been fifteen inches high when Mr. Peldo first saw him. Now he stood over thirty inches.

Still time, though. Time for everything.

Mr. Peldo looked at the animal until his eyes hurt; then he saw the newspaper on the floor. It was soaked with what looked like shreds of liquid soap-jelly, greenish, foul with the odor of seaweed and other things. On it lay a bird and a small dog.

He felt sad for a moment. But then he thought again of some of the things he had dreamed a long time ago, of what he had now, and he determined to make certain telephone calls.

A million dollars, or almost, probably. They'd—oh, they'd stuff Fritzchen, at all odds, or something like that.

"Dirty rotten lousy—"

Luther had come back. He had a crumpled-up magazine saturated with oil and lighter fluid. The magazine was on fire.

The monkeys and the rabbits and the mice and the goldfish and the cats and birds and dogs shrilled in fear. But Fritzchen didn't.

Fritzchen howled only once. Or lowed: a deep sound from somewhere in the middle of his body that seemed to come from his body and not just his mouth. It was an eerily mournful sound that carried a new tone, a tone of helplessness. Then the creature was silent.

By the time Mr. Peldo reached the cage, Luther had thrown inflammable fluid from a can. The fire burned fiercely.

"I *told* you," Luther said, pettishly.

When the fire was pulled and scattered and trampled out, an ugly thing remained in the cage. An ugly blackened thing that made no noise.

Luther began to cry.

Then he stopped.

And Mr. Peldo stopped chasing him.

Sol and Edna in the doorway didn't move either.

They all listened.

It could have been a crazed elephant shambling madly through a straw village . . .

Or a whale blind with the pain of sharp steel, thrashing and leaping in illimitable waters . . .

Or it could have been a massive hawk swooping in outraged vengeance upon the killers of her young . . .

The killers of her young!

In that moment before the rustling sound grew huge, before the windows shattered and the great nightmarish shadow came into the shop, Mr. Peldo understood the meaning of Fritzchen's inconsolable cries.

They were the cries of a lost infant for its mother.

You Can't Have Them All

Upon entering the hotel room and glancing at its occupant, Doctor Lenardi assumed that hearty, cheerful manner which is characteristic of all physicians once they have abandoned hope. His eyes flicked over the luxurious appointments—the thick-piled rug, the hearth, the high-fidelity phonograph—and across the towel-wrapped ice bucket, from which extruded a magnum of champagne, and the single guttering candle: then he smiled. He rubbed his hands together, professionally. "Well, now," he said, "and what seems to be the trouble here?"

The man in bed moaned, softly. "Women," he said.

"I beg your pardon?"

"Women," the man repeated, in a faint, almost inaudible whisper.

Doctor Lenardi sighed. He had come out of the rainswept streets like an angry raven, cursing, muttering; yet now he was ashamed. For he could not recall a time in his existence when he had been so instantaneously moved to pity. Why? The patina of weariness, of ineffable exhaustion, perhaps; the absolute incapacity that shone dully from the fellow's eyes... *Poor devil!* he thought.

Forgetting entirely the difficulty with his wife, an almost omnipresent burden on his mind these days, forgetting his own unhappy state, he walked briskly to the bed and began to unsnap his bag. "Can you understand me?" he asked gently.

The man nodded.

"Good. Then I want you to tell me this. Are you in any pain? Dizzy? Nauseated?"

"No." The man trembled. "That is, not exactly."

"I see." Doctor Lenardi uncoiled a stethoscope and applied

it. He said, "Hmmm," and took from the bag a number of vari-sized articles with which he proceeded to peer, thump, prod, and listen.

Some minutes later he put everything away and sat for a time stroking his nose. Not even in Nairobi, during the plague, had he encountered a human being whose thread with life seemed quite so frayed, whose *élan vital* and resistance had sunk to such abysmal depths. "Tell me," he said spontaneously, "if you can—how in the world did you manage to get yourself into this wretched condition. Mister——"

"Simms," the man said. "Edward Simms." He surrendered to a rather violent shudder, which sent his dressing gown to rippling like a troubled scarlet sea. His face was seamed and wasted; obviously once striking, the features had fallen into a mandarin desiccation. It was an old man's face, sure enough. "Well, you know, that's quite a question; yes. I called room service around seven, I think it was, and that's when the, the weakness came over me. A terrible weakness, in all my bones . . ."

Doctor Lenardi glanced at the two empty wine glasses on the coffee table. "Yes. Go on."

"That's all there is. I think that I just sort of blacked out, then. Must have knocked the phone off its hook." The man swallowed: it bobbled the knot of his white silk scarf. "Am I . . . all right?" he murmured.

"That," Doctor Lenardi said, making no effort whatever to conceal his astonishment, "is a moot question. There does not appear to be anything the matter with you, in particular——"

"Thank Heaven!"

"On the other hand, Mister Simms, I would say—and the opinion is based upon some twenty-five years of intensive practice—that you are, in general, the most singularly run-down human I've ever dealt with. There may be nothing wrong with you, but I give you my word that there is nothing right. May I ask your age?"

"Certainly," Edward Simms said. "I am twenty-eight."

"Please be serious."

"Twenty-eight is my exact age, I tell you. Here, look at my driver's license!"

Doctor Lenardi emitted a gust of wind. With difficulty he restrained himself from remarking that the patient looked closer to *forty*-eight. "Then," he said, "you are tremendously overworked."

The man called Simms smiled strangely. "Perhaps." He glanced at his watch and made a futile effort to rise. "Doctor," he said, with considerable urgency, "I apologize for having detained you this long. I am perfectly all right now. If you will only give me a slight stimulant, something to get me ticking again, that is, I'll be much obliged."

"My dear chap, what you need is precisely the reverse. A sedative—"

"No, no!" Simms was looking at his watch again, and shaking his head. "You don't understand. It's absolutely vital that I get a *stimulant*. Doctor——" His voice grew meaningful, edged with innuendo. "If I were to tell you that I am expecting a young lady, would that change your mind?"

Doctor Lenardi sat down abruptly. He gazed at the thin young man who did not appear to have the strength to pull himself off the bed, and tried to assimilate what he'd heard. He looked at the champagne. At the man's dressing gown . . .

"You're joking, Simms."

"Not a bit of it. See here now, I happen to be a man of science, too, and I know perfectly well what I need. I'm willing, if necessary, to *buy* what I ask. Name your price. Ten dollars? Fifty? A hundred?" Edward Simms reached out and grasped the other's lapels. "*Please*," he said desperately; there was the fire of delirium in his eyes. The eyes searched for agreement, then hardened. "I'll—I'll tell you *exactly* why I need your help in this. Will you listen?"

Doctor Lenardi was about to answer in the negative, but he paused. It occurred to him, suddenly, that this man was familiar. In a peculiar, elusive way, familiar . . .

Well, let the fellow rave, let the poor wretch rave on, perhaps it would put him to sleep. "Very well, Mister Simms. But I will have to administer a sedative afterwards in any case."

"No; you'll see." The young man fell back against the pillows like a crumbling tower. "I've kept it to myself so long," he whispered, in a voice already distant; "So terribly long. It's good to be able to tell someone, at last, now that it's almost finished . . ."

Doctor Lenardi pulled his chair closer to the bed.

He removed his glasses.

"Go on, Mister Simms. I'm listening."

*   *   *

Beautiful women (the young man began, in muted tones) are my sickness; I know that now, but I did not always know it. Years ago, when I was terribly young and very naive, when life was hopscotch and marbles and jam sandwiches, and I had no glimpse of the adult world, I realized one thing: that boys and girls were *different*. And the difference disturbed me, though for what reason I could scarcely guess. I was one thing and girls were another, you see. But what? *How* were we different, in what way?

I used to wander about, turning the problem over in my mind. And it seemed to make no sense. But then I would catch sight of a particularly striking six-year-old with golden pigtails, and I knew that I must be right.

It was a thorny problem, but one which did not, apparently, concern my friends, or disturb them, so I tried earnestly to dismiss it. But I was not successful in this.

I found that while I went about my boyhood in a normal fashion, playing football and baseball and the like, my mind was ever ready to stray. I would be in the act of executing a forward pass, or bunting for a one-base hit, when my eyes would fall upon the smiling face of a beautiful girl, and I would be lost, lost.

Of course, later, in the private schools my parents sent me to, I learned that my earlier suspicions had been correct—there was indeed a difference between boys and girls—and the vaguely disturbed feeling became one of intense curiosity. But *a priori* knowledge was insufficient to quell my interest: you cannot appreciate the bouquet of a rare wine if it is forever sealed in the bottle. So I was more than pleased when a young coed named Bobbi indicated a fondness for me. She was an entrancing creature, 34-24-36, as attractive as she was cooperative, and we saw the stars up close. And that, I felt sure, was the end of my obsession. The bottle, so to speak, had been unsealed.

Time passed. I'd buried myself in my hobbies, which were science, mathematics and chemistry—with an occasional belt at electronics—as, I suppose, compensation for my obsessive curiosity; now I returned to them with vigor. All was well.

Then, on a day no different than any other, the terrible trouble began.

I'd set out for the parts house to purchase a coil of light wire, part of a perpetual motion experiment. I was crossing the street, with no other thought in my head, when, utterly without warning, I saw her walking toward me—a tall, slender yet curvesome female, regal as a goddess, with skin the color of white marble and hair the exotic tint of burnished copper: 35-24-36.

The old feeling had returned! I couldn't understand it. I had thought all my problems were solved. With Bobbi's sweet help, that feeling had been routed—for good, I'd thought. But *now!* . . .

I was deeply disturbed. That did not, however, prevent me from acting.

With what amounted to ferocity, I wheeled, overtook the girl, and, before I knew what was happening, made my overtures. They were rebuffed, needless to say, but I persisted, and (to spare you the details) it was not long before Clara and I had got to the hand-holding stage.

I think it was my relative inexperience that charmed her. Like a feminine Virgil, to my Dante, she seemed to take a grim delight in her role of guide, and would often laugh at my enthusiastic but hopelessly amateur stumblings. But whatever her shortcomings in matters of finesse, it must be said of Clara that she was thorough. I had entered the Undiscovered Country a stranger; now, thanks to her, I was a pioneer.

It was an enormously pleasant idyll, satisfactory in every sense.

Bobbi had begun my education, Clara had completed it. Surely now, I felt, I would be rid of the Feeling, and could devote myself to other, less earthly, pursuits.

But——

Some weeks later, a very odd thing happened. On my way to Clara's apartment, I caught a glimpse of a blonde college girl. She was like the rest of them—young; uniformed in dark skirt and white sweater; approximately 36-24-36—but there was a then indefinable something about her that compelled me to stop in my tracks. The sway of her hips, perhaps; the jaunty bounce of her hair—I didn't know. I knew only that the Feeling was back, and in full force.

I stared after her until she'd disappeared from view, then continued to Clara's. All evening I tried to analyze what it was that was wrong. Then, at a horribly ironic moment, I discovered the answer.

Clara was wonderful, she gave me all I could possibly ask

and I could not have been fonder of her; yet I wanted this stranger.

It was a crushing discovery, and one which caused no little self-examination.

But I could no longer think of anything but that college girl, I tell you! She permeated my dreams. I saw her everywhere. She would not, absolutely would *not* leave me.

I am here to tell you that locating her was no easy task. But perseverance pays. I found her eventually at a malt shop, in the company of a dozen football players...

Well, Eunice and I began to see a bit of each other, as the phrase goes. I think it was my relative experience that charmed her. We traveled to remote picnic grounds, attended fairs and carnivals, and presently the Feeling, and my sadness at parting with Bobbi and Clara, abated.

Until I saw Carmen, 37-25-36...

I spent an entire month and a great deal of my parents' money barraging this one with my attentions, and finally, with great reluctance, she granted me a date. We had no more than stepped out of her house, however, when I saw the flashing ankles of a honey blonde in a tight jersey. It all but drove me out of my mind. I could hardly wait to be done with Carmen and go after the blonde!

And so, I am afraid, it went.

A psychiatrist allayed my fears somewhat—and I had begun to wonder what the devil was the matter with me, anyway—by reporting that there was nothing really unusual in my case. "It is as if you owned an original painting by Rembrandt," he said. "It is beautiful. You love it. No other painting is more satisfying to you. But—there are other pictures in the gallery; and, because you are exceptionally sensitive to beauty, you cannot ignore them. You pass a Botticelli and your heart stops. You pause by a Van Gogh. Again the frustration. You see a fine Picasso..."

Shortly afterwards, my father offered a similar diagnosis. "My son," he said, placing an affectionate hand upon my shoulder, "I know what you feel, believe me. And it's a terrible, terrible thing. But there's no way around it. You can't have them all."

Which seemed logical enough. At the time.

I waited for the calm acceptance to come, of course; for that moment when, fully matured, I would realize the patent impossibility of what must be my subconscious ambition and, like other men, content myself with a less rewarding arrangement.

Unfortunately, nothing happened.

Except that my condition, if we may refer to it as that, worsened. I was disturbed most of the time now, riddled with nameless hungers at the increasingly frequent sights of beautiful women. And whenever I would hear someone say, joshingly, "Well, remember, Simms boy, just remember now—you can't have 'em all!" I would find myself bristling.

At last, when I was sure that I could not continue to exist in the midst of such intolerable frustration, I sat down and took stock.

They say you cannot have them all, I thought.

And then I thought: Why not?

It was a beginning. In just such a way, I imagine, are most great advances made. One man asking himself: *Why not?*

The answer did not come exactly in a flash. I thought about it until my mind was all but paralyzed, and things looked very dark, indeed. In the first place, I ruminated, there were countless thousands—perhaps millions—of beautiful women on Earth. And even if I could locate them, what guarantee was there I would be uniformly successful? I was handsome enough then, charming enough, rich enough; but there would always be obstinate cases, there had been before. Also, counting time for courting, wooing, and what not, there would—and this was an important point—be *a new crop* before I had even made a dent in the first! Mathematically, it was far from encouraging.

Then, in the very act of loading the pistol that would disperse my woe, I asked myself the question that was to become, so to speak, the opening wedge.

I asked myself what I meant when I said *beautiful woman*. What did the term imply? Was it *really* as indefinable as all that?

I remembered the women who had attracted me, and thought about them carefully, seeking a connecting link. There had to be one.

And there was.

You've heard the expression, "She may be pretty, but she's just not my type?"

It was this that gave me my greatest lead. Every man is

attracted by a particular *type* of female; and there should be more-or-less consistent characteristics determining these types.

Things started to look up. This information meant that the field was unquestionably narrower than I'd thought. Three more questions remained, however; and they were not unimportant.

Number One: Exactly how many women of my type existed?

Number Two: Where were they?

Number Three: How could I get at them?

There was, you understand, no available method of answering these questions. But I knew that equally complex problems were being solved in the various universities and laboratories by electronic calculators, and—call it faith, call it desperation, or sheer naiveté—I was confident that a machine could be constructed to do the work.

However, such a machine would cost a large fortune, and I had but a small fortune, left to me by my parents, God rest them. So I was thrown upon the resources of my imagination. In time the answer came, though, I am proud to say.

At the local university, there was one of the largest and most modern electronic calculators in existence. It was an incredibly complex device, considerably more advanced than its rather primitive predecessors. It could do everything but dance a hornpipe, I was told, and they were working on that. So, in high fettle, and with respect for the instinct which had early turned me to a study of electronics, I immediately set to the problem of building what we may term an "extension" of the machine. Endless weeks passed, and failure after failure confronted me, but at last all that remained was devising a method of attaching the addition to the main body without calling the attention of officials or guards. It was a knotty business, but a way was found.

By now I knew to the last minute detail what sort of women I wanted—they had to be no younger than eighteen, no older than forty; they had to possess an intellectual potential; etc.—and had these specifications broken down in code upon a series of tapes. My extension would be fed these data and would then submit them to the giant calculator (which, in a moment of whimsy, I had decided to call Procurer One).

Upon receiving the information, my machine lit up like a grotesque Christmas tree and began to whine. It was almost frightening, the noises it made; but after a few hours, it quieted and was still, and presently a scroll dropped into the tray.

I breathed a silent hallelujah.

Procurer One had ingested my data and had ascertained exactly the geographical and climatical, also the generic, conditions likely to produce the type of women I sought.

It gave the number and the locations.

There were five hundred and sixty-three of them. Mostly they were in America—which was no handy coincidence, for I knew that however exotic and *interesting* the foreign product might be, it was seldom more than that. There were exceptions, of course, primarily in Sweden and Britain and France; and a number of surprising contradictions—a Tahitian, for example, was on the list; a total of four in Rangoon; and so on—but the bulk lay within the boundaries of my own continent.

You can consider my delight.

I attacked the last phase of the project with something akin to frenzy. Knowing the address of Tiffany's, I realized, did not automatically put a diamond necklace about one's throat. One must be able to afford the necklace, or—one must be an accomplished thief.

In this connection, I elminated all of the obvious answers and reduced the matter to one incontrovertible equation: Mutual attraction—Success of the plan. There could be no slip-ups, no depending upon circumstances, and certainly no unrealistic faith in my own charm, however devastating. No: there must be, simply, a straightforward method by which I could be absolutely assured of at least acquiescence to my designs—a problem, as you can see, chockablock with difficulties.

An aphrodisiac, of course, was what I needed. But in what form? Perfume? Perhaps; but there would be imponderable drawbacks—an unruly wisp of breeze, for instance, might throw everything off balance. One would have to be sure to "hit the target," as it were, yet if the target happened to be in a mixed crowd . . .

I decided at length upon a potion. Potions were once very much the vogue, and a careful survey of Medieval literature convinced me that here was the one sure way; it also convinced me that although we take it for granted that the so-called Love Draught is a mythical and non-existent form of wish fulfillment, it is nothing of the kind. As with stained glass, it is merely an art we had lost.

Reviving the art was not an easy matter, you may be sure, but I believe I mentioned that chemistry was one of my childhood loves. You will therefore not be shocked to learn that, in due time, I evolved sort of an herbal tea—I shan't become tiresome by going into the exact recipe—and that this brew sufficed for the purpose. One sip of it, in fact, was quite enough to engender *rapport* in the stoniest female heart, and two sips—ah well, enough to say that I was satisfied.

So, I must admit, were the first stray recipients of my experimentation.

But there was still work to be done. To go about it haphazardly would spell doom as surely as if nothing had been accomplished; for there was the unalterable fact that scores of *girls* would be leaping out of their chrysalises, so to say, and becoming *women*. As I've pointed out, nothing below the age of eighteen would do for me, but consider the sixteen and seventeen-year-olds all crouched, waiting to spring into the fray!

I therefore made up a schedule.

It was, as one might suspect, fantastically demanding. It granted me an absolute maximum of two days per case. Fortunately, there were certain areas where overlapping and doubling-up were feasible; otherwise I'd have been licked. In any event, it *could* be done. On paper, at least.

My work was now cut out for me.

I girded my loins, as they say, and began at once, enplaning the following morning for Europe. According to Procurer One, a ravishing brunette by the name of Françoise Simon, 37-25-36, lived on the outskirts of Montauban. She was married, without children, and of a generally sunny temperament. The machine, of course, had not been able to supply all of this information—I'd had to fall back on a number of private detectives—but I was certain of my facts. About the husbands, or similar ties, I knew nothing; but it didn't matter, particularly, as my system was sufficiently flexible to allow for contingencies.

I went straight to the village, located the cottage, and, making sure that the phial containing the potion was with me, rapped on the door.

It was opened by a young woman in a peasant blouse and full skirt.

Procurer One had not been whistling *Dixie*! From her frank Norman features there shone a warmth and honesty and fire that sent excitement flashing through me.

I recovered my aplomb and inquired, in French, the way to the nearest bus stop.

She told me that there were not such things as buses in this vicinity, but would I not step inside to take the chill off?

"Is your husband home?" I asked, noncommittally. She shook her head. I stepped inside.

Francoise blushed and made conversation about the weather, but I could see that she was thinking of other thinngs. When she leaned over to light my cigarette, I could almost feel the heat of her blood. "Monsieur," she said—actually it was "Monsieur l'Americain"—"would you care for a glass of brandy?" I nodded enthusiastically and, when the drinks were poured, managed to add a drop of my herbal tea to hers—though it did seem piling Scylla on Charybdis, or however that goes.

Upon the first swallow, Francoise lost even the vestigial reticence she had displayed and, literally, sprang across the room. I was not quite prepared, but I managed to catch her, and soon it was raining clothes.

The whole thing was enormously pleasant. But my schedule did not permit of divertissement. I told her that she was exquisite, said "Merci beaucoup" or something like that, and beat a hasty exit. From the way she sobbed and clung to my legs, I knew that I would have to cut down on the quantity of the draughts: even a single drop was entirely too powerful!

I seemed to hear her savage cries of woe all the way to my plane.

I proceeded to Boulogne, and there called upon a delightful creature named Laurette, 38-25-37; it was an equally satisfactory interlude. Laurette lived alone, fortunately, and so it did not require more than an hour, all told. Then I was off again, headed for Paris.

Procurer One had come through magnificently! With the foreign entries out of the way, I returned to America and settled down to a program of activity which, owing to its rigorousness, if not to its nature, would have impressed the most earnest toiler. Implacably I kept to the schedule, and there were not, I'm proud to say, more than a dozen occasions when the allotted time was exceeded. These were due to sudden moves, biological upsets over which no man has dominion, slight difficulties with relatives, and what have you.

Of course, there were problems with the philtre, particularly in the case of Mildred C., a teetotaler, but these were circumvented in divers ways. With Mildred, for example, it was necessary to tamper with the morning milk; whereas with Josie F., the hypochondriac, I was forced to modify the contents of her throat spray. Frequently I was thrown for a loss, but never for very long: nothing deflected me seriously from my course then.

Cutting a swath through California, an unusually rich vein, I began to work my way across the States. Albuquerque, Boise, Snohomish, Portland, Oklahoma City, Chicago, Wheeling, Detroit—these were the greatest concentrations, though there were hundreds of tiny outposts, some not even listed on the map, which yielded plenty, too. Tall ones, short ones, dark ones, light ones; the intellectual type with glasses and the innocent farm type; redheads, blondes, brunettes—they fell like wheat under the scythe. I left a wake of memorable evenings, and shattered reputations. True, some were more diverting than others; howbeit, I rolled on, relentless, dauntless, a veritable juggernaut. No power on Earth could stop me!

After a while, however, I must confess that some of the edge had gone out of the project. Not that I was tiring spiritually, you understand; but one is, after all, flesh and blood. Subsequent to number three hundred and seventy-four, I think there was less spontaneous joy than determination in it for me. To be brutally honest, I was becoming physically fagged of the whole thing—and I shudder now to think of the times when I came so close to throwing in the towel. Although I was in bed most of the while, I slept but little; and when I passed the four hundred mark, I found that my weight was dropping precipitously. From a robust one-ninety-six, I now weighed in at one hundred and fourteen pounds! My eyes had taken on their present glaze. I felt tired all of the time. Everything began to ache.

But Simmses are not quitters. When they start a thing, they finish it.

I went on.

The days melted into the nights. Each conquest became a supreme effort of will. I traveled like a somnambulist, dumbly carrying out my duties; and by the time the number had been whittled down to less than fifty, I was in the position of having to be constantly fortified with drugs, hormones, and other medications. I cannot describe to you the agonies of spirit and body I endured as the end approached. Logically I ought to have collapsed from overwork then; but, somehow, I was able to forge ahead.

Then, one day, as I lay gasping, I discovered a remarkable thing. I was down to ten. Ten more, and the project would be a *fait accompli*!

Despite my haggard look, and the fact that I was weak to the point of total exhaustion, I gathered together every last trace of my strength, and continued.

Isabella R., 39-23-35, number ten—Indianapolis—was shocked by my appearance, but overwhelmed by my potion. In less than twenty minutes, she succumbed.

A practical nurse in Dubuque, Dorothy S., 40-25-37, offered to look after me, and in a way she did. A day for her.

Sondra the stenographer, Old Lyme, Conn., 41-24-38, was a pushover.

Then there was Ivy, formerly Miss Improved Ball Bearings and in 1953 voted "The Girl We'd Most Like to Retouch" by the Association of Commercial Photographers—42-25-37: a two-day job.

Gloria the proper Bostonian, at an astounding 42½-24-34, followed; and the genuinely accomplished stripper Emma Samuelson (known professionally as "Peachy" Kean); and Pearl and Sally and Bertha. Then there was Detroit's Natasha, a fiery, mordant pseudo-intellectual with advanced views and retarded intentions. . . . Procurer One had shrewdly pierced her frosty exterior and added her to the list. I wasted no time.

But their names are unimportant. Important only that I was able to check them off.

It was at this point—this crucial, critical point—that an accident occurred. An accident that nearly ruined all my plans.

On my way to this city, where the remaining two women resided, the plane encountered foul weather. The pilot made the announcement: an announcement that was merely annoying to the other passengers, but which struck me with unnameable horror. He had been advised, by radio, to ground the plane at a small rural airport and wait for clearer weather...

Weak though I was, the news wrenched me to my feet,

tore a cry of frustration and despair from my throat: "*Wait!?* I cannot wait! I must be there on schedule! Time . . . is of the essence . . . my plans . . . all my plans . . ." But the effort had proved too much for my weakened body. I blacked out, and I was soon to find myself marking time—precious, irrevocable time!—in a cheerless hotel in a cheerless town the name of which I never bothered to learn. Hours. Priceless hours! Do they seem unimportant to you, Doctor? Yes, they do, I am sure. But, you see—the nearer I drew to the end of my task, the more critical the time element became! One slip—such as this—one delay, and the delicate balance of the whole cycle might well be upset! The seventeen-year-olds would attain maturity, become eligible for my conquest, become part of the symbolic All that was now my *raison d'etre*, my obsession, my curse . . .

Do you understand? If this thing happened—if that immense armada of girls blossomed into womanhood before I completed my task—*I would have to begin all over again!* All over again: consider that, Doctor! Look at me, think of my condition, and then consider what that would mean. All over again? A wasted, spent, exhausted man, near death? Impossible! I waited six hours, but the weather did not clear. I asked about trains. There were no trains. And buses: I asked about buses. Yes, there was a bus . . . if you could call it that. It seems you took it to the adjacent county, where you transferred to another bus which took you to a place where you got a taxi (if you were lucky) which would transport you to the Greyhound station . . .

I looked once at the overcast sky, and took the bus. If you could call it that.

And, twenty-eight hours later, shaken to jelly, wracked with pain, held together only by tenacity and vitamin pills, I arrived here to make my last two conquests.

The first, a waitress over on Fifth Street, gasped when I entered the restaurant.

"What will you have, sir?" she asked, obviously uncertain whether to give me a glass of water or call an emergency clinic.

"What have you got?" I joshed, being careful not to chuckle. The drugs kept the pain down, and it hurt only when I laughed.

She leaned forward to place the silverware, and I felt like a tourist at the base of Mount Rushmore. "Poached eggs," I murmured, and when the meal was finished, I tucked half of a hundred dollar bill underneath my napkin, together with a note reading: "For the other half, meet me after work." A crude maneuver, perhaps, but generally effective.

We met and had cocktails. Then we went to my hotel. Poor creature, I think it was the first time she'd ever tasted good champagne . . .

When she left, I tried to sleep, but I could not sleep. How did Edison feel a few hours before he switched on the first electric light? Or Shakespeare, just before he dashed off *Hamlet*? I could only taste, again and again, the heady draught of Victory. One more, I kept saying, and the everlasting, long-enduring dream of my life would be realized! I'd be satisfied, for in essence I would have had every beautiful woman—beautiful, to me—on the list. All that existed when the list was made.

All.

The next morning I saw that in my excitement I had neglected to bring along the proper drugs, and even the vital hormones—but it didn't trouble me. I would need no artificial aids now. I therefore showered and shaved and dressed in one of my better-padded suits (so that I would not look quite so resurrected) and checked out.

Then, shaking with anticipation, I registered at a hotel hard by the site of Number Five Hundred and Sixty-three— this very hotel—and proceeded to the lady's house. It was a brownstone, very old and mellow-mossy. I opened the wicket gate and went to the heavy oak door and knocked.

It was opened presently by the queen of them all, a truly incredible woman. Short, curly black hair, a Mona Lisa smile, blue-green burning eyes; 43-25-36, give or take a quarter-inch. She was clad in a dainty flowered house dress.

"What," she asked, in a throaty contralto, "can I do for you?"

I couldn't help smiling at that. "I represent a new firm, Kool-Kola, Inc.," I said, "and I have here a sample of our product. It is a dietetic soda pop, yet it has all the zest and effervescence of sweet drinks. Won't you try a taste?" I opened the bottle of pop and handed it to her.

"Well," she said, "if you'll leave it here, I'll be glad——"

"Please," I interrupted: this time I simply could not wait. "It's necessary for me to make a report, and I have a great many more houses to visit. Just a taste, just to tell me your reaction..."

She cocked her head to one side, and I was afraid I'd gone too far, then she laughed, shrugged, and put the bottle to her lips. She swallowed.

"Very nice," she said; then all but swooned. I'd put in four drops, to be doubly, or quadruply, safe: at this stage of the game, I could take no chances. There was no longer a margin for error. I had to attain this final one that night—or fail forever in my task.

I caught her and asked if I might come in. She told me no, this was impossible, as her husband was home and, she went on to explain, he was many years older than she and of a violently jealous nature. "I don't dare think of what he'd do..."

I said, "Very well, then it's up to you to make the necessary arrangements. I shall be waiting at this address."

She kissed me hard on the mouth, nodded and whispered: "I'll be there, tonight. Somehow. I promise!"

I returned to the hotel and spent the day trembling. At five-thirty I changed into my dressing gown. At seven I called room service for the champagne and candle.

Then I collapsed.

You know the rest...

Edward Simms was shaking like a blade of grass in a sirocco. He had spoken slowly and carefully, as if each word were a separate achievement; now he lay back, panting.

"So you see," he said, "why it is important for me to regain my strength. If I am the slightest bit tardy in this matter, everything will be thrown off. A new crop will spring up. And—you *do* understand?"

Doctor Lenardi, who had a somewhat dazed expression on his face, said, "Yes," in a voice equally dazed. "Yes, indeed."

"Then you'll do it? Now? At once?"

"Do it?" The elderly man shook his head and seemed to claw his way back to reality. "Mister Simms, you know, I think that from now on you're going to be rid of your troubles. Yes, now, I really think that."

"Thank you, sir!"

"Not at all." Doctor Lenardi's face had become a complacent mask. He got up and went to the telephone and mumbled something into the black mouthpiece. Then he returned and withdrew a hypodermic from the black bag. "Your arm, please."

"Doctor, you do believe me, don't you? I realize it's a pretty farfetched story, but it's essential that you understand I'm telling the absolute truth."

"Now, now. Your arm."

Simms lifted his right arm. "This is, I presume," he said weakly, "the stimulant——"

The physician grunted. He held the needle so that it hovered directly above the large vein. "As it happens, I had to phone down to the drugstore for what we need, but it'll be here in a jiffy. Meanwhile this will keep you calm. But first, you know, I would appreciate one last piece of information regarding your extraordinary adventure. Call it plain old scientific curiosity . . ."

"Yes?"

"This woman you're expecting—the one who'll, ah, round out the experiment . . . Do you recall her name?"

Edward Simms furled his brow and fell into deep concentration; then he snapped his fingers. "Alice," he said, "Alice Lenardi."

"Ah."

The needle descended.

The young man winced. Then he was quiet for many long minutes. "Doctor——"

There was a rap at the door. Doctor Lenardi leaped from his chair, crossed the room and returned with a small package in his hands. "Now, then," he said pleasantly, removing a bottle from the cardboard and pouring a quantity of the bottle's contents into a wine glass. "Drink this down."

Edward Simms blinked questioningly and gulped the odd fluid.

Once he'd finished, he said: "When will I begin to feel fit again?"

"Oh, I should say in about two weeks."

Simms' eyes widened. "T-two weeks! But——"

"You see," Doctor Lenardi said, chuckling, "I thought I recognized you, but I wasn't sure. When you grow old, that's what happens. You're not sure about things. I was in the living room when you called at our house, heard some of your talk, caught a glimpse of you; didn't think much of it at the time."

Now Simms's eyes threatened to leap from their sockets. The gaunt man struggled to rise from the bed and failed.

"I have, of course, known about you and Alice for a long while—that's why I made a point of returning home this morning unexpectedly. Eh? Oh, she's clever; always was; but . . . so am I." The physician chuckled again. "Thing is, I was only fifty when she married me, and for a while it looked as though it might work out; but now I'm sixty-two, and she's barely thirty-five. And like all women in their prime, she's getting restless. Tied to an antique, an 'elderly gentleman.' Longing for strong, young arms—although I really don't quite see how yours qualify." Doctor Lenardi sighed; then he frowned. "I've known about the recondite meetings, Simms. The trips she made into town—to do the shopping!—and all the shoddy, sneaking ruses by which you both hoped to deceive me!"

"It isn't true!" Edward Simms made a strangulated sound. "You've got it all wrong. I never met your wife before this morning."

"Come, *come*, I'm not as old as all that. Nor am I naive!"

"But—Good Lord, do you think for a moment that I'd have told you my story if your suspicions were correct? Would I have——"

"Don't, please, take me for a fool, Simms. You got a room as near to Alice as you could without actually moving in with us. For reasons I'd rather not dwell on, you collapsed; and, since I am the closest doctor in the neighborhood, they naturally called me. Recognizing me, you thought fast and told me this fantastic tale, doubtless in the hope that I would consider you insane and therefore not liable. A low sort of dodge, boy, and an unsuccessful one."

The young man, who looked older than ever, moaned. His eyelids were coming together. "I swear to you," he whispered, "that every word was the truth. It was nothing personal; I'd never even laid eyes on your wife. As far as I was concerned, she was just Number Five Hundred and Sixty-three . . ."

Doctor Lenardi smiled. "You're a convincing actor," he said. "Really a remarkable talent—you should have gone on the stage! I don't, of course, believe you. But never let it be said that Leo Lenardi lacked vision. The injection I administered was a sedative, very powerful; the oral medication, on the other hand——"

Edward Simms was by this time a definition of terror, a synonym for fright; he stared out from frog eyes. "The oral medication——" he croaked.

"Well," the older man said, "let's just say that it will keep you 'on the bench' for a couple of weeks. By which time, if there *is* anything to your story, a number of girls—a considerable number—will have celebrated their eighteenth birthdays. And then I suppose you'll have to start all over again. Except, you won't be in any condition for that, will you?"

Doctor Lenardi recognized the quick, tentative, feminine knocking at the door. He snapped his bag and rose.

"You see, Mister Simms," he said, "it's true. You *can't* have them all!"

Mother's Day

His hair was red, but his face was redder, and I never saw such sadness in the eyes of a man before. Not a new sadness, either, but something old and strong and buried deep inside. He sat down at my table.

"Good evening to you," I said, smiling.

He looked up, wrenched off his helmet, and rubbed his sweaty face into an even brighter red brightness.

"Good evening," I said again, but without the smile.

"Beer!" he said to the little Venusian who had rolled up. "Earth beer. American beer—understand?" The waiter shook his tendrils angrily and made motions in the air: *"Please use Accepted Signs, wise-fellow."*

The sad red man did so, following a gigantic shrug. He sat quiet as death until the beer arrived, and the waiter had rolled away. He swigged loudly and belched louder still. He looked at me. "Cop?" he said.

"No."

"It would be my luck. I practically live with these overgrown spiders, and the first Earthman I see, what is he: a goddam cop." He snorted disgustedly.

"You're wrong," I said, and offered him a cigarette. He examined it carefully, saw it was a Terran make. He lit up, sighing.

I extended my hand. "Looks like we're going to be together a while," I said. "The *Ginger* isn't due for three more hours. I suppose you're headed for Earth? My name is—"

"Stop play-acting, sonny! You know who I am and you're about to wet your pants over it. Well, I don't care, understand? Not one little bit. Go ahead and laugh your fool head off!"

"I'm sorry. I've not been in touch with Earth for quite a while. Why *should* I laugh at you?"

He examined me with a beady eye; then he sank back in the booth. "Reasons," he said.

"Care to talk about them?" I poured him another beer.

"I only thank the Lord my dear sweet mother—bless her bones—was spared the shame," he murmured. "It would have killed her dead."

"Tell me about it," I said.

"I will, by God!" he said, and he began to talk.

They never would have found out I killed that jasper (*the man with the red hair said*) if it hadn't been my black Irish luck to leave fingerprints all over the house. Of course, there was the fact that it was well known that this here particular fella had announced his intention to marry my youngest sister, Amarantha, which made it look pretty suspicious, I suppose, considering my public sentiments. Besides which, three people seen me do it. But otherwise, who would have known? Nobody, that's who.

So they caught me—not without the best kind of fight, I want you to know—and in less time than it takes, Mrs. McCreigh's favorite son was thrown in the pokey.

Now there is no worse place on the face of the earth, nor elsewhere for that matter, than these new-fangled jails. Used to be they had bars made of steel and so you was spared temptation: Nowadays it looks just exactly like you're in a swell apartment with the windows wide open. Course, you *touch* them windows and you get enough charge to knock you back to yesterday. I know. I tried.

Well, sir: "Gavin McCreigh," the judge says to me, "for the willful murder of Edgar Johnson, we hereby sentence you to spend the rest of your natural life in exile upon the asteroid *Spartanburg.*"

Sent a chill right through my stummick. Spartanburg! On that mess of mud, a man's 'natural life' couldn't be expected to exceed a day and a half at the outside!

But being Irish-American and a human being of the White race, I took her on the chin. Says I: That's how the cards fall! That's how the big ball bounces!

Spartanburg, as you well know, or ought to if you've ever looked inside a micronews, is crawling with giant bugs and disease of the absolute worst kind. A body would be dead before he started.

So, I mean to say, me loving life and brooking no desire to perish out in the middle of space any more than the next one, maybe you can see why I give her some thought when they come to me with their proposition.

"Gavin McCreigh," says they, "choose. Life or death—which'll you have?"

"Life," says I enthusiastically.

"Come with us."

It almost shook the teeth out of my head when they told me what it was all about—me, of all people, me: Gavin McCreigh: American!

(*Give me some more to drink. Get that hoppin' toad over here with some beer!*)

"For the advancement of science," they said. I truly thought they was joking, swear I did, but it was no joke.

I, Gavin Patrick Quentin McCreigh, was to be the first Earthman to marry a Martian!

Needless to say, I told them where they could put *that* noise. "Let's go," says I. "Let's go to Spartanburg. I'll walk if need be, or you can tie me with a rope at the jet-end and *drag* me—anything, my buckos, anything; but not this."

Some choice they give me, wouldn't you say? Die of a lingering disease a million miles from home, or take the Holy Vows with an outsize cockroach!

"If it's such an honor," says I, "then why don't you do it yourself?"

They shoveled me back into my hole, and I set there ticking off the days. You ever hear stories about Spartanburg? Man don't have a chance. Longest *anybody* was known to last in that slime was two weeks. They watch you on the screens—everybody does—sitting at home with their TVs. All over the world. Watch you take sick and die.

They put a TV in my room and so as I could watch old films of that ax murderer—what was his name—Buechner?—going stark raving crazy mad. Poor fella run around nutty as a squirrel until finally the bugs got him. Took the varmints two minutes by the clock, and poor old Buechner was just parched bones.

Well, that did her. I swallowed my fierce Irish pride and give them a buzz and told them all right, by God, I'd marry their Martian beetle and would they please get the thing over with in a hurry.

What a change! You'd think I was the King of England the way they puttered and spit over me, getting me this, getting me that—never letting me out of the cell, you understand, but treating me to cocktails and squab under glass and—it was okay. That part of it was all right.

'Course the papers was coming out with their headlines all about it, like and similar with TV and ekcetra. All the high mucky-mucks from Mars was here and twice as happy about the whole thing as we was, mainly because they had been angling to move in on us before their country went plumb dry. Dis*gust*ing the way them creechures sucked around!

For myself, I always figured we had enough race problem as it was, but I guess you know what happened. It had started even when I was there: They flooded in like crickets, took over, and set up their housing projects, messing up the land with big old glass bubbles. Ha! Guess maybe they was sorry they used glass, hey? Imagine some of our boys threw a couple of stones that just accidentally landed somewheres.

But then, I warned them. Said, looky: It ain't as if we don't have enough trouble trying to live on the same planet with all the yellow ones and black ones and the rest, we got to 'adjust' to people who ain't even people in the first place, but more like common roaches. I asked, ain't we got enough of a burden as it is?

They wouldn't listen. Deef and dumb. Now look what they got on their hands. Earth ain't even Earth no more. Swear, I'm glad I didn't stick around to see what happened *afterwards*...

I mean, referring to after the day when it all really begun.

They got me out and decked me in finery from my neck to my toes and, keeping guard, waltzed me into the Prison Hospital. It was crowded to the living rafters with folks: reporters, newsboys, diplomats and ekcetra.

And then—I fainted. Swear I did—fainted. Or like to. I was introduced to my future wife!

"This is Jane of Mars," the warden says to me. "Shake hands," says he with a frown.

Ever shake hands with a Martian? It's like taking holt of a wet sponge. But I thought of Buechner and grabbed on.

This Jane—she wasn't no different from any of the others.

Big as I was, standing there on four legs, twittering them aunt-emmies. "How do you do," says she with her thumbs.

By a stroke of good fortune, I managed not to throw up right then and there, you may be sure.

Well, the officials come and told me as how Jane was elected by unanimous decision—Miss Mars!—and what we was supposed to do, why we was gathered together and the rest of the malarkey.

Then they got a Martian and one of our own men and, next thing I knew they was saying (one aloud, the other in this sign language):

"Blahblahblah and ekcetra: Do you, Jane of Mars, take this Earthman to be your lawful wedded husband?"

"I do," says the cockroach.

"Do you, Gavin Patrick McCreigh, take this girl, Jane of Mars, for your lawful wedded wife?"

My intruls was boiling with the shame and the humiliation. "I do," says I.

"I now pronounce you man and wife."

"Well?" says the warden.

"Well?" says I.

"Aren't you going to kiss the bride?"

I'll make a long story short right about here, because it's a matter of considerable pain for me to go into the details of what followed then.

We was given a house, a regular house, but specially treated so we could both live in it—which must have cost a pretty penny. Half of it was hers, though, and this here part was full of rocks and stuff and all that stuff the Martians live around like lizards.

They kept a strict watch. Guess because maybe they knew I'd hightail it the minute I could. Particularly at night, we was kept tabs on. I don't know what they expected—but I just kept my mouth shut and talked civil as I could to this Jane and stayed out of her way.

She stayed out of mine too. Always looking sad and forlorn like, always telling me how we had to make a go of it for the sake of this and the sake of that. But when I let her know I had hid the meat cleaver, well, she just says: "I don't understand, I don't understand." But she steered clear after that.

After a week of this misery and hell, with me halfway wishing I *had* of gone to Spartanburg to begin with and upheld to the limit my honor and dignity as a white man, the boys trouped in.

Says: "Gavin McCreigh." Says: "Jane of Mars. We must talk to you."

And when they told me what it was they wanted to talk *about*, what they demanded and insisted on, for the "interests of science"—well, this was one healthy red-blooded American male who wished he'd of been borned a eunuch.

What could I do? What chance did I have?

It was essential, we was told, to find out what would happen. No other way of telling. And since these here Martians looked like cockroaches only to *me* (due no doubt to the manner in which I was brought up)—aside from all them legs and aunt-emmies they pretty well resembled human beings—and there'd be a lot of mixing going on—well, this was really, says they, the whole point of marrying me off to one!

I let 'em all know what I thought about it, you can bet your bottom credit on that. I let 'em know they was going against every natural law and that they'd be punished sure as there's a hell below.

But they told me: "We'll be watching, Gavin McCreigh!"—which any way you look at it is downright obscene—"and unless you want a vacation on a certain asteroid, we suggest you follow through."

So—because an Irishman can do anything he's got to do, and do it well—I followed through.

Next week afterwards a peculiar thing happened.

They sent me back to jail.

Talk about your reliefs! I lazed around watching the TV and reading newspapers and wondering in a sort of vague way about it all. What was next? Would I get to stay here smarting from my shame, or would they toss me back with that Martian? But I figured, well, I've done my bit, the good Lord knows, so maybe they'll leave me alone.

Everything went jimdandy until about, oh, I'd say about two-three weeks had gone by. Then I woke up one morning feeling like the last rose of summer pulled up by the roots and stomped on. Got out of bed and fell flat on my face just exactly like I was Lord High. Dizzy I was, and fuzzheaded. When they brought in the breakfast, damn if I didn't heave all over the floor!

Now I want you to understand that for Gavin McCreigh, who'd never seen a sick day in his whole life, this here was mighty peculiar indeed. I didn't say nothing, and it passed and I felt fine for a while—until the next morning.

'Twas the same thing, only twice as bad. Couldn't even keep boiled eggs down.

Then the pains begun.

I set there cramped up, the pains shooting through me like lightning bugs for quite a spell. Finally I got to the visiscreen and hollered for help.

The doctors all come on the double, almost like as if they was waiting for just such a thing to happen. I wouldn't know. Anyway, they rolled me over, and punched and poked and shook their heads and give me some slimy stuff to take, and the pains stopped so I said: "Leave go of me, I'm all right!"

But they wouldn't. They made X-ray pictures, and drew up charts, and I didn't spend fifteen minutes to myself all that day.

And that's the way it went. They took away my TV. They took away my reading newspapers. The tapes—everything, every touch with the outside. Put me to bed, too, they did and said, "Now don't you get alarmed, now don't you get alarmed."

Alarmed!

By damn, I near like to fell out of the bed when I seen the weight I was putting on. When you're sick, thought I, you're supposed to get all thin and piney; and here I was pooching out like a fed hog.

"Amazing!" says they. "Fantastic!" Then: "The gestation period seems to be the same as with the ordinary Martian."

Fortunately, I didn't know the meaning of that word then, or I would probably of killed myself, since there were numerous sharp things still left laying around.

But I see the word ain't new to you. You're wondering, are you?

All right. Come about five weeks, with me looking like the blue ribbon sow—only sicker'n a dog—and *still* not understanding it all, they come in, their old lips drawn back in Chessy smiles a yard wide—but worried too.

"Gavin," says the warden, "we got a little news for you."

Then they told me.

I, Gavin Patrick Quentin McCreigh, son of Mrs. Samuel

Denis McCreigh, Irish-American from Atlanta, Georgia, forty-two years of age, male and in my right senses—was about to have a baby.

You don't remember none of this? Well then, maybe you just don't believe, is that it? All right, by Neddie Jingo, you see this here scar? I didn't get it in no duel, sonny.

I got it when three days later they rushed me to the hospital—and me in agony—for what is known as a see-sarian section.

Don't ask me how it happened. I ain't no damn doctor. They went on about 'backwash' or something and talked about a lad named Gene, but it didn't make no sense to me at all, at all.

All I knew was, I was under that ether a long old time, and when I got out I had this scar and I was normal size again.

"This puts a new shading on our relations with Mars," says the warden.

"Puts a new shading," says I, "on a whole hell of a lot of things."

Says he: "Well, my bucko, that's the way she goes."

Says I quick as a wink: "That may be the way she goes now, but that sure ain't the way she used to go."

Then they brought it in.

Now understand. I don't and never did hold with the common notion that any newborn young'n is necessarily the prettiest sight on this here earth. But when they toted *this* thing in, thought I: Gavin, you should have been borned a bald-headed Englishman. Because it was—and I don't color the facts—far and away the ugliest piece of meat ever beholden on the face of the globe.

All red it was and bellering to the top of its lungs—if it had lungs.

Didn't have no aunt-emmies, and right down to the waist could have been a healthy normal child. Except for the fact it had twice the healthy normal number of legs: four, to be exact. Four little cockroachy legs, and them kicking and flailing in my face till I had to scream to get the crawly thing off of me.

It was an experience.

Well, I thought, anyway this'll sure as the devil put a crimp into the idea of intermarriage if the whole shooting match don't come to nothing else. But you know what? They claimed it was *cute*. You hear me?

"As beautiful a child as anyone could wish" was the way I heard it put.

It takes a lot to sour an Irishman on his own home soil, that it does, but this did the trick, you may bet your spaceboots. I had to do something and do it mighty quick, or it'd be curtains for Gavin McCreigh.

Do you know what they had planned? Planned to put us back in the house and see if it worked out! Just like that: one-man's-family style!

Says I: "You can't make me do it."

Says they: "Spartanburg is reached in two weeks by the direct route."

Says I: "If I may call your gentlemen's kind attention to one fact: According to law, and tradition, only women have babies—correct?"

"Well..."

"And according to lawful records, one Gavin Patrick Quentin McCreigh, *male*, was found guilty of murder and sentenced to The Rock. Correct?"

"Well..."

"All right. Inasmuch as *I* have just given birth to a bairn, and inasmuch and notwithstanding as men can't have children, that makes me a mother. Correct?"

"Hmmm," says they.

"And being as how I'm a mother and therefore no longer the same person, and the thought of sending a *mother* to Spartanburg is unconstitutional on the grounds of being against God and law—"

Thanks be for my golden Irish tongue, is all I can say. For when I was finished, they was so screwjeed they didn't know whether to shoot me or send me a Mother's Day card.

Anyway, they dropped the charges against me and—legally anyway—I was a free man.

Free to endure my shame. They came after me like buzzards: Sign this; sign that; would I make a testimonial? Would I endorse two dozen and fifty things, from high chairs (with an extra foot rest) to oatmeal. You wouldn't believe it! I had half the diaper laundries in town after me.

Well, I saw it was financially to my good to stay a spell in the same house with this Martian woman Jane. Wasn't easy, but the big hurt had been done, and so I acted out the part of the changed man: pretended I was right in love with my little family. Phew! Some family—three people and ten legs!

Finally, though, I had enough money from these testimonials and digest articles and lectures in Denmark and ekcetra to make my move. Junior never did have a name: they was having a contest at the time—he was exactly one year old, and according to the rest of the damfool world the cutest tyke that ever was, but according to me a blooming four-legged monsterosity.

The Irish don't forget. And this Irishman had endured more pain and torment than St. Patrick with the snakes—though on the whole I'd say they was more agreeable creechures. I waited until I knew for fair we weren't being watched in any of the secret ways they'd cooked up. Then I got me a good stout shillelagh and went into the bedroom and woke up that Martian shrew that was palming herself off as my wife and working it through me and my unfortunate situation that her whole damn race of bugs could infest our world.

"Get up!" says I.

"I'm not asleep," says she.

I told her what I aimed to do, but it didn't seem to scare her none: these Martians don't know fear nor any other decent emotion. Just stared at me with them crocus-eyes full of confusion and sorrow, all calculated to make me drop my shillelagh and leave her be.

Made me so dingdong mad I let out a cuss that turned the air blue and hove to. But she wouldn't yell, damn her! Just—took it. If she'd yelled or asked me to quit—anything *human*—maybe it wouldn't of happened.

When I seen what I'd done, I looked around and there was this other little brute, little four-legs, standing up in his crib, wiggling all over and glaring out at me with the fires of Hades in his eyes. Then he begun to bawl fit to wake the whole block. So I left, pretty fast.

It didn't take long for me to grab a ride on a space scow headed far away.

I escaped some things. But some things I didn't. I been give scars I'll never get over, never if I live to be a hundred years. I can't go back. And even if I could, I wouldn't. Not back to my shame—not to a world that ain't my world any more, crawling with the filth of the universe.

They got no room for me there now. They gave me eternal shame and cast me out and Gavin McCreigh will never have a home again...

The man whose name was Gavin McCreigh got to his feet. "Forget what I told you, sonny," he said. "It was stoppered up; now it's out, and I'm better for it. But you forget. And if you want my advice, stay away from Earth—just remember it the way it was before they all went crazy with this brotherhood business."

He started to leave, putting on his helmet, pressing the restaurant's inner air-lock button. I called to him: "Wait."

He turned around.

"I'm sorry, Gavin," I said, "but you're right. An Irishman *can't* forget, not even if he wants to. You're a dead thing now, the last of your kind in all the Galaxy; but I've looked for you a long time. A very long time... Mother."

He started to run, but it wasn't difficult to overtake him.

After all, four legs are better than two.

Last Rites

Somewhere in the church a baby was shrieking. Father Courtney listened to it, and sighed, and made the sign of the Cross. Another battle, he thought, dismally. Another grand tug of war. And who won this time, Lord? Me? Or that squalling infant, bless its innocence?

"In the Name of the Father, and of the Son, and of the Holy Ghost. Amen."

He turned and made his way down the pulpit steps, and told himself, Well, you ought to be used to it by now, Heaven knows. After all, you're a priest, not a monologist. What do you care about "audience reaction"? And besides, who ever listens to these sermons of yours, anyway—even under the best of conditions? A few of the ladies of the parish (though you're sure they never hear or understand a word), and, of course, Donovan. But who else?

Screech away, little pink child! Screech until you—no.

No, no. Ahhh!

He walked through the sacristy, trying not to think of Donovan, or the big city churches with their fine nurseries, and sound-proof walls, and amplifiers that amplified...

One had what one had: it was God's will.

And were things really so bad? Here there was the smell of forests, wasn't there? And in what city parish could you see wild flowers growing on the hills like bright lava? Or feel the earth breathing?

He opened the door and stepped outside.

The fields were dark silver and silent. Far above the fields, up near the clouds, a rocket launch moved swiftly, dragging its slow thunder behind it.

Father Courtney blinked.

Of course things were not so bad. Things would be just

fine, he thought, and I would not be nervous and annoyed at little children, if only—

Abruptly he put his hands together. "Father," he whispered, "let him be well. Let that be Your will!"

Then, deciding not to wait to greet the people, he wiped his palms with a handkerchief and started for the rectory.

The morning was very cold. A thin film of dew coated each pebble along the path, and made them all glisten like drops of mercury. Father Courtney looked at the pebbles and thought of other walks down this path, which led through a wood to Hidden River, and of himself laughing; of excellent wine and soft cushions and himself arguing, arguing; of a thousand sweet hours in the past.

He walked and thought these things, and did not hear the telephone until he had reached the rectory stairs.

A chill passed over him, unaccountably.

He went inside and pressed a yellow switch. The screen blurred, came into focus. The face of an old man appeared, filling the screen.

"Hello, Father."

"George!" the priest smiled and waved his fist, menacingly. "George, why haven't you contacted me?" He sputtered. "Aren't you out of that bed yet?"

"Not yet, Father."

"Well, I expected it, I knew it. *Now* will you let me call a doctor?"

"No—" The old man in the screen shook his head. He was thin and pale. His hair was profuse, but very white, and there was something in his eyes. "I think I'd like you to come over, if you could."

"I shouldn't," the priest said, "after the way you've been treating all of us. But, if there's still some of that Chianti left . . ."

George Donovan nodded. "Could you come right away?"

"Father Yoshida won't be happy about it."

"Please. Right away."

Father Courtney felt his fingers draw into fists. "Why?" he asked, holding onto the conversational tone. "Is anything the matter?"

"Not really," Donovan said. His smile was brief. "It's just that I'm dying."

"And I'm going to call Doctor Ferguson. Don't give me any argument, either. This nonsense has gone far—"

The old man's face knotted. "No," he said, loudly. "I forbid you to do that."

"But you're ill, man. For all we know, you're *seriously* ill. And if you think I'm going to stand around and watch you work yourself into the hospital just because you happen to dislike doctors, you're crazy."

"Father, listen—*please*. I have my reasons. You don't understand them, and I don't blame you. But you've got to trust me. I'll explain everything, if you'll promise me you won't call *anyone*."

Father Courtney breathed unsteadily; he studied his friend's face. Then he said, "I'll promise this much. I won't contact a doctor until I've seen you."

"Good." The old man seemed to relax.

"I'll be there in fifteen minutes."

"With your Little Black Bag?"

"Certainly not. You're going to be all right."

"Bring it, Father. Please. Just in case."

The screen blurred and danced and went white.

Father Courtney hesitated at the blank telephone.

Then he walked to a table, and raised his fists, and brought them down hard, once.

You're going to get well, he thought. It isn't going to be too late.

Because if you are dying, if you really are, and I could have prevented it . . .

He went to the closet and drew on his overcoat.

It was thick and heavy, but it did not warm him. As he returned to the sacristy he shivered and thought that he had never been so cold before in all his life.

The Helicar whirred and dropped quickly to the ground. Father Courtney removed the ignition key, pocketed it, and thrust his bulk out the narrow door, wheezing.

A dull rumbling sifted down from the sky. The wake of fleets a mile away, ten miles, a hundred.

It's raining whales in our backyard, the priest thought, remembering how Donovan had described the sound once to a little girl.

A freshet of autumn leaves burst against his leg, softly, and for a while he stood listening to the rockets' dying rumble, watching the shapes of gold and red that scattered in the wind, like fire.

Then he whispered, "Let it be Your will," and pushed the picket gate.

The front door of the house was open.

He walked in, through the living-room, to the study.

"George."

"In here," a voice answered.

He moved to the bedroom, and twisted the knob.

George Donovan lay propped on a cloudbank of pillows, his thin face white as the linen. He was smiling.

"I'm glad to see you, Father," he said, quietly.

The priest's heart expanded and shrank and began to thump in his chest.

"The Chianti's down here in the night-table," Donovan gestured. "Pour some: morning's a good enough time for a dinner wine."

"Not now, George."

"Please. It will help."

Father Courtney pulled out the drawer and removed the half-empty bottle. He got a glass from the bookshelf, filled it. Dutifully, according to ritual, he asked, "For you?"

"No," Donovan said. "Thank you all the same." He turned his head. "Sit over there, Father, where I can see you."

The priest frowned. He noticed that Donovan's arms were perfectly flat against the blanket, that his body was rigid, outlined beneath the covering. No part of the old man moved except the head, and that slowly, unnaturally.

"That's better. But take off your coat—it's terribly hot in here. You'll catch pneumonia."

The room was full of cold winds from the open shutters.

Father Courtney removed his coat.

"You've been worried, haven't you?" Donovan asked.

The priest nodded. He tried to sense what was wrong, to smell the disease, if there was a disease, if there was anything.

"I'm sorry about that." The old man seemed to sigh. His eyes were misted, webbed with distance, lightly. "But I wanted to be alone. Sometimes you have to be alone, to think, to get things straight. Isn't that true?"

"Sometimes, I suppose, but—"

"No. I know what you're going to say, the questions you want to ask. But there's not enough time . . ."

Father Courtney arose from the chair, and walked quickly

to the telephone extension. He jabbed a button. "I'm sorry, George," he said, "but you're going to have a doctor."

The screen did not flicker.

He pressed the button again, firmly.

"Sit down," the tired voice whispered. "It doesn't work. I pulled the wires ten minutes ago."

"Then I'll fly over to Milburn—"

"If you do, I'll be dead when you get back. Believe that: I know what I'm talking about."

The priest clenched and unclenched his stubby fingers, and sat down in the chair again.

Donovan chuckled. "Drink up," he said. "We can't have good wine going to waste, can we?"

The priest put the glass to his lips. He tried to think clearly. If he rushed out to Milburn and got Doctor Ferguson, perhaps there'd be a chance. Or—He took a deep swallow.

No. That wouldn't do. It might take hours.

Donovan was talking now; the words lost—a hum of locusts in the room, a far-off murmuring; then, like a radio turned up: "Father, how long have we been friends, you and I?"

"Why . . . twenty years," the priest answered. "Or more."

"Would you say you know me very well by now?"

"I believe so."

"Then tell me first, right now, would you say that I've been a good man?"

Father Courtney smiled. "There've been worse," he said and thought of what this man had accomplished in Mount Vernon, quietly, in his own quiet way, over the years. The building of a decent school for the children—Donovan had shamed the people into it. The new hospital—Donovan's doing, his patient campaigning. Entertainment halls for the young; a city fund for the poor; better teachers, better doctors—all, all because of the old man with the soft voice, George Donovan.

"Do you mean it?"

"Don't be foolish. And don't be treacly, either. Of course I mean it."

In the room, now, a strange odor fumed up, suddenly.

The old man said, "I'm glad." Still he did not move. "But I'm sorry I asked. It was unfair."

"I don't have the slightest idea what you're talking about."

"Neither do I, Father, completely. I thought I did, once, but I was wrong."

The priest slapped his knees, angrily. "Why won't you let me get a doctor? We'll have plenty of time to talk afterwards."

Donovan's eyes narrowed, and curved into what resembled a smile. "You're my doctor," he said. "The only one who can help me now."

"In what way?"

"By making a decision." The voice was reedy: it seemed to waver and change pitch.

"What sort of a decision?"

Donovan's head jerked up. He closed his eyes and remained this way for a full minute, while the acrid smell bellied and grew stronger and whorled about the room in invisible currents.

"'... the gentleman lay braveward with his furies...' Do you remember that, Father?"

"Yes," the priest said. "Thomas, isn't it?"

"Thomas. He's been here with me, you know, really; and I've been asking him things. On the theory that poets aren't entirely human. But he just grins. 'You're dying of strangers,' he says; and grins. Bless him." The old man lowered his head. "He disappointed me."

Father Courtney reached for a cigarette, crumpled the empty pack, laced and unlaced his fingers. He waited, remembering the times he had come to this house, all the fine evenings. Ending now?

Yes, Whatever else he would learn, he knew that, suddenly: they were ending.

"What sort of a decision, George?"

"A theological sort."

Father Courtney snorted and walked to a window. Outside, the sun was hidden behind a curtain of gray. Birds sat black and still on the telephone lines, like notes of music; and there was rain.

"Is there something you think you haven't told me?" he asked.

"Yes."

"About yourself?"

"Yes."

"I don't think so, George." Father Courtney turned. "I've known about it for a long time."

The old man tried to speak.

"I've known very well. And now I think I understand why you've refused to see anyone."

"No," Donovan said. "You don't. Father, listen to me: it isn't what you think."

"Nonsense." The priest reverted to his usual gruffness. "We've been friends for too many years for this kind of thing. It's *exactly* what I think. You're an intelligent, well-read, mule-stubborn old man who's worried he won't get to Heaven because sometimes he has doubts."

"That isn't—"

"Well, rubbish! Do you think I don't ask questions, myself, once in a while? Just because I'm a priest, do you think I go blindly on, never wondering, not even for a minute?"

The old man's eyes moved swiftly, up and down.

"Every intelligent person doubts, George, once in a while. And we all feel terrible about it, and we're terribly sorry. But I assure you, if this were enough to damn us, Heaven would be a wilderness." Father Courtney reached again for a cigarette. "So you've shut yourself up like a hermit and worried and stewed and endangered your life, and all for nothing." He coughed. "Well, that's it, isn't it?"

"I wish it were," Donovan said, sadly. His eyes kept dancing. There was a long pause; then he said, "Let me pose you a theoretical problem, Father. Something I've been thinking about lately."

Father Courtney recalled the sentence, and how many times it had begun the evenings of talk—wonderful talk! These evenings, he realized, were part of his life now. An important part. For there was no one else, no one of Donovan's intelligence, with whom you could argue any subject under the sun—from Frescobaldi to baseball, from colonization on Mars to the early French symbolists, to agrarian reforms, to wines, to theology...

The old man shifted in the bed. As he did, the acrid odor diminished and swelled and pulsed. "You once told me," he said, "that you read imaginative fiction, didn't you?"

"I suppose so."

"And that there were certain concepts you could swallow—such as parallel worlds, mutated humans, and the like—, but that other concepts you couldn't swallow at all. Artificial life, I believe you mentioned, and time travel, and a few others."

The priest nodded.

"Well, let's take one of these themes for our problem. Will you do that? Let's take the first idea."

"All right. Then the doctor."

"We have this man, Father," Donovan said, gazing at the ceiling. "He looks perfectly ordinary, you see, and it would occur to no one to doubt this; but he is not ordinary. Strictly speaking, he isn't even a man. For, though he lives, he isn't alive. You follow? He is a thing of wires and coils and magic, a creation of other men. He is a machine . . ."

"George!" The priest shook his head. "We've gone through this before: it's foolish to waste time. I came here to help you, not to engage in a discussion of science fiction themes!"

"But that's how you *can* help me," Donovan said.

"Very well," the priest sighed. "But you know my views on this. Even if there were a logical purpose to which such a creature might be put—and I can't think of any—I still say they will never create a machine that is capable of abstract thought. Human intelligence is a spiritual thing—and spiritual things can't be duplicated by men."

"You really believe that?"

"Of course I do. Extrapolation of known scientific advances is perfectly all right; but this is something else entirely."

"Is it?" the old man said. "What about Pasteur's discovery? Or the X-ray? Did Roentgen correlate a lot of embryonic data, Father, or did he come upon something brand new? What do you think even the scientists themselves would have said to the idea of a machine that would see through human tissue? They would have said it's fantastic. And it was, too, and is. Nevertheless, it exists."

"It's not the same thing."

"No . . . I suppose that's true. However, I'm not trying to convince you of my thesis. I ask merely that you accept it for the sake of the problem. Will you?"

"Go ahead, George."

"We have this man, then. He's artificial, but he's perfect: great pains have been taken to see to this. Perfect, no detail spared, however small. He looks human, and he acts human, and for all the world knows, he *is* human. In fact, sometimes even he, our man, gets confused. When he feels a pain in his heart, for instance, it's difficult for him to remember that he has no heart. When he sleeps and awakes refreshed, he must remind himself that this is all controlled by an automatic switch somewhere inside his brain, and that he doesn't *actually* feel refreshed. He must think, I'm not real, I'm not real, I'm not real!

"But this becomes impossible, after a while. Because he doesn't believe it. He begins to ask, Why? *Why* am I not real? Where is the difference, when you come right down to it? Humans eat and sleep—as I do. They talk—as I do. They move and work and laugh—as I do. What they think, I think, and what they feel, I feel. Don't I?

"He wonders, this mechanical man does, Father, what would happen if all the people on earth were suddenly to discover they were mechanical also. Would they feel any the less human? Is it likely that they would rush off to woo typewriters and adding machines? Or would they think, perhaps, of revising their definition of the word, 'Life'?

"Well, our man thinks about it, and thinks about it, but he never reaches a conclusion. He doesn't believe he's nothing more than an advanced calculator, but he doesn't really believe he's human, either: not completely.

"All he knows is that the smell of wet grass is a fine smell to him, and that the sound of the wind blowing through the trees is very sad and very beautiful, and that he loves the whole earth with an impossible passion..."

Father Courtney shifted uncomfortably in his chair. If only the telephone worked, he thought. Or if he could be sure it was safe to leave.

"... other men made the creature, as I've said; but many more like him were made. However, of them all, let's say only he was successful."

"Why?" the priest asked, irritably. "Why would this be done in the first place?"

Donovan smiled. "Why did we send the first ship to the moon? Or bother to split the atom? For no very good reason, Father. Except the reason behind all of science: Curiosity. My theoretical scientists were curious to see if it could be accomplished, that's all."

The priest shrugged.

"But perhaps I'd better give our man a history. That would make it a bit more logical. All right, he was born a hundred years ago, roughly. A privately owned industrial monopoly was his mother, and a dozen or so assorted technicians his father. He sprang from his electronic womb fully formed. But, as the result of an accident—lack of knowledge, what have you—he came out rather different from his unsuccessful brothers. A mutant! A mutated robot, Father—now there's an idea that ought to appeal to you! Anyway, *he* knew who, or what, he was. He remembered. And so—to make it brief— when the war interrupted the experiment and threw things into a general uproar, our man decided to escape. He wanted his individuality. He wanted to get out of the zoo.

"It wasn't particularly easy, but he did this. Once free, of course, it was impossible to find him. For one thing, he had been constructed along almost painfully ordinary lines. And for another, they couldn't very well release the information that a mechanical man built by their laboratories was wandering the streets. It would cause a panic. And there was enough panic, what with the nerve gas and the bombs."

"So they never found him, I gather."

"No," Donovan said, wistfully. "They never found him. And they kept their secret well: it died when they died."

"And what happened to the creature?"

"Very little, to tell the truth. They'd given him a decent intelligence, you see—far more decent, and complex, than they knew—so he didn't have much trouble finding small jobs. A rather old-looking man, fairly strong—he made out. Needless to say, he couldn't stay in the same town for more than twenty years or so, because of his inability to age, but this was all right. Everyone makes friends and loses them. He got used to it."

Father Courtney sat very still now. The birds had flown away from the telephone lines, and were at the window, beating their wings, and crying harshly.

"But all this time, he's been thinking, Father. Thinking and reading. He makes quite a study of philosophy, and for a time he favors a somewhat peculiar combination of Russell and Schopenhauer—unbitter bitterness, you might say. Then this phase passes, and he begins to search through the vast theological and metaphysical literature. For what? He isn't sure. However, he is sure of one thing, now: He *is*, indubitably, human. Without breath, without heart, without blood or bone, artificially created, he thinks this and believes it, with a fair amount of firmness, too. Isn't that remarkable!"

"It is indeed," the priest said, his throat oddly tight and dry. "Go on."

"Well," Donovan chuckled, "I've caught your interest, have I? All right, then. Let us imagine that one hundred years have passed. The creature has been able to make minor repairs on himself, but—at last—he is dying. Like an ancient motor, he's gone on running year after year, until he's all paste and hairpins, and now, like the motor, he's falling apart. And nothing and no one can save him."

The acrid aroma burned and fumed.

"Here's the real paradox, though. Our man has become religious. Father! He doesn't have a living cell within him, yet he's concerned about his soul!"

Donovan's eyes quieted, as the rest of him did. "The problem," he said, "is this: Having lived creditably for over a century as a member of the human species, can this creature of ours hope for Heaven? Or will he 'die,' and become only a heap of metal cogs?"

Father Courtney leapt from the chair, and moved to the bed. "George, in Heaven's name, let me call Doctor Ferguson!"

"Answer the question first. Or haven't you decided?"

"There's nothing to decide," the priest said, with impatience. "It's a preposterous idea. No machine can have a soul."

Donovan made the sighing sound, through closed lips. He said, "You don't think it's conceivable, then, that God could have made an exception here?"

"What do you mean?"

"That He could have taken pity on this theoretical man of ours, and breathed a soul into him after all? Is that so impossible?"

Father Courtney shrugged. "It's a poor word, impossible," he said. "But it's a poor problem, too. Why not ask me whether pigs ought to be allowed to fly?"

"Then you admit it's conceivable?"

"I admit nothing of the kind. It simply isn't the sort of question any man can answer."

"Not even a priest?"

"Especially not a priest. You know as much about Catholicism as I do, George; you ought to know how absurd the proposition is."

"Yes," Donovan said. His eyes were closed.

Father Courtney remembered the time they had argued furiously on what would happen if you went back in time and killed your own grandfather. This was like that argument. Exactly like it—exactly. It was no stranger than a dozen other discussions (What if Mozart had been a writer instead of a composer? If a person died and remained dead for an hour and were then revived, would he be haunted by his own ghost?). Plus, perhaps, the fact that Donovan might be in a fever. Perhaps and might and why do I sit here while his life may be draining away . . .

The old man made a sharp noise. "But you can tell me this much," he said. "If our theoretical man were dying, and you knew that he was dying, would you give him Extreme Unction?"

"George, you're delirious."

"No, I'm not: please, Father! Would you give this creature the Last Rites? If, say, you knew him? If you'd known him for years, as a friend, as a member of the parish?"

The priest shook his head. "It would be sacrilegious."

"But why? You said yourself that he might have a soul, that God might have granted him this. Didn't you say that?"

"I—"

"Father, remember, he's a friend of yours. You know him *well*. You and he, this creature, have worked together, side by side, for years. You've taken a thousand walks together, shared the same interests, the same love of art and knowledge. For the sake of the thesis, Father. Do you understand?"

"No," the priest said, feeling a chill freeze into him. "No, I don't."

"Just answer this, then. If your friend were suddenly to reveal himself to you as a machine, and he was dying, and wanted very much to go to Heaven—what would you do?"

The priest picked up the wine glass and emptied it. He noticed that his hand was trembling. "Why—" he began, and stopped, and looked at the silent old man in the bed, studying the face, searching for madness, for death.

"What would you do?"

An unsummoned image flashed through his mind. Donovan, kneeling at the altar for Communion, Sunday after Sunday; Donovan, with his mouth firmly shut, while the others' yawned; Donovan, waiting to the last moment, then snatching the Host, quickly, dartingly, like a lizard gobbling a fly.

Had he ever seen Donovan eat?

Had he seen him take even one glass of wine, ever?

Father Courtney shuddered slightly, brushing away the images. He felt unwell. He wished the birds would go elsewhere.

Well, answer him, he thought. *Give him an answer. Then*

get in the helicar and fly to Milburn and pray it's not too late...

"I think," the priest said, "that in such a case, I would administer Extreme Unction."

"Just as a precautionary measure?"

"It's all very ridiculous, but—I think that's what I'd do. Does that answer the question?"

"It does, Father. It does." Donovan's voice came from nowhere. "There is one last point, then I'm finished with my little thesis."

"Yes?"

"Let us say the man dies and you give him Extreme Unction; he does or does not go to Heaven, provided there is a Heaven. What happens to the body? Do you tell the townspeople they have been living with a mechanical monster all these years?"

"What do you think, George?"

"I think it would be unwise. They remember our theoretical man as a friend, you see. The shock would be terrible. Also, they would never believe he was the only one of his kind: they'd begin to suspect their neighbors of having clockwork interiors. And some of them might be tempted to investigate and see for sure. And, too, the news would be bound to spread, all over the world. I think it would be a bad thing to let anyone know, Father."

"How would I be able to suppress it?" the priest heard himself ask, seriously.

"By conducting a private autopsy, so to speak. Then, afterwards, you could take the parts to a junkyard and scatter them."

Donovan's voice dropped to a whisper. Again the locust hum.

"... and if our monster had left a note to the effect that he had moved to some unspecified place, you..."

The acrid smell billowed, all at once, like a steam, a hiss of blinding vapor.

"George."

Donovan lay unstirring on the cloud of linen, his face composed, expressionless.

"George!"

The priest reached his hand under the blanket and touched

the heart-area of Donovan's chest. He tried to pull the eyelids up: they would not move.

He blinked away the burning wetness. "Forgive me!" he said, and paused and took from his pocket a small white jar and a white stole.

He spoke softly, under his breath, in Latin. While he spoke, he touched the old man's feet and head with glistening fingertips.

Then, when many minutes had passed, he raised his head.

Rain sounded in the room, and swift winds, and far-off rockets.

Father Courtney grasped the edge of the blanket.

He made the sign of the Cross, breathed, and pulled downward, slowly.

After a long while he opened his eyes.

Blood Brother

"Now, then," said the psychiatrist, looking up from his note pad, "when did you first discover that you were dead?"

"Not dead," said the pale man in the dark suit. "Undead."

"I'm sorry."

"Just try to keep it straight. If I were dead, I'd be in great shape. That's the trouble, though. I can't die."

"Why not?"

"Because I'm not alive."

"I see." The psychiatrist made a rapid notation. "Now, Mr. Smith, I'd like you to start at the beginning, and tell me the whole story."

The pale man shook his head. "At twenty-five dollars an hour," he said, "are you kidding? I can barely afford to have my cape cleaned once a month."

"I've been meaning to ask you about that. Why do you wear it?"

"You ever hear of a vampire without a cape? It's part of the whole schmear, that's all. *I* don't know why!"

"Calm yourself."

"Calm myself! I wish I could. I tell you, Doctor, I'm going right straight out of my skull. Look at this!" The man who called himself Smith put out his hands. They were a tremblous blur of white. "And look at this!" He pulled down the flaps beneath his eyes, revealing an intricate red lacework of veins. "Believe me," he said, flinging himself upon the couch, "another few days of this and I'll be ready for the funny farm!"

The psychiatrist picked a mahogany letter opener off his desk and tapped his palm. "I would appreciate it," he said, "if you would make an effort to avoid those particular terms."

"All right," said the pale man. "But you try living on blood for a year, and see how polite you are. I mean—"

"The beginning, Mr. Smith."

"Well, I met this girl, Dorcas, and she bit me."

"Yes?"

"That's all. It doesn't take much, you know."

The psychiatrist removed his glasses and rubbed his eyes. "As I understand it," he said, "you think you're a vampire."

"No," said Smith. "I *think* I'm a human being, but I *am* a vampire. That's the hell of it. I can't seem to adjust."

"How do you mean?"

"Well, the hours, for instance. I used to have very regular habits. Work from nine to five, home, a little TV, maybe, into bed by ten, up at six-thirty. Now—" He shook his head violently from side to side. "You know how it is with vampires."

"Let's pretend I don't," said the psychiatrist, soothingly. "Tell me. How is it?"

"Like I say, the hours. Everything's upside-down. That's why I made this appointment with you so late. See, you're supposed to sleep during the *day* and work at *night.*"

"Why?"

"Boy, you've got me. I asked Dorcas, that's the girl that bit me, and she said she'd try and find out, but nobody seems to be real sure about it."

"Dorcas," said the psychiatrist, pursing his lips. "That's an unusual name."

"Dorcas Schultz is an unusual girl, I'll tell you. A real nut. She's on that late-late TV show, you know? The one that runs all those crummy old horror movies?" Smith scraped a stain from his cloak with his fingernail. "Maybe you know her. She recommended you."

"It's possible. But let's get back to you. You were speaking of the hours."

Smith wrung his hands. "They're murdering me," he said. "Eight fly-by-night jobs I've had—eight!—and lost every one!"

"Would you care to explain that?"

"Nothing to explain. I just can't stay awake, that's all. I mean, every night—I mean every *day*—I toss and turn for hours and then when I finally *do* doze off, boom, it's nightfall and I've got to get out of the coffin."

"The coffin?"

"Yeah. That's another sweet wrinkle. The minute you go bat, you're supposed to give up beds and take to a casket. Which is not only sick, but expensive as *hell.*" Smith shook his head angrily. "First you got to buy the damn thing. Do you know the cost of the average casket?"

"Well—" began the psychiatrist.

"Astronomical! Completely out of proportion. I'm telling you, it's a racket! For anything even halfway decent you're going to drop five bills, easy. But that's just the initial outlay. Then there's the cartage and the cleaning bills."

"I don't—"

"Seventy-five to a hundred every month, month in, month out."

"I'm afraid I—"

"The grave dirt, man! Sacking out in a coffin isn't bad enough, no, you've got to line it with *soil from the family plot.* I ask you, who's got a family plot these days? Have you?"

"No, but—"

"Right. So what do you do? You go out and buy one. Then you bring home a couple pounds of dirt and spread it around in the coffin. Wake up at night and you're *covered* with it." Smith clicked his tongue exasperatedly. "If you could just wear pajamas—but no, the rules say the full bit. Ever *hear* of anything so crazy? You can't even take off your *shoes,* for cry eye!" He began to pace. "Then there's the bloodstains."

The psychiatrist lowered his pad, replaced his glasses, and regarded his patient with a not incurious eye.

"I must go through twenty white shirts a month," continued Smith. "Even at two-fifty a shirt, that's a lot of dough. You're probably thinking, Why isn't he more careful? Well, listen, I try to be. But it isn't like eating a bowl of tomato soup, you know." A shudder, or something like a shudder, passed over the pale man. "That's another thing. The diet. I mean, I always used to like my steaks rare, but this is ridiculous! Blood for breakfast, blood for lunch, blood for dinner. Uch—just the thought of it makes me queasy to the stomach!" Smith flung himself back onto the couch and closed his eyes. "It's the monotony that gets you," he said, "although there's plenty else to complain about. You know what I mean?"

"Well," said the psychiatrist, clearing his throat, "I—"

"Filthy stuff! And the routines I have to go through to get it! What if you had to rob somebody every time you wanted a hamburger—I mean, just supposing. That's the way it is with me. I tried stocking up on plasma, but that's death warmed over. A few nights of it and you've got to go after the real thing, it doesn't matter *how* many promises you've made to yourself."

"The real thing?"

"I don't like to talk about it," said Smith, turning his head to the wall. "I'm actually a very sensitive person, know what I mean? Gentle. Kind. Never could stand violence, not even as a kid. Now..." He sobbed wrackingly, leaped to his feet, and resumed pacing. "Do you think I *enjoy* biting people? Do you think I don't *know* how disgusting it is? But, I tell you, *I can't help it!* Every few nights I get this terrible urge...."

"Yes?"

"You'll hate me."

"No, Mr. Smith."

"Yes you will. Everybody does. Everybody hates a vampire." The pale man withdrew a large silk handkerchief from his pocket and daubed at sudden tears. "It isn't fair," he choked. "After all, we didn't *ask* to become what we are, did we? Nobody ever thinks of that."

"You feel, then, that you are being persecuted?"

"Damn right," said Smith. "And you know why? I'll tell you why. Because I *am* being persecuted. That's why. Have you ever heard a nice thing said about a vampire? Ever in your whole life? No. Why? Because people hate us. But I'll tell you something even sillier. They *fear* us, too!" The pale man laughed a wild, mirthless laugh. "*Us,*" he said. "The most helpless creatures on the face of the Earth! Why, it doesn't take *anything* to knock us over. If we don't cut our throats trying to shave—you know the mirror bit: no reflection—we stand a chance to land flat on our back because the neighbor downstairs is cooking garlic. Or bring us a little running water, see what happens. We flip our lids. Or silver bullets. *Daylight,* for crying out loud! If I'm not back in that stupid coffin by dawn, zow, I'm out like a light. So I'm out late, and time sort of gets away from me, and I look at my watch and I've got ten minutes. What do I do? Any other vampire in his right mind, he changes into a bat and flies. Not me. You know why?"

The psychiatrist shook his head.

"Because I can't stand the ugly things. They make me sick just to look at, let alone *be*. And then there's all the hassle of taking off your clothes and all. So I grab a cab and just pray there isn't any traffic. Boy. Or take these." He smiled for the first time, revealing two large pointed incisors. "What do you imagine happens to us when our choppers start to go? I've had this one on the left filled it must be half a dozen times. The dentist says if I was smart I'd have 'em all yanked out and a nice denture put in. Sure. Can't you just see me trying to rip out somebody's throat with a pair of false teeth? Or take the routine with the wooden stake. It used to be that was kind of a secret. Now with all these lousy movies, the whole *world* is in on the gag. I ask you, Doctor, how are you supposed to be able to sleep when you know that everybody in the block is just itching to find you so they can drive a piece of wood into your heart? Huh? Man, you talk about *sick!* Those people are in *really* bad shape!" He shuddered again. "I'll tell you about the jazz with crosses, but frankly, even thinking about it makes me jumpy. You know what? I have to walk three blocks out of my way to avoid the church I used to go to every Sunday. But don't get the idea it's just churches. No; it's *anything*. Cross your fingers and I'll start sweating. Lay a fork over a knife and I'll probably jump right out the window. So then what happens? I splatter myself all over the sidewalk, right? But do I die? Oh, hell, no. Doc, listen! You've got to help me! If you don't, I'm going to go off my gourd, I know it!"

The psychiatrist folded his note pad and smiled. "Mr. Smith," he said, "you may be surprised to learn that yours is a relatively simple problem . . . with a relatively simple cure."

"Really?" asked the pale man.

"To be sure," said the psychiatrist. "Just lie down on the couch there. That's it. Close your eyes. Relax. Good." The psychiatrist rose from his chair and walked to his desk. "While it is true that this syndrome is something of a rarity," he said, "I do not foresee any great difficulty." He picked something off the top of the desk and returned. "It is primarily a matter of adjustment and of right thinking. Are you quite relaxed?"

Smith said that he was.

"Good," said the psychiatrist. "Now we begin the cure." With which comment he raised his arm high in the air, held it there for a moment, then plunged it down, burying the mahogany letter opener to its hilt in Mr. Smith's heart.

Seconds later, he was dialing a telephone number.

"Is Dorcas there?" he asked, idly scratching the two circular marks on his neck. "Tell her it's her fiancé."

The New People

If only he had told her right at the beginning that he didn't like the house, everything would have been fine. He could have manufactured some plausible story about bad plumbing or poor construction—something; anything!—and she'd have gone along with him. Not without a fight, maybe: he could remember the way her face had looked when they stopped the car. But he could have talked her out of it. Now, of course, it was too late.

For what? he wondered, trying not to think of the party and all the noise that it would mean. Too late for what? It's a good house, well built, well kept up, roomy. Except for that bloodstain, cheerful. Anyone in his right mind . . .

"Dear, aren't you going to shave?"

He lowered the newspaper gently and said, "Sure." But Ann was looking at him in that hurt, accusing way, and he knew that it was hopeless.

Hank-what's-wrong, he thought, starting toward the bathroom.

"Hank," she said.

He stopped but did not turn. "Uh-huh?"

"What's wrong?"

"Nothing," he said.

"Honey. Please."

He faced her. The pink chiffon dress clung to her body, which had the firmness of youth; her face was unblemished, the lipstick and powder incredibly perfect; her hair, cut long, was soft on her white shoulders: in seven years Ann hadn't changed.

Resentfully, Prentice glanced away. And was ashamed. You'd think that in this time I'd get accustomed to it, he thought. *She* is. Damn it!

"Tell me," Ann said.

"Tell you what? Everything is okay," he said.

She came to him and he could smell the perfume, he could see the tiny freckles that dotted her chest. He wondered what it would be like to sleep with her. Probably it would be very nice.

"It's about Davey, isn't it?" she said, dropping her voice to a whisper. They were standing only a few feet from their son's room.

"No," Prentice said; but, it was true—Davey was part of it. For a week now Prentice had ridden on the hope that getting the locomotive repaired would change things. A kid without a train, he'd told himself, is bound to act peculiar. But he'd had the locomotive repaired, and brought it home, and Davey hadn't even bothered to set up the track.

"He appreciated it, dear," Ann said. "Didn't he thank you?"

"Sure, he thanked me."

"Well?" she said. "Honey, I've *told* you: Davey is going through a period, that's all. Children do. Really."

"I know."

"And school's been out for almost a month."

"I know," Prentice said, and thought: *Moving to a neighborhood where there isn't another kid in the whole damn block for him to play with, that might have something to do with it, too!*

"Then," Ann said, "it's me."

"No, no, no." He tried a smile. There wasn't any sense in arguing: they'd been through it a dozen times, and she had an answer for everything. He could recall the finality in her voice . . . "I love the house, Hank. And I love the neighborhood. It's what I've dreamed of all my life, and I think I deserve it. Don't you?" (It was the first time she'd ever consciously reminded him.) "The trouble is, you've lived in dingy little apartments so long you've come to *like* them. You can't adjust to a really *decent* place—and Davey's no different. You're two of a kind: little old men who can't stand a change, even for the better! Well, I can. I don't care if *fifty* people committed suicide here, I'm happy. You understand, Hank? Happy."

Prentice had understood, and had resolved to make a real effort to like the new place. If he couldn't do that, at least he could keep his feelings from Ann—for they were, he knew, foolish. Damned foolish. Everything she said was true, and he ought to be grateful.

Yet, somehow, he could not stop dreaming of the old man who had picked up a razor one night and cut his throat wide open...

Ann was staring at him.

"Maybe," he said, "I'm going through a period, too." He kissed her forehead, lightly. "Come on, now; the people are going to arrive any second, and you look like Lady Macbeth."

She held his arm for a moment. "You are getting settled in the house, aren't you?" she said. "I mean, it's becoming more like home to you, isn't it?"

"Sure," Prentice said.

His wife paused another moment, then smiled. "Okay, get the whiskers off. Rhoda is under the impression you're a handsome man."

He walked into the bathroom and plugged in the electric shaver. Rhoda, he thought. First names already, and we haven't been here three weeks.

"Dad?"

He looked down at Davey, who had slipped in with nine-year-old stealth. "Yo." According to ritual, he ran the shaver across his son's chin.

Davey did not respond. He stepped back and said, "Dad, is Mr. Ames coming over tonight?"

Prentice nodded. "I guess so."

"And Mr. Chambers?"

"Uh-huh. Why?"

Davey did not answer.

"What do you want to know for?"

"Gee." Davey's eyes were red and wide. "Is it okay if I stay in my room?"

"Why? You sick?"

"No. Kind of."

"Stomach? Head?"

"Just sick," Davey said. He pulled at a thread in his shirt and fell silent again.

Prentice frowned. "I thought maybe you'd like to show them your train," he said.

"Please," Davey said. His voice had risen slightly, and Prentice could see tears gathering. "Dad, please don't make me come out. Leave me stay in my room. I won't make any noise, I promise, and I'll go to sleep on time."

"Okay, okay. Don't make such a big deal out of it!" Prentice ran the cool metal over his face. Anger came and went, swiftly. Stupid to get mad. "Davey, what'd you do, ride your bike on their lawn or something? Break a window?"

"No."

"Then why don't you want to see them?"

"I just don't."

"Mr. Ames likes you. He told me so yesterday. He thinks you're a fine boy, so does Mr. Chambers. They—"

"*Please*, Dad!" Davey's face was pale; he began to cry. "Please, please, please. Don't let them get me!"

"What are you talking about? Davey, cut it out. Now!"

"I saw what they were doing there in the garage. And they know I saw them, too. They know. And—"

"Davey!" Ann's voice was sharp and loud and resounding in the tile-lined bathroom. The boy stopped crying immediately. He looked up, hesitated, then ran out. His door slammed.

Prentice took a step.

"No, Hank. Leave him alone."

"He's upset."

"Let him be upset." She shot an angry glance toward the bedroom. "I suppose he told you that filthy story about the garage?"

"No," Prentice said, "he didn't. What's it all about?"

"Nothing. Absolutely nothing. Honestly, I'd like to meet Davey's parents!"

"We're his parents," Prentice said, firmly.

"All right, all right. But he got that imagination of his from *some*body, and it wasn't from us. You're going to have to speak to him, Hank. I mean it. Really."

"About what?"

"These wild stories. What if they got back to Mr. Ames? I'd—well, I'd die. After he's gone out of his way to be nice to Davey, too."

"I haven't heard the stories," Prentice said.

"Oh, you will." Ann undid her apron and folded it, furiously. "Honestly! Sometimes I think the two of you are trying to make things just as miserable as they can be for me."

The doorbell rang, stridently.

"Now make an effort to be pleasant, will you? This is a *house*warming, after all. And do hurry."

She closed the door. He heard her call, "Hi!" and heard Ben Roth's baritone booming: "Hi!"

Ridiculous, he told himself, plugging the razor in again. Utterly goddam ridiculous. No one complained louder than I did when we were tripping over ourselves in that little upstairs coffin on Friar. *I'm* the one who kept moaning for a house, not Ann.

So now we've got one.

He glanced at the tiny brownish blood stain that wouldn't wash out of the wallpaper, and sighed.

Now we've got one.

"Hank!"

"Coming!" He straightened his tie and went into the living room.

The Roths, of course, were there. Ben and Rhoda. Get it right, he thought, because we're all going to be pals. "Hi, Ben."

"Thought you'd deserted us, boy," said the large, pink man, laughing.

"No. Wouldn't do that."

"Hank," Ann signaled. "You've met Beth Cummings, haven't you?"

The tall, smartly dressed woman giggled and extended her hand. "We've seen each other," she said. "Hello."

Her husband, a pale man with white hair, crushed Prentice's fingers. "Fun and games," he said, tightening his grip and wheezing with amusement. "Yes, sir."

Trying not to wince, Prentice retrieved his hand. It was instantly snatched up by a square, bald man in a double-breasted brown suit. "Reiker," the man said. "Call me Bud. Everyone does. Don't know why; my name is Oscar."

"*That's* why," a woman said, stepping up. "Ann introduced us, but you probably don't remember, if I know men. I'm Edna."

"Sure," Prentice said. "How are you?"

"Fine. But then, I'm a woman: I *like* parties!"

"How's that?"

"Hank!"

Prentice excused himself and walked quickly into the kitchen. Ann was holding up a package.

"Honey, look what Rhoda gave us!"

He dutifully handled the salt and pepper shakers and set them down again. "That's real nice."

"You turn the rooster's head," Mrs. Roth said, "and it grinds your pepper."

"Wonderful," Prentice said.

"And Beth gave us this lovely salad bowl, see? And we've needed *this* for *cen*turies!" She held out a gray tablecloth with gold bordering. "Plastic!"

"Wonderful," Prentice said. Again, the doorbell rang. He glanced at Mrs. Roth, who had been staring thoughtfully at him, and returned to the living room.

"How you be, Hank?" Lucian Ames walked in, rubbing his hands together briskly. "Well! The gang's all here, I see. But where's that boy of yours?"

"Davey? Oh," Prentice said, "he's sick."

"Nonsense! Boys that age are never sick. Never!"

Ann laughed nervously from the kitchen. "Just something he ate!"

"Not the candy we sent over, I hope."

"Oh, no."

"Well, tell him his Uncle Lucian said hello."

A tan elf of a man, with sparkling eyes and an ill fitting mustache, Ames reminded Prentice somewhat of those clerks who used to sit silently on high wooden stools, posting infinitesimal figures in immense yellow ledgers. He was, however, the head of a nationally famous advertising agency.

His wife Charlotte provided a remarkable contrast. She seemed to belong to the era of the twenties, with her porcelain face, her thin, delicately angular body, her air of fragility.

Nice, Prentice told himself.

He removed coats and hung them in closets. He shook hands, and smiled until his face began to ache. He looked at presents and thanked the women and told them they shouldn't have. He carried out sandwiches. He mixed drinks.

By eight-thirty, everyone in the block had arrived. The Johnsons, the Ameses, the Roths, the Reikers, the Klementaskis, the Chamberses; four or five others whose names Prentice could not remember, although Ann had taken care to introduce them.

What it is, he decided, looking at the people, at the gifts they had brought, remembering their many kindnesses and how, already, Ann had made more friends than she'd ever had before, is, I'm just an antisocial bastard.

After the third round of whiskeys and martinis, someone turned on the FM and someone else suggested dancing. Prentice had always supposed that one danced only at New

Year's Eve parties, but he said the hell with it, finally, and tried to relax.

"Shall we?" Mrs. Ames said.

He wanted to say no, but Ann was watching. So he said, "Sure, if you've got strong toes," instead.

Almost at once he began to perspire. The smoke, the drinks, the heat of the crowded room, caused his head to ache; and, as usual, he was acutely embarrassed at having to hold a strange woman so closely.

But, he continued to smile.

Mrs. Ames danced well, she followed him with unerring instinct; and within moments she was babbling freely into his ear. She told him about old Mr. Thomas, the man who had lived here before, and how surprised everyone had been at what had happened; she told him how curious they'd all been about The New People and how relieved they were to find him and Ann so very nice; she told him he had strong arms. Ann was being twirled about by Herb Johnson. She was smiling.

An endless, slow three-step came on, then, and Mrs. Amos put her cheek next to Prentice's. In the midst of a rambling sentence, she said, suddenly, in a whisper, "You know, I think it was awfully brave of you to adopt little Davey. I mean, considering."

"Considering what?"

She pulled away and looked at him. "Nothing," she said. "I'm awfully sorry."

Blushing with fury, Prentice turned and strode into the kitchen. He fought his anger, thinking, God, God, is she telling strangers about it now? Is it a topic for backfence gossip? *"My husband is impotent, you know. Is yours?"*

He poured whiskey into a glass and drank it, fast. It made his eyes water, and when he opened them, he saw a figure standing next to him.

It was—who? Dystal. Matthew Dystal; bachelor; movie writer or something; lives down the block. Call him Matt.

"Miserable, isn't it?" the man said, taking the bottle from Prentice's hand.

"What do you mean?"

"Everything," the man said. He filled his glass and drained it smartly. "Them. Out there." He filled the glass again.

"Nice people," Prentice forced himself to say.

"You think so?"

The man was drunk. Clearly, very drunk. And it was only nine-thirty.

"You think so?" he repeated.

"Sure. Don't you?"

"Of course. I'm one of them, aren't I?"

Prentice peered at his guest closely, then moved toward the living room.

Dystal took his arm. "Wait," he said. "Listen. You're a good guy. I don't know you very well, but I like you, Hank Prentice. So I'm going to give you some advice." His voice dropped to a whisper. "Get out of here," he said.

"What?"

"Just what I said. Move away, move away to another city."

Prentice felt a quick ripple of annoyance, checked it. "Why?" he asked, smiling.

"Never mind that," Dystal said. "Just do it. Tonight. Will you?" His face was livid, clammy with perspiration; his eyes were wide.

"Well, I mean, Matt, that's a heck of a thing to say. I thought you said you liked us. Now you want to get rid of us."

"Don't joke," Dystal said. He pointed at the window. "Can't you see the moon? You bloody idiot, can't you—"

"Hey, hey! Unfair!"

At the sound of the voice, Dystal froze. He closed his eyes for a moment and opened them, slowly. But he did not move.

Lucian Ames walked into the kitchen. "What's the story here," he said, putting his arm on Dystal's shoulder, "you trying to monopolize our host all night?"

Dystal did not answer.

"How about a refill, Hank?" Ames said, removing his hand.

Prentice said, "Sure," and prepared the drink. From the corner of his eye, he saw Dystal turn and walk stiffly out of the room. He heard the front door open and close.

Ames was chuckling. "Poor old Matt," he said. "He'll be hung over tomorrow. It seems kind of a shame, doesn't it? I mean, you know, of all people, you'd think a big Hollywood writer would be able to hold his liquor. But not Matt. He gets loaded just by staring at the labels."

Prentice said, "Huh."

"Was he giving you one of his screwball nightmares?"

"What? No—we were just sort of talking. About things."

Ames dropped an ice cube into his drink. "Things?" he said.

"Yeah."

Ames took a sip of the whiskey and walked to the window, looking lithe, somehow, as well as small. After what seemed a long time, he said, "Well, it's a fine night, isn't it. Nice and clear, nice fine moon." He turned and tapped a cigarette out of a red package, lighted the cigarette. "Hank," he said, letting the gray smoke gush from the corners of his mouth, "tell me something. What do you do for excitement?"

Prentice shrugged. It was an odd question, but then, everything seemed odd to him tonight. "I don't know," he said. "Go to a movie once in a while. Watch TV. The usual."

Ames cocked his head. "But—don't you get bored?" he asked.

"Sure, I guess. Every so often. Being a C.P.A., you know, that isn't exactly the world's most fascinating job."

Ames laughed sympathetically. "It's awful, isn't it?"

"Being a C.P.A.?"

"No. Being bored. It's about the worst thing in the world, don't you agree? Someone once remarked they thought it was the only real sin a human could commit."

"I hope not," Prentice said.

"Why?"

"Well, I mean—everybody gets bored, don't they?"

"Not," Ames said, "if they're careful."

Prentice found himself becoming increasingly irritated at the conversation. "I suppose it helps," he said, "if you're the head of an advertising agency."

"No, not really. It's like any other job: interesting at first, but then you get used to it. It becomes routine. So you go fishing for other diversions."

"Like what?"

"Oh . . . anything. Everything." Ames slapped Prentice's arm good naturedly. "You're all right, Hank," he said.

"Thanks."

"I mean it. Can't tell you how happy we all are that you moved here."

"No more than we are!" Ann walked unsteadily to the sink with a number of empty glasses. "I want to apologize for Davey again, Lucian. I was telling Charlotte, he's been a perfect beast lately. He should have thanked you for fixing the seat on his bike."

"Forget it," Ames said, cheerfully. "The boy's just upset because he doesn't have any playmates." He looked at Prentice. "Some of us elders have kids, Hank, but they're all practically grown. You probably know that our daughter, Ginnie, is away at college. And Chris and Beth's boy lives in New York. But, you know, I wouldn't worry. As soon as school starts, Davey'll straighten out. You watch."

Ann smiled. "I'm sure you're right, Lucian. But I apologize, anyway."

"Nuts." Ames returned to the living room and began to dance with Beth Cummings.

Prentice thought then of asking Ann what the devil she meant by blabbing about their personal life to strangers, but decided not to. This was not the time. He was too angry, too confused.

The party lasted another hour. Then Ben Roth said, "Better let these good folks get some sleep!" and, slowly, the people left.

Ann closed the door. She seemed to glow with contentment, looking younger and prettier than she had for several years. "Home," she said, softly, and began picking up ash trays and glasses and plates. "Let's get all this out of the way so we won't have to look at it in the morning," she said.

Prentice said, "All right," in a neutral tone. He was about to move the coffee table back into place when the telephone rang.

"Yes?"

The voice that answered was a harsh whisper, like a rush of wind through leaves. "Prentice, are they gone?"

"Who is this?"

"Matt Dystal. Are they gone?"

"Yes."

"All of them? Ames? Is he gone?"

"Yes. What do you want, Dystal? It's late."

"Later than you might think, Prentice. He told you I was drunk, but he lied. I'm not drunk. I'm—"

"Look, what is it you want?"

"I've got to talk with you," the voice said. "Now. Tonight. Can you come over?"

"At eleven o'clock?"

"Yes. Prentice, listen to me. I'm not drunk, and I'm not kidding. This is a matter of life and death. Yours. Do you understand what I'm saying?"

Prentice hesitated, confused.

"You know where my place is—fourth house from the

corner, right-hand side. Come over now. But listen, carefully: go out the back door. The back door. Prentice, are you listening?"

"Yes," Prentice said.

"My lights will be off. Go around to the rear. Don't bother to knock, just walk in—but be quiet about it. They mustn't see you."

Prentice heard a click, then silence. He stared at the receiver for a while before replacing it.

"Well?" Ann said. "Man talk?"

"Not exactly." Prentice wiped his palm on his trousers. "That fellow Matt Dystal, he's probably sick. Wants me to come over."

"Now?"

"Yeah. I think I better; he sounded pretty bad. You go on to sleep, I'll be back in a little while."

"Okay, honey. I hope it isn't anything serious. But, it *is* nice to be doing something for *them* for a change, isn't it?"

Prentice kissed his wife, waited until the bathroom door had closed; then he went outside, into the cold night.

He walked along the grass verge of the alleyway, across the small lawns, up the steps to Dystal's rear door.

He deliberated with himself for a moment, then walked in.

"Prentice?" a voice hissed.

"Yes. Where are you?"

A hand touched his arm in the darkness and he jumped, nervously. "Come into the bedroom."

A dim lamp went on. Prentice saw that the windows were covered by heavy tan drapes. It was chilly in the room, chilly and moist.

"Well?" Prentice said, irritably.

Matthew Dystal ran a hand through his rope-colored hair. "I know what you're thinking," he said. "And I don't blame you. But it was necessary, Prentice. It was necessary. Ames has told you about my 'wild nightmares' and that's going to stick with you, I realize; but get this straight." His hand became a fist. "Everything I'm about to say is true. No matter how outlandish it may sound, it's *true*—and I have proof. All you'll need. So keep still, Prentice, and listen to me. It may mean your life: yours and your wife's and your boy's. And, maybe, mine..." His voice trailed off; then, suddenly, he said, "You want a drink?"

"No."

"You ought to have one. You're only on the outskirts of confusion, my friend. But, there are worse things than confusion. Believe me." Dystal walked to a bookcase and stood there for almost a full minute. When he turned, his features were slightly more composed. "What do you know," he asked, "about the house you're living in?"

Prentice shifted uncomfortably. "I know that a man killed himself in it, if that's what you mean."

"But do you know why?"

"No."

"Because he lost," Dystal said, giggling. "He drew the short one. How's that for motivation?"

"I think I'd better go," Prentice said.

"Wait." Dystal took a handkerchief from his pocket and tapped his forehead. "I didn't mean to begin that way. It's just that I've never told this to anyone, and it's difficult. You'll see why. Please, Prentice, promise you won't leave until I've finished!"

Prentice looked at the wiry, nervous little man, and cursed the weakness that had allowed him to get himself into this miserably uncomfortable situation. He wanted to go home. But he knew he could not leave now.

"All right," he said. "Go on."

Dystal sighed. Then, staring at the window, he began to talk. "I built this house," he said, "because I thought I was going to get married. By the time I found out I was wrong, the work was all done. I should have sold it, I know, I see that, but I was feeling too lousy to go through the paperwork. Besides, I'd already given up my apartment. So I moved in." He coughed. "Be patient with me, Prentice: this is the only way to tell it, from the beginning. Where was I?"

"You moved in."

"Yes! Everybody was very nice. They invited me to their homes for dinner, they dropped by, they did little favors for me; and it helped, it really did. I thought, you know, what a hell of a great bunch of neighbors. Regular. *Real*. That was it: they were real. Ames, an advertising man; Thomas, a lawyer; Johnson, paint company; Chambers, insurance; Reiker and Cummings, engineers—I mean, how average can you get?" Dystal paused; an ugly grin appeared on his face, disappeared. "I liked them," he said. "And I was really delighted with things. But, of course, you know how it is when a woman gives you the business. I was still licking my wounds. And I guess it showed, because Ames came over one evening. Just dropped by, in a neighborly way. We had some drinks. We talked about the ways of the female. Then, bang, out of nowhere, he asked me the question. Was I bored?"

Prentice stiffened.

"Well, when you lose your girl, you lose a lot of your ambition. I told him yes, I was plenty bored. And he said, 'I used to be.' I remember his exact words. 'I used to be,' he said. 'The long haul to success, the fight, the midnight oil: it was over. I'd made it,' he said. 'Dough in the bank. Partnership in a top agency. Daughter grown and away to school. I was ready to be put out to pasture, Matt. But the thing was, I was only fifty-two! I had maybe another twenty years left. And almost everybody else in the block was the same way— Ed and Ben and Oscar, all the same. You know: they fooled around with their jobs, but they weren't interested any more—not really. Because the jobs didn't *need* them any more. They were bored.'" Dystal walked to the nightstand and poured himself a drink. "That was five years ago," he murmured. "Ames, he pussy-footed around the thing for a while—feeling me out, testing me; then he told me that he had decided to do something about it. About being bored. He'd organized everyone in the block. Once a week, he explained, they played games. It was real Group Activity. Community effort. It began with charades, but they got tired of that in a while. Then they tried cards. To make it interesting, they bet high. Everybody had his turn at losing. Then, Ames said, someone suggested making the game even *more* interesting, because it was getting to be a drag. So they experimented with strip poker one night. Just for fun, you understand. Rhoda lost. Next time it was Charlotte. And it went that way for a while, until finally, Beth lost. Everyone had been waiting for it. Things became anticlimactic after that, though, so the stakes changed again. Each paired off with another's wife; lowest scoring team had to—" Dystal tipped the bottle. "Sure you won't have a bracer?"

Prentice accepted the drink without argument. It tasted bitter and powerful, but it helped.

"Well," Dystal went on, "I had one hell of a time believing all that. I mean, you know: *Ames,* after all—a little book-keeper type with gray hair and glasses... Still, the way he talked, I knew—somehow, I *knew*—it was the truth. Maybe because I didn't feel that a guy like Ames could make it all up! Anyway: when they'd tried all the possible combinations, things got dull again. A few of the women wanted to stop, but, of course, they were in too deep already. During one particular Fun Night, Ames had taken photographs. So they had to keep going. Every week, it was something new. Something different. Swapsies occupied them for a while, Ames told me: Chambers took a two-week vacation with Jacqueline, Ben and Beth went to Acapulco, and that sort of thing. And that is where I came into the picture." Dystal raised his hand. "I know, you don't need to tell me. I should have pulled out. But I was younger then. I was a big writer, man of the world. Training in Hollywood. I couldn't tell him I was shocked: it would have been betraying my craft. And he figured it that way, too: that's why he told me. Besides, he knew I'd be bound to find out eventually. They could hide it from just about everybody, but not someone right in the block. So, I played along. I accepted his invitation to join the next Group Activity—which is what he calls them.

"Next morning, I thought I'd dreamed the whole visit, I really did. But on Saturday, sure enough, the phone rings and Ames says, 'We begin at eight, sharp.' When I got to his house, I found it packed. Everybody in the neighborhood. Looking absolutely the same as always, too. Drinks; dancing; the whole bit. After a while, I started to wonder if the whole thing wasn't an elaborate gag. But at ten, Ames told us about the evening's surprise." Dystal gave way to a shudder. "It was a surprise, all right," he said. "I told them I wanted nothing to do with it, but Ames had done something to my drink. I didn't seem to have any control. They led me into the bedroom, and..."

Prentice waited, but Dystal did not complete his sentence. His eyes were dancing now.

"Never mind," he said. "Never mind what happened! The point is, I was drunk, and—well, I went through with it. I *had* to. You can see that, can't you?"

Prentice said that he could see that.

"Ames pointed out to me that the only sin, the *only* one, was being bored. That was his justification, that was his incentive. He simply didn't want to sin, that was all. So the Group Activities went on. And they got worse. Much worse. One thing, they actually plotted a crime and carried it off: the Union bank robbery, maybe you read about it: 1953. I drove the car for them. Another time, they decided it would ward off ennui by setting fire to a warehouse down by the docks. The fire spread. Prentice—do you happen to remember that DC-7 that went down between here and Detroit?"

Prentice said, "Yes, I remember."

"Their work," Dystal said. "Ames planned it. In a way, I think he's a genius. I could spend all night telling you the things we did, but there isn't time. I've got to skip." He placed his fingers over his eyes. "Joan of Arc," he said, "was the turning point. Ames had decided that it would be diverting to re-enact famous scenes from literature. So he and Bud went down to Main Street, I think it was, and found a beat doll who thought the whole thing would be fun. They gave her twenty-five dollars, but she never got a chance to spend it. I remember that she laughed right up to the point where Ames lit the pile of oil-soaked rags...Afterward, they re-enacted other scenes. The execution of Marie Antoinette. The murder of Hamlet's father. You know *The Man in the Iron Mask?* They did that one. And a lot more. It lasted quite a while, too, but Ames began to get restless." Dystal held out his hands suddenly and stared at them. "The next game was a form of Russian roulette. We drew straws. Whoever got the short one had to commit suicide—in his own way. It was understood that if he failed, it would mean something much worse—and Ames had developed some damned interesting techniques. Like the nerve clamps, for instance. Thomas lost the game, anyway. They gave him twelve hours to get it over with."

Prentice felt a cold film of perspiration over his flesh. He tried to speak, but found that it was impossible. The man, of course, was crazy. Completely insane. But—he had to hear the end of the story. "Go on," he said.

Dystal ran his tongue across his lower lip, poured another drink and continued. "Cummings and Chambers got scared then," he said. "They argued that some stranger would move into the house, and then there'd be all sorts of trouble. We had a meeting at Reiker's, and Chris came out with the idea of us all chipping in and buying the place. But Ames didn't go for it. 'Let's not be so darned exclusive,' he said. 'After all, the new people might be bored, too. Lord knows we could use some fresh blood in the Group.' Cummings was pessimistic. He said, 'What if you're wrong? What if they don't want to join us?' Ames laughed it off. 'I hope,' he said, 'that you don't think we're the only ones. Why, every city has its neighborhoods just like ours. We're really not that unique.' And then he went on to say that if the new people don't work out, he would take care of the situation. He didn't say how."

Dystal looked out the window again.

"I can see that he's almost ready to give you an invitation, Prentice. Once that happens, you're finished. It's join them or accept the only alternative."

Suddenly the room was very quiet.

"You don't believe me, do you?"

Prentice opened his mouth.

"No, of course you don't. It's a madman's ravings. Well, I'm going to prove it to you, Prentice." He started for the door. "Come on. Follow me; but don't make any noise."

Dystal walked out the back door, closed it, moved soundlessly across the soft, black grass.

"They're on a mystic kick right now," he whispered to Prentice. "Ames is trying to summon the devil. Last week we slaughtered a dog and read the Commandments backward; the week before, we did some chants out of an old book that Ben found in the library; before that it was orgies—" He shook his head. "It isn't working out, though. God knows why. You'd think the devil would be so delighted with Ames that he'd sign him up for the team."

Prentice followed his neighbor across the yards, walking carefully, and wondering why. He thought of his neat little office on Harmon Street, old Mrs. Gleason, the clean, well-lighted restaurant where he had his lunch and read newspaper headlines; and they seemed terribly far away.

Why, he asked himself, am I creeping around backyards with a lunatic at midnight?

Why?

"The moon is full tonight, Prentice. That means they'll be trying again."

Silently, without the slightest sound, Matthew Dystal moved across the lawns, keeping always to the shadows. A minute later he raised his hand and stopped.

They were at the rear of the Ameses' house.

It was dark inside.

"Come on," Dystal whispered.

"Wait a minute." Somehow, the sight of his own living room, still blazing with light, reassured Prentice. "I think I've had enough for this evening."

"Enough?" Dystal's face twisted grotesquely. He bunched

the sleeve of Prentice's jacket in his fist. "Listen," he hissed, "listen, you idiot. I'm risking my life to help you. Don't you understand yet? If they find out I've talked . . ." He released the sleeve. "Prentice, *please*. You have a chance now, a chance to clear out of this whole stinking mess; but you won't have it long—Believe me!"

Prentice sighed. "What do you want me to do?" he said.

"Nothing. Just come with me, quietly. They're in the basement."

Breathing hard now, Dystal tiptoed around to the side of the house. He stopped at a small, earth-level window.

It was closed.

"Prentice. *Softly*. Bend down and keep out of view."

In invisible, slow movements, Dystal reached out and pushed the window. It opened a half inch. He pushed it again. It opened another half inch.

Prentice saw yellow light stream out of the crack. Instantly his throat felt very dry, very painful.

There was a noise. A low, murmurous sound; a susurrus like distant humming.

"What's that?"

Dystal put a finger to his lips and motioned: "Here."

Prentice knelt down at the window and looked into the light.

At first he could not believe what his eyes saw.

It was a basement, like other basements in old houses, with a large iron furnace and a cement floor and heavy beams. This much he could recognize and understand. The rest, he could not.

In the center of the floor was a design, obviously drawn in colored chalks. It looked a bit, to Prentice, like a Star of David, although there were other designs around and within it. They were not particularly artistic, but they were intricate. In the middle was a large cup, similar to a salad bowl, vaguely familiar, empty.

"There," whispered Dystal, withdrawing.

Slightly to the left were drawn a circle and a pentagram, its five points touching the circumference equally.

Prentice blinked and turned his attention to the people.

Standing on a block of wood, surrounded by men and women, was a figure in a black robe and a serpent-shaped crown.

It was Ames.

Introducing the first and only complete hardcover collection of Agatha Christie's mysteries

Now you can enjoy the
greatest mysteries ever written
in a magnificent
Home Library Edition.

Discover Agatha Christie's world of mystery, adventure and intrigue

Agatha Christie's timeless tales of mystery and suspense offer something for every reader—mystery fan or not—young and old alike. And now, you can build a complete hardcover library of her world-famous mysteries by subscribing to The Agatha Christie Mystery Collection.

This exciting Collection is your passport to a world where mystery reigns supreme. Volume after volume, you and your family will enjoy mystery reading at its very best.

You'll meet Agatha Christie's world-famous detectives like Hercule Poirot, Jane Marple, and the likeable Tommy and Tuppence Beresford.

In your readings, you'll visit Egypt, Paris, England and other exciting destinations where murder is always on the itinerary. And wherever you travel, you'll become deeply involved in some of the most ingenious and diabolical plots ever invented ... "cliff-hangers" that only Dame Agatha could create!

It all adds up to mystery reading that's so good ... it's almost criminal. And it's yours every month with The Agatha Christie Mystery Collection.

Solve the greatest mysteries of all time. The Collection contains all of Agatha Christie's classic works including *Murder on the Orient Express, Death on the Nile, And Then There Were None, The ABC Murders* and her ever-popular whodunit, *The Murder of Roger Ackroyd.*

Each handsome hardcover volume is Smythe sewn and printed on high quality acid-free paper so it can withstand even the most murderous treatment. Bound in Sussex-blue simulated leather with gold titling, The Agatha Christie Mystery Collection will make a tasteful addition to your living room, or den.

Ride the Orient Express for 10 days without obligation. To introduce you to the Collection, we're inviting you to examine the classic mystery, *Murder on the Orient Express*, without risk or obligation. If you're not completely satisfied, just return it within 10 days and owe nothing.

However, if you're like the millions of other readers who love Agatha Christie's thrilling tales of mystery and suspense, keep *Murder on the Orient Express* and pay just $7.95 plus postage and handling.

You will then automatically receive future volumes once a month as they are published on a fully returnable, 10-day free-examination basis. No minimum purchase is required, and you may cancel your subscription at any time.

This unique collection is not sold in stores. It's available only through this special offer. So don't miss out, begin your subscription now. Just mail this card today.

☐ Yes! Please send me *Murder on the Orient Express* for a 10-day free-examination and enter my subscription to <u>The Agatha Christie Mystery Collection</u>. If I keep *Murder on the Orient Express*, I will pay just $7.95 plus postage and handling and receive one additional volume each month on a fully returnable 10-day free-examination basis. There is no minimum number of volumes to buy, and I may cancel my subscription at any time. 07013

☐ I prefer the deluxe edition bound in genuine leather for $24.95 per volume plus shipping and handling, with the same 10-day free-examination. 07054

Name_____

Address_____

City_____State_____Zip_____

Z 1 2 3
Send No Money...
But Act Today!

NO POSTAGE
NECESSARY
IF MAILED
IN THE
UNITED STATES

BUSINESS REPLY CARD

FIRST CLASS   PERMIT NO. 2154   HICKSVILLE, N.Y.

Postage will be paid by addressee:

The Agatha Christie
Mystery Collection
Bantam Books
P.O. Box 956
Hicksville, N.Y. 11802

His wife, Charlotte, dressed in a white gown, stood next to him. She held a brass lamp.

Also in robes and gowns were Ben and Rhoda Roth, Bud Reiker and his wife, the Cummingses, the Chamberses, the Johnsons—

Prentice shook away his sudden dizziness and shaded his eyes.

To the right, near the furnace, was a table with a white sheet draped across it. And two feet away, an odd, six-sided structure with black candles burning from a dozen apertures.

"Listen," Dystal said.

Ames' eyes were closed. Softly he was chanting:

All degradation, all sheer infamy,
    Thou shalt endure. Thy head beneath the mire.
    And dung of worthless women shall desire
As in some hateful dream, at last to lie;
    Woman must trample thee till thou respire
        That deadliest fume;
    The vilest worms must crawl, the loathliest vampires
        gloom . . .

"The Great Beast," chuckled Dystal.

"I," said Ames, "am Ipsissimus," and the others chanted, "He is Ipsissimus."

"I have read the books, dark Lord. *The Book of Sacred Magic of Abra-Melin the Mage* I have read, and I reject it!"

"We reject it!" murmured the Roths.

"The power of Good shall be served by the power of Darkness, always."

He raised his hands. "In Thy altar is the stele of Ankf-f-n-Khonsu; there, also, *The Book of the Dead* and *The Book of the Law*, six candles to each side, my Lord, Bell, Burin, Lamen, Sword, Cup, and the Cakes of Life . . ."

Prentice looked at the people he had seen only a few hours ago in his living room, and shuddered. He felt very weak.

"We, your servants," said Ames, singing the words, "beseech your presence, Lord of Night and of Life Eternal, Ruler of the Souls of men in all Thy vast dominion . . ."

Prentice started to rise, but Dystal grasped his jacket. "No," he said. "Wait. Wait another minute. This is something you ought to see."

" . . . we live to serve you; grant us . . ."

"He's begging the devil to appear," whispered Dystal.

". . . tonight, and offer the greatest and most treasured gift. Accept our offering!"

"Accept it!" cried the others.

"What the hell is this, anyway?" Prentice demanded, feverishly.

Then Ames stopped talking, and the rest were silent. Ames raised his left hand and lowered it. Chris Cummings and Bud Reiker bowed, and walked backwards into the shadows where Prentice could not see them.

Charlotte Ames walked to the six-sided structure with the candles, and picked up a long, thin object.

She returned and handed this to her husband.

It was a knife.

"*Killnotshaltthou!*" screamed Ed Chambers, and he stepped across the pentagram to the sheet-shrouded table.

Prentice rubbed his eyes.

"Shhh."

Bud Reiker and Chris Cummings returned to the center of light then. They were carrying a bundle. It was wrapped in blankets.

The bundle thrashed and made peculiar muffled noises. The men lifted it onto the table and held it.

Ames nodded, and stepped down from the block of wood. He walked to the table and halted, the long-bladed butcher knife glittering in the glow of the candles.

"To Thee, O Lord of the Underground, we make this offering! To Thee, the rarest gift of all!"

"What is it?" Prentice asked. "What is this gift?"

Dystal's voice was ready and eager. "A virgin," he said.

Then they removed the blanket.

Prentice felt his eyes bursting from their sockets, felt his heart charging the walls of his chest.

"Ann," he said, in a choked whisper. "Ann!"

The knife went up.

Prentice scrambled to his feet and fought the dizziness. "Dystal," he cried. "Dystal, for God's sake, what are they doing? Stop them. You hear me? Stop them!"

"I can't," said Matthew Dystal, sadly. "It's too late. I'm afraid your wife said a few things she shouldn't have, Prentice. You see—we've been looking for a real one for such a long time . . ."

Prentice tried to lunge, but the effort lost him his balance.

He fell to the ground. His arms and legs were growing numb, and he remembered, suddenly, the bitter taste of the drink he'd had.

"It really couldn't have been avoided, though," Dystal said. "I mean, the boy knew, and he'd have told you eventually. And you'd have begun investigating, and—oh, you understand. I told Lucian we should have bought the place, but he's so obstinate; thinks he knows everything! Now, of course, we'll have to burn it, and that does seem a terrible waste." He shook his head from side to side. "But don't you worry," he said. "You'll be asleep by then, and, I promise, you won't feel a thing. Really."

Prentice turned his eyes from the window and screamed silently for a long time.

Father, Dear Father

To Mr. Pollet, Time was a highway: a vast, gleaming, empty highway, waiting to be traveled. "It has roadblocks, to be sure," he would say, "and there are altogether too many dangerous curves, much too sharp for even the minimum speed. Still, it's not unlikely that a really clever man will get through someday."

Of course, Mr. Pollet hoped to be that man. To this end he had devoted thirty-seven of his fifty-three years; unswervingly, tirelessly, and with almost monomaniacal faith. Friends he had none. Acquaintances, few. His wife was afraid of him. And in the scientific clubs he was *persona non grata:* for when he was not mumbling jiggery-pokery about the "space-time continuum" and "the pretzel of the Past," he was nudging people and asking them his famous, and perpetually wearisome question:

"Well, now, what about you, what is *your* opinion? If I were to go back in Time and kill my own father—what would happen?"

"Perhaps it is wishful thinking on my part," one beleaguered physicist had replied, "but I am of the notion that you would vanish instantly."

Among other shortcomings, however, Mr. Pollet had no appreciation for subtlety. "Oh?" he'd said, tapping his nose; "you think so? I wonder. It's an interesting theory, but somehow it doesn't seem possible. And yet—"

The question haunted him. He went to sleep with it and arose with it and carried it about with him through the days.

Indeed, it was for no other purpose than to solve this perennial riddle that he labored on his Time Machine. History certainly did not intrigue him. He was not excited over the prospect of visiting past ages. Nor was he unduly concerned with the fame that would surely come to the first man to pierce the time barrier. The Future? It was a bore.

Mr. Pollet wanted little. Only the answer to the question. *What would happen . . . ?*

It was a late summer evening when the lean man with the sallow cheeks and wispy black hair stepped, for the eight-hundred-and-thirteenth time, into the large metal cylinder in his laboratory basement, pulled a lever, waited, and, also for the eight-hundred-and-thirteenth time, stepped out. Another failure, Mr. Pollet mused. Another botched job of it.

It was enough to discourage a saint.

He was a man not normally given to emotional excess; yet now he found himself yielding to a thoroughly wild impulse. He stamped his foot, cursed loudly but not well, picked up a heavy crescent wrench, and threw it at the Time Machine.

A bank of lights came on.

The metal cylinder began to whine, softly.

Mr. Pollet stared. Was it possible? He advanced. Yes; there was no denying it—the weight and angle of curve had accomplished what he had tried to accomplish a thousand times with signal lack of success. The delicate balance was, at last, achieved!

In short, the Time Machine was ready to go.

Wondering where Science would be without its share of accidents, Mr. Pollet beamed, and prepared to enter. Then he paused. No: it must be done methodically. He mustn't take any chances whatever.

He ran upstairs, pushed his wife aside, and got a faded photograph from the bedroom trunk. Hand-tinted, it pictured a clear-eyed, square-jawed, heavy-set middle-aged man with a fierce shock of red hair.

"Dad," Mr. Pollet said reverently, pocketing the snapshot and loading a blue-steel .38 revolver.

He changed into proper clothing, went back downstairs, and entered the cylinder. He made a careful adjustment of the dials; then pulled the main lever.

There was a whirring of gears. Things fizzed. The machine bucked, smoked, clanged, whistled. Mr. Pollet felt dizzy. Blackness reached for him. He fought it.

Things settled down again.

He stepped out of the cylinder.

The landscape was immediately familiar to him: it was, without doubt, the Ohio Valley region, the playground of his youth. But Mr. Pollet's mission was not to be delayed by sentiment. He looked about; then, certain that he was unobserved, rolled the Time Machine over to a clump of trees and locked it securely.

He began to walk across the field of alfalfa, and soon the town came into view, and he was confident that his calculations had been correct. He was in Middleton.

But what about the date? He would have to check that. It would not do to kill Dad after he, Pollet, Jr., had been conceived: for then, what would be accomplished?

He withdrew the photograph one more time. Pollet, Sr., was a stern-looking fellow. He remembered him dimly as a strict disciplinarian, at all times cold and distant, and prey to a brooding disposition—but he could remember no more about his father, and nothing specific. After all, Pollet, Sr., had passed away in 1922. And he was only six years old then.

It is almost ironic, Mr. Pollet, Jr., thought, as he jogged along, that Dad shall see his son grown to manhood, only to be slaughtered by him...

Having been hatched a scrawny, prune-wrinkled, four-pound mummy, Mr. Pollet had never enjoyed an abundance of stamina. He slowed to a walk.

At the edge of town he stopped, checked the action of his revolver to be sure it would not misfire, and felt his heart beating fast. He smiled wanly. Then he entered the main street of Middleton, Ohio.

The community was abustle. Children played with hoops and bricks, and men sat on porches and women shopped. Some looked curiously at Mr. Pollet, and one, a lanky, dark-haired fellow, went so far as to stare; but this was only because a stranger had come to town, doubtless.

The stranger nodded genially and made his way down the main artery. At a drugstore he paused. Inside the window was a calendar.

It read: *February 19, 1916.*

Mr. Pollet frowned slightly. He was cutting it close, quite close. But he was still early. In fact, he could not even be a gleam in his father's eye now!

He walked to Elm Avenue, where he turned right and walked three blocks more. At a large yellow house on the corner, he stopped.

Memories came and went.

He started up the path. Never had he been so full of excitement; never so nervous.

He rapped on the door.

It was opened presently by a clear-eyed, square-jawed, heavy-set middle-aged man with a fierce shock of red hair. "Yes?"

"Mr. James Agnew Pollet?"

"That's right," the man said. Pollet, Jr., caught a glimpse of a slight, tall, exceedingly fair and moderately attractive woman seated in the living room. It was his mother. He experienced a pang.

"Are you selling something?" James Agnew Pollet asked, brusquely.

"Not exactly," Mr. Pollet, Jr., said, and plucked out the .38.

"What's the meaning—"

The revolver roared, once. A small, neat hole appeared in James Agnew Pollet's forehead. He gasped and toppled backward, and lay still.

There was a scream from the living room.

Mr. Pollet pocketed the gun, turned, and ran down the street. As he ran, he tried to absorb the fact that, so far, nothing had happened to him.

People turned to stare. He saw the same man who had gazed so intently at him before, only now the man was open-mouthed. There was something familiar about him . . .

Mr. Pollet went leaping and bounding across the field, panting heavily. Cars could not follow him: they were too primitive. Men could, but they were still reacting to shock. He had time.

He ran to the trees, got the key in the lock, and entered the cylinder. He slammed the door. He pulled the return lever.

The blackness reached, but did not find him.

After a minute, he opened the door again and stepped into his basement laboratory.

His wife was waiting. She looked confused and frightened. "Did you—go through with it?" she asked.

Mr. Pollet nodded glumly. The gun, he saw, was still hot from its recent firing.

"I killed him," he said. "Gave it to him right between the eyes. Saw him die."

"Shame!" Mrs. Pollet declared, paling. "You may not have

actually *known* him well, and perhaps it's true he was cruel to you as a child—but to murder your own father! That is terribly unkind."

"Nonsense," Mr. Pollet snapped. "It was an impersonal gesture: purely scientific. I killed him and—nothing happened. Absolutely nothing." The lanky, dark-haired man stomped his foot. "Do you understand?" he bellowed, furiously. *"Nothing happened!"*

He reached out and grasped a crowbar, and brought the heavy iron down upon the banks of delicate instruments, smashing them and the years that went into their making into a million bright pieces. "Impossible!" he raged. *"Something should have happened!"*

Mrs. Pollet watched him destroy the machine. When he had quite finished, she inquired, "Are you sure that he—that it *was* your father?"

Mr. Pollet froze, the crowbar raised high. He blinked and lowered his arm.

"What do you mean?" he asked softly.

"Nothing," his wife said, "except that I never did think you looked much like the picture, you know. It's very old. Perhaps you found a man who resembled the snapshot and it wasn't your father at all. Perhaps—"

"Be quiet," Mr. Pollet said. "I must think."

He thought.

He thought of the undeniable truth of Mrs. Pollet's observation, of the myriad dissimilarities between himself and the man in the photograph.

Especially he thought of the lanky, sallow-cheeked, dark-haired man in Middleton, who had stared so intently . . .

Mr. Pollet dropped the crowbar. He looked at the wreckage of the machine he would never be able to rebuild.

"Well, I'm a son of a bitch," he said.

And, in a manner of speaking, so he was.

A Classic Affair

It took her quite a while to get around to it, but that's the way Ruth is, and there's nothing you can do except wait. The direct line doesn't work. I'd tried it once, and she'd married Hank. So I sat there, watching her wind up, and waiting, wishing she weren't so damned pretty; it didn't make me feel much like the friend of the family I was supposed to be.

Finally I couldn't take it any more. I finished the coffee and got up and started to go. But she caught my arm and looked at me, very hard, and said, "Dave, I've got to talk to you about something." I kept quiet. "I've got to talk to you about Hank," she said.

Of course, at first I thought she was kidding. There was a time when she might have pulled such a gag; but I reminded myself that this wasn't *my* Ruth. This was Hank's, another person entirely. A housewife. Feet on the ground, eyes on the budget, not the sort to pull gags.

But even so, I couldn't quite believe what she was saying. I'd been gone almost a year—the Europe thing: partly to reorient myself and get it all straight, partly as a dirty trick: Ruth and I had planned the trip together—but a year isn't very long. Not long enough, anyway, for a person to reverse his character. And yet this was apparently what had happened. Because Ruth was telling me that she and Hank were breaking up, because she had discovered that he was no longer faithful to her. It boiled down to that.

You'd have to know the guy to understand what a blast it was. I mean, I never was crazy about him, we weren't the Best Friends some people thought, but I guess I knew Hank Osterman as well as anyone did. And the biggest thing I knew was that he was just exactly what he seemed. A solid, substantial citizen. No-nonsense type. Mr. Average, in every way. Except that he loved Ruth. Almost as much as I did, maybe; and when you feel this way about Ruth, extra-curricular activities simply don't interest you much. They couldn't.

"When did you find out?" I asked. She was getting ready for a cry, but that was all right.

"About three months ago," she said. And then she told me the whole story. It was classic stuff. How he had failed to come home on time one night, and how he had gradually turned moody and secretive, and the rest of the routine. When she came to the part where she followed him, she looked away.

I told her never mind, get on with it.

"Well . . ." She glanced at the clock; it was three-thirty. We were safe.

"Come on," I said.

She started talking to herself. "It was ten-something. He'd been fidgeting, pretending to read a magazine, but you could tell—I mean, I could. I could tell something was wrong. Always before, Hank would get sleepy around this time. Now he wasn't sleepy at all. He'd turn a page and look at it, and then look up—not at anything, actually—and keep doing this until I thought I'd go insane. Then he said he was going for a walk. I asked him if he wanted company, but he said no, he was nervous and had a headache, and a walk all by himself would probably clear it up. So he went out. This was about the seventh or eighth time it had happened, and he'd been acting so strangely, that—"

"That you decided to see what was up."

"Yes." She faced me now.

"And what *was* up?"

"I followed him for around seven blocks," she said, "down to where Riverside and Alameda come together, you know. He stopped at the corner there."

She was having a hard time, so I helped her out a little. "So far nothing to get excited about."

"No? What about this, then? He went into the car lot there and looked around over his shoulder, like a—criminal. And then he got into one of the cars in the back, in the shadows, where nobody could see him."

"And?"

"How should I know?" She blew up. "Do you think I wanted to stand there and watch the whole filthy thing?"

"Why not?"

"Oh, Dave, for heaven's sake! Am I supposed to be a child? Isn't that enough?"

I walked over to the stove—still afraid that this was all too good to be true—and got the pot and poured some more coffee. "You mean you didn't really see him meet anyone?"

"No," she said, "I didn't. I didn't have to. I mean, isn't it plain enough? Must I show you pictures or something?"

"Take it easy."

"It's a woman, all right," she said. "I don't see what else it could be except a woman, do you? He's got all the symptoms; believe me. All of them." She raised her eyes at that. "He hasn't come close to me for months," she said, and waited for it to sink in. It did.

I changed the subject in a hurry. "How many times have you gone after him?" I asked.

"Five or six."

"Always the same thing?"

"Exactly the same."

I threw down the coffee. Everything was getting too warm. I had to be careful. "I'll see what I can do," I told her.

"You won't tell him—" She came close to me. "You know what I mean."

"The soul of discretion," I said, and moved toward the back door. "Will he be there tonight, you suppose?"

She came closer. "He's there every night." I remembered the smell of her hair and the softness of her arms, suddenly, all in sharp focus, and I wanted to run.

"Dave," she said, touching my hand. "I want this thing to work. I want it to be all right between Hank and me. You grew up with him; maybe he'll tell you. Please help and make it all right."

"I'll do what I can."

She tried to give me one of those noncommittal kisses, but I managed to get out the door.

I went home, and took a shower and thought about quite a number of things. About what Ruth was *really* telling me, for instance. Try to patch it up, Dave, try your best. If it can't be done, let's talk some more. Wasn't that it?"

I thought about what she had told me about Hank, and it was certainly peculiar, but it didn't make me feel bad. Not bad at all.

*   *   *

I parked four blocks away and looked at my watch. It was crowding ten now, and Ruth had said that would be plenty of time, so I got out and started walking toward Riverside and Alameda. The streets were pretty quiet. I walked and tried to figure things out, but they wouldn't fit together. With somebody else, maybe, but somehow not with Hank.

One thing I knew for sure: I'd play it straight. She loves the guy, I kept telling myself, and if I can fix it, I will. Yes, by God, that's what I'll do. For Ruth's sake. Then I'll go right back to being a friend of the family, old buddy-buddy Dave.

Like hell.

I'll just help Hank shake the girl—and it's a girl, all right: probably a secretary, one of the standard bits—and then I'll get out. And stay out.

Across the street I saw him. There couldn't be any mistake: cheap suit, stooped shoulders, that old man's walk he'd had even as a kid.

"Hey, Hank!"

He whipped around and blinked until I was close enough for him to make me out, then he smiled and stuck his hand forward. He'd looked bad the one night I'd spent over at his house last week, the welcome home party, but now he looked worse.

"What are you doing around here?" he asked.

I told him. "Looking for you." Then I said, "Hank, I want to talk with you. Let's grab a drink."

He shook his head. "No, thanks. I'd rather not, not this time, anyway." He kept glancing over his shoulder at the corner, nervously; it was pretty obvious.

I let him have both barrels. "I saw Ruth this afternoon."

"Oh?" It didn't register.

"She called me up. That's why I came over while you were at work."

He nodded, but I could see it still hadn't penetrated.

"Look, Hank," I said, "we've been friends for about fifteen years. I guess we can talk to each other by now. Can't we?"

"Why, of course," he said. "I mean, hell yes, of course. But—couldn't we make it tomorrow, Dave? For lunch, maybe?"

He was headed down the street for the corner. I got his sleeve. "Why? Do you have a pressing engagement?"

"So to speak, Dave. That is, I do have something on."

I walked in front of him. "Ruth told me a story," I said. "Now I'd like to hear your version of it."

"What?" For the first time he seemed to come out of it. His eyes lost that glassy look. "What do you mean?"

"You want to discuss it here, in the middle of the street?"

"Yes," he said. "Here in the middle of the street will be just fine."

I told him everything that Ruth had told me. He listened intently, never interrupting.

When it was over, he smiled.

"Well?" I was getting a little sore.

"I'm afraid it's true," he said. "I *have* been unfaithful to Ruth."

The urge to swing on him passed, and I found myself feeling confused. "She's waiting for you now, I suppose?"

He nodded. "She waits every night for me."

All I could say was, "Who is she?"

"Come along," he said, "I'll introduce you."

I said no, of course, but he insisted, so I followed him to the corner, still not completely able to accept things.

Hank turned, then, and started into the lot. It was dark, no strings of bulbs, no flashy Christmas-tree come-ons, just a dark place with a lot of parked cars that you couldn't see very well.

"Do you remember this?" he asked softly. "It's really amazing. We used to pass it every day—hundreds of times. And never gave it a second look."

I adjusted my eyes to the blackness. The cars, I saw, were antique models mostly; big square boats, the kind you see in Chaplin and Fields revivals. Reos and Auburns and old Lincolns, I guessed. Over the salesman's shack a sign read: SPRINGFIELD'S VINTAGE AUTOMOBILES.

Well, it was an original trysting spot, anyway.

Hank pulled me along, past all the ancient crates. Some of them were orange with rust, nothing but heaps of rotten metal, twenty and thirty years old. A few didn't seem to be anything but shells.

He stopped by the tiny wooden house, and grinned. Then he leaned against one of the boats. "You still want the introduction?"

I nodded. Why not? I was this far already. Sure, trot her out, and we'll all have a nice sticky scene.

He stepped back. By this time I could see perfectly. "All right, then," he said. "Come over here."

I did. He walked around and opened the door of the car. "David, please meet Miss Duesenberg. Miss Duesenberg, my good friend David Jenkinson."

I looked inside the car.

It was empty.

"You understand?" Hank said.

I said "No," and I never spoke a truer word.

He was staring at the car now. I'd tried to light a ciagarette, but he'd knocked it out of my hand, explaining that there might be police around. We stood quietly.

"No woman," I said.

He shook his head. "No woman." He wasn't touching the car, or leaning against it; just staring. It was a huge thing. Dark blue or black, it looked something like a Rolls-Royce, I thought, only sportier. There was just room for two in it, or at the outside three. I couldn't tell much else. A big convertible, around twenty years old.

"Let's go somewhere and talk," I said, almost in a whisper.

"I can't," he said. "I've got to stay here, Dave. Look." He opened the door again. "Look at this leather. Smell it. It's top grain, you can't get any better. Feel how soft it is, and rich. Go on."

I ran my hand over the seat. It was good leather, all right.

"Now think of what one kid with a pocketknife could do to that," Hank said. "I mean, you know what kids are. They slash the seats in theatres, in drug stores, you know that. I don't know why. But they do, and think of what would happen if one of them found out about *this*..." His voice turned angry and hard. "And these fools won't lock it!" He glared in the direction of the shack, and swallowed. "I know, you're going to tell me that I ought to bring it to their attention. I almost did, believe it or not. But then I thought, if it's locked, I won't ever be able to sit in it. I don't know."

"Hank," I said, "let's go somewhere. I really think we'd better do that."

"I just told you, I *can't*. If you want to talk, do it here."

I was going to argue, but I could tell from his tone that it wouldn't do any good. "Okay."

"Not outside, though," he said. "Here."

I got into the car; Hank settled himself beside me and closed the door.

"By the way, I want you to notice the wheel," he said. "Leather-covered. Horn button, too. And take ahold of that emergency."

It was all chromed, longer than the gearshift; something you'd expect to find aboard a steamship.

Hank was smiling again. He pointed to a small lever on the dash—there were dozens of them. "This gadget is your brake adjustment," he murmured. "See? You can adjust the brakes for any road condition, no matter what. This here is the altimeter. Tells you how high up you are. And this little thing—"

"Hey."

He stopped talking. After a bit he sighed and turned toward me. "I can't explain, Dave," he said. "I've fallen in love with a car, that's all. I can't explain."

"Give it a try."

"No use. It's something that's happened. I can tell you how, how's easy; but not why."

"That's good enough."

He leaned back and closed his eyes. "Well—I was coming home from work. I guess it must be almost three months ago. The bus went down Riverside, as usual. I was looking out the window. When we passed Springfield's, I glanced in at the old cars, and—well, I saw it."

"You saw this car."

"That's right. The sun was still fairly high, and it sort of glittered off the paint, and I remember thinking at the time, My God, you know, what a fine-looking piece of machinery. Didn't think much about it, of course. But the funny thing is, I kept seeing it, even after the bus had passed. At home I still saw it, that quick flash of dark blue . . ." He got lost in his remembering. But I wasn't about to interrupt. "It wouldn't go away, Dave. The next day when the bus passed, I stopped and got out and walked back. I stood around the lot for a long time, looking in at the car—I mean, I didn't even know what kind it was!—and I felt something happening. You used to say it happened to you: kind of hurting, the way you feel when you see a beautiful girl that you don't really want, but you do, too. With you it was paintings and plays and things like that. But, God this was the first time for me, and I couldn't understand what was wrong!"

"Go on."

"There isn't much more," he said. "I came back the next

day and asked the dealer what it was, and he told me, a Duesenberg. That night I decided to take another look; at the engine. He wouldn't let me see it, you know. The lot was closed. It was sitting alone, two big Mercedes-Benz jobs on either side. For the first time I examined it closely. I touched it, and saw how wonderful it was."

Now he was going. Talking more than I'd ever heard him do, he told me how he'd worked up the nerve to try the door. How he'd sweated over the decision: to get in or not to get in. How he had then gone to libraries and book stores and read everything he could get ahold of pertaining to the car.

"It was an astonishing thing," he said, "really and truly astonishing." His eyes were lit, and I think he was trembling; maybe not. "The facts—Dave, listen. This automobile, the one you're in now, how fast would you say it goes?"

"Hell," I said. "I don't know anything about cars."

"Take a guess. Go on."

"Seventy?"

"*Seventy?*" He chuckled. "Dave, this automobile will turn an honest one-thirty. One hundred and thirty miles per hour. But that's not it, of course," he said, hurriedly. "I mean, a lot of cars will go fast."

"Then what is it?"

"Everything," he said, helplessly. "The way it looks so goddamn regal and efficient and luxurious, and—the way it's put together. That Augie Duesenberg, you know, he didn't fool around. I mean, this car isn't one of your assembly-line jobs like they have nowadays. It just isn't, Dave. Like—well, you remember that house we looked at on Benedict Canyon, the big stone one that you said it looked like it had its feet planted in the ground right up to its knees? You remember that house?"

"Yeah."

"This is the same. The same exactly. It's a work of art, Dave; I'm telling you!" His voice got a little louder. "This guy Briggs Cunningham, he goes around saying he wants to be the first American car to win at Le Mans—he's nuts. An American car won Le Mans. The French G. P., anyway. Which American car? The Duesenberg. Yes, and, listen, the tolerances on the engine are still just as fine as any of your European makes. Hell, they didn't have anything else but Duesie powerplants at Indianapolis! Not for years! God, Dave, you know what they did? They had this one man, a mechanic. He was an artist. Responsible for the whole engine, just him. They'd finish the car, and take it out on the track, and run it at top speed for twenty-four hours or something. Then they'd take it back in and this mechanic, he'd take it apart and see if anything was worn. If it wasn't absolutely perfect, he'd start all over again. I mean, that's something that's gone, it's gone forever, I'm telling you. And—I suppose I sound like an advertisement!"

"A little."

"Well, never mind. It's all true." He opened the door. "Look here: three hinges. Or there, the running board. Get out for a minute."

He had me bang my fist on the fender. It was hard and solid. Then he started showing me other things: the taillights, the gigantic wheels with their special tires, the rumble seat. There wasn't anything for me to do but follow him around and wait it out.

"Shall we take a peek at the engine?"

We took a peek.

"Four hundred horses, Dave. A '29, remember."

He must have talked for hours, showing me every square inch of the car, giving me a complete history. I could see that it was for real, however fantastic it might seem. Old gray Hank had flipped his wig over an auto, and since people like Hank usually live out their whole lives without flipping their wigs over anything, he was taking it hard.

"I may be insane," he said, "but there's nothing to be done about it. I'm telling you, when I'm away from the car, I'm—in hell. I keep thinking of what might happen to it, just sitting here, unlocked at night. I keep dreading the day when somebody buys it. Some ape, some fat cigar-smoking ape without the sense to know what he's got . . . Here it is, the finest automobile ever built, the absolute best of them all. Sitting here." His fists were clenched tightly. "I want you to know this, if some idiot comes in here and buys it, I'll kill him. So help me God, that's what I'll do."

I let him calm down, then I said, "Hank, listen. If you're so nuts about the car, if it means all this to you, why don't you buy the damn thing and get it over with? Why all this creeping around at night, why such a big deal?"

He laughed, the coldest laugh I think I've ever heard. "That's a real brainstorm," he said. "Now why didn't I think of that? Just go ahead and buy it . . ."

"Well, you want it, don't you?"

"Of course I want it. Unfortunately, I don't have seven thousand, five hundred dollars, which is the price. I don't even have five hundred dollars."

We sat still for a while. The idea I'd been fighting off broke through finally, and when it did, I opened the door and got out of the car.

"You don't understand, do you?" he said.

I told him yes, I thought I did.

"Then you see why I haven't told Ruth. What could I tell her—that I'm in love with a car?"

"No, you couldn't do that."

"Besides," he said, "she's a woman."

I thought, yes, she is, she is that. A beautiful and desirable woman, and I'm in love with her. Not with a hunk of machinery . . .

I walked to the edge of the lot. Then, almost scared, I started back. I knew that if I thought much about it, I wouldn't do it. And it was the only real chance I'd seen.

"What's your plan?" I asked him.

"I don't have any," he said.

"Think it'll wear off?"

"Maybe. I don't know. I've never been through anything like this before. Do you think I ought to see a doctor?"

"No," I said. "You'd spend two hundred dollars just to learn that you've got a fixation on a car. I've got fixations, too. Who doesn't?" I took a deep breath. "Hank, how badly do you want this boat, anyway?"

He didn't answer.

"I'm serious. Tell me exactly what it would mean to you."

"To own it?"

"That's right."

His hands gripped the steering wheel. You could see that he wasn't really considering the question. It was too much for him.

"What I mean is, to know that it was completely yours. Hank Osterman's own car. To know that you could keep it in the garage, and work on it whenever you wanted to, and shine it up every morning." I gave the knife a twist. "Or drive it whenever you got the urge. Maybe early in the morning . . ." I remembered how Hank liked five o'clock. "You know, take it out and really wind it up. Wait for one of the new bombs, idle him along, and then let him see what you have."

"Stop it."

"Or tool it downtown and park it, just to let everybody have a look."

"Dave, goddamn it, shut up. I want that more than anything else in the world. I told you, didn't I?"

"More than *anything* else?"

"Yes!"

"That's all I wanted to know," I said.

I left him sitting in the car.

I had a rough time with the loan, but there are ways. People like Hank don't know that. If I'd asked for five hundred they'd have tossed me out on my ear; getting eight thousand was a different story.

Once I knew it was set up, I called Ruth and told her to be patient, everything was going to be all right. When she told me that nothing had changed, I let her know she was wrong. Things would be changing very soon.

It was pretty close to perfect.

I'd buy the car while Hank was at work. Then I'd drive it over and catch him as he broke for lunch. Let him take the wheel for a few blocks—to get the feel of it. Sink the hook good and deep.

Then make him the deal.

"It's yours, Hank, old scout. All yours. There's only one little thing I'd like in return—really not very much at all, considering. In exchange for the car—this one here, the one you said you'd give anything for—I'd like Ruth. Fair enough?"

Oh, yes. It would work, too: I knew that. It would work. Of course, he'd come to his senses eventually, but then it'd be too late. Ruth and I would be long ago and far away . . .

The money came from the bank last Monday, a week ago. I'd been giving Ruth a good stall and managed to keep her quiet, so I knew that conditions were ripe.

I was at Springfield's when they opened. The salesman, a short man with a mustache and an accent, just about fainted when he saw he had a live one. "The Duesenberg? Oh, yes, sir; a genuine classic, indeed. Tyrone Power had one quite a bit like it, you know, but not in anything like this condition. The engine's been completely overhauled, only five hundred miles on it, and those are all new tires. New paint—the original color, by the way . . ."

I offered him six grand, and he boggled it up. Then he told me how to work the gears, and I had to listen to a story about the Duesenberg Owner's Club, and what rare taste I had and all like that.

While he spieled, I glanced over at the car. The paint glistened, because of the sun; it was a rich, dark blue. I hadn't actually seen the thing before, and you had to admit it was a handsome job. Every part of it seemed to be made of cast iron. There was a lot of chrome, but somehow it managed to look good, for once, not gaudy and useless.

I thought of Hank, suddenly, of his sneaking around at night, peeping at the car, worrying over it, scared that someone might hurt it. He really must love the old heap. Maybe I'm not kidding myself after all, I thought, maybe I *am* doing him a favor!

Finally I was permitted to get in and start it up. It caught right away. The engine began to pulse, smoothly, but with a power you could feel. The salesman was smiling. "Be very careful," he said. "You've got a thoroughbred under you."

I waved at him, and put it in gear and touched the accelerator pedal.

The car lunged forward like a mad thing. Low in the seat—you're like a midget in that cab, it's so big—I pressed the brake, fast.

"See what I mean?" the salesman said.

I nodded, and took off more cautiously. I'd been driving for years, but now I was a beginner again, trying to keep the whole works from running away with me.

When I finally got it out on the highway, just for fun I fed it a little more gas. The engine took on a different pitch, there was a surge, and I saw by the speedometer that I was traveling almost seventy! It told you plainly that you had a long way to go before you strained *this* baby.

Poor old Hank, I thought: God, he's in love with it and he hasn't even driven it yet. Just wait'll he gets behind the wheel and sees what it will do.

Out toward the valley a couple of hot-rods got smart. Cut-down Fords, I think they were. They tooted and roared past, dribbling exhaust. I floored the Duesenberg, and, believe me, before I even started thinking about third those boys were out of sight behind me.

It was a hell of a feeling.

I'd planned, of course, to take the car over to Hank's office that afternoon. It was all rehearsed and ready to go.

But I was miles away, headed for open highway. The salesman had said something about suspension, and I wanted to try a few curves—nothing fancy or anything. And besides, that evening would do just as well. There wasn't any rush about it. Just a few curves and a straight run, to see how the old bus behaved.

That was a week ago. Since then I've taken the Duesie over the ridge route, along Highway One—you know what that is—and into Beverly Hills, for kicks. Parked it across from Romanoff's, where the boys in their new Detroit tubs could get a nice long look. And then over to the Derby—and wasn't that fine, though. I mean, I'd spent a couple of hours getting it all shined up, and I felt like a damn king there, a regular damn king.

Hank's probably going crazy—I went back and told the salesman not to give out any information—but then, he'll have it for a long time to come, won't he?

Meanwhile, I figure why not enjoy it a little. It really is a work of art. You're always discovering strange new things about it, hidden compartments, extra switches and levers and buttons. God knows what they're all for. It's for sure they're for something, though. That's the kind of car it is.

I'll probably turn it over to Hank some time next week, before he goes berserk, and then Ruth and I will take up where we left off.

But first I would like to see if the Duesie actually does an honest hundred and thirty mph.

I wouldn't be a bit surprised if it did.

I mean, it's a hell of a car.

Perchance to Dream

"Please sit down," the psychiatrist said, indicating a somewhat worn leather couch.

Automatically, Hall sat down. Instinctively, he leaned back. Dizziness flooded through him, his eyelids fell like sashweights, the blackness came. He jumped up quickly, and slapped his right cheek, then he slapped his left cheek, hard.

"I'm sorry, Doctor," he said.

The psychiatrist, who was tall and young, and not in the least Viennese, nodded. "You prefer to stand?" he asked gently.

"Prefer?" Hall threw his head back and laughed. "That's good," he said. "*Prefer!*"

"I'm afraid I don't quite understand."

"Neither do I, Doctor." He pinched the flesh of his left hand until it hurt. "No, no: that isn't true. I do understand. That's the whole trouble. I do."

"You—want to tell me about it?"

"Yes. No." It's silly, he thought. You can't help me. No one can. I'm alone! "Forget it," he said and started for the door.

The psychiatrist said, "Wait a minute." His voice was friendly, concerned; but not patronizing. "Running away won't do you much good, will it?"

Hall hesitated.

"Forgive the cliché. Actually, running away is often the best answer. But I don't know yet that yours is that sort of problem."

"Did Dr. Jackson tell you about me?"

"No. Jim said he was sending you over, but he thought you'd do a better job on the details. I only know that your name is Philip Hall, you're thirty-one, and you haven't been able to sleep for a long time."

"Yes. A long time . . ." To be exact, seventy-two hours, Hall thought, glancing at the clock. Seventy-two horrible hours . . .

The psychiatrist tapped out a cigarette. "Aren't you—" he began.

"Tired? God yes. I'm the tiredest man on earth! I could sleep forever. But that's just it, you see: I would. I'd never wake up."

"Please," the psychiatrist said.

Hall bit his lip. There wasn't, he supposed, much point to it. But, after all, what *else* was there for him to do? Where would he go? "You mind if I pace?"

"Stand on your head, if you like."

"Okay. I'll take one of your cigarettes." He drew the smoke into his lungs and walked over to the window. Fourteen floors below, the toy people and the toy cars moved. He watched them and thought, this guy's all right. Sharp. Intelligent. Nothing like what I expected. Who can say—*maybe* it'll do some good. "I'm not sure where to begin."

"It doesn't matter. The beginning might be easier for you."

Hall shook his head, violently. The beginning, he thought. Was there such a thing?

"Just take it easy."

After a lengthy pause, Hall said, "I first found out about the power of the human mind when I was ten. Close to that time, anyway. We had a tapestry in the bedroom. It was a great big thing, the size of a rug, with fringe on the edges. It showed a group of soldiers—Napoleonic soldiers—on horses. They were at the brink of some kind of cliff, and the first horse was reared up. My mother told me something. She told me that if I stared at the tapestry long enough, the horses would start to move. They'd go right over the cliff, she said. I tried it, but nothing happened. She said, 'You've got to *think* about it.' So every night, before I went to bed, I'd sit up and stare at that damn tapestry. And finally, it happened. Over they went, all the horses, all the men, over the edge of the cliff . . ." Hall stubbed out the cigarette and began to pace. "Scared hell out of me," he said. "When I looked again, they were all back. It got to be a game with me. Later on, I tried it with pictures in magazines, and pretty soon I was able to move locomotives and send balloons flying and make dogs open their mouths: everything, anything I wanted."

He paused, ran a hand through his hair. "Not too unusual,

you're thinking," he said. "Every kid does it. Like standing in a closet and shining a flashlight through your finger, or sewing up the heel of your palm . . . common stuff?"

The psychiatrist shrugged.

"There was a difference," Hall said. "One day it got out of control. I was looking at a coloring book. One of the pictures showed a knight and a dragon fighting. For fun I decided to make the knight drop his lance. He did. The dragon started after him, breathing fire. In another second the dragon's mouth was open and he was getting ready to eat the knight. I blinked and shook my head, like always, only—nothing happened. I mean, the picture didn't go back. Not even when I closed the book and opened it again. But I didn't think too much about it, even then."

He walked to the desk and took another cigarette. It slipped from his hands.

"You've been on Dexedrine," the psychiatrist said, watching as Hall tried to pick up the cigarette.

"Yes."

"How many grains a day?"

"Thirty, thirty-five, I don't know."

"Potent. Knocks out your co-ordination. I suppose Jim warned you?"

"Yes, he warned me."

"Well, let's get along. What happened then?"

"Nothing," Hall allowed the psychiatrist to light his cigarette. "For a while, I forgot about the 'game' almost completely. Then, when I turned thirteen, I got sick. Rheumatic heart—"

The psychiatrist leaned forward and frowned. "And Jim let you have thirty-five—"

"Don't interrupt!" He decided not to mention that he had gotten the drug from his aunt, that Dr. Jackson knew nothing about it. "I had to stay in bed a lot. No activity; might kill me. So I read books and listened to the radio. One night I heard a ghost story. 'Hermit's Cave' it was called. All about a man who gets drowned and comes back to haunt his wife. My parents were gone, at a movie. I was alone. And I kept thinking about that story, imagining the ghost. Maybe, I thought to myself, he's in that closet. I knew he wasn't; I knew there wasn't any such thing as a ghost, really. But there was a little part of my mind that kept saying, 'Look at the closet. Watch the door. He's in there, Philip, and he's going to come out.' I picked up a book and tried to read, but I couldn't help glancing at the closet door. It was open a crack. Everything dark behind it. Everything dark and quiet."

"And the door moved."

"That's right."

"You understand that there's nothing terribly unusual in anything you've said so far?"

"I know," Hall said. "It was my imagination. It *was*, and I realized it even then. But—I got just as scared. Just as scared as if a ghost actually *had* opened that door! And that's the whole point. The mind, Doctor: It's everything. If you *think* you have a pain in your arm and there's no physical reason for it, you don't hurt any less... My mother died because she thought she had a fatal disease. The autopsy showed malnutrition, nothing else. But she died just the same!"

"I won't dispute the point."

"All right. I just don't want you to tell me it's all in my mind. I *know* it is."

"Go on."

"They told me I'd never really get well. I'd have to take it easy the rest of my life. Because of the heart. No strenuous exercise, no stairs, no long walks. No shocks. Shock produces excessive adrenalin, they said. Bad. So that's the way it was. When I got out of school, I grabbed a soft desk job. Unexciting: numbers, adding numbers, that's all. Things went okay for a few years. Then it started again. I read about where some woman got into her car at night and happened to check for something in the back seat and found a man hidden there. Waiting. It stuck with me; I started dreaming about it. So every night, when I got into my car, I automatically patted the rear seat and floorboards. It satisfied me for a while, until I started thinking, 'What if I forget to check?' Or, 'What if there's something back there that isn't human?' I had to drive across Laurel Canyon to get home, and you know how twisty that stretch is. Thirty, fifty-foot drops, straight down. I'd get this feeling halfway across. 'There's someone... something... in the back of the car!' Hidden, in darkness. Fat and shiny. I'll look in the rearview mirror, and I'll see his hands ready to circle my throat... Again, Doctor: understand me. *I knew it was my imagination*. I had no doubt at all that the back seat was empty—hell, I kept the car locked and I double-checked! But, I told myself, you keep thinking this way, Hall, and you'll see those hands. It'll be a reflection, or somebody's headlights, or nothing at all—but you'll see them! Finally, one night, I did see them! The car lurched a couple of times and went down the embankment."

The psychiatrist said, "Wait a minute," rose, and switched the tape on a small machine.

"I knew how powerful the mind was, then," Hall continued. "I know that ghosts and demons did exist, they did, if you only thought about them long enough and hard enough. After all, one of them almost killed me!" He pressed the lighted end of the cigarette against his flesh; the fog lifted instantly. "Dr. Jackson told me afterwards that one more serious shock like that would finish me. And that's when I started having the dream."

There was a silence in the room, compounded of distant automobile horns, the ticking of the ship's-wheel clock, the insectival tapping of the receptionist's typewriter, Hall's own tortured breathing.

"They say dreams last only a couple of seconds," he said. "I don't know whether that's true or not. It doesn't matter. They *seem* to last longer. Sometimes I've dreamed a whole lifetime; sometimes generations have passed. Once in a while, time stops completely; it's a frozen moment, lasting forever. When I was a kid I saw the Flash Gordon serials; you remember? I loved them, and when the last episode was over, I went home and started dreaming more. Each night, another episode. They were vivid, too, and I remembered them when I woke up. I even wrote them down, to make sure I wouldn't forget. Crazy?"

"No," said the psychiatrist.

"I did, anyway. The same thing happened with the Oz books and the Burroughs books. I'd keep them going. But after the age of fifteen, or so, I didn't dream much. Only once in a while. Then, a week ago—" Hall stopped talking. He asked the location of the bathroom, and went there and splashed cold water on his face. Then he returned, and stood by the window.

"A week ago?" the psychiatrist said, flipping the tape machine back on.

"I went to bed around eleven thirty. I wasn't too tired, but I needed the rest, on account of my heart. Right away the dream started. I was walking along Venice Pier. It was close to midnight. The place was crowded, people everywhere; you know the kind they used to get there. Sailors, dumpy looking dames, kids in leather jackets. The pitchmen were going through their routines. You could hear the roller coasters thundering along the tracks, the people inside the roller coasters, screaming; you could hear the bells and the guns cracking and the crazy songs they play on calliopes. And, far away, the ocean, moving. Everything was bright and gaudy and cheap. I walked for a while, stepping on gum and candy apples, wondering why I was there." Hall's eyes closed. He opened them quickly and rubbed them. "Halfway to the end, passing the penny arcade, I saw a girl. She was about twenty-two or -three. White dress, very thin and tight, and a funny white hat. Her legs were bare, nicely muscled and tan. She was alone. I stopped and watched her, and I remember thinking, 'She *must* have a boy friend. He *must* be here somewhere.' But she didn't seem to be waiting for anyone, or looking. Unconsciously, I began to follow her. At a distance.

"She walked past a couple of concessions, then she stopped at one called 'The Whip', and strolled in and went for a ride. The air was hot. It caught her dress as she went around and sent it whirling. It didn't bother her at all. She just held onto the bar and closed her eyes, and—I don't know, a kind of ecstasy seemed to come over her. She began to laugh. A high-pitched, musical sound. I stood by the fence and watched her, wondering why such a beautiful girl would be laughing in a cheap carnival ride, in the middle of the night, all by herself. Then my hands froze on the fence, because suddenly I saw that she was looking at me. Every time the car would whip around, she'd be looking. And there was something in her eyes, something that said, Don't go away, don't leave, don't move . . .

"The ride stopped, and she got out and walked over to me. As naturally as if we'd known each other for years, she put her arm in mine, and said, 'We've been expecting you, Mr. Hall.' Her voice was deep and soft, and her face, close up, was even more beautiful than it had seemed. Full, rich lips, a little wet; dark, flashing eyes; a warm gleam to her flesh. I didn't answer. She laughed again and tugged at my sleeve. 'Come on, darling,' she said. 'We haven't much time.' And we walked, almost running, to The Silver Flash—a roller coaster, the highest on the pier. I knew I shouldn't go on it because of my heart condition, but she wouldn't listen. She said I had to, for her. So we bought our tickets and got into the first seat of the car . . ."

Hall held his breath for a moment, then let it out, slowly.

As he relived the episode, he found that it was easier to stay awake. Much easier.

"That," he said, "was the end of the first dream. I woke up sweating and trembling, and thought about it most of the day, wondering where it had all come from. I'd only been to Venice Pier once in my life, with my mother. Years ago. But that night, just as it'd happened with the serials, the dream picked up exactly where it had left off. We were settling into the seat. Rough leather, cracked and peeling, I recall. The grab bar iron, painted black, the paint rubbed away in the center.

"I tried to get out, thinking, Now's the time to do it; do it now or you'll be too late! But the girl held me, and whispered to me. We'd be together, she said. Close together. If I'd do this one thing for her, she'd belong to me. 'Please! Please!' Then the car started. A little jerk; the kids beginning to yell and scream; the *cluck-clack* of the chain pulling up; and up, slowly, too late now, too late for anything, up the steep wooden hill . . .

"A third of the way to the top, with her holding me, pressing herself against me, I woke up again. Next night, we went up a little farther. Next night, a little farther. Foot by foot, slowly, up the hill. At the halfway point, the girl began kissing me. And laughing. 'Look down!' she told me. 'Look down, Philip!' And I did, and saw little people and little cars and everything tiny and unreal.

"Finally we were within a few feet of the crest. The night was black, and the wind was fast and cold now, and I was scared, so scared that I couldn't move. The girl laughed louder than ever, and a strange expression came into her eyes. I remembered then how no one else had noticed her. How the ticket-taker had taken the two stubs and looked around questioningly.

" 'Who are you?' I screamed. And she said, 'Don't you know?' And she stood up and pulled the grab-bar out of my hands. I leaned forward to get it.

"Then we reached the top. And I saw her face and I knew what she was going to do, instantly: I knew. I tried to get back into the seat, but I felt her hands on me then and I heard her voice, laughing, high, laughing and shrieking with delight, and—"

Hall smashed his fist against the wall, stopped and waited for calm to return.

When it did, he said, "That's the whole thing, Doctor. Now you know why I don't dare to go to sleep. When I do—and I'll have to, eventually; I realize that!—the dream will go on. And my heart won't take it!"

The psychiatrist pressed a button on his desk.

"Whoever she is," Hall went on, "she'll push me. And I'll fall. Hundreds of feet. I'll see the cement rushing up in a blur to meet me and I'll feel the first horrible pain of contact—"

There was a click.

The office door opened.

A girl walked in.

"Miss Thomas," the psychiatrist began, "I'd like you to—"

Philip Hall screamed. He stared at the girl in the white nurse's uniform and took a step backward. "Oh, Christ! No!"

"Mr. Hall, this is my receptionist, Miss Thomas."

"No," Hall cried. "It's her. It is. And I know who she is now, God save me! I know who she is!"

The girl in the white uniform took a tentative step into the room.

Hall screamed again, threw his hands over his face, turned and tried to run.

A voice called, "Stop him!"

Hall felt the sharp pain of the sill against his knee, realized in one hideous moment what was happening. Blindly he reached out, grasping. But it was too late. As if drawn by a giant force, he tumbled through the open window, out into the cold clear air.

"Hall!"

All the way down, all the long and endless way down past the thirteen floors to the gray, unyielding, hard concrete, his mind worked; and his eyes never closed...

"I'm afraid he's dead," the psychiatrist said, removing his fingers from Hall's wrist.

The girl in the white uniform made a little gasping sound. "But," she said, "only a minute ago, I saw him and he was—"

"I know. It's funny; when he came in, I told him to sit down. He did. And in less than two seconds he was asleep. Then he gave that yell you heard and..."

"Heart attack?"

"Yes." The psychiatrist rubbed his cheek thoughtfully. "Well," he said, "I guess there are worse ways to go. At least he died peacefully."

The Customers

The room was quiet, and the old woman sat in the room looking out the window, out into the steel-gray afternoon. At the cheddar-sharp little fingers of wind playing with icy bits of weeds and leaves; at the sickly rays of sunlight tumbling to the ashen earth; at the soft, clean fragrance of moist grass and moldering pine needles; the gray wind, the gray sunlight.

She fretted the neck of the brown tomcat asleep in her lap, and watched. Then she leaned forward, squinted and rubbed away some window-frost with her hand.

"Henry," the old woman said.

The old man's hand fell from the arm of his chair. He made a small noise.

"Henry."

His head bobbled. His lips moved.

"Wake up."

The old man's eyes opened. "All right," he said. "Just give me a second."

"Second nothing. Wake up now."

"Well, what is it? What is it?"

The old woman's voice sounded filled with fear. "It's Him," she said. "He's coming."

The old man sat up, and yawned, and wiped the sleep from his face. He smiled. "Didn't I tell you to quit staring out that blamed window? Didn't I say that you'd go imagining things?"

"Henry Ludlow, nobody's imagining nothing. Get up from there and come look."

Mr. Ludlow braced his fingers on the chair. He walked to the window, patted his wife upon her wrists and parted the curtains. He squinted.

"Hmm!" Mr. Ludlow said.

"Mr. Know-it-all. You see or don't you see?"

"I see," the old man said, dropping the curtains again. "But we can't be sure, Myrtle. Not actually."

Mrs. Ludlow turned her head. "Just look at Him," she said. "*You* ever see such an elegant person around these parts? Black suit, briefcase, even a little bitty old mustache. Now who in thunder else could it be?"

Mr. Ludlow laid a finger alongside his nose and shook his head. "I ain't saying it don't look like Him."

"Of *course* it's Him." Mrs. Ludlow removed a lace handkerchief from her sleeve.

"You said that about them others too, remember. That last feller, what was he? A census taker, that's what. I'm only saying you don't want to go jumping to conclusions."

"Jump, jump—*tsk*! Aunt Lucia said we'd get fooled the first few times, didn't she? Said He'd be everywhere inside and out, a feeling of Him in the air. We never was right certain *sure* the last times—just sort of hoped or feared, like. Besides, the sun was shining them times. And my bones didn't ache, neither."

Mr. Ludlow caressed a small amulet shaped like an elk's tooth. "Myrtle, your bones—they feeling pretty shipshape now?"

"Ache like the dickens. Feel just right, they do: conditions is right everywhere. Watch at how He walks—mincey-like, like He don't even touch the ground."

Mr. Ludlow sighed. "Well," he said. "Well—guess maybe you're right this time, my dear. Come to think about it, I got the feeling myself."

The old woman clutched suddenly at her husband's arm. She searched his face. "You don't suppose—I mean, He wouldn't want just one of us, would He? It wouldn't happen like that."

"Shh. Still now. You want Him to see you all broke up and whiny?" Mr. Ludlow paused. "Either way, it wouldn't be for long."

The brown tomcat put its head to one side, and stood with arched back, listening. Steps on the outside porch sounded briskly, then stopped.

Mrs. Ludlow held to her husband's hand.

"Henry—Oh, tarnation! Go and answer the blame door. Said I wouldn't act like this, and I ain't. Go on now."

Mr. Ludlow brushed the tops of his shoes along the backs of his legs and walked out into the hall. He looked at the old woman sitting in the chair by the window, paused a moment, and then unlatched the door.

A man in black stood smiling. "How do you do, sir. Do I have the pleasure of addressing Mr. Henry L. Ludlow?"

Mr. Ludlow wet his lips and looked at the man, at the man's tailored suit, gray homburg hat, briefcase, small waxed mustache. "Yes, sir, you do."

"*Excellent.* Now, my name is—"

"Come on in."

The man stepped lightly into the hall and took the homburg hat carefully from his head so that no single hair was disturbed.

"Thank you. Thank you very much. My goodness, sir, such a charming house! And so secluded—I tell you, I had the devil's own time finding it. Yes indeedy." The man examined a wooden hat rack briefly before depositing his homburg thereupon. "Exquisite," he said.

Mr. Ludlow looked curious. "Had trouble finding us, you say?"

"Well, a slight exaggeration. Although, well, I *did* get a little bit lost once or twice."

"*You* got lost?"

"I certainly did. In fact, I called on two other homes by mistake."

"Say, I'll have to tell Myrtle that one! The wrong house—twice!"

The man looked sheepish. "But now then," he said, "I imagine you're wondering who I am and why I'm here."

"Well, wouldn't exactly say that, no."

"No?" The man furled his brows. "Oh, the print on the briefcase, eh? Ha ha, now that's very perspicacious of you, sir. I mean, for a man of your age—what I mean is—"

"Never mind, son. That's all right."

"Most folks getting along in years," the man said, "why, they never give us a second thought. You might not believe it, but they wait right up to the last minute, wait until it's too late."

"You don't mean to tell me!"

The man looked sad. "Yes. You'd be amazed. No perception, no acceptance of reality. Why, if we'd known you were thinking of us, we would never have troubled you in this way. Most people, you see, somehow don't take to the idea. Can you countenance it, sir: eighty-seven per cent of people above age seventy must be sought out by us!"

"Huh!"

"Oh yes. Those that do call are pretty generally goaded into it by others. Therefore, if I may, I'd like to congratulate you, Mr. Ludlow, on your down-to-earth common-sense attitude."

Mr. Ludlow scratched his head.

The man in black went through some papers. "Now let's see," he said. "According to our records, we understand you have a wife—Myrtle Louisa Ludlow. May I ask if she is present?"

"Will you be wanting her, too?"

"By all means, sir. By all means! This is something for all of us to talk over. I—that is, I take it you have something definite in mind?"

"Something definite . . ."

"What I mean to say is, I gather from what you've said that you've been considering us?"

"Oh. Yes—we've had you in mind, all right. For quite a spell. Ever since Myrtle—that's my wife—well, since she had that heart attack about four, five months back. We've been sort of sitting around waiting, you might say."

"Good! I can't tell you how pleased that makes me. For your sake as well as my own. You simply would not believe it: I usually have to plead with people, beg them."

"That a fact?"

"Yes indeedy. They're that stubborn."

"Well," Mr. Ludlow said, "I guess you ain't been turned down by nobody."

The man in black brightened and smoothed his mustache. "No sir, I am glad to say that that has not happened yet. I take a certain pride in the fact."

"I imagine you do."

"Oh yes, they all come around in time. But I've always said, why drag it out—when all the details can be taken care of in an afternoon?"

Mr. Ludlow hooked his thumbs in his vest and began to walk toward the big living-room doors. "The wife's in here," he said. "She's probably wondering what we've been up to."

They went in.

Mrs. Ludlow looked up and sighed deeply. "Henry, you

gave me a scare. I couldn't even move, I was so scared."

"Just a little preliminary talk, Myrtle. My dear, this here is—"

"I know who it is. How do, young man?"

Mrs. Ludlow stared at the man and a faint pink flushed her thin cheeks. She turned her eyes to her husband and whispered, "Henry—something happened while you was in the hall talking. No mistake about it now. I—had it."

Mr. Ludlow answered in a loud voice full of admiration. "The vision? You had the vision, like Aunt Lucia said?"

"Clear as creekwater. There she was, tapping her foot, smiling away. 'That's Him,' she says, 'that's Him.'"

The young man bowed uncertainly and sat down. "Very happy to meet you, Mrs. Ludlow," he said.

"Expect you are."

The man in black opened his mouth and then closed it. He put the briefcase on his lap. "Now then, folks, shall we get down to business?"

Mrs. Ludlow put a hand to her throat and the sternness went from her face. "So soon?" She looked about the room, at the pictures, at the walls, at the big brown tomcat. She looked at her husband.

"Oh, all right. Go ahead then."

"Thank you. My!" The man's face lost its look of annoyed confusion. "You can't even guess what a pleasure it is to deal with you folks. My job isn't as easy as some might think."

"No," Mr. Ludlow said. "Can't say I'd want to swap with you."

"Not easy work," the man went on. "But it does have its reward. I like to think that I—one should say, 'we'—are giving a lot of people a lot of happiness. Even if some of them won't admit it at the time."

"You look terrible young," Mrs. Ludlow said. "You been at this here kind of work long?"

"Not actually—at least, not in this particular section. I've only been in Martinburg for, oh, two years. Before that I was with the army."

Mrs. Ludlow gasped. "Then it was *you*—all them poor boys—you hear that, Henry?"

"No," Mr. Ludlow said, "can't say I'd swap places with you."

The young man was working his fingers through papers,

swiftly, meticulously. "As I was saying to your husband, Mrs. L., if you folks had anything special in mind—?"

"Well sir, to tell the truth, we ain't give the matter much thought. Didn't rightly know we had anything to say about it."

"Why, but you have everything to say about it!"

"We do?"

"Certainly! Indeedy yes, you do!"

Frost was forming heavily on the windows; the room was going dark.

"Now Henry," Mrs. Ludlow said, "that's right thoughtful of them, ain't it."

Mr. Ludlow didn't seem to hear. "I think," he said, "we ought to get one thing die-straight right off the bat here. Is this for certain for both of us, my wife and I?"

"Mr. Ludlow, there are innumerable fine things about Murmuring Everglades, but the finest, possibly, is this policy. *Definitely* for both of you."

Mr. Ludlow walked to his wife and stroked her head. He waited a long moment, then he said, "This Murmuring Everglades, that there's a good spot you say?"

The young man looked momentarily confused. "A good spot? Why, it is, if I may say so, the very best. Did you happen to have any other cemetery—no, but of course you didn't."

Mrs. Ludlow shook her head. The brown tomcat leapt into her lap, purring, stretching.

"Very well. Now then, as I say, to business. Did you folks prefer a vault, the regular mausoleum, or something a bit less expensive?"

Mr. Ludlow bit off the end of a cigar. "You handle all that, too?" he said.

"Oh, yes indeedy."

"Well, I'll be darned. What do you think of that, Myrtle? Well—for myself, I can't say I much relish the idea of six foot of dirt on top of me."

Mrs. Ludlow shuddered and looked out the window.

"But then again, I don't reckon it'd make much difference one way or the other. What say, my dear?"

"You take care of it, Henry. Ain't my place to."

The man in black produced a sheet of paper and held it before his eyes. "If you think the vault is too expensive," he said, "let me say, *there* is where you're off on the wrong track. Yes indeed. For a fine vault on selected property, the cost to you is negligible—in comparison with the rates of other similar establishments. For example—Mr. Ludlow, you see on this table I have—for a twelve-by-eighteen, completely air-tight, guaranteed Italian marble and imported granite vault—or Rest Haven—you pay only one thousand dollars down and—how old did you say you were, sir?"

"Eighty-four."

"And the Missus?"

"Same."

"Serious illnesses—tuberculosis, et cetera?"

"Well, not exactly. Just those heart attacks of Myrtle's."

"Oh yes, of course—*those.*" The young man scribbled on a piece of paper, consulted columns of figures. "Well," he said at last, "that would come to twelve hundred down with the balance insured. Can you beat that?"

"I don't quite understand," Mr. Ludlow said.

"Well, sir, it only means that Murmuring Everglades bets that you will live the two years necessary to pay up the balance."

"And you let them do that?"

"I beg your pardon?" the young man said. "You see, Murmuring Everglades sets up this guarantee so that if anything *should* happen to you, the vault will still be yours. No risk that way, on your part. I think you'll find it all quite in order."

"Sounds all right to me," Mrs. Ludlow said. "Henry?"

The old man nodded.

"The vault, then?" the man in black said.

"Yes, the vault."

"Good. A splendid choice. So many people—well, you know, they simply don't care *how* they're put to their peace. The intelligent ones—like yourselves—always, I have found, *always* make adequate provisions. Now, there's a Rest Haven on one half of an acre, overlooking the town. I've a picture—there, you see?"

Mr. and Mrs. Ludlow gazed thoughtfully at the brightly tinted photograph. Centered at the crest of a knoll was a large whitewash-white crypt, clean-lined, solemn despite the colors around it.

"As you might guess," the man was saying, "that construction is A-1. Completely impregnable to atom bombs, excepting direct hits. The statue, by the way, is a perfect reproduction of Rodin's 'The Kiss.' "

Mr. Ludlow showed the photograph again to his wife.

"Well," she said, "it's right pretty, but I *have* seen prettier places in my time. We'll take it—you can tell them so."

The man in black beamed. He extracted two other forms and wrote things upon these. "Yes indeedy," he smiled, "a real pleasure to do business with you folks. Don't often run up against such co-operation."

Mr. Ludlow touched his wife's shoulder. "It's nice of you to say, my boy."

"Tah!" The young man busied himself. "Most of the others feel it's sort of looking on the dark side of things, and, well, that makes me feel bad. It's a reality everyone has to face; but they don't seem to understand."

Mrs. Ludlow pulled her chair around quickly and stared into the frost. The voices and the talk and the papers faded into gray silence; time began to gather up like a hurricane, time and memory and presence. The old woman stroked the back of the brown tomcat and held the delicate lace handkerchief to her eyes. Minutes went by unheard.

Mrs. Ludlow started at the gentle pressure. She looked up and smiled, took the pen in her thin fingers, and signed her name on five black lines.

Then the young man in black took all the papers and returned them to his briefcase. He rose, smiled. "May I congratulate you both? A great burden has been lifted from your minds; and in these twilight moments of your life, you can know that the best possible thing has been done, the best possible resting place chosen for your final peace. No trouble, no more bother—all arrangements waiting for you."

Mrs. Ludlow put her hands about the arms of her chair. "How—how long will it be?" she said.

"How long? Before—" The young man straightened his suit. "Well, Murmuring Everglades will have all preparations completed by next week, I should say."

"Just—a week?"

"We try to be prompt."

Mrs. Ludlow held to the chair. "Only a week . . ."

"Yes indeedy, folks. But that old vault might stand empty for ten more years!"

Mr. Ludlow unhanded his elk's tooth. "What was that?"

"Um? Oh, merely that you might not see the inside of your

property—unless on routine inspection, of course—for ten years or longer. It's entirely possible. Just because we look at reality doesn't mean we ought to be pessimists, no indeedy. You may both have many wonderful years ahead of you. And that's the beauty of it! You can spend them now without worries and heartaches about the Afterwards."

Mr. Ludlow stared at the young man. "I don't understand."

"Who does?" the young man said. "Who does? Just for an example: I called on a gentleman of ninety-two a year and a half ago. He purchased his property—a modest but very pleasant plot very near the Kirche by the Heide—and I haven't seen him since. Understand he's in excellent health, all things considered—a little weak, but the doctors aren't particularly concerned."

"Is that so?" Mr. Ludlow's mouth was open. "You really—you really mean all that?"

The man in black walked toward the hall. "I do indeed, I do."

"And you came here—only to make these arrangements for later on?"

"That's right."

"And—" Mr. Ludlow was gasping. "And we can stay here, right here, stay on for ten more years? We won't have to sit waiting for you and looking for you, scared all the time, scared you'll come?"

"Not unless some question arises about your property. But I don't think that's very likely, heh? You both look in fine shape to me, and, well, I see no reason whatever to believe an estimate of ten years is anything but skimpy." The man grinned. "After all, you know," he said, "Murmuring Everglades is betting on it."

Mrs. Ludlow picked up the tomcat and held it to her breast. Her body trembled slightly.

The young man stood silently, looking at the two old people. "And, of course, if anything should come up, if you should ever need me for anything, don't hesitate to call. Yes indeedy."

Mr. Ludlow took his hand gently from his wife's cheek. His face glistened. He switched off the light. "I don't think we'll be needing you for anything, young feller."

"Fine." The young man walked into the hall. "Don't bother," he called. "I can find my way."

The house waited for the crisp sharp steps to disappear, and then it was silent.

Mr. Ludlow went to the door and watched the figure walk down the little path, on past the twin gates; watched the figure turn and wave, standing tall against the sulphurous sky; then he closed the door, leaned against it for a moment, and returned to the living room.

"Henry, now what's happened to the air? Ain't it warm, all of a sudden? Warm like honey!"

Mr. Ludlow took off his jacket and tie-pin and replaced them in the closet. He sat down in his chair and scooted it nearer his wife.

"And look at the window," Mrs. Ludlow said. "The frost is going away. It's melting."

Mr. Ludlow leaned back in the chair.

"Henry, look! The moon's come out!"

"That so?"

"It's big, and yellow; it's lighting up the whole yard. You can see every tree!"

The old man smiled and put his head on his chest.

In moments he was asleep, and his wife was asleep, and there was only the sound of the brown cat, purring.

Hair of the Dog

"Arterio—what was that you said?"

"—sclerosis."

"Bunky?"

"Yes."

"*Our* Bunky?"

"Yes."

"God!"

"*Sic transit gloria mundi*. A rare case. Poor chap—went out like a light. Just like a light."

"But I mean—Bunky, of all people! Up in his studies, young, well off, good looking, everything to live for!"

"*Ave atque vale*, old boy."

"I can't believe it."

"Here today, gone tomorrow."

"God!"

Up until now, Lorenzo Gissing had thought about death, when he thought about it at all, which was practically never, as one of those things one didn't think about. The frequency of its occurrence among the lower classes especially made it impossible. None of his relatives had ever died, to his knowledge. Nor had any of his good chums. In fact, he had never once looked upon a human corpse. The entire subject, therefore, was dismissed as pointless, morbid, and not a little scatological, no more to be worried over than the other diseases that came as direct sequels to unclean living habits.

So the news of Bunky Frith's rather pell-mell departure from this world affected Lorenzo as few things had. His reaction was one of total disbelief, followed by an angry sense of betrayal. He took to his rooms. He refused to eat. He slept little, and then fitfully, leaping to the floor from time to time and cursing, knocking the blue china about and gazing at his image in the mirror.

"God!" he exclaimed every so often.

The funeral was the usual sort of thing, though perhaps a shade more elaborate than most. Lorenzo sat dazed throughout. The flowers made him ill at the stomach. The music was unbearable. And Rev. Bottomly's oration struck a new low. Presently, however, services ended and it was time to line up for a last look at old Bunky.

"Dear old pal!" cried Lorenzo, when his turn had come to stand before the dead man. *"What has happened here?"*

They had to carry him away. His eyes had rolled up in his head, his skin had paled and, all things considered, he looked not quite as good as the late Frith.

His studies immediately took a dip; such had been his scholastic standing at the university that this was fatal. He left the ivied walls and took up residence in the city. He became a changed person. From a happy-go-lucky Pierrot to a fog-bound Raskolnikov. Overnight. He lost touch with his parents, with his friends, and even with his tailor. He thought of only one thing: Death. His money went for any literature connected with the subject, and when he was not thinking about it he was reading about it. The books were without exception humorless and dispiriting, though the medical publications were the worst of all. They had pictures. In color.

He bought every manner of medicine imaginable. He was inoculated against, or given reason to believe he would not contract, diphtheria, smallpox, chicken pox, elephantiasis, polio, jungle rot, cirrhosis of the liver, Bright's disease, hoof and mouth disease, and the common cold. He avoided drafts and stuffy rooms. He checked daily with four doctors to make sure he did not have cancer, heart trouble, or perforated ulcers.

Then he read a book on the statistics of death. It floored him. He gave up all thought of travel, almost of movement of any kind. It nearly drove him insane. With disease one could fight back, take precautions, guard oneself—but what chance did one have against accidents? If you went into the streets a safe might fall on your head, if you stayed at home a thief might murder you and then set the house afire.

Lorenzo was thinking these things one night when he found that he had wandered far from home. The gurgle of the

Thames could be heard beyond a fogbank. It was late. He remembered poor old Bunky and how frightful he had looked—like dried paste there in the coffin, and dead, dead, dead. He ran a pale hand through his thick, bushy hair.

Why not? Do it yourself and at least you won't have to go on waiting for it. There were worse things than drowning. Arteriosclerosis, for one.

He took a step. A finger tapped his shoulder. He let loose a strangulated cry.

"Mr. Gissing?" The man was dressed in execrable taste: jaunty bowler, plus fours, a dun jacket of reprehensible fit. "Mr. Lorenzo Gissing?"

"Yes. Who are you? What are you going about prodding people for? I might have had a heart attack!"

"I'm sorry—I didn't mean to startle you. But you were about to jump into the river."

Mr. Gissing said "Coo" or something that sounded like coo.

"I represent a firm," the man said, "whose services you may find attractive. Shall we talk?"

Lorenzo nodded dumbly. His armpits discharged cold pellets of perspiration as he became aware of what he had been about to do.

"Very well," the man said. "Now then. Does the thought of death keep you up nights, plague you, torture you, prevent you from full enjoyment of life's rich bounty? Does it?"

"In a manner of speaking."

"And do you wish to be rid of this nagging worry?"

"Good heavens, yes! But how?"

"I'll tell you how, sir. I represent the Eternal Life Insurance Company and—"

"What was that?"

"—and we are in a position to help you. Our plan is roughly this: We offer Eternal Life to our clients. Now, we've been established since—"

"Oh dear, is this some sort of quiz program? Because, if it is—"

"Of course, we'll have to sit down and discuss this in more detail. Get your signature on some contracts and the like. But a run-down of our services may be stated in this way: For a very nominal fee—very nominal indeed, sir—to be paid to us monthly, we give you immortality."

"You're not the de—"

"Oh no. I merely work for the company. Mr. Asmodeus,

our president, has given up canvassing. It's a very old firm."

"Well..."

"Think of it, Mr. Gissing! No more worry about death! But life—happy, content, healthy, eternal, free to do what you choose without thought to consequences."

"Hmm."

"And all for a very low monthly payment."

"What sort of payment?"

"There will be, of course, the usual waiting period. Then— by the way, which do you prefer, the first or the fifteenth?"

"Oh, I don't know—the first, I guess."

"Then on the first of the month and every subsequent month, you will just slip your payment in the mails to us, and, why Mr. Gissing, you'll just go on living, that's all!"

"What *sort* of payment?"

"One hair. Plucked from your head on exactly the day the payment comes due—never before."

"Did you say one hair?" Lorenzo started calculating and remembering his wild heavy brown bush.

"One hair. No more, no less." The man dug in his briefcase for some papers. "Each shall represent a month of life to you."

Lorenzo gulped. "Well now," he said, "that's not exactly eternity."

"Rather close though," the man smiled, "wouldn't you say?"

"Yes," Lorenzo agreed, remembering approximately how many hundreds of thousands of hairs one is supposed to have on one's dome.

"Are you interested?"

"I'm interested. But tell me this—what happens when they're all gone?"

"Then you die."

"Oh."

"It's the best we can do. You won't get a better offer."

"Well, I mean, is that all? I just—die? Where's *your* profit?"

"Ah, Mr. Gissing, I wouldn't have suspected such business acumen in one so young. But you're quite right. There is one other little matter."

"I supposed as much. My soul, eh?"

"You won't miss it. They're sort of like an appendix, nowadays."

"Well..."

"Shall we talk business? I do have other calls to make."

"All right."

The man spoke for almost an hour. Then he gave Lorenzo the contract to read. It seemed in order. Lorenzo signed all copies in a peculiar reddish ink provided by the man. Then he was given a brochure, a number of self-addressed envelopes, a carbon of the contract, and a payment book.

"It will be renewed every hundred years or so," the man said, beginning to put things away. "Well!" he said. "That seems to take care of about everything. We're all fixed up now. I think you'll be quite happy with the arrangement—our firm does quite a volume business. You'd be amazed. Good evening, Mr. Gissing. Remember now, the first payment falls due on the first, which is forty-five days from now."

"Good evening," Lorenzo said. But the man was already gone.

"Lorenzo, you're looking peculiar."

"Peculiar, Mama?"

"So healthy! That *savoir vivre*, that smile, that twinkle in the eye! Is this my boy?"

"It is, Mama. In the flesh. Quick now, what has happened? Father ill?"

"No—worse luck. Dead."

"What? Dad? Dad dead?"

"Quite."

"Oh."

"Last week. Fell off his horse whilst hunting a fox. Cracked his skull, poor thing."

"Well, that's the way it goes. *Sic transit gloria mundi.*"

"You're taking it remarkably well, Lorenzo."

"Here today, gone tomorrow, Mama, I always say. Part of the game, what? Well, at least we shan't have to suffer. I imagine poor old Dad's estate is tidied up. That is—"

"Oh Lorenzo!"

"Yes, Mama?"

"Your father, bless his departed soul, has kept something from us."

"And what might that be, Mama?"

"He—I mean to say, your father—well, he—"

"Yes? Yes? Yes?"

"Stony."

"Oh no!"

"Yes. Not a sou. How he ever managed to keep us in such luxury, why, it must have taken everything! Such a good man, not to worry us."

"Yes, quite so, quite so. Mama, when you say 'not a sou' I assume you're indulging in a slight overstatement of the situation. That is to say, surely—"

"Nothing. Except debts. Whatever shall we do? There's scarcely enough for the funeral expenses."

"Good heavens!"

"What is it, Lorenzo?"

"I've just remembered something. An appointment in the city—business; you know. I must leave at once!"

"But my son, you've just arrived!"

"I know. Well, chin up! I'm off!"

Back in the city, Lorenzo Gissing thrashed a good bit at this blow. How ludicrous, after all. Here one is offered eternal life, or very nearly that, and the next thing one knows, one has no money with which to enjoy it. He took to brooding, and might have continued to do so indefinitely, had not a happy thought occurred. He smiled. He visited his tailor.

"My dearest!" he said not long afterwards to the Lady Moseby, formerly of Tunbridge Wells now of London, rich, widowed and lonely. "My very dearest only one!"

Anastasia Moseby had heretofore been spared the attentions of bachelors both eligible and ineligible owing to the genuineness of her despair at the death by his own hand of her husband, Sir Malcolm Peterhenshaw Moseby, Bart. This despair was transmitted by the pallor in her face and the quietness of her speech, which qualities actually made her more attractive and generally desirable. She was known as a woman who had loved and would not love again.

Lorenzo Gissing demonstrated the fallacy of this notion by walking down the old aisle with the now beamingly radiant lady, to the incipient dismay of certain other parties in attendance.

She was a woman transformed.

"Lorenzo, duck," she enthused later, at the proper time and place. "I do love you."

"And I love you," Lorenzo responded.

"I love you more than anyone or anything else on Earth!"

"And I love you more than anyone or anything else in the entire galaxy."

"We shall be so very happy."

"Fantastically, deliriously, I'm sure."

"And will you love me all your life?"

"I resent the question's implication."

"Sweet, we are such a pair, we two. I know and understand you so well, Lorenzo. The others—"

"Yes, what about the others?"

"They are saying—no, I cannot even repeat it!"

"What, what? Is this to be a marriage of secrecy and deception?"

"They're saying, Lorenzo my dearest plum, that you married me only for my money."

"The swine! Who said it? Who? I'll beat him to within an inch—"

"Hush, my duck! You and I know differently, don't we."

"Indeed me do. By the bye, what *does* the bally old bank book come to?"

"Oh, I don't know. A few hundred thousand, I should imagine. What does it matter?"

"Matter? Not at all. Only, well, you see—I've had some baddish luck."

"Not really."

"Yes. Wiped out. Utterly."

"I see."

"Yes. Well, never mind; I've my application in at the terminal for a clerk's position. It won't be much, but by the almighty, we'll make it, and without your having to dip—"

"Lorenzo! Kiss me!"

"There!"

"You'll never have to worry about money, so long as you kiss me like that and are faithful to me. This one must go right."

"I beg pardon?"

"Nothing. Only that just before Sir Malcolm's tragic death, the details of which you must have read, I—well, I discovered he had been faithless to me."

"The fool. Darling, oh my darling!"

It did not consume a great deal of time for Lorenzo to arrange for the account to be put in both their names. As soon as this was accomplished, and he had withdrawn the greater portion of it, there was a marked change in the relationship. Anastasia's fey charm was all well and good for a while, downright pleasant once or twice, but as Lorenzo put it to her one evening, there were other fish to fry.

The day before he left for Cannes, he received an unstamped letter in the mails, which read:

A FRIENDLY REMINDER!

Your first payment falls
due in exactly two (2)
days.

Thank you.

> Asmodeus, Pres.
> ETERNAL LIFE INS. CO.
> Gehenna

It made him feel good somehow, in a creepy kind of way, and he left whistling. He did not kiss his wife goodbye.

Having plucked one hair from his head, placed it into an envelope and included a covering letter, Mr. Gissing set forth to enjoy himself. He learned rapidly the extent to which this was going to be possible.

Having made certain improper overtures to a bronzed and altogether statuesque beauty sunning herself in the Riviera warmth, he was annoyed at the approach of said beauty's husband: tall, angry, and, Lorenzo felt sure, a circus giant. There followed an embarrassing scene. The husband actually hit him. In the mouth.

But he didn't feel a thing. And though he had never previously been athletically inclined, Lorenzo's amazing staying power—this extra dividend—eventually tired the irate husband to a point whereat it was possible to kick him senseless. It made quite an impression on the bronzed statuesque beauty, and they subsequently enjoyed a relationship which, though brief, was nothing if not satisfactory.

Mr. Gissing proceeded to cut what may be described as a wide swath. He became increasingly mindless of consequences. He traveled from point to point with the unconcerned purpose of a bluebottle fly, leaving untold damaged reputations and memorable evenings in his wake. Each month, on the first exactly, he mailed away the hair, praised his good fortune, and went on to newer conquests. He set records for derring-do, performing publicly such feats as diving three hundred feet into a bathtub, and wrestling a giant ape to the death.

At length, however, as is often the case with the most adventuresome of hearts, he tired of the gaiety, the lights and the tinsel, and began to long for the comforts of hearth, dog-at-the-feet, and wife. He therefore gave up his apartment in Tangier, composed an effusive letter of apology to Anastasia—explaining that the death of his father had sent him temporarily balmy—and returned home.

Nothing had changed. Anastasia was as lovely as ever: forgiving, understanding, loving. She tended to his wants as though he had not been gone for the better part of five years. There was not one word of recrimination at his having spent most of the money. They settled in their cozy little cottage and, aside from noticing a slightly peculiar look in his wife's eyes once in a great while, Lorenzo Gissing partook of the pleasures of domesticity, content until the old urges should again assail him.

It was during dinner, with Heine the spaniel lying on his feet and roast beef lying on his plate, that Mr. Gissing dropped his coffee cup to the floor.

"What did you say?" he demanded.

"I merely remarked, dear," answered his wife, "that it's a pity you should be losing your hair so rapidly."

"It's a lie!" Mr. Gissing raced for the mirror and stood transfixed before it, running his hands over his head. "It's a lie!"

"Well, you needn't get so broken up about it. Lots of people lose their hair. I shall still love you."

"No, no, no, that isn't the point. Do you really think that I am?"

"No question about it."

"God!"

It was quite true. It was going fast. How strange that he hadn't noticed before—

He noticed now. It was as if it were all rotting off, so to speak. "My God!" cried Mr. Gissing. "I'm shedding!"

It thinned first at the front of his head: the hairline receding some ten or fifteen inches. In short order it was reduced to a definite tonsure, giving him the curious appearance of a profane monk. He became frantic, finally to the point of spilling the beans to Anastasia.

"But how dreadful!" Anastasia said, "Oughtn't you to complain to the Better Business Bureau? I'm sure it must be some terrible fraud."

"What shall I do? I'm going bald, don't you understand?"

"Now I wonder," Anastasia said, "if that's what's happening to all the men that go bald? I mean, are they clients of Mr.—what's his name—Asmodeus—too?"

"You don't believe me!"

"Now, dear, you've always had a vivid imagination. But if you insist, I'll believe you. Why not see a scalp specialist?"

"Of course! Yes, I will!"

He did. The specialist, a Dr. Fatt, shook his head sadly. "Sorry, old man. One of those rare things. Nothing we can do."

He went to other specialists. They also shook their heads. He thought of saving the hairs as they fell. But no. In the contract it was clearly put forth:

"—that this hair shall be plucked from the head on the exact day payment falls due; never before, otherwise client risks forfeiture of his security..."

"The fiends!" he groaned. "They're responsible for this! Why didn't somebody warn me I'd go bald?"

Mr. Gissing lived the life of a tortured man, running from scalp specialist to scalp specialist, inundating his almost totally unhirsute head with a great variety of oils, herbs, juices and powders. He submitted to treatments by diet, magnet, X-ray, vibrator, and once tried hanging a dead toad from the lattice at midnight. Nothing helped. He grew balder and balder and—

At last, down to no more than twenty single hairs, he waited for the first of the month to roll 'round, and then carefully sliced the plucked hair into two sections, and mailed one of the sections off. He received a letter the same day.

> Dear Mr. Gissing:
> In Hades, we do not split hairs.
> Very truly yours,
> Asmodeus

He got off the remaining section hurriedly.

Finally, when only one solitary tendril protruded from his pate, one tiny hair flourishing like a lone palm tree in a gigantic desert, Mr. Gissing, nearly speechless with anxiety, contacted the newly founded Binkley Clinic.

"You've come to the right place," said Dr. Binkley, saturnine of expression and comfortingly beshocked and tressed with carrot-colored filaments.

"Thank God," said Mr. Gissing.

"Not a bit of it," said the doctor. "Thank me."

"Can you really keep me from going bald?"

"My dear sir, the Binkley method will grow hair on a billiard ball." He pointed to a green-felt-covered table, on which rested three billiard balls, each covered with a thick hairy matting.

"That's all quite nice," Mr. Gissing said, "but will it grow hair on *me*?"

"I guarantee that in one month you will begin to feel the effects."

"*Feel the effects*—be specific, man. In one month's time, will there be any growth?"

"My method is expensive, but rightly so. Yes, Mr. Gissing: though slight, there will definitely be hairs upon your head in one month's time."

"You *promise*? That is, you've done it before?"

"With scalp conditions such as yours, which are uncommon, yes, I can say unequivocally, I have."

"Let's begin immediately."

It was necessary for Mr. Gissing to stand on his head for several hours and then submit to having his dome raked with a strange electrical device rather like a combination cotton gin and sewing machine.

"Be careful," he reminded the doctor every few minutes, "do not on your life disturb that last hair. Don't even go near it."

Upon leaving the Binkley Clinic, Mr. Gissing put a bandaid over the hair and returned to his cottage, tired but happy.

"It's all right now," he said with jubilance to his wife. "I've this month's payment. And by next month I am guaranteed a new growth. Isn't that *wonderful*?"

"Yes, dear. Supper is ready now."

After stowing away his first undyspeptic meal in some time, Mr. Gissing turned to his wife and was shocked to observe how wan and beautiful she looked in the firelight. He felt a surge of sorts.

"Anastasia," he said. "You're looking fit."

"Thank you, Lorenzo."

"Very fit indeed."

"Thank you, Lorenzo."

"In fact, if I may remark, you're looking positively pretty, somehow."

"You are very gallant."

"Nonsense. See here, you're not angry about what happened as a direct result of poor old Dad's death, I mean my skipping off and all that—"

"Not angry, no."

"Good girl. Good *girl*. It's the way a man's constructed, one supposes. Well, it's all over now. I mean, we were barely getting to know one another."

"Yes . . ."

"Say, pretty sage of the old boy—meaning me—outsmarting the devil himself, what?"

"Very sage indeed, Lorenzo. I'm tired. Do you mind if I go to bed?"

Mr. Gissing smiled archly and delivered a pinch to his wife's backside. "Oh," he exclaimed, "I can feel it growing already. The hair. I can make the payment tomorrow—it *is* the first, isn't it?—and by next month I'll be able to start all over again without any fears. Dr. Binkley says *his* hair won't shed. Think of it!"

They retired and after a certain amount of wrestling and one thing and another, Mr. Gissing dropped off to a very sound sleep. He dreamed.

"Anatasia! Oh my Lord!"

"Yes dear, yes, what is it?"

"You mean *where* is it! It's gone, that's where. *Gone*, you understand?"

"I don't know what you're talking about."

"The hair, you idiot. It fell off. Lost. You must help me look for it."

They looked. Frantically. In the bedroom. In the bed. In the bedclothes. The mattress. The sheets. The pillows. Nothing. No hair.

"Again, we must look again. Carefully this time. Oh, *carefully*!"

They covered every inch of the room, then every other room, on hands and knees.

"Are you sure you had it when you came in?"

"Yes. I checked."

"Well, have you looked in all your pockets?"

"Yes. No—wait. No. Not there."

"Then where did you lose it?"

Mr. Gissing gave his wife a withering look, and continued his prayerful search. He inspected his clothes minutely. His shoes, his socks. The bathroom drain. The combs. Everything, everywhere.

"We must find it. It's getting near midnight."

"But dear, we've looked all day and all night. Can't you just sort of forget about it?"

"Anastasia, from the way you talk one would think you *wanted* to see me sizzle!"

"Lorenzo, what a discourteous and utterly unattractive thing to say!"

"Just keep looking."

At last, exhausted, breathless, hungry, his mind a kaleidoscope of fear, Mr. Gissing hurled himself onto the bed and lay there trembling.

"Would this be it?"

He leapt to his feet. He took the hair from his wife's hand. "Yes! Yes, it is! I'm sure of it—see, how brown it is. It isn't yours, yours is all black. Oh Anastasia, we're saved! I'll get it in the mails right away."

He started back from the post office still shaken by the experience and was almost to the door. A finger tapped his shoulder.

"Mr. Gissing?"

"Yes, yes?" He turned. It was the man he'd encountered by the Thames, so long ago. Still badly dressed.

"Well, what is it? Almost had me, didn't you?"

"Come with me," the man said.

"In a pig's eye I will. The payment's already in, old boy, and on time too. According to the con—"

The man's clothes suddenly burst into flame and in a moment Mr. Gissing found himself confronted by a creature unlike any in his experience. He quailed somewhat.

"*Come—with—me.*"

A hand of hot steel clutched Mr. Gissing's arm, and they

began to walk down an alley where no alley had ever seemed to be before. It was quite dark.

"What," Mr. Gissing shrieked, "is the meaning of this, may I inquire? The contract clearly states that as long as I get a hair off to you on the first of every month everything's in order."

"That is not quite correct," said the creature, exuding the kind of aroma one smells at barbeques. "One of *your* hairs."

"But—but that *was* my hair. I saw it. No one else was in the house. Certainly not in the bedroom. Except my wife—and she's brunette."

The creature laughed. "It was not yours."

"Then what—oh surely not! Anastasia, unfaithful? I can hardly believe it."

They walked in silence. The creature said nothing.

"My heart is broken!" Mr. Gissing wailed. "Another man in *our* bedroom! What sort of world is this where such iniquity is permitted to exist! Surely it can be no worse where we are going."

They disappeared into the blackness.

Anastasia Gissing never saw her husband again. She was left to seek solace from her thoughts and a small brown-haired spaniel named Heine. She bore up well.

Insomnia Vobiscum

I cannot say how it was that we fell into a discussion of so-called psychic phenomena that night at the Kings—our interest in spirits was generally limited to those found in bottles—but I suppose it is the sort of topic which must inevitably crop up among the very young, the very old, and the addled. Crenshaw, our ex-senator, was holding forth, loudly, on a trip he had taken to Haiti, and of the voodoo rites he had witnessed with his own two eyes. At the conclusion of this tale, which demonstrated either the fragility of memory or the plasticity of truth, Henderson, the retired banker, took over. In sepulchral tones he related the story of how his life had been saved by a gypsy phrenologist who, out of her fund of arcane knowledge, had warned him to stay out of single-engined aircraft. The elder of the club, Mycroft, a spry octogenarian, told of his encounter with a London spiritualist who put him in direct communication with his deceased wife. ("Thought I'd seen the last of the old termagant," commented Mycroft wryly, "but there she was, plain as pigs. Worst fright I've ever had.") Jenkins, our explorer, was cajoled into repeating his story of the Abominable Snowman, and I offered a variant of my one experience with the Great Unknown—correctly diagnosed by the group at large as a case of too much mince pie and too little regard for the facts.

We laughed, then, all but our newest member, the Scotsman, Creel—who sat, as he had done throughout the evening, absolutely still and expressionless. No one knew much about Creel, except that he was a stockbroker, single, and reportedly rich. He never said much, but from that little it was evident that he was a realist, a dweller in the here and now. It occurred to me suddenly that he must be thinking us all a hopeless bunch of nincompoops, which was true enough;

still, it annoyed me, and for that reason I twisted in my chair and addressed him.

"See here, Creel, surely you've a contribution to make."

He seemed to rouse from a deep reverie. "Contribution?"

"Yes." I winked at the others. "You must have bumped up against the unknown a few times in your life, seen a phantom or two." The vacancy of his stare drove me on. "Come on, Creel. As a King, it's your duty to give us a ghost story."

"Nonsense," he said. "Such talk is pointless."

"I can't agree. The unknown surrounds us."

I expected a snort. Instead, Creel continued to stare. "Well?"

"I've never seen a ghost," he said. "And I don't think anyone else has, either. But an odd thing did happen to me, once, a number of years ago . . ."

There was a quick hush in the room, as though a curtain had fallen. Creel had never before made such a long speech.

"I was visiting an acquaintance in the country," he continued, more to himself than to us. "It was a big house. There was a party. We ate a good meal and then, about ten o'clock, I decided to retire. I got into bed and tried to sleep, but I couldn't." He lit his pipe, thoughtfully. "Too much noise from downstairs. Yelling and screaming and dancing and cursing. Right below me. I never heard such noise. All night it lasted."

We waited. Finally someone said, "Well? Go on."

"That's all," said Creel.

"You were visiting someone, and you couldn't sleep because people were having a party downstairs and that's the whole story?"

"Aye," said Creel. "That's my brush with the unknown." He sucked at his pipe until he'd got it going, then he looked up at our astonished faces. "Oh," he said, "I forgot one part. There was no downstairs at this house. My bedroom was on the ground floor."

The Crooked Man

"Professing themselves to be wise, they became fools...who changed the truth of God into a lie...for even their women did change the natural use into that which is against nature: and likewise also the men, leaving the natural use of the woman, burned in their lust one toward another; men with men working that which is unseemly..."

—St. Paul: Romans, 1

He slipped into a corner booth away from the dancing men, where it was quietest, where the odors of musk and frangipani hung less heavy on the air. A slender lamp glowed softly in the booth. He turned it down: down to where only the club's blue overheads filtered through the beaded curtain, diffusing, blurring the image thrown back by the mirrored walls of his light, thin-boned handsomeness.

"Yes, sir?" The barboy stepped through the beads and stood smiling. Clad in gold-sequined trunks, his greased muscles seemed to roll in independent motion, like fat snakes beneath his naked skin.

"Whiskey," Jesse said. He caught the insouciant grin, the broad white-tooth crescent that formed on the young man's face. Jesse looked away, tried to control the flow of blood to his cheeks.

"Yes, sir," the barboy said, running his thick tanned fingers over his solar plexus, tapping the fingers, making them hop in a sinuous dance. He hesitated, still smiling, this time questioningly, hopefully, a smile deep drenched in admiration and desire. The Finger Dance, the accepted symbol, stopped: the pudgy brown digits curled into angry fists. "Right away, sir."

Jesse watched him turn; before the beads had tinkled together he watched the handsome athlete make his way imperiously through the crowd, shaking off the tentative hands of single men at the tables, ignoring the many desire symbols directed toward him.

That shouldn't have happened. Now the fellow's feelings were hurt. If hurt enough, he would start thinking, wondering—and that would ruin everything. No. It must be put right.

Jesse thought of Mina, of the beautiful Mina—It was such a rotten chance. It *had* to go right!

"Your whiskey, sir," the young man said. His face looked like a dog's face, large, sad; his lips were a pouting bloat of line.

Jesse reached into his pocket for some change. He started to say something, something nice.

"It's been paid for," the barboy said. He scowled and laid a card on the table and left.

The card carried the name E. J. Two HOBART, embossed, in lavender ink. Jesse heard the curtains tinkle.

"Well, hello. I hope you don't mind my barging in like this, but—you didn't seem to be with anyone . . ."

The man was small, chubby, bald; his face had a dirty growth of beard, and he looked out of tiny eyes encased in bulging contacts. He was bare to the waist. His white, hairless chest drooped and turned in folds at the stomach. Softly, more subtly than the barboy had done, he put his porky stubs of fingers into a suggestive rhythm.

Jesse smiled. "Thanks for the drink," he said. "But I really am expecting someone."

"Oh?" the man said. "Someone—special?"

"Pretty special," Jesse said smoothly, now that the words had become automatic. "He's my fiancée."

"I see." The man frowned momentarily and then brightened. "Well, I thought to myself, I said: E. J., a beauty like that couldn't very well be unattached. But—well, it was certainly worth a try. Sorry."

"Perfectly all right," Jesse said. The predatory little eyes were rolling, the fingers dancing in one last-ditch attempt. "Good evening, Mr. Hobart."

Bluey veins showed under the whiteness of the man's nearly female mammae. Jesse felt slightly amused this time: it was the other kind, the intent ones, the humorless ones like—like the barboy—that repulsed him, turned him ill, made him want to take a knife and carve unspeakable ugliness into his own smooth, ascetic face.

The man turned and waddled away crabwise. The club was becoming more crowded. It was getting later, and heads full of liquor shook away the inhibitions of the earlier hours. Jesse tried not to watch, but he had long ago given up trying to rid himself of his fascination. So he watched the men together. The pair over in the corner, pressed close together, dancing with their bodies, never moving their feet, swaying in slow lissome movements to the music, their tongues twisting in the air, jerking, like pink snakes, contracting to points and curling invitingly, barely making touch, then snapping back. The Tongue Dance . . . The couple seated by the bar. One a Beast, the other a Hunter, the Beast old, his cheeks caked hard and cracking with powder and liniments, the perfume rising from his body like steam; the Hunter, young but unhandsome, the fury evident in his eyes, the hurt anger at having to make do with a Beast—from time to time he would look around, wetting his lips in shame. . . . And those two just coming in, dressed in Mother's uniforms, tanned, mustached, proud of their station. . . .

Jesse held the beads apart. *Mina must come soon.* He wanted to run from this place, out into the air, into the darkness and silence.

No. He just wanted Mina. To see her, touch her, listen to the music of her voice. . . .

Two women came in, arm in arm, Beast and Hunter, drunk. They were stopped at the door. Angrily, shrilly, told to leave. The manager swept by Jesse's booth, muttering about them, asking why they should want to come dirtying up The Phallus with their presence when they had their own section, their own clubs—

Jesse pulled his head back inside. He'd gotten used to the light by now, so he closed his eyes against his multiplied image. The disorganized sounds of love got louder, the singsong syrup of voices: deep, throaty, baritone, falsetto. It was crowded now. The Orgies would begin before long, and the couples would pair off for the cubicles. He hated the place. But close to Orgy time you didn't get noticed here—and where else was there to go? Outside, where every inch of pavement was patrolled electronically, every word of conversation, every movement recorded, catalogued, filed?

Damn Knudson! Damn the little man! Thanks to him, to the Senator, Jesse was now a criminal. Before, it wasn't so bad—not this bad, anyway. You were laughed at and shunned and fired from your job, sometimes kids lobbed stones at you, but at least you weren't hunted. Now—it was a crime. A sickness.

He remembered when Knudson had taken over. It had been one of the little man's first telecasts; in fact, it was the platform that got him the majority vote:

> "Vice is on the upswing in our city. In the dark corners of every Unit, perversion blossoms like an evil flower. Our children are exposed to its stink, and they wonder— *our children wonder*—why nothing is done to put a halt to this disgrace. We have ignored it long enough! The time has come for *action*, not mere words. The perverts who infest our land must be flushed out, eliminated *completely*, as a threat not only to public morals but to society at large. These sick people must be cured and made normal. The disease that throws men and women together in this dreadful abnormal relationship and leads to acts of retrogression—retrogression that will, unless it is stopped and stopped fast, push us inevitably back to the status of animals—this is to be considered as any other disease. It must be conquered as heart trouble, cancer, polio, schizophrenia, paranoia, all other diseases have been conquered. . . ."

The Women's Senator had taken Knudson's lead and issued a similar pronunciamento, and then the bill became a law, and the law was carried out.

Jesse sipped at the whiskey, remembering the Hunts. How the frenzied mobs had gone through the city at first, chanting, yelling, bearing placards with slogans: WIPE OUT THE HETEROS! KILL THE QUEERS! MAKE OUR CITY CLEAN AGAIN! And how they'd lost interest finally after the passion had worn down and the novelty had ended. But they had killed many, and they had sent many more to the hospitals. . . .

He remembered the nights of running and hiding, choked dry breath glued to his throat, heart rattling loose. He had been lucky. He didn't look like a hetero. They said you could tell one just by watching him walk—Jesse walked correctly. He fooled them. He was lucky.

And he was a criminal. He, Jesse Four Martin, no different from the rest, tube-born and machine-nursed, raised in the Character Schools like everyone else—was terribly different from the rest.

It had happened—his awful suspicions had crystallized—on his first formal date. The man had been a Rocketeer, the best high quality, even out of the Hunter class. Mother had arranged it carefully. There was the dance. And then the ride in the spacesled. The big man had put an arm about Jesse and—Jesse knew. He knew for certain, and it made him very angry and very sad.

He remembered the days that came after the knowledge; bad days, days fallen upon evil, black desires, deep-cored frustrations. He had tried to find a friend at the Crooked Clubs that flourished then, but it was no use. There was a sensationalism, a bravura to these people, that he could not love. The sight of men and women together, too, shocked the parts of him he could not change, and repulsed him. Then the vice squads had come and closed up the clubs, and the heteros were forced underground, and he never sought them out again or saw them. He was alone.

The beads tinkled.

"Jesse—" He looked up quickly, afraid. It was Mina. She wore a loose man's shirt, an old hat that hid her golden hair: her face was shadowed by the turned-up collar. Through the shirt the rise and fall of her breasts could be faintly detected. She smiled once, nervously.

Jesse looked out the curtain. Without speaking, he put his hands about her soft thin shoulders and held her like this for a long minute.

"Mina—" She looked away. He pulled her chin forward, and ran a finger along her lips. Then he pressed her body to his, tightly, touching her neck, her back, kissing her forehead, her eyes, kissing her mouth. They sat down.

They sought words. The curtains parted.

"Beer," Jesse said, winking at the barboy, who tried to come closer, to see the one loved by this thin, handsome man.

"Yes sir."

The barboy looked at Mina very hard, but she had turned, and he could see only the back. Jesse held his breath. The barboy smiled contemptuously then, a smile that said: You're insane—I was hired for my beauty. See my chest, look—a pectoral vision. My arms, strong; my lips—come, were there ever such sensuous ones? And you turn me down for this bag of bones. . . .

Jesse winked again, shrugged suggestively and danced his fingers: *Tomorrow, my friend; I'm stuck tonight. Can't help it. Tomorrow.*

The barboy grinned and left. In a few moments he returned with the beer. "On the house," he said, for Mina's benefit. She turned only when Jesse said, softly:

"It's all right. He's gone now."

Jesse looked at her. Then he reached over and took off the hat. Blond hair rushed out and over the rough shirt.

She grabbed for the hat. "We mustn't," she said. "Please— what if somebody should come in?"

"No one will come in. I told you that."

"But what if? I don't know—I don't like it here. That man at the door—he almost recognized me."

"But he didn't."

"Almost, though. And then what?"

"Forget it. Mina, for God's sake. Let's not quarrel."

She calmed. "I'm sorry, Jesse. It's only that—this place makes me feel—"

"—what?"

"Dirty." She said it defiantly.

"You don't really believe that, do you?"

"No. I don't know. I just want to be alone with you."

Jesse took out a cigarette and started to use the lighter. Then he cursed and threw the vulgarly shaped object under the table and crushed the cigarette. "You know that's impossible," he said. The idea of separate Units for homes had disappeared, to be replaced by giant dormitories. There were no more parks, no country lanes. There was no place to hide at all now, thanks to Senator Knudson, to the little bald crest of this new sociological wave. "This is all we have," Jesse said, throwing a sardonic look around the booth, with its carved symbols and framed pictures of entertainment stars— all naked and leering.

They were silent for a time, hands interlocked on the table top. Then the girl began to cry. "I—I can't go on like this," she said.

"I know. It's hard. But what else can we do?" Jesse tried to keep the hopelessness out of his voice.

"Maybe," the girl said, "we ought to go underground with the rest."

"And hide there, like rats?" Jesse said.

"We're hiding here," Mina said, "like rats."

"Besides, Parner is getting ready to crack down. I know, Mina—I work at Centraldome, after all. In a little while there won't be any underground."

"I love you," the girl said, leaning forward, parting her lips for a kiss. "Jesse, I do." She closed her eyes. "Oh, why won't they leave us alone? Why? Just because we're que—"

"Mina! I've told you—don't ever use that word. It isn't true! *We're* not the queers. You've got to believe that. Years ago it was *normal* for men and women to love each other: they married, and had children together; that's the way it was. Don't you remember anything of what I've told you?"

The girl sobbed. "Of course I do. I do. But, darling, that was a long time ago."

"Not so long! Where I work—listen to me—they have books. You know, I told you about books? I've read them, Mina. I learned what the words meant from other books. It's only been since the use of artificial insemination—not even five hundred years ago."

"Yes dear," the girl said. "I'm sure, dear."

"Mina, stop that! We are not the unnatural ones, no matter what they say. I don't know exactly how it happened—maybe, maybe as women gradually became equal to men in every way—or maybe solely because of the way we're born—I don't know. But the point is, darling, the whole world was like us, once. Even now, look at the animals—"

"Jesse! Don't you dare talk as if we're like those horrid little dogs and cats and things!"

Jesse sighed. He had tried so often to tell her, show her. But he knew, actually, what she thought. That she felt she was exactly what the authorities told her she was—God, maybe that's how they all thought, all the Crooked People, all the "unnormal" ones. . . .

The girl's hands caressed his arms, and the touch became suddenly repugnant to him. Unnatural. Terribly unnatural.

Jesse shook his head. Forget it, he thought. Never mind. She's a woman, and you love her, and there's nothing wrong nothing wrong nothing wrong in that . . . or am I the insane person of old days who was insane because he was so sure he wasn't insane because—

"Disgusting!"

It was the fat little man, the smiling masher, E. J. Two Hobart. But he wasn't smiling now.

Jesse got up quickly and stepped in front of Mina. "What do you want? I thought I told you—"

The man pulled a metal disk from his trunks. "Vice squad, friend," he said. "Better sit down." The disk was pointed at Jesse's belly.

The man's arm went out the curtain, and two other men came in, holding disks.

"I've been watching you quite a while, mister," the man said. "Quite a while."

"Look," Jesse said, "I don't know what you're talking about. I work at Centraldome and I'm seeing Miss Smith here on some business."

"We know all about that kind of business," the man said.

"All right—I'll tell you the truth. I forced her to come here. I—"

"Mister—didn't you hear me? I said I've been watching you. All evening. Let's go."

One man took Mina's arm, roughly; the other two began to propel Jesse out through the club. Heads turned. Tangled bodies moved embarrassedly.

"It's all right," the little fat man said, his white skin glistening with perspiration. "It's all right, folks. Go on back to whatever you were doing." He grinned, and tightened his grasp on Jesse's arm.

Mina didn't struggle. There was something in her eyes—it took Jesse a long time to recognize it. Then he knew. He knew what she had come to tell him tonight: that even if they hadn't been caught—she would have submitted to the Cure voluntarily. No more worries then, no more guilt. No more meeting at midnight dives, feeling shame, feeling dirt. . . .

Mina didn't meet Jesse's look as they took her out into the street.

"You'll be okay," the fat man was saying. He opened the wagon's doors. "They've got it down pat now—couple days in the ward, one short session with the doctors; take out a few glands, make a few injections, attach a few wires to your head, turn on a machine: presto! You'll be surprised."

The fat officer leaned close. His sausage fingers danced wildly near Jesse's face.

"It'll make a new man of you," he said.

Then they closed the doors and locked them.

The Jungle

Suddenly it was there. On foxfeet, invisibly, it had crept, past all the fences and traps he had laid, past all the barriers. And now it sat inside his mind, a part of him, like his pulse, like the steady beat of his heart.

Richard Austin became rigid in the chair. He closed his eyes, and strained the muscles in his body until they were silent and unmoving as granite; and he listened to the thing that had come again, taking him by surprise even while he had been waiting. He listened to it grow—it *seemed* to grow; he couldn't be sure: perhaps he was merely bringing it into sharper focus by filtering out the other constant sounds: the winds that whispered through the foliage of balloon-topped trees, the murmurous insect-drone of all the machines that produced this wind and pumped blood through the city from their stations far beneath the night-heavy streets. Or, perhaps, it was because he was searching, trying to lay hands on it that the thing seemed to be different tonight, stronger, surer. Or—what did it matter?

He sat in the darkened room and listened to the drums; to the even, steady throb that really neither rose nor diminished, but held to that slow, dignified tempo with which he'd become so familiar.

Then, quickly, he rose from the chair and shook his head. The sounds died and became an indistinguishable part of the silence. It was only concentration, he thought, and the desire to hear them that gave them life...

Richard Austin released a jagged breath from his swollen lungs, painfully. He walked to the bar and poured some whiskey into a glass, and drank most of it in a single swallow; it went down his dry throat like knives, forcing the salivary glands back into action.

177

He shook his head again, turned, and walked back across the living room to the far door. It swung out noiselessly as his hand touched the ornamented circle of hammered brass.

The figure of his wife lay perfectly still under the black light, still and pale, as she had lain three hours before. He walked toward her, feeling his nostrils dilate at the acrid medicine smells, harshly bitter and new to his senses. He blinked away the hot tears that had rushed, stinging, to his eyes; and stood for a time, quietly, trying not to think of the drums.

Then he whispered, "Mag... Mag, don't die tonight!"

Imbecile words! He clenched his fists and stared down at the face that was so full of pain, so twisted with defeat, that now you could not believe it had once been different, a young face, full of laughter and innocence and courage.

The color had gone completely. From the burning splotchy scarlet of last week to this stiff white mask, lifeless, brittle as drying paste. And covered over with perspiration that glistened above her mouth in cold wet buttons and over her face like oil on white stone. The bedding under and around her was drenched gray.

Austin looked at the bandage that covered his wife's head, and forced away the memory, brutally. The memory of her long silver hair and how it had fallen away in clumps in his hands within a week after she had been stricken...

But the thoughts danced out of control, and he found himself remembering all the terrible steps in this nightmare.

The scientists had thought it malaria, judging from the symptoms, which were identical. But that was difficult to accept, for malaria had been effectively conquered—powerful new discoveries in vaccines having been administered first, and then the primary cause of the disease itself—the Anopheles mosquito—destroyed completely. And the liquid alloys which formed the foundations for this new city eliminated all the likely breeding places, the bogs and marshlands and rivers. No instance of re-occurrence of the disease had been reported for half a century. Yet—malarial parasites were discovered in the bloodstreams of those first victims, unmistakable parasites that multiplied at a swift rate and worked their destruction of the red corpuscles. And the chemists immediately had to go about the business of mixing medicines from now-ancient prescriptions, frantically working against time. A disquieting, even a frightening thing; but without terror for the builders of the new city; not sufficient to make them abandon their work, or to spark mass evacuations. Panic was by now so forgotten by most that it had become a new emotion, to be learned all over again.

It had not taken very long to relearn, Austin recalled. Terror had come soon enough. The stricken—some thirty husky workmen, engineers, planners—had rallied under the drugs and seemed to be out of critical condition when, one night, they had all suffered relapses, fallen into fevered comas, and proceeded to alternate between unconsciousness and delirium. The scientists were baffled. They tried frenziedly to arrest the parasites, but without success. Their medicines were useless, their drugs and radium treatments and inoculations—all, useless. Finally, they could only look on as the disease took new turns, developed strange characteristics, changed altogether from what they had taken to be malaria to something utterly foreign. It began to assume a horrible regular pattern: from prolonged delirium to catatonia, whereby the victim's respiratory system and heartbeat diminished to a condition only barely distinguishable from death. And then, the most hideous part: the swift decomposition of the body cells, the destruction of the tissues . . .

Richard Austin carefully controlled a shudder as he thought of those weeks that had been the beginning. He fingered out a cigarette from his pocket, started to strike it, then broke the cylinder and ground its bright red flakes into his palms.

No other real hint had been given then: only the disease. Someone had nicknamed it "Jungle Rot"—cruel, but apt. The victims *were* rotting alive, the flesh falling from them like rain-soaked rags; and they did not die wholly, ever, until they had been transformed into almost unrecognizable mounds of putrescence . . .

He put out a hand and laid it gently against his wife's cheek. The perspiration was chill and greasy to his touch, like the stagnant water of slew banks. Instinctively, his fingers recoiled and balled back into fists. He forced them open again, and stared at the tiny dottles of flesh that clung to them.

"Mag!" It had started already! Wildly, he touched her arm, applying very slight pressure. The outer skin crumbled away, leaving a small wet gray patch. Austin's heart raced; an involuntary movement caused his fingers to pinch his own wrists, hard. A wrinkled spot appeared and disappeared, a small, fading red line.

She's dying, he thought. Very surely, very slowly, she'd begun to die—Mag. Soon her body will turn gray and then it will come loose; the weight of the sheet will be enough to tear big strips of it away... She'll begin to rot, and her brain will know it—they had discovered that much: the victims were never completely comatose, could not be adequately drugged—she will know that she is mouldering even while she lives and thinks...

And why? His head ached, throbbed. *Why?*

The years, these past months, the room with its stink of decay—everything rushed up, suddenly, filling Austin's mind.

If I had agreed to leave with the rest, he thought, to run away, then Mag would be well and full of life. But—I didn't agree...

He had stayed on to fight. And Mag would not leave without him. Now she was dying, and that was the end of it.

Or—he turned slowly—was it? He walked out to the balcony. The forced air was soft and cool; it moved in little patches through the streets of the city. Mbarara, *his* city; the one he'd dreamed about and then planned and designed and pushed into existence; the place built to pamper five hundred thousand people.

Empty now, and deserted as a gigantic churchyard...

Dimly he recognized the sound of the drums, with their slow, muffled rhythm, directionless as always, seeming to come from everywhere and from nowhere. Speaking to him. Whispering.

Austin lit a cigarette, and sucked the calming smoke into his lungs. He remained motionless until the cigarette was down to the cork.

Then he walked back into the bedroom, opened a cabinet and took a heavy silver pistol.

He loaded it carefully.

Mag lay still; almost, it seemed to Austin, expectant, waiting. So very still and pale.

He pointed the barrel of the pistol at his wife's forehead and curled his finger around the trigger. Another slight pressure and it would be over. Her suffering would be over. Just a slight pressure!

The drums droned louder until they were exploding in the quiet room.

Austin tensed and fought the trembling, gripped the pistol with his other hand to steady it.

But his finger refused to move on the curved trigger.

After a long moment, he lowered his arm and dropped the gun into his pocket.

"No." He said it quietly, undramatically. The word hit a barrier of mucus and came out high-pitched and child-like.

He coughed.

That was what they wanted him to do—he could tell, from the drums. That's what so many of the others had done. Panicked.

"No."

He walked quickly out of the room, through the hall, to the elevator. It lowered instantly, but he did not wait for it to reach bottom before he leapt off and ran across the floor to the barricaded front door.

He tore at the locks. Then the door swung open and he was outside; for the first time in three weeks—outside, alone, in the city.

He paused, fascinated by the strangeness of it. Impossible to believe that he was the only white man left in the entire city.

He strode to a high-speed walkway, halted it, and stepped on. Setting the power at half with his passkey, he pressed the control button and sagged against the rail as the belt whispered into movement.

He knew where he was going. Perhaps he even knew why. But he didn't think about that; instead, he looked at the buildings that slid by silently, the vast rolling spheres and columns of colored stone, the balanced shapes that existed now and that had once existed only in his mind. And he listened to the drums, wondering why the sound of them seemed natural and his buildings suddenly so unnatural, so strange and disjointed.

Like green balloons on yellow sticks, the cultured Grant Wood trees slipped by, uniform and straight, arranged in aesthetically pleasing designs on the stone islands between belts. Austin smiled: The touch of nature. Toy trees, ruffling in artificial winds . . . It all looked, now, like the model he had presented to the Senators. About as real and lifelike.

Austin moved like a carefully carved and painted figurine, incredibly small and lonely-looking on the empty walkway. He thought about the years of preparation; the endless red tape and paperwork that had preceded the actual job. Then of the natives, how they had protested and petitioned to influence the Five-Power governments, and how that had slowed them down. The problem of money, whipped only by pounding at the point of over-population, again and again, never letting up for a moment. The problems, problems...

He could not recall when the work itself had actually begun—it was all so joined. Laying the first railroad could certainly not have been a particle as beset with difficulty. Because the tribes of the Kenya territory numbered into the millions; and they were all filled with hatred and fury, opposing the city at every turn.

No explanation had satisfied them. They saw it as the destruction of their world and so they fought. With guns and spears and arrows and darts, with every resource at their disposal, refusing to capitulate, hunting like an army of mad ants scattered over the land.

And, since they could not be controlled, they had to be destroyed. Like their forests and rivers and mountains, destroyed to make room for the city.

Though not, Austin remembered grimly, without loss. The white men had fine weapons, but none more fatal than machetes biting deep into neck flesh or sharp wooden shafts coated with strange poisons. And they did not all escape. Some would wander too far, unused to this green world where a man could become hopelessly lost within three minutes. Others would forget their weapons. And a few were too brave.

Austin thought of Joseph Fava, the engineer, who had been reported missing. And of how Fava had come running back to the camp after two days, running and screaming, a bright crimson nearly dead creature out of the worst dreams. He had been cleanly stripped of all his skin, except for the face, hands, and feet....

But the city had grown, implacably, spreading its concrete and alloy fingers wider every day over the dark and feral country. Nothing could stop it. Mountains were stamped flat. Rivers were dammed off or drained or put elsewhere. The marshes were filled. The animals shot from the trees, and then the trees cut down. And the big gray machines moved forward, gobbling up the jungle with their iron teeth, chewing it clean of its life and all its living things.

Until it was no more.

Leveled, smoothed as a highway is smoothed, its centuries choked beneath millions and millions of tons of hardened stone.

The birth of a city... It had become the death of a world.

And Richard Austin was its murderer.

As he traveled, he thought of the shaman, the half-naked, toothless Bantu medicine man who had spoken for most of the tribes. *"You have killed us, and we could not stop you. So now we will wait, until you have made your city and others come to live here. Then YOU will know what it is to die."* Bokawah, who lived in superstition and fear, whom civilization had passed, along with the rest of his people. Who never spoke again after those words, and allowed himself to be moved to the wide iron plateau that had been built for the surviving natives.

Bokawah, the ignorant shaman, with his eternal smile... How distinct that smile was now!

The walkway shuddered suddenly, and jarred to a noisy grinding stop. Austin pitched forward and grasped the railing in order to break his fall.

Awareness of the silence came first. The eerie dead silence that hung like a pall. It meant that the central machines had ceased functioning. They had been designed to operate automatically and perpetually; it was unthinkable that these power sources could break down!

As unthinkable as the drums that murmured to life again beyond the stainless towers, so loud now in the silence, so real.

Austin gripped his pistol tightly and shook away the panic that had bubbled up like acid in his chest. It was merely that the power had gone off. Strike out impossible, insert improbable. Improbabilities happen. The evil spirits do not summon them, they *happen*. Like strange diseases.

I am fighting, he thought, *a statistical paradox. That's all. A storage pile of coincidences. If I wait*—he walked close to the sides of the buildings—*and fight, the graph will change. The curve will* ...

The drums roared out a wave of scattered sound, stopped, began again ...

He thought a bit further of charts; then the picture of Mag materialized, blocking out the thick ink lines, ascending and descending on their giant graphs.

Thinking wasn't going to help...

He walked on.

Presently, at the end of a curve in the city maze, the "village" came into view, suspended overhead like a gigantic jeweled spider. It thrust out cold light. It was silent.

Austin breathed deeply. By belt, his destination was only minutes away. But the minutes grew as he walked through the city, and when he had reached the lift, hot pains wrenched at his muscles. He stood by the crystal platform, working action back into numbed limbs.

Then he remembered the silence, the dead machines. If they were not functioning, then the elevator—

His finger touched a button, experimentally.

A glass door slid open with a pneumatic hiss.

He walked inside, and tried not to think as the door closed and the bullet-shaped lift began to rise.

Below, Mbarara grew small. The treated metals glowed in a dimming lace of light. And the city looked even more like the little clay model he had built with his hands.

At last, movement ceased. Austin waited for the door to slide open again, then he strode out onto the smooth floor.

It was very dark. The artificial torches did not even smolder: their stubs, he noticed, were blackened and cold.

But the gates to the village lay open.

He looked past the entrance into the frozen shadows.

He heard the drums, throbbing from within, loud and distinct. But—ordinary drums, whose sound-waves would dissipate before ever reaching the city below.

He walked into the village.

The huts, like glass blisters on smooth flesh, sat silent. Somehow, they were obscene in the dark, to Austin. Built to incorporate the feel and the atmosphere of their originals, and yet to include the civilized conveniences; planned from an artistic as well as a scientific standpoint—they were suddenly obscene.

Perhaps, Austin thought, as he walked, perhaps there was something to what Barney had been saying... No—these people had elected to stay of their own free will. It would have been impossible to duplicate *exactly* the monstrous conditions under which they had lived. If not impossible, certainly wrong.

Let them wallow in their backward filth? In their disease and corruption, let them die—merely because their culture had failed to absorb scientific progress? No. You do not permit a man to leap off the top of a hundred-story building just because he has been trained to believe it is the only way to get to the ground floor—even though you insult him and blaspheme against his gods through your intervention. You restrain him, at any cost. Then, much later, you show him the elevator. And because he is a man, with a brain no smaller than yours, he will understand. He will understand that a crushed superstition is better than a crushed head. And he will thank you, eventually.

That is logic.

Austin walked, letting these thoughts form a thick crust. He felt the slap of the pistol against his thigh and this, also, was comforting.

Where were they now? Inside the huts, asleep? All of them? Or had they, too, contracted the disease and begun to die of it? . . .

Far ahead, at the clearing which represented the tip of the design, a glow of light appeared. As he approached, the drums grew louder, and other sounds—voices. How many voices? The air was at once murmurous and alive.

He stopped before the clearing and leaned on the darkness and watched.

Nearby, a young woman was dancing. Her eyes were closed, tightly, and her arms were straight at her sides like black roots. She was in a state of possession, dancing in rhythm to the nearest drum. Her feet moved so fast they had become a blur, and her naked body wore a slick coat of perspiration.

Beyond the dancing woman, Austin could see the crowd, squatted and standing, swaying; over a thousand of them— surely every native in the village!

A clot of brown skin and bright white paint and brilliant feathers, hunched in the firelight.

An inner line of men sat over drums and hollow logs, beating these with their palms and with short sticks of wood. The sounds blended strangely into one—the one Austin had been hearing, it seemed, all his life.

He watched, fascinated, even though he had witnessed Bantu ceremonies countless times in the past, even though he was perfectly familiar with the symbols. The little leather bags of hex-magic: nail-filings, photographs, specks of flesh; the rubbing boards stained with fruit-skins; the piles of bones at the feet of the men—old bones, very brittle and dry and old.

Then he looked beyond the natives to the sensible clean crystal walls that rose majestically, cupping the area, giving it form.

It sent a chill over him.

He walked into the open.

The throng quieted, instantly, like a scream cut off. The dancers caught their balance, blinked, drew in breath. The others lifted their heads, stared.

All were turned to dark, unmoving wax.

Austin went past the gauntlet of eyes, to one of the painted men.

. "Where is Bokawah?" he said loudly, in precise Swahili. His voice regained its accustomed authority. "Bokawah. Take me to him."

No one moved. Hands lay on the air inches above drums, petrified.

"I have come to talk!"

From the corner of his eyes, Austin felt the slight disturbance. He waited a moment, then turned.

A figure crouched beside him. A man, unbelievably old and tiny, sharp little bones jutting into loose flesh like pins, skin cross-hatched with a pattern of white paint, chalky as the substance some widows of the tribes wore for a year after the death of their mates. His mouth was pulled into a shape not quite a smile, but resembling a smile. It revealed hardened, toothless gums.

The old man laughed, suddenly. The amulet around his chicken neck bobbled. Then he stopped laughing and stared at Austin.

"We have been waiting," he said, softly. Austin started at the perfect English. He had not heard English for a long time; and now, coming from this little man... Perhaps Bokawah had learned it. Why not? "Walk with me, Mr. Austin."

He followed the ancient shaman, dumbly, not having the

slightest idea why he was doing so, to a square of moist soil. It was surrounded by natives.

Bokawah looked once at Austin, then reached down and dipped his hands into the soil. The horny fingers scratched away the top-dirt, burrowed in like thin, nervous animals, and emerged, finally, holding something.

Austin gasped. It was a doll.

It was Mag.

He wanted to laugh, but it caught in his throat. He knew how the primitives would try to inflict evil upon an enemy by burying his effigy. As the effigy rotted, symbolically, so would...

He snatched the doll away from the old man. It crumbled in his hands.

"Mr. Austin," Bokawah said, "I'm very sorry you did not come for this talk long ago." The old man's lips did not move. The voice was his and yet not his.

Austin knew, suddenly, that he had not come to this place of his own accord. He had been summoned.

The old man held a hyena's tail in his right hand. He waved this, and a slight wind seemed to come up, throwing the flames of the fire into a neurotic dance.

"You are not convinced, even now, Mr. Austin. Aiii. You have seen suffering and death, but you are not convinced." Bokawah sighed. "I will try one last time." He squatted on the smooth floor. "When you first came to our country, and spoke your plans, I told you—even then—what must happen. I told you that this city must not be. I told you that my people would fight, as *your* people would fight if *we* were to come to your land and build jungles. But you understood nothing of what I said." He did not accuse; the voice was expressionless. "Now Mbarara lies silent and dead beneath you, and still you do not wish to understand. What must we do, Mr. Austin? How shall we go about proving to you that this Mbarara of yours will *always* be silent and dead, that your people will never walk through it?"

Austin thought of his old college friend Barney—and of what Barney had once told him. Staring at Bokawah, at this scrawny, painted savage, he saw the big Texan clearly, and he remembered his wild undergraduate theories—exhuming the antique view of primitives and their religions, their magics.

"Go on, pal, laugh at their tabus," Barney, who was an anthropologist, used to be fond of saying, *"sneer, while you*

throw salt over your shoulder. Laugh at their manas, while you blab about your own 'geniuses'!"

He had even gone beyond the point of believing that magic was important because it held together the fabric of culture among these natives, because it—and their religious superstitions—gave them a rule for behavior, therefore, in most cases, happiness. He had even come to believe that native magic was just another method of arriving at physical truths.

Of course, it was all semantic nonsense. It suggested that primitive magic could lift a ship into space or destroy disease or . . .

That had been the trouble with Barney. You could never tell when he was serious. Even a social anthropologist wouldn't go so far as to think there was more than one law of gravity.

"Mr. Austin, we have brought you here for a purpose. Do you know what that purpose is?"

"I don't know and I don't—"

"Have you wondered why you, alone, of all your people, have been spared? Then—listen to me, very carefully. Because if you do not, then what has happened in your new city is merely the beginning. The winds of death will blow over Mbarara and it will be far more awful than what has been." The medicine man stared down at the scattered piles of bones. Panther bones, Austin knew—a divination device. Their position on the ground told Bokawah much about the white people.

"Go back to your chiefs. Tell them that they must forget this city. Tell them that death walks here, and that it will always walk, and that their magic is powerful but not powerful enough. It cannot stand against the spirits from time who have been summoned to fight. Go and talk to your chiefs and tell them these things. Make them believe you. *Force* them to understand that if they come to Mbarara, they will die, in ways they never dreamed, of sickness, in pain, slowly. Forever."

The old man's eyes were closed. His mouth did not move at all and the voice was mechanical.

"Tell them, Mr. Austin, that at first you thought it was a strange new disease that struck the workers. But then remind them that your greatest doctors were powerless against the contagion, that it spread and was not conquered. Say these things. And, perhaps, they will believe you. And be saved."

Bokawah studied the panther bones carefully, tracing their arrangement.

Austin's voice was mechanical, also. "You are forgetting something," he said. He refused to let the thoughts creep in. He refused to wonder about the voice that came through closed lips, about where the natives could have found soil or fresh panther bones, or... "No one," he said to the old man, "has fought back—yet."

"But why would you do that, Mr. Austin, since you do not believe in the existence of your enemy? Whom shall you fight?" Bokawah smiled.

The crowd of natives remained quiet, unmoving, in the dying firelight.

"The only fear you hold for us," Austin said, "is the fear that you may prove psychologically harmful." He looked at the crushed doll at his feet. The face was whole; otherwise, it lay hideously disfigured.

"Yes?"

"Right now, Bokawah, my government is sending men. They will arrive soon. When they do, they will study what has happened. If it is agreed that your rites—however harmless in themselves—cause currents of fear—are in *any* way responsible for the disease—you will be given the opportunity to go elsewhere or—"

"Or Mr. Austin?"

"—you will be eliminated."

"Then people will come to Mbarara. Despite the warnings and the death, they will come?"

"Your magic sticks aren't going to scare away five hundred thousand men and women."

"Five hundred thousand..." The old man looked at the bones, sighed, nodded his head. "You know your people very well," he murmured.

Austin smiled. "Yes, I do."

"Then I think there is little left for us to talk about."

Austin wanted to say, No, you're wrong. We must talk about Mag! She's dying, and I want to keep her from dying. But he knew what these words would mean. They would sketch his real feelings, his fears and doubts. And everything would be lost. He could not admit that the doll was anything more than a doll. He must not!

The old man picked up a calabash, and ran water over his hands. "I am sorry," he said, "that you must learn the way you must."

A slow chant rose from the natives. It sounded to Austin

like Swahili, yet it was indistinct. He could recognize none of the words, except *gonga* and *bagana*. Medicine? The man with the medicine? It was a litany, not unlike the Gregorian chants he had once heard, full of overpowering melancholy. Calm and ethereal, and sad as only the human voice can be sad. It rode on the stale air, swelling, diminishing, cutting through the stench of decay and rot with profound dignity.

Austin felt the heaviness of his clothes. The broken machines had stopped pumping fresh breezes, so the air was like oil, opening the pores of his body, running coldly down his arms and legs.

Bokawah made a motion with his hand and sank back onto the smooth floor. He breathed wrackingly, and groaned as if in pain. Then he straightened and looked at Austin and hobbled quickly away.

The drums began. Movement eased back into the throng and soon the dancers were up, working themselves back into their possessed states.

Austin turned, and walked quickly away from the ceremony. When he had reached the shadows, he ran. He did not stop running until he had reached the lift, even while his muscles, long dormant, unaccustomed to this activity, turned to stone, numb and throbbing stone.

He stabbed the button and closed his eyes, while his heart pumped and roared sound into his ears and colored fire into his mind. The platform descended slowly, unemotional and calm as its parts.

Austin ran out and fell against a building, where he tried to push away the image of the black magic ceremony, and what he had felt there.

He swallowed needles of pain into his parched throat.

And the fear mounted and mounted, strangling him slowly...

The Towers of Mbarara loomed, suddenly, to Austin, more unreal and anachronistic than the tribal rites from which he had just come. Stalagmites of crystal pushing up to the night sky that bent above them; little squares and diamonds and circles of metal and stone. Office buildings; apartments; housing units; hat stores and machine factories and restaurants; and, cobwebbing among them, all these blind and empty shells, the walkways, like colored ribbons, like infinitely long reptiles, sleeping now, dead, still.

Or, were they only waiting, as he wanted to believe?

Of course they're waiting, he thought. People who know the answers will come to Mbarara tomorrow. Clear-headed scientists who have not been terrorized by a tribe of beaten primitives. And the scientists will find out what killed the workers, correct it, and people will follow. Five hundred thousand people, from all over the closet-crowded world, happy to have air to breathe once more—air that hasn't had to travel down two hundred feet—happy to know the Earth can yet sustain them. No more talk, then, of "population decreases"—murder was a better word—; no more government warnings screaming "depopulation" at you...

The dream would come true, Austin told himself. Because it must. Because he'd promised Mag, and they'd lived it all together, endless years, hoped and planned and fought for the city. With Mbarara, it would begin: the dark age of a sardine-can world would end, and life would begin. It would be many years before the worry would begin all over—for half the earth lay fallow, wasted. Australia, Greenland, Iceland, Africa, the Poles... And perhaps then the population graph would change, as it had always changed before. And men would come out of their caverns and rat-holes and live as men.

Yes. But only Mbarara worked. If he could show them his success here...

Austin cursed the men who had gone back and screamed the story of what had happened to the other engineers. God knew there were few enough available, few who had been odd enough to study a field for which there seemed little further use.

If they'd only kept still about the disease! Then others would have come and...

Died. The word came out instantly, uncalled, and vanished.

Austin passed the Emperor, the playhouse he had thought of that night with Mag, ten years before. As he passed, he tried to visualize the foyer jammed with people in soup-and-fish and jeweled gowns, talking of whether the play had meat or not. Now, its marbled front putting out yellow glow, it looked foolish and pathetic. The placard case shone through newly gathered dust, empty.

Austin tried to think of what had been on this spot original-ly. Thick jungle growth alone. Or had there been a native village—with monkeys climbing the trees and swinging on vines and white widows mourning under straw roofs?

Now playing: JULIUS CAESAR. Admission: Three coconuts.

Be still. You've stayed together all this time, he thought, you can hold out until tomorrow. Tcheletchew will be here, sputtering under his beard, and they'll fly Mag to a hospital and make her well and clear up this nonsense in a hurry.

Just get home. Don't think, and get home, and it will be all right.

The city was actually without formal streets. Its plan did not include the antiquated groundcars that survived here and there in old families. Therefore, Mbarara was literally a maze. A very pretty maze. Like an English estate—Austin had admired these touches of vanished gentility—the areas were sometimes framed by green stone hedges, carved into functional shapes.

He had no difficulty finding his way. It was all too fresh, even now, the hours of planning every small curve and design, carefully leaving no artistic "holes" or useless places. He could have walked it blindfolded.

But when he passed the food dispensary and turned the corner, he found that it did not lead to the 'copter-park, as it should have. There were buildings there, but they were not the ones they ought to have been.

Or else he'd turned the wrong— He retraced his steps to the point where he had gone left. The food dispensary was nowhere in sight. Instead he found himself looking at the general chemistry building.

Austin paused and wiped his forehead. The excitement, of course. It had clouded his mind for a moment, making him lose his way.

He began walking. Warm perspiration coursed across his body, turning his suit dark-wet, staining his jacket.

He passed the food dispensary.

Austin clenched his fists. It was impossible that he could have made a complete circle. He had built this city, he knew it intimately. He had walked through it without even thinking of direction, in the half-stages of construction, and never taken a wrong step.

How could he be lost?

Nerves. Nothing strange in it. Certainly enough had happened to jar loose his sense of direction.

Calmly, now. Calmly.

The air hung fetid and heavy. He had to pull it into his lungs, push it out. Of course, he could go below and open the valves—at least *they* could be operated by hand. He could, but why? It would mean hunching down in a dark shaft—damn, should have made that shaft larger! And there were, after all, enough openings in the sealing-bubble to keep a breathable flow of oxygen in circulation. If the air was heavy and still outside the bubble, he could scarcely expect it to be different within...

He looked up at the half-minaretted tower that was one of the 'copter repair centers. It was located in exactly the opposite direction to the one he thought he'd taken.

Austin sank onto a stone bench. Images floated through his mind. He was lost; precisely as lost as if he had wandered into the jungle that had stood here before the building of Mbarara, and then tried to find his way back.

He closed his eyes and saw a picture, startlingly clear, of himself, running through the matted growths of dark green foliage, stumbling across roots, bumping trees, face grotesque with fear, and screaming...

He opened his eyes quickly, shook away the vision. His brain was tired; that was why he saw such a picture. He must keep his eyes open.

The city was unchanged. The park, designed for housewives who might wish to pause and rest or chat, perhaps feed squirrels, surrounded him.

Across the boating lake was the university.

Behind the university was home.

Austin rose, weakly, and made his way down the grassy slope to the edge of the artificial lake. Cultured city trees dotted the banks: the lake threw back a geometrically perfect reflection.

He knelt and splashed water into his face. Then he gulped some of it down, and paused until the ripples spread to the center of the lake.

He studied his image in the water carefully. White skin, smooth cheeks, iron-colored hair. Good clothes. A dolichocephalic head, evenly spaced, the head of a twenty-second century civilized...

Above his reflection, Austin detected movement. He froze and blinked his eyes. As the water smoothed, the image of an animal appeared on the surface, wavering slightly. A small animal, something like a monkey. Like a monkey hanging from the branches of a tree.

Austin whirled around.

There was only the darkness, the golfing-green lawn, the cultured trees—smooth-barked, empty.

He passed a hand through his hair. It was a trick of the lights. His subconscious fear, the shimmering water...

He walked quickly to the darkened boathouse, across its floor, his footsteps ringing against the stone, echoing loudly.

At the end of the miniature pier, he untied a small battery boat and jumped into it. He pulled a switch at the side, waited, forced himself to look back at the deserted bank.

The boat moved slowly, with only a whisper of sound, through the water.

Hurry, Austin thought. *Hurry— Oh God, why are they so slow!*

The boat, whose tin flag proclaimed its name to be Lucy, sliced the calm lake with its toy prow, and, after many minutes, reached the center.

The glow was insufficient to make the approaching bank distinct. It lay wrapped in darkness, a darkness that hid even the buildings.

Austin narrowed his eyes and stared. He blinked. It was the fuzziness of the luminescence, of course, that gave movement to the bank. That made it seem to seethe with unseen life.

It was only that his position to the shadows kept changing that made them turn into dark and feral shapes; trees, where buildings surely were, dense growth...

It was the milky phosphorescence of the metals that rose like marsh-steam from the nearing water...

He thought of stepping off the boat into a jungle, a magical forest, alive and waiting for him.

He closed his eyes and gripped the sides of the boat.

There was a scraping. Austin felt the cement guard, sighed, switched off the battery and leapt from the little boat.

There was no jungle. Only the lime-colored city trees and the smooth lawn.

The university sat ahead like a string of dropped pearls: blister-shaped, connected by elevated tunnels, twisting, delicate strands of metal and alloy.

Austin scrambled up the embankment. It must be very late now. Perhaps nearly morning. In a few hours, the others would arrive. And—

He halted, every muscle straining.

He listened.

There were the drums. But not only the drums, now. Other sounds.

He closed his eyes. The airless night pressed against him. He heard a rustling noise. Like something traveling through dense brush. He heard, far away, tiny sounds, whistlings, chitterings. Like monkeys and birds.

He tore open his eyes. Only the park, the city.

He went on. Now his feet were on stone and the park was behind him. He walked through the canyons of the city again, the high buildings, metal and crystal and alloy and stone.

The rustling noises did not cease, however. They were behind him, growing nearer. Bodies, moving through leaves and tall grass.

Austin suddenly remembered where he'd heard the sound before. Years ago, when he'd first visited this land. They had taken him on a hunting expedition, deep into the wild country. They were going to bag something—he forgot exactly what. Something strange. Yes; it was a wild pig. They had walked all day, searching, through the high tan grass, and then they had heard the rustling sounds.

Exactly like the sound he heard now.

Austin recalled the unbelievable fury of the boar, how it had disemboweled two dogs with a couple of swipes of those razor-sharp fangs. He recalled clearly the angry black snout, curled over yellow teeth.

He turned and stared into the darkness. The noises grew steadily louder, and were broken by yet another sound. Deep and guttural, like a cough.

As the sound behind him came closer, he ran, stumbled and fell, pulled himself from the stone, and ran until he had reached a flight of steps.

The coughing noise was a fast, high-pitched scream now, a grunting, snorting, a rush of tiny feet galloping across tamped earth, through dry grass. Austin stared blindly, covered his face with his arms, and sank back until the sound was almost upon him.

His nostrils quivered at the animal smell.

His breath stopped.

He waited.

It was gone. Fading in the distance, the rustling, the

coughing, and then there was the silence of the drums again.

Austin pressed the bones of his wrist into his throbbing skull to quiet the ache.

The panic drained off slowly. He rose, climbed the steps and walked through the shadowed courtyard onto the campus

It was a vast green plain, smooth and grassy.

Across from it, in sight, was Austin's home.

He gathered his reason about him like a shield, and decided against taking the other routes. If he had gotten lost before, it could happen again. Certainly now, with his imagination running wild.

He must cross the campus.

Then it would be all right.

He began treading, timorously at first, listening with every square inch of his body.

The shaman's voice slithered into his mind. Chanting. "... *you were destroying us against our will, Mr. Austin. Our world, our life. And such is your mind, and the mind of so-called 'civilized' men, that you could not see this was wrong. You have developed a culture and a social structure that pleased you, you were convinced that it was right; therefore, you could not understand the existence of any that differed. You saw us as ignorant savages—most of you did— and you were anxious to 'civilize' us. Not once did it occur to you that we, too, had our culture and our social structure; that we knew right and wrong; that, perhaps, we might look upon you as backward and uncivilized ...*"

The sound of birds came to Austin; birds calling in high trees, circling impossibly in the night sky.

"... *we have clung to our 'magic,' as you call it, and our 'superstitions' for longer than you have clung to yours. Because—as with your own—they have worked for us. Whether magic can be explained in Roman numerals or not, what is the difference, so long as it works? Mr. Austin, there is not only one path to the Golden City—there are many. Your people are on one path—*"

He heard the chatter of monkeys, some close, some far away, the sound of them swinging on vines, scolding, dropping to mounds of foliage, scrambling up other trees.

"—*my people are on another. There is room in this world for both ways. But your failure to grasp this simple fact has killed many of us, and it will kill many more of you. For we have been on our path longer. We are closer to the Golden City . . ."*

Austin clapped his hands to his ears. But he did not stop walking.

From the smooth stone streets, from the direction of the physics department, came the insane trumpeting of elephants, their immense bulks crashing against brittle bark, their huge feet crunching fallen limbs and branches . . .

The shaman's voice became the voice of Barney Chadfield . . . He spoke again of his theory that if one could only discover the unwritten bases of black magic and apply formulae to them, we would find that they were merely another form of science . . . perhaps less advanced, perhaps more.

The sounds piled up, and the feelings, and the sensations. Eyes firmly open, Austin thought of Mag, and felt needled leaves slap invisibly against his legs; he smelled the rot and the life, the heavy, wild air of the jungle, like animal steam; the odors of fresh blood and wet fur and decaying plants; the short, rasping breath of a million different animals—the movement, all around him, the approaches, the retreats, the frenzied unseen . . .

Eyes open, he felt and smelled and heard all these things; and saw only the city.

A pain shot through his right arm. He tried to move it: it would not move. He thought of an old man. The old man had a doll. The old man was crushing the doll's arm, and laughing . . . He thought of reflexes and the reaction of reflexes to emotional stimuli.

He walked, ignoring the pain, not thinking about the arm at all.

" . . . tell them, Mr. Austin. Make them believe. Make them believe . . . Do not kill all these people . . ."

When he had passed the Law College, he felt a pain wrench at his leg. He heard another dry-grass rustle. But not behind him: in front. Going forward.

Going toward his apartment.

Austin broke into a run, without knowing exactly why.

There was a pounding, a panting at his heels: vaguely, he was aware of this. He knew only that he must get inside, quickly, to the sanity of his home. Jaws snapped, clacked. Austin stumbled on a vine, his fingers pulled at air, he leapt away and heard the sound of something landing where he had just been, something that screamed and hissed.

He ran on. At the steps, his foot pressed onto something soft. It recoiled madly. He slipped and fell again, and the feel of moist beaded skin whipped about his legs. The thunder was almost directly above. He reached out, clawed loose the thing around his leg and pulled himself forward.

There was a swarming over his hands. He held them in front of his eyes, tried to see the ants that had to be there, slapped the invisible creatures loose.

The apartment door was only a few feet away now. Austin remembered his pistol, drew it out and fired it into the night until there were no more bullets left.

He pulled himself into the lobby of the unit.

The door hissed closed.

He touched the lock, heard it spring together.

And then the noises ceased. The drums and the animals, all the wild nightmare things—ceased to be. There was his breathing, and the pain that laced through his arm and leg.

He waited, trembling, trying to pull breath in.

Finally he rose and limped to the elevator. He did not even think about the broken machines. He knew it would work.

It did. The glass doors whirred apart at his floor, and he went out into the hall.

It was soundless.

He stood by the door, listening to his heart rattle crazily in his chest.

He opened the door.

The apartment was calm, silent. The walls glowed around the framed Mirós and Mondrians and Picassos. The furniture sat functionally on the silky white rug, black, thin-legged chairs and tables...

Austin started to laugh, carefully checked himself. He knew he probably would not be able to stop.

He thought strongly about Tcheletchew, and of the men who would come to Mbarara in the morning. He thought of the city teeming with life. Of the daylight streaming onto the streets of people, the shops, the churches, the schools. His work. His dream...

He walked across the rug to the bedroom door.

It was slightly ajar.

He pushed it, went inside, closed it softly.

"Mag," he whispered. "Mag—"

There was a noise. A low, throaty rumble. Not of anger; of warning.

Richard Austin came close to the bed, adjusted his eyes to the black light.

Then he screamed.

It was the first time he had ever watched a lion feeding.

Sorcerer's Moon

When he heard the screams, Carnaday stopped walking. A fist closed about his heart. He stood perfectly still, waiting, knowing that the end had come and that he had lost. He sniffed the air for sulphur, and wondered what form it would take, how it would happen. The screams grew louder, raking across his eardrums like angry claws. He forced himself to look up.

"Damn!"

He sighed. Two crows. Just that. Two crows, on a telephone pole, fighting. And what else could it have been? He cursed again and wiped the cold film of perspiration from his face. Why should he be afraid? It was Farrow who ought to be worrying now, if only the fool knew.

He glanced at the crows and smiled. If I were fanciful, he thought, I'd see a symbol there. A high, majestic perch with room for one, and two black creatures fighting for possession of it. Farrow and me, I'd say, if I were fanciful. Equal power in the legs. No advantage either way. But one will win and one will lose.

He listened to the battle cries and watched the war above, telling himself that he was not listening, not watching. The crow he identified as Farrow fought gamely, but the other resisted all assaults, and eventually the Farrow-crow shot, wounded, into the air and out of sight. Beaten.

Simon Carnaday nodded and hurried on, forgetting the episode. Although in his time, which was now approaching four hundred years, he had fetched corpses back to life, turned lead into gold, and joked with the Devil, he was nevertheless a skeptic at heart. What he did not understand, and he understood a great deal more than most people, he did not believe. Symbolism, to Carnaday, was superstitious nonsense. Psychiatry, though, was worse. It was the purest sort of buncombe, hardly as respectable as spiritualism. Which compounded Farrow's insult, made it insupportable, the last, the final straw.

As he strode down the dingy street, his shoeleather grinding the dark coat of soot and cinders, Carnaday recalled again that climactic conversation; and again it made his blood run hot. He could see Farrow's vulpine face, hear his soft, mocking voice...

"Really, Simon, you ought to see a good psychiatrist. I'm quite serious. This persecution complex of yours is beginning to worry me."

"It isn't a complex. It's a fact. I *am* being persecuted, and by you."

"Oh, nonsense. Be reasonable, Simon: why should I want to persecute you? For what purpose? I have everything I want—and so, for that matter, do you. Riches, comfort, eternal life. What could I possibly gain?"

"The one thing you don't have."

"Which is?"

"Distinction, Farrow. Distinction. We're the only two warlocks left on Earth, but that's one too many for you, isn't it? It upsets you. It gnaws at you. If I were a little less powerful, then it wouldn't be so bad. You'd at least have seniority. But our power is equal. And you can't stand it."

"Simon, Simon—what can I say? You're being absurd."

"Am I? Yesterday a car missed me by less than an inch. The day before, I nearly stepped into a manhole where no manhole should have been. Accidents, Farrow?"

"Of course! I mean, give me *some* credit, old man. If I were really trying to do away with you, do you suppose I'd go about it so crudely?"

"Well—"

"Believe me, Simon, what you need is psychiatric treatment. We may be sorcerers, but we're human, too, don't forget that. I'll find a good man, someone to trust, and send you his address..."

The letter had arrived the following day. But it had not contained an address.

Carnaday took the rune from his pocket and glared at it. Just a piece of parchment, with strange markings scrawled across its surface; yet it was a more powerful, a *surer* instrument of destruction than all the silly bombs in the world. "Damn Farrow!" he said, superfluously—they were, of course, both damned in any case—but then he remembered his cleverness, and smiled once more. For a while, he'd been numbed by panic. The rune had given him three days, and he had tried desperately to pass it back; but always without success. Farrow shrewdly resisted all attempts. He did not accept telegrams or special delivery letters. He did not respond to shouts of "Fire!" He did not touch papers. He stayed inside. And the time had drawn nearer, and nearer. Then Carnaday had had his inspiration, and he knew that all would now be well.

He walked up the evil-smelling, rickety staircase, and opened the cracked door.

"Mr. Bryan?"

A bald, thin, tiny-eyed man with dewlaps that hung like limp flags, looked up, squinting, through a haze of cigarette smoke. "Yeah," he said.

"My name is Carnaday. I called."

"Yeah."

"Let us be frank. I've heard, Mr. Bryan, that you are one of the best private detectives in the state, and that as a process server you recognize no peer. If that is true, then you stand to make a fair amount of money for a few hours' work. If it isn't true, then we are wasting our time."

The thin man shrugged, blinked, exhaled.

"Well?"

"Put it this way, Jack. I been in business twenty-five years. You stay in business twenty-five years, you ain't exactly inexperienced. Check-o?"

"A good point. But please be honest with me. In your capacity as process server, have you ever . . . failed?"

"Not yet."

Carnaday frowned. "This job," he said, "will be difficult."

The thin man smirked. "Tell you something, Jack. They're all difficult. All these bastards, they try to give you the dodge." He laughed, harshly. "But I know the tricks. I know tricks they never even thought of. In the end, I get them."

Carnaday rubbed his hands together. "Excellent. Then you'll work for me?"

"I work for anybody, any time."

"Yes; but there is one catch, Mr. Bryan. The paper must be delivered—personally, into the party's hands—before midnight tonight. That is absolutely essential. Can you do it?"

Bryan shrugged.

Carnaday placed five hundred-dollar bills on the glass-top desk. "Can you do it?" he repeated.

The thin man stared at the bills, then he picked them up, folded them, and put them into his pocket. "Let's have the paper," he said.

Carnaday took a last look at the markings on the rune, then inserted the parchment into an envelope and handed it, along with Farrow's address, to the detective. "You will find him at home," he said. "I'll wait here."

Bryan nodded and went out.

Carnaday leaned back in the chair. He prayed to the daemons of the Outer Circle, then to those of the Inner Circle, and, finally, to each of the Black Powers. He walked to the window and raised it, and stared at the moon, which was low and close, like a gigantic eye.

Nine o'clock came and went.

Then ten.

At eleven, Carnaday began to perspire. He knocked his hands together and paced, glaring at the moon.

Then the cracked door opened and the private detective walked in.

"Well?" croaked Carnaday anxiously.

The thin man grinned. "I thought you said it was gonna be difficult."

"It—wasn't?"

"Nah. Piece of cake. He played cute awhile, but then I gave him Routine Six. Routine Six always works."

Carnaday felt weary with relief. For the first time, he was pleased at Farrow's low opinion of his intelligence. It allowed him to catch the fool off guard. Hiring a process server to cast a rune—could there be a grander joke? He glanced again at the moon, which seemed closer and lower, and started out of the office.

"Just a second."

Carnaday turned around. "Yes? What is it?"

The detective smiled and pressed an envelope swiftly into the sorcerer's hands. "You forgot your receipt. For the five bills."

"Oh." Carnaday nodded, turned and got nearly to the door before his heart congealed into a hard icy knot. He tore the envelope apart. He looked at its contents.

"Like I told you," said Bryan, shrugging, "I work for anybody, any time."

Slowly, suggestively, the moon outside the window blinked.

The Trigger

It was a warm room; one, Ives decided, that had been lived in, despite its enormity. Real logs lay in a real fireplace. Originals by Wyeth and Benton and Hopper studded the walls. In a corner, near the concert grand piano, stood a fine mahogany bar, with a tasteful assortment of bottles—most of them half-full—on the shelves behind.

Not at all the sort of room a man would choose to commit suicide in.

Ives tapped the gleaming hardwood floor with his toe.

Lieutenant Bracker, a four-square giant of a man, turned and smiled. "Rug's out getting cleaned, I imagine," he said. "He used a .45. They make quite a mess."

"Yes." Phillip Ives brushed away the quick image that had sprung into his mind. He walked over to the mantel and inspected, for the tenth time, one of the numerous model racing cars that decorated the house. This was a bright red roadster, shark-snouted and, somehow, vicious.

"That's called a Ferrari," Bracker said. "Around twenty thousand bucks. Lawrence has a garage full of them."

"Had," Ives corrected, replacing the model. "Had."

Bracker shrugged. "Miserable word," he said. "But I don't hear much else lately."

A door opened and a woman entered the room. She might have been attractive; you couldn't tell. Now she looked lost and afraid.

"I'm sorry to have kept you waiting," she said. "I—wasn't dressed."

"That's perfectly all right, Mrs. Lawrence," Bracker said. in a surprisingly tender voice. "We won't stay long." He nodded his head toward the lean, short man in the corner, the man whose painfully plain suit and drugstore tie gave him

204

a meek, apologetic air. "This," Bracker said, "is Mr. Phillip Ives. He's connected with the Homicide Division in San Francisco. I hope you won't mind if he asks you a few questions."

The woman studied Ives, then went to the bar; she made three scotch-and-waters before replying. "Do you think Oscar was murdered?" she asked.

"No," Ives said, taking the drink. "The department has definitely ascertained that your husband took his own life."

"But—"

"Now that you've had some time to think, perhaps you can help us find a motive." There was something hard and metallic, expressionless, about the lean man's voice. It told you that he was more than just a policeman, more than a man with a job. A specialist called in to perform a delicate operation on a patient he'd never seen before would speak this way. Upon the patient's death, he would express sorrow; but only because he had failed in his duty—not because a life had been lost. He wouldn't be interested in life.

"There was no motive," the woman said, a bit angrily. "Oscar was a happy man."

"It has been my experience, Mrs. Lawrence," Ives commented, "that people who commit suicide are seldom happy. And they always have a reason. In your husband's case, can you recall any differences in his behavior prior to the . . . incident?"

"No."

"Are you quite sure?"

The woman walked to a window, then turned. "For the past year and a half," she said, "my husband was happier and more content than he'd ever been. Sports cars, as Mr. Bracker knows, were his hobby. He'd always wanted to be a sort of impresario, but business obligations never gave him the time. Then he retired, suddenly, and devoted himself completely to the thing he loved most. He was like a child—like a child who'd finally gotten the toys he had always dreamed about. Anyone can tell you!" She took a swallow of the scotch and shuddered. "He was the happiest man I've ever known!"

Ives set his drink aside. His eyes were cold. "Then you can say, *for certain*, that he was not behaving at all oddly toward the last?"

"For Christ's sake, man," Bracker said, taking a step.

"Well?" Ives demanded.

The woman stood very still; then, slowly, as if in defeat, she nodded. "He was—I don't know—moody the last week, you might say. Not a lot, actually. But—"

"But he was withdrawn, quiet, thoughtful?"

"Yes."

"Thank you, Mrs. Lawrence." Ives put on his sweat-stained Stetson, turned, and walked out of the room, out the door, into the damp and rain-flecked air. Bracker followed, an annoyed expression on his face.

"You don't care much for my tactics, do you, Lieutenant?" Ives asked.

"To be frank, no."

"Neither do I. Unfortunately, it is the only way I can get results."

"What results?"

"I'm not too sure. For one thing, we know that the pattern is unbroken. I spoke earlier with Mrs. Addison and Mrs. Vaile. They said essentially the same things. No reason for their husbands to commit suicide; yet each man had grown moody the week before. 'Thoughtful' . . ." The two policemen paused for a light to change. "May I have a look at that note again, Lieutenant? Lawrence's."

Bracker fished a photostat from his wallet. The words on it read, "Dearest Louise: I'm sorry. I know how unhappy this will make you, but it's the only way out."

"Out of what?" Ives murmured.

"You tell me," Bracker said. "That's why you're here."

The lean man smiled. "Of course." In eight months there had been four suicides. In each instance, the man had been a celebrated figure, or had been wealthy, all had achieved much in life. The local police had suspected murder, but that was out of the question.

So they had called in Phillip Ives, who possessed a reputation in his field. He was known as a fanatic. To him, there were Open Files, but never, never Unsolved Cases. The thwarting of criminals (not the undoing of crime) was his life. He had no special hours. No special home. No special office. Except in name: he was "with" the San Francisco Division of Homicide. A loner, they said, remembering vaguely that he was supposed to have had a wife, once. Just the man.

"I suppose you've observed that all four men belonged to the same club, Lieutenant?"

"Of course," Bracker said, exasperatedly. "The Sportsman's Haven. We're not stupid, Mr. Ives. We're just tired."

"I can understand that. I was merely thinking out loud." They stopped at a 1938 Chrysler sedan; it was faded gray, covered with forgotten dents and bruises; it sat, askew, as if victim to some horrible accident. "The answer," Ives said, clambering into the car, "is, nevertheless, at that place."

Bracker removed a handkerchief and wiped his face. "Mr. Ives," he said, "I hate to argue with you, because the chief thinks you're pretty hot. But after the second time we saw the coincidence, and I personally covered every member of the club. And there's nothing there; I mean, inside. But look—four guys are supposed to've knocked themselves off. First was Fred Addison. He got at least five hundred grand a year out of his lumber business. Nice wife, plenty of stuff on the side; and I checked 'em all out, too. No problems. Suddenly he decides to swallow half a can of lye. Lye! I mean, he knew what it'd do to his stomach, he was smart enough to know that! Okay. Next we have that young Parker kid. Millions, from his old man. Broads to burn. He shoves a letter opener into his chest, that's what they say. Just like that. And Vaile—you know, it's real easy to believe that a guy who's two steps from being governor of the state all of a sudden decides to jump out of a window. Real easy."

"What are you getting at, Lieutenant?" Ives asked, something of a smile at the corners of his mouth.

"Well," the big man said, "I know what the doc says; he says there wasn't any foul play. And I went over the whole business with a comb, and I couldn't find anything out of line, either. But, four suicides in eight months—all connected—it just doesn't happen."

"Yes, go on."

"I'll tell you the truth, Ives. I think it's murder. I think somebody, somewhere, has figured out a way to bump these guys so it won't show. The Cap thinks I'm in the bag, but—" Bracker gave a final swipe at his face with the handkerchief and flipped away the cigarette he'd been smoking. "I suppose that's what you think, too."

"To the contrary," the lean detective said. "There is no doubt whatever that the men were murdered. I'll talk to you later, Lieutenant."

Ives slammed the door and drove off, tires spinning on the wet cement.

*   *   *

The Sportsman's Haven was a squat, rather ugly building, constructed of tan bricks and hung with nautical symbols. In place of a doorknob was a small ship's wheel. A rusted bell, marked THISTLEDOWN, supplanted a buzzer. Ives rang the bell.

The door was opened by a sumptuously clad Negro. He said, "Yes?" after a good look up and down.

Ives removed a bulging plastic wallet from his hip pocket, plucked out his identification.

"Yes, sir," the Negro said.

The interior of the club was dimly lit; it resembled a high class cocktail lounge. Fish netting covered the walls. There were etchings of whalers and ancient four-masters, and photographs of yachts, mostly white. In the corners, tiny fires wriggled in chafing dishes. Exactly eighteen men occupied the room.

Ives put a cigarette in his mouth and ambled over to the far wall. Here a picture window gave a splendid view of the Sound: of the two immense yet graceful yachts sitting solidly, as though buried in cement, and of the numerous smaller craft, bobbing and rolling with the swells. And beyond, the mist-grayed water, rippling endlessly out of sight.

"May I be of some assistance to you?"

A large man in a flannel suit, topped with the inevitable cap, stood unsmiling. Clearly he was displeased. And, perhaps, nervous.

"It might be," Ives said. "Who are you?"

"The owner. Eric Korngold."

"Mr. Korngold, I'm with the police. We're troubled at the number of incidents that have taken place among the members of this club."

The large man nodded. "Terrible," he said. "Simply awful. I've thought a good deal about it; but it makes no sense whatever. When I heard about Mr. Lawrence I nearly fainted. Yes."

An inch-long ash fell, trailing gray down Ives's suit. "I'm going to speak frankly with you, Mr. Korngold. I know you've been bothered quite a bit with questions and snooping, but that can't be helped."

"Of course. I understand completely."

Ives nodded. "People kill themselves for a lot of reasons," he said. "Money is number one. Number two, however, is women. Now I've been informed that women are not allowed in the Sportsman's Haven. Is that correct?"

"Absolutely," Korngold said. "Without exception."

"Formally speaking, you mean."

"How's that?"

"Mr. Korngold, do you provide call girls for your club members?"

The man's face hardened into tight lines. For a moment he seemed unable to speak. Then he said, "No."

Ives shrugged. "Well," he said, "it was a thought. Thanks for your cooperation."

Korngold wheeled and strode angrily away.

He wouldn't lie, Ives thought. It would be too easy to check. Besides, Bracker has probably done it already. A smart cop. Damn!

He glanced over at the bar, which was dark and quiet. A tall, angular man in a white jacket stood wiping pony glasses. Another man sat over a drink, talking softly. That would be Carter Sexton, of the Sexton paper mills. Forty-three, married, father of two boys, rich.

Ives was suddenly overcome by a feeling of frustration. He had gone into the case with his usual sure-footed, imperious calm. And why not? Hadn't it been he who'd cracked the eight-year-old Yedor mystery, sending the benevolent Horton directly to the gas chamber? And who but Ives had hounded unhappy Mrs. Gottlieb into a full confession of her various poisonings? "It's the difficult cases that are easy," he'd often said. "The more complicated you get, the more likely you are to leave clues. Really *simple* murders are much, much harder to solve."

Well, there was nothing simple about this. It was a murder case without a murderer.

He sat down on the bar stool.

"Yes, sir?"

"Something strong," Ives said, his eyes closed. "Something that will warm my insides."

As he tried to sort out the pieces and fit them together, he heard, vaguely, the drone of voices. Mr. Sexton was whispering now. And the bartender was whispering, too, as he put various liquids into a short, thick glass.

"It is called a Black Russian," the angular man in the white jacket said. "I think you'll be pleased."

Ives threw it down recklessly. It did the job. "Another," he said. He noticed and did not notice that Sexton had gone out the door. "What's your name?" he asked when the bartender returned.

"Morrow," the man said. "Harold Morrow."

"Do *you* have any ideas?"

"About what, sir?"

"About the deaths."

"Of course, Mr. Ives." The bartender smiled. "Oh, you're famous, sir—that is, to anyone who dabbles in true crime. I recognized you at once."

"Flattered." Ives took another swallow of the drink, which was a rum concoction. "Also, baffled. Are you?"

The bartender retained his smile, which exuded small delight. "Baffled, sir, and fascinated. I knew the gentlemen well, and I can't imagine any reason for them to have done what they did. It's not my business to pry; still, they seemed such, well, such *happy* men!"

Ives murmured something indistinct. For three days he had been investigating, examining, thinking; now his brain was tired, as he was tired. Perhaps it was coming home, after so many years. No; Seattle wasn't home. It was just a place.

"It's certainly a pity, sir, that you'll finally have to admit to an unsolved case. Rodney Brown mentioned in his study of California murders that you would never recognize the existence of such a thing—an unsolved case, that is. But here you are."

"Yes. Here I am. Morrow, how is it that you know so much about me?"

"As I said, sir, true crime is a hobby of mine. I'm no expert or anything, but I read the books—Boucher, Roughead, Pearson, Brown. And you figure quite prominently in most of them."

Ives hiccuped. He found that he liked this fellow, wanted to stay and hear more. The voice had a soothing, melodious quality to it; Morrow seemed to understand, the way bartenders are supposed to.

". . . but think they're unfair," he was saying. "Picturing you as such an inhuman machine. That's what Sherlock Holmes was, but he was an imaginary character. Boucher mentions that you had a wife, sir. Is that true?"

"Yes," Ives said.

The voice went on, and suddenly, his mind loosened by the

drinks, and by the memory of familiar landmarks, he began to think of Greta. After such a long time. For a while he dwelled on the happy days; then, as he knew it must, the final picture—the picture of the apartment and its odd smell; of the doctor, leaning over the bed of Greta, still and unmoving—came into focus. God, if he'd only stayed home. If he hadn't gone out on that ridiculous, miserable case . . . she might have lived. But, alone, with no way to reach the telephone, no way to call out—

". . . it must be a lonely life," the bartender said.

"It is," Ives responded, distantly.

"I don't know what I'd do if I were in your shoes," Morrow went on. "Brown hints that it was your ambition that killed your wife, but that seems terribly harsh . . ."

On and on the man talked, slowly, carefully, in the melodious voice.

On. And on.

When the remembering crowded in his head, Ives tossed down the drink, placed two dollars on the bar, and went outside.

The air did no good. He knew that it was true: he had killed Greta, and he was lonely, and that was why he was such a fanatic, such a droll Sleuth. And also true he had failed in this case. It made no sense and it would never make sense.

He walked across the slimy boards, up the stairs, to the edge of the street.

When the light turned to green, he stepped out; from another street a bus came groaning, preparing for a left turn. Ives continued, hardly seeing at all. He thought of Greta. And he thought, if this is failure, then what is the usefulness of Phillip Ives?

A part of him whispered, the pain could end. It could end. All you have to do is wait a second longer, take a step; just one.

The memories exploded. He started forward.

"Hey, buddy—watch it!"

Ives automatically jumped aside; the vast, helpless bulk of the bus swept within inches of him, its horn bleating.

"You okay?" a man asked.

Ives shook his head. "Yes. I—" Suddenly he realized what he had almost done and it chilled him. "Thank you."

The man hurried off.

Ives stood still, while people brushed by him, thinking.

Then he clenched his fists and ran to the parked Chrysler, hoping, praying that he would not be too late.

He was precisely one hour too late. By the time he reached the gray-white mansion on the hill, Carter Sexton was dead. The millionaire lay sprawled across an Oriental rug, a bullet lodged somewhere inside his skull.

"Ives," Lieutenant Bracker barked, "how in the holy hell did you know about this? I just got the call twenty minutes ago myself!"

"There is no time for explanations," Ives said, replacing his hat. "Let's say this. If I'd been a little smarter, Sexton would be alive. If I'd been a little dumber, I'd be dead along with him."

"Hold on, damn it. You can't just toss something off like that. I want to know how you—"

The lean detective whirled around and walked briskly out of the room. He went to a public telephone booth and placed a call. Then he got into his car and drove to Queen Anne Hill.

Two hours and thirty minutes later he reappeared at the Sportsman's Haven.

"Bartender!"

The angular man in the white jacket looked up. A flicker of surprise crossed his face. "Mr. Ives, I thought you'd gone."

Ives stared at the man. "A Black Russian, Harold," he said. "Have one with me. I wish to celebrate."

The drinks were prepared with uncertain haste.

"Mr. Sexton is dead, by the way," Ives said. "Did you know?"

The bartender gasped. "But—are you serious? I was talking to him only a few hours ago! How—did it happen?"

"Oh, shot himself," Ives said, casually.

"That's very bad news. He was one of our finest members."

"Yes." Ives lifted the glass. "Mr. Morrow?"

The bartender frowned. "I honestly can't see what you find to celebrate, in view of this shocking—"

"Why," Ives interrupted, "the conclusion of the case."

Morrow smiled, wryly. "I'm afraid I made those first ones a bit too strong."

"Not at all. Harold, and I hope I may call you Harold—I believe I have figured out this riddle. Would you care to hear my answer?"

"Yes," the bartender said. "I would, very much."

"Well," Ives said, scraping a fleck of egg from his tie, "it's this way. And bear with me, for it does get complicated in parts. Well: four people—I beg your pardon; five people—commit suicide. They are supposedly happy, however, and have no apparent reason for committing suicide. But now, Harold, as any psychologist will tell us, this is a very doubtful sort of a proposition. It takes an awful lot to get a man to conquer his natural instinct for survival. Were they the victims of foul play, we wondered? No. Though the view was held by certain officers, it was merely a desperate reaction, one might say. These deaths were, most definitely, suicides.

"We had only one pattern: the men belonged to this club. Beyond that there was no logic, no thread. Or so we thought. Then I discovered another pattern, and it was damned important. *These were all human beings.* May I have another drink?"

The bartender mixed the fluids hurriedly, served someone else who had appeared, returned. "Please go on, Mr. Ives."

"Well, I dropped the criminological approach, because it wasn't getting us anywhere, and tried to remember what I'd read of human psychology. One thing came back, clearly. I forget the book. 'Within each human heart there is a trigger. When a person destroys himself, we know then that something, or someone, has pulled that trigger.' You wouldn't recall who said that, would you, Harold?"

The angular man was silent.

"Anyway," Ives went on, "it meant that every human being on Earth is a potential suicide. Every person on Earth is capable of it, just as he's capable of murder; and needs only the right combination of circumstances—mental or physical. So: obviously, Harold, something or someone was activating the trigger mechanism on each of our unfortunate club members. I preferred to think, some*one*. Which is really quite extraordinary. In fact, the first new method of murder I've encountered in ten years!"

"It's certainly an interesting theory, I'll say that," the bartender said; "but it isn't much more than that, is it, Mr. Ives?"

"Oh, I suppose not. Still, let me go on. I did some investigating, some digging around in the pasts of the recently departed. Starting chronologically, I looked up the facts on Fredric Addison, our first case. He had a hundred and sixty-two thousand in the bank, a loving wife, et cetera. But there was something else. I hit upon it in one of the newspapers. In 1943, Mr. Addison got into some trouble with a Marine. The Marine claimed Addison had made 'untoward advances' on him after inviting him up to the apartment for a non-existent party. Of course, Addison paid off, and the episode was blown away. But it's interesting, wouldn't you say?"

The bartender picked up a towel and began, slowly, to wipe a martini glass. The hum of conversation from the main room filtered in. "I don't believe I follow you, sir."

"You will. Next I examined Ray Vaile's record. A clean one, on the surface. But deeper down, do you know what I found? Vaile had once been in love with a certain motion picture actress; they'd been engaged. Then she dumped him, and he married a local girl. But he wrote impassioned letters to the actress for years afterwards. Parker, a draft-dodger, a coward. Oscar Lawrence was a humanitarian sort. A driver had been killed in one of his racing cars. Some columnists put the blame on Lawrence's shoulders. As for Sexton, he'd washed out of college. Plagued with doubts about his intelligence. Felt bad about it. Now do you see, Harold?"

"No," the bartender said, the light from the martini glass reflecting in white slivers on his face.

"Oh, come. Those were the *triggers* of the men! Their Achilles' heels, if you like. Of course, they'd hidden them, even from themselves; but, now, Harold, if someone were to uncover these sore points, bring them out into the open . . . it's not too difficult to understand their actions then."

"It's quite a theory, Mr. Ives."

"But I'm not finished. I began to think on all cylinders once I'd reached that hypothesis. Very well, very well. I had a method: but what about the other details? How did this fit in with the coincidence of all the men belonging to the same club? It got easier once I'd licked that problem."

"And did you lick it?"

"Yes. Obviously, Harold, there would have to be one person at the club—the murderer—busily engaged in pulling triggers, as it were. One person all the others would instinctively trust, regard almost as a friend—or perhaps as a father confessor. I began to think about him. What was he like? What would his motive be?"

Ives deliberately peeled the cellophane off a package of

cigarettes, tore out a folded square of silver foil, removed a cigarette.

"Smoke?"

"No."

"Well, the motive. He'd have to be interested in psychology, needless to say. More than likely, his apartment would be filled with textbooks on the subject. Secondly, he would have to be either a bored millionaire, indulging in the game for the intellectual sport of it, or—"

"Or what?" the bartender asked.

"Or," Ives continued, lighting the cigarette at last, "he'd have to be a frustrated fellow—one who felt he ought to be as successful as those around him, for, of course, he was a good deal brighter than they. Frustrated and vengeful, I thought, and a little batty, too. There are a lot of people like that, you know, Harold: people who can't abide the good fortune of others. Sometimes they feel that Fate has cheated them, and this is good, because then their fury is impotent; they can only blame Fate. Sometimes, though, they blame society or even, in advanced cases, the very persons they envy so. In that event it's nasty, because eventually they go off their heads and start shooting.

"I decided that my man was among this group: a self-styled god, only without worshippers. He'd knocked around for years, hanging to the periphery of the high social world in one capacity or another, letting his hate build up. Then he'd hit upon his truly unique method of murder—perhaps the cruelest I've ever heard of—and that was that. Well, what do you think, Harold?"

"Mr. Ives," the bartender said, "they certainly didn't exaggerate when they said you were a man of imagination. But—" He picked up another glass, began polishing it. "But granting the theory, I'd say you were in a bad way."

"Oh?"

"Well, I mean, even if you found this fellow and he admitted—to you—that it was true, there'd be nothing you could do to him. What if he told you that he had every intention of going on with his 'murders,' as you call them? What then? You'd have to spend the rest of your life watching, helplessly, while he killed whoever he cared to."

Ives sucked smoke into his lungs and grinned; it was not a nice thing to see. "You're assuming, Harold, that I'm an honest cop. But I'm just as much of a fanatic in my own way as he is in his. One failure, just *one*, and it will all have been for nothing. So, if I ever find him (and I don't mind admitting this; you'll never get anyone to believe you if you repeated it) I'll simply frame him. It would be my word against him, you see. And—well, I know a couple of doctors who would be glad to do me a favor, make a suicide look exactly like a murder."

The bartender stopped wiping the glass.

"However," Ives said, "since he *is* a fanatic, such measures really won't be necessary."

There was a silence.

The next suicide occurred on the following morning. It was phoned in by one of two policemen who had been diverted from their usual route and sent to the home.

Bracker sat down. "You were right," he said, in a voice filled with suspicion and awe. "He shot himself through the mouth."

Phillip Ives nodded, somewhat wearily.

"Now would you mind explaining how the devil you knew about it? He hasn't been dead over six hours. No one heard the shot. You've been with me, here, all night—come on, Ives, before I go out of my mind! How did you know Harold Morrow was going to kill himself?"

"He didn't," Ives said. "I killed him. In a way."

Lieutenant Bracker looked on the verge of hysteria. He got up, walked to the tiny window, came back, and slammed his palm down on the table. "Goddamn it! I—"

"Sit back down, Lieutenant. I'll be glad to tell you what happened."

Ives spoke carefully, with his eyes closed, as if dictating the story for later transcription in a memoir.

When he stopped talking, Bracker's jaw had dropped. The big policeman shook his head.

"You see, your theory of murder was correct, after all."

"Just a second," Bracker said. "The framing part I get—I can even see this maybe scaring Morrow into suicide. But you didn't use that?"

"No. Once I'd realized, standing there in front of the bus, ready to stay rooted and be killed, once I knew that he was our boy, I phoned information for his address. Getting into the apartment was simple enough; it was a common lock. There I found several hundred books on psychology and true crime (which, doubtless, one of your men saw, without really seeing); also, in one of the volumes, information on all Sportsman's Haven members. Three more were slated to die, incidentally. Morrow had spent a lot of time finding their weak spots, and he'd found them, all right. Anyway, it was enough to show the extent of his psychosis. It was enough to show that the man considered himself perfect. To such a person, failure was unthinkable."

"So?"

Ives smiled. "So I simply pointed out to him that there would always be *one* failure, one person whose hidden trigger he would never find."

"Yours?"

"No. His. Even God, I told him, did not have it within His power to commit suicide. When Morrow saw that this was true, he became so depressed that he killed himself."

Bracker opened his mouth and closed it again.

"Then again," Ives said, "perhaps he wanted to prove that I was wrong, and that he *was* perfect. In any event, the case is closed. May I buy you a coffee, Lieutenant?"

The Love-Master

"My wife is frigid," said the young man, getting directly to the point. "That's the long and the short of it."

"Nonsense!" Salvadori raised a dessicated finger to his fine Roman nose. "Women," he declared, "are creatures of milk and blood and fire; they are cradles of delight, ships of spices, doorways leading to lands of wonder!"

"That may be," responded the young man. "But my wife Beatrice—"

"—is no different." Candlelight shot the rapids of the Love-Master's brook-gray hair as he nodded impatiently. "I assure you of that."

"You don't know her."

"She is a woman? Young? Healthy?"

"Yes."

"Then I do not need to know her." Salvadori rolled the wheelchair up close to his visitor and studied the lean, pale features. There was something vaguely disturbing here, something a bit off-center, but he could not place it. Perhaps the hat, a large and incongruous Stetson. "Mr. Cubbison, I trust that you, yourself, are not—ah—"

The young man flushed. "There is nothing wrong with me," he said. "Physically."

"Then," Salvadori said, "you have little to worry about. Only remember this: There is no such thing as a frigid woman. They are all as alike as locks, and want but the proper key."

"Nice simile," Cubbison granted, "but not very believable. I've tried everything."

At that the Love-Master grinned, crookedly, like an ancient tiger. He was incredibly old, that much one could see in the parchmented flesh, the veined and white-whiskered arms, the woollen shawl tucked under tremblous knees; but there was power of a kind in that creaking hull of skin, and from those dark olive eyes there shone a light that told of other years, better days.

"*Everything*, Mr. Cubbison?"

Once again the visitor flushed. His glance traveled uncomfortably over the dusty room, returning at last to the old man in the wheelchair. "I think perhaps we ought to get down to business," he said nervously. "But I warn you, I haven't much faith in love potions or spells or any of that sort of thing."

"Nor do I," replied Salvadori. "They are buncombe."

Cubbison's eyes flickered. "I'm afraid I don't understand," he said. "I'd heard that you were some kind of a wizard."

"And so I am," the old man laughed. "In a way. But I am no thief. I offer no magical formulae for success: merely the benefit of personal experience. This disappoints you?"

"It surprises me."

"Then you are typical. I cannot count the number of young frustrates who have come to me expecting miracles, hoping for pentagrams or, at the very least, genii. They all felt quite cheated when I offered them, instead, conversation. But that attitude changed soon enough."

"Indeed?"

"Oh, yes. For, you see, I have never had an unsuccessful case."

"Never?"

Salvadori adjusted his white silk scarf. "Never," he said, humbly. His eyes momentarily gathered the distance of years. "There is actually nothing complex or sinister about it," he said. "Had I been a great matador in my youth, I would today be dispensing advice to neophyte *toreros;* similarly if I had been a great race driver, or hunter, or soldier. As it happens, I was a great lover." He sighed. "Alas, the rewards for my endeavors were not tangible. They could not be carried in the pocket, like a bull's ear, or mounted on the mantel, like a gold cup; yet they were real enough, and I have them all—*here*." Salvadori tapped his forehead.

Cubbison coughed, and the old man's mind surfaced.

"Well, young fellow, do you want to avail yourself of my services, or not?"

"I can't see that it would do any harm."

"Very well, then. Pull up a chair."

The thin, hatted man dusted the seat of a harp-back with a handkerchief of fine linen, and moved forward. "About the price—" he began.

"Afterward," Salvadori chuckled. He settled his iron-maned head against the pillow, closed his eyes and murmured: "Describe the subject. High points only, please."

"Well, she's . . . fairly attractive. Twenty-seven years of age. Hundred and ten pounds, I imagine. Good shape. May I smoke?"

"Describe the subject, Mr. Cubbison."

The young man took a long puff on the cigarette, then blurted, "Dammit, she's a fish, that's all. When we married, I understood that she'd been everywhere, done everything; you know, woman of the world. But I can't believe it. No matter what one tries, Beatrice simply shakes her head and treats the whole thing as if it were a pathetic joke. Of course, she *claims* to want to love—don't they all?—and she *pretends* to co-operate, but the end is always the same. Sometimes she cries, or laughs, or sits awake all night smoking; mostly she just says, 'Sorry, no good.'"

Salvadori listened carefully. Occasionally he would open one eye, then close it again. At length, when the visitor had concluded, he put his hands together and said, "Mr. Cubbison, I am glad to report that yours is one of the more basic dilemmas. I anticipate no difficulty whatever."

The young man's eyes widened. "You can say that?" he asked. "After all I've told you?"

"Of course." Salvadori leaned forward in the wheel chair. The guttering candle brought his handsome profile into sharp relief. "In fact, I shall prescribe a comparatively mild, but highly effective, remedy. Cubbison, have you ever heard of 'The Chinese Flip' method?"

"No, I can't say that I have."

"Then listen. Performed with anything approaching accuracy, this should put an end to your problem." Upon which remark, Salvadori went on to describe in minute detail Method #12 which he'd learned a half-century before in Bechuanaland. He observed the shocked expression on his visitor's face and went through it all a second time.

"Good Lord," said the young man.

"Nothing, really, once you get the hang of it. But a word of caution—don't overdo. And now, good evening. I will see you tomorrow at midnight."

The Love-Master watched the gaunt young client walk dazedly from the room; then, when the door was closed, he fell into a sleep of dreams.

Next evening at twelve the soft knock came, and Salvadori wheeled his aging body to the door. It was Mr. Cubbison, looking frailer and paler than ever before.

"No saccharine displays of gratitude," the Love-Master murmured, "and, please, no lurid descriptions. A simple check for one hundred dollars will suffice."

But the young man did not smile or make a move toward his checkbook.

"What's the trouble; are you ill?" Salvadori inquired, frowning. "It went well, needless to say?"

"No," the visitor said. "It didn't."

"Not at all?"

"No."

"Hmm." Salvadori looked startled for an instant, then regained his composure. "Well," he smiled, "it appears I underestimated the subject. Score one for her!"

"I'm afraid it isn't any use," Cubbison said, sighing deeply. "Of course, if you could meet her—that is—"

"Sorry! I no longer make house calls. It's a cardinal policy I've had to adopt, for reasons that should be manifest. For almost twenty years, Cubbison, women have tried to seduce me out of retirement; they have come by the hundreds and employed every low trick known to the female mind, but always they have failed. In the School for Scandal I am a professor *emeritus*, and so it must and shall remain. Besides, we're in no trouble yet. Merely a call for stronger medicine . . ."

The old man tented his fingers and thought for a long time.

"Cubbison, I think we are going to try a little something called 'The Australian Hop'—a facetious-sounding but nonetheless lethal technique, originally developed for a certain recalcitrant maiden in the brush country, who—but never mind that. Tell me, how are your muscles?"

"All right, I suppose."

"Then pay strict attention. The first step . . ."

In a way, Salvadori felt ashamed, for Method 18 was nominally for advanced students. It was a lot of technique for an amateur to handle. Still, there was one's reputation to consider; and though one might become old and jaded, one had to eat . . .

* * *

When the gloved knock sounded again the following night, Salvadori chuckled, imagining the beatific expression of his client.

"Well?"

Cubbison shook his head sadly: there was a look of ineffable weariness—and defeat—about his eyes. "No go," he said.

Salvadori blinked. "This," he hawked, "is difficult to believe. You followed my instructions?"

"To the letter."

"And the subject... did not respond?"

"Oh, she responded, all right. Like a dead eel. Like a frozen trout— See here, Mr. Salvadori, I'm very much afraid that Beatrice is beyond even your powers. I think we ought to give up. She and I will just go on living like sister and brother."

"What?" The Love-Master reached out a trembling hand and laid it across his client's face. "Mr. Cubbison, don't be obscene. You have not, I hope, orally capitulated with your wife?"

"Beg pardon?"

"Let it go. Be quiet a moment; I must think." Salvadori made fists and put them to his temples. "In the summer of '04," he said slowly, "in Florence, I made the acquaintance of a certain princess, an altogether ravishing vessel but, alas, caught up like a fly in the web of virtue. It was perhaps my second most trying case, hard fought and won at no small expense. However, *won*. As I recall, it was Method 26—'*The Drunken Reptile*'—that turned the trick."

Mr. Cubbison, looking thin and wan beneath the Stetson, shrugged.

"My boy, my boy," Salvadori said gently, in a voice thick with confidence, "you mustn't despair. Remember: 'No tree so tall/it cannot fall.' Now listen..."

As the Love-Master spoke, seated there like a time-lost fragment of Roman sculpture, Cubbison's eyes grew large and frightened and occasionally he gasped.

Then he grinned. "Salvadori," he said, "what you have just described is without doubt the most shocking thing I've ever heard. But," he rose, "it might work!"

"Might? It will," the old man said. "You can count on that. Beatrice will love you forever!"

But when the visitor left Salvadori did not find sleep so easy. It had been a long time since he'd heard of a woman whose defenses could withstand both *The Chinese Flip* and *The Australian Hop*. He could not even imagine a woman in *this* age upon whom Method 26 would not work its fiendish spell.

And yet . . .

"She laughed at me," the hatted Cubbison said, hotly. "Called me a damned acrobat!"

"You are surely exaggerating!"

"Not a bit. Laughed, I tell you. Said, 'Bunny, that's a scream!'"

"At what point?"

"The penultimate point. Where, according to your thesis, she ought to have been undulating in helpless frenzies."

"Gad." Salvadori bit his lip. "In this case, I fear it's time we brought out The Big Guns. Mr. Cubbison, yours has turned out, I must confess, to be a rare case; most rare, indeed. But the battle is not lost."

At which time the Love-Master, throwing caution to the winds, explained the workings of Method 34. *'The Tasmanian Trounce, Double Switchback and Rebound!'* It shocked even *his* hardened sensibilities; but it was fool-proof. No female could resist its insidious puissance; not possibly!

"She fell asleep," Cubbison said, one night later.

Salvadori got a wild, frantic look in his eyes. He outlined the dreadful Method 37—*'The Creeping Terror'*—which, he recalled, had driven the Marquis de Silva Ramos's wife mad as a March hare thirty summers previous.

"She yawned," said Cubbison.

And Salvadori thought, *What a woman! She must indeed have been everywhere and done everything!* Carefully, he went through his entire repertoire, not excluding the nerve-shattering *'Belgian Carousel'* (Method 51) nor even *'Roman Times'* (Method 60), held in reserve since its first use on the adamant Lady Titterington, long gone to her reward.

But always it was the same. Always Cubbison would return with his report of failure. "She giggled," he would say; or, "She just looked at me."

Until at last, Salvadori saw clearly that there was but one thing to do.

"Mr. Cubbison, I have reached a decision. It violates my strictest rule of business, but, under the circumstances, there is, unhappily, no choice."

"Yes?" said Mr. Cubbison.

"There is one technique," Salvadori whispered, "which I have not mentioned. Method 100. It bears no name. It is absolutely guaranteed: on that, sir, I would stake my life." His countenance reddened with fierce pride. "However—to describe it to you would (and I mean no offense) be tantamount to handing a jar of nitroglycerin to a three-year-old baboon. I shudder to think of the consequences of even one small error . . . Only two men have ever mastered Method 100. The first, or so the rumor goes, was Don Giovanni. The second, myself. Therefore—"

The young client leaned forward, breathing heavily.

"Therefore, I shall make my first house call in fifteen years!"

Cubbison leaped to his feet; he seemed on the edge of tears. "Salvadori, can you mean it?" he quavered. "Would you?"

The old man raised a claw. "I dislike emotional excess," he said with distaste. "Please sit down and pay attention. Now: you will make very certain that the room is in darkness. Understood?"

"Yes, of course."

"And do not call me until the subject is nearly asleep. That is quite important. Should my identity be discovered"—Salvadori gave way to a paroxysm—"I'd have no peace for the rest of my days. The subject would be at my door constantly, entreating, imploring, threatening . . . It would be horrible."

"But," said Cubbison, "here is something. If *I* cannot repeat Method 100—"

"Once," Salvadori said, "is enough. She will, of course, go on hoping, but meanwhile (the ice having been broken, as it were) the other techniques will suffice."

The young man took the Love-Master's bony shoulders. "I—I hardly know what to say."

"Say good night, Mr. Cubbison. I do this only because it is necessary, and do not wish to dwell on it. I shall see you later."

Having braved the strumpet winds, Salvadori sat panting wearily in the darkened alcove, ruminating with displeasure on the ordeal before him. When a knight is old, he mused, heavy lie the cudgels. Heavy the mace and heavy the dirk, and hard the battle.

He began to nod sleepily.

Then a voice whispered, "Now!" and the Love-Master straightened, senses alert. He rolled the chair in rubbery silence to the black room and entered.

"Cubbison?" he hissed softly.

No answer.

Well enough. Instinct brought him to the panoplied bed. Reflex put him into it.

He lay still for a time, going over Method 100 in his mind; then, listening to the steady breathing, absorbing the feral warmth, reluctantly he struck.

It went perfectly.

At the precise moment planned, he hurled his wizened frame back into the chair, exited the room, whispered "Cubbison, hop to it!" and caromed clattering out of the house, into the dark and wind-swept streets.

All over. He rumbled loose a mighty sigh. Reputation or no reputation, he told himself, rolling up the concrete ramp to his quarters, he would never again break the rule.

Sleep for the Love-Master was immediate.

Promptly at midnight the next evening, there came again the gloved knock. Salvadori set aside his dish of smoked oysters. He was weak and racked with bamboo shoots of pain, but no longer disturbed.

"Come in, Mr. Cubbison."

The young man entered; he was smiling peculiarly.

"The charge," Salvadori said crisply, "is one thousand dollars. Cash, if you don't mind."

The visitor laid ten one-hundred-dollar bills on the scarred table.

"I trust it went well?"

"Oh, yes!"

"Everything satisfactory?"

"Yes!"

"Then, Cubbison, good-by to you."

The visitor, however, made no indication that he was prepared to leave. His smile grew broader. Then, suddenly, he rushed forward and planted a kiss on Salvadori's forehead.

"Damn it, boy," the old man spluttered, "get away!" Then Salvadori, the Love-Master, touched his assailant and gasped. His eyeballs threatened to roll from their sockets.

For the visitor, still smiling, had stepped back and, for the first time, removed the large Stetson; and golden locks of hair had cascaded forth.

"Cubbison, in the name of decency!"

"I hope that you'll forgive me, darling," the visitor said, taking off coat, trousers, shirt and other encumbrances, "but it was the only way I could have you. And I couldn't take less!"

Salvadori's knuckles bleached against the chair arms. Within moments, to his profound dismay, he was staring at a woman of immense beauty—full-rounded, soft, and white as an elephant's tusk.

"Cubbison!" Salvadori croaked, refusing to believe the trick that had been played. *"Cubbison!"*

The woman paused. "Call me Beatrice," she said.

And then she sprang.

Three Thirds of a Ghost

I.
THE BARON'S SECRET
or
A CURIOUS INCIDENT
Being a Complete
Chronicle of the Extraordinary Events
of a Particular Night
in the Life of Sir F—;
Together with an Inquiry Regarding
the Limitations of Human Knowledge
and a Moral as to the Proper
Conduct of British Gentlemen.

It came to pass that on a lovely autumnal day in the year 18—, a certain Sir F— set off on a walking tour of Germany. Although equipped with a full complement of navigational apparatus, he took a wrong turning near the picturesque village of K— and, on the fourth day, found himself hopelessly lost in the dreaded B— Forest. Calling upon his ample reserve of good humor, Sir F— essayed a chuckle, dined upon the last of his provender, and struck off down a likely-seeming path. The shades of evening descended, and with them the first ominous portents of storm. Soon the heavens opened to release a cataract of rain, accompanied by freezing gales and a celestial cannonade of singular intensity; and Sir F— counted himself more than fortunate when, some hours later, he espied what appeared and subsequently proved to be a castle.

Guided by nature's erratic beacon, the traveler fought his way through the storm to the great stone edifice. Hesitating not at all, he proceeded to apply the knocker. At length the door was opened.

Within stood a man of extraordinary visage. Bearded, monocled, clad entirely in black, he held aloft an ornate silver candelabrum and smiled crookedly through a webwork of old sabre scars.

"Ja?" demanded he, in German. "What is it?"

Sir F— identified himself and stated, succinctly, the substance of his dilemma. "I realize, of course, that it is a frightful imposition—"

"Not a bit of it," interrupted the bearded man, this time in perfect English. "It is not often I have guests, so perhaps you will forgive the lack of preparations." He gazed out at the raging storm, sniffed the air like a great dark animal and gestured Sir F— inside.

Baron von T— (for that was his name) proved to be a thoughtful and considerate host, despite his somewhat forbidding appearance. Sir F— was led through the stone halls of the castle to an immense bedroom, where he was given a complete change of clothing and an opportunity for regaining his composure, after which dinner was announced. On his way downstairs, the Englishman took notice of a large oil-portrait, which depicted a young and, to Sir F—, extremely beautiful woman. "Hulloa," exclaimed he, pausing; "Who's this?"

"My wife, the Baroness von T—," answered the bearded man, and they continued to the dining area.

It was a vast cave of a room, feebly illuminated by two candelabra and the great open hearth. Several moments passed before Sir F— observed the presence of a third party. As his eyes became accustomed to the gloom, he saw that a woman was seated near the far end of the long wooden table. His heartbeat accelerated when he recognized the woman as none other than Baroness von T—, whose likeness he had so lately admired, and he thrilled to the prospect of an introduction; however, as the Baron continued to speak of his various passions, which included falconry, dueling, and the study of warfare, it was evident that no introduction would be forthcoming. Sir F— seated himself at the foot of the table, which placed him in close juxtaposition with the Baroness—who was, he found upon closer scrutiny, even lovelier than he had imagined, lovelier, indeed, than any other woman he had seen; so lovely, in fact, that he could scarcely concentrate upon the Baron's penetrating analysis of the current political scene.

"I entirely agree," stated Sir F— at what he took to be an appropriate juncture. His voice quavered, however, for at this exact moment he felt the pressure of what could be nothing if it was not a leg. Flushing, Sir F— downed the remainder of his veal and toasted the Baron's hospitality. Again he felt the pressure, more definite than before. From the corner of his left eye he could see the wine-red dress, the night-black hair, the crimson lips of Baroness von T—. Unable to believe the testimony of his senses, he looked directly at her. To his amazement, she smiled, dropped her hand below the table and rested it, for a brief moment, upon his knee.

"Now," stated the Baron, "you must be very weary."

"Yes," agreed Sir F—. "Very."

"Tomorrow morning I will ride with you to G—. A railway will take you where you wish to go."

Rising unsteadily, for he had partaken liberally of the excellent Napoleon, Sir F— bowed in the direction of the baroness, saluted the baron, turned, and walked through the halls and up the stairs to his room.

The gigantic four-poster proved to be the most comfortable bed he had ever encountered, just as the dinner was the finest he could recall ever having eaten, and the brandy certainly superior to all other brandies in his experience. Warmed and exhilarated by the memory of the evening, Sir F— blew out the candle and settled in for sleep; but sleep would not come. In his mind he continued to see the face of Baroness von T—, inscrutable, mysterious, inviting. Ruminating thus, Sir F— was startled to hear the creak of the door. He sat upright in the bed, and allowed his jaw to drop when he recognized the figure of the baron's wife.

If she was beautiful in the dining room, she was ethereal here. A nightgown surely made of butterflies' wings and spiders' webs concealed, without concealing, her body, which Sir F— decided must be the most perfectly proportioned extant. Her dark hair wafted in a weightless tumble across her china-white shoulders, and in the flickering light of the tiny candle which she held, it seemed as if her face had been carved from a single exquisite piece of ivory.

"Baroness," exclaimed Sir F—, "is anything the matter?"

"Hush," quoth she, touching a slender finger to her full lips; whereupon the baroness set the candle upon the floor, went to the bed and, smiling a smile of utmost friendship, delivered unto Sir F— a kiss which he subsequently described as "two parts fire, one part honey."

It would be agreeable to record that Sir F— comported himself in a meritorious and honorable fashion, but such, unhappily, was not the case. Instead, perhaps owing to the Napoleon, he yielded *in toto* to instincts the existence of which surprised even Sir F—.

"————," whispered Baroness von T—, when Sir F— made so bold as to ——.

"——," answered he.

"————"

"——"

While the storm howled outside the unshuttered windows, they ———— the night long; then, at the —'s first crow, the baroness bestowed a last —— on Sir F—'s —— and, smiling again the friendly smile, picked up the spent candle and darted silently from the room.

Sir F— sank into the suppliant arms of Morpheus, and did not awaken for several hours. When at length he felt rested, he rose, dressed in his own dry clothes, and walked downstairs. The baron greeted him and together they rode, on flame-red stallions, to the village of G—. But Sir F— could not but observe that in contrast to his manner of the previous evening, Baron von T— seemed moody and uncommunicative. As they waited at the railway depot, Sir F— felt a twinge of conscience, and blurted, "I suppose it's about your wife."

"Yes," offered the baron, his eyes widening. "How did you guess?"

"Guess?" put in Sir F—.

"Today would be our anniversary."

"Would be?"

Suddenly the Baron grasped Sir F— by the shoulders and cried, "My good friend! What would you do if you discovered that your wife had been unfaithful to you?"

"I would work fearful punishment," replied Sir F—, "on her."

"Ja, ja! You understand! Six months ago we had a guest. A man. In the middle of the night I awoke with fear in my heart. I went to the guest's room—the same occupied by yourself. There—there—"

"Yes?"

"I found them. Together!"

Vaguely, Sir F— heard the approaching thunder of the train. "And?" hissed he.

The baron beat a harsh tattoo upon his chest. "I ordered the guest from my home."

"And the baroness?"

"I confess! Too long has it been hidden! I killed her. With my hands! These hands! And now she is dead. Do you understand?"

Unable to answer, Sir F— boarded his train. And for years afterward, he could not hear the expression, "laying a ghost," without suffering a reaction variously described by his friends as hysteria, Sydenham's chorea, and fantods.

Place of Meeting

It swept down from the mountains, a loose, crystal-smelling wind, an autumn chill of moving wetness. Down from the mountains and into the town, where it set the dead trees hissing and the signboards creaking. And it even went into the church, because the bell was ringing and there was no one to ring the bell.

The people in the yard stopped their talk and listened to the rusty music.

Big Jim Kroner listened too. Then he cleared his throat and clapped his hands—thick hands, calloused and work-dirtied.

"All right," he said loudly. "All right, let's us settle down now." He walked out from the group and turned. "Who's got the list?"

"Got it right here, Jim," a woman said, coming forward with a loose-leaf folder.

"All present?"

"Everybody except that there German, Mr. Grunin—Grunger—"

Kroner smiled; he made a megaphone of his hands. "Grüninger—Barthold Grüninger?"

A small man with a mustache called out excitedly, "Ja, ja!... s'war schwer den Friedhof zu finden."

"All right. That's all we wanted to know, whether you was here or not." Kroner studied the pages carefully. Then he reached into the back pocket of his overalls and withdrew a stub of pencil and put the tip to his mouth.

"Now, before we start off," he said to the group, "I want to know is there anybody here that's got a question or anything to ask?" He looked over the crowd of silent faces. "Anybody don't know who I am? No?"

232

It came another wind then, mountain-scattered and fast: it billowed dresses, set damp hair moving; it pushed over pewter vases, and smashed dead roses and hydrangeas to swirling dust against the gritty tombstones. Its clean rain smell was gone now, though, for it had passed over the fields with the odors of rotting life.

Kroner made a check mark in the notebook. "Anderson," he shouted. "Edward L."

A man in overalls like Kroner's stepped forward.

"Andy, you covered Skagit valley, Snohomish and King counties, as well as Seattle and the rest?"

"Yes, sir."

"What you got to report?"

"They're all dead," Anderson said.

"You looked everywhere? You was real careful?"

"Yes, sir. Ain't nobody alive in the whole state."

Kroner nodded and made another check mark. "That's all, Andy. Next: Avakian, Katina."

A woman in a wool skirt and gray blouse walked up from the back, waving her arms. She started to speak.

Kroner tapped his stick. "Listen here for a second, folks," he said. "For those that don't know how to talk English, you know what this is all about—so when I ask my question, you just nod up-and-down for yes (like this) and sideways (like this) for no. Makes it a lot easier for those of us as don't remember too good. All right?"

There were murmurings and whispered consultations and for a little while the yard was full of noise. The woman called Avakian kept nodding.

"Fine," Kroner said. "Now, Miss Avakian. You covered what?... Iran, Iraq, Turkey, Syria. Did you—find—an-ybody a-live?"

The woman stopped nodding. "No," she said. "No, no."

Kroner checked the name. "Let's see here. Boleslavsky, Peter. You go on back, Miss Avakian."

A man in bright city clothes walked briskly to the tree clearing. "Yes, sir," he said.

"What have you got for us?"

The man shrugged. "Well, I tell you; I went over New York with a fine-tooth comb. Then I hit Brooklyn and Jersey. Nothin', man. Nothin' nowhere."

"He is right," a dark-faced woman said in a tremulous voice. "I was there too. Only the dead in the streets, all over, all over the city; in the cars I looked even, in the *offices*. Everywhere is people dead."

"Chavez, Pietro. Baja California."

"All dead, señor chief."

"Ciodo, Ruggiero. Capri."

The man from Capri shook his head violently.

"Denman, Charlotte. Southern United States."

"Dead as doornails..."

"Elgar, David S...."

"Ferrazio, Ignatz..."

"Goldfarb, Bernard..."

"Halpern..."

"Ives...Kranek...O'Brian..."

The names exploded in the pale evening air like deep gunshots; there was much head-shaking, many people saying, "No. No."

At last Kroner stopped marking. He closed the notebook and spread his big workman's hands. He saw the round eyes, the trembling mouths, the young faces; he saw all the frightened people.

A girl began to cry. She sank to the damp ground, and covered her face and made these crying sounds. An elderly man put his hand on her head. The elderly man looked sad. But not afraid. Only the young ones seemed afraid.

"Settle down now," Kroner said firmly. "Settle on down. Now, listen to me. I'm going to ask you all the same question one more time, because we got to be sure." He waited for them to grow quiet. "All right. This here is all of us, every one. We've covered all the spots. Did anybody here find one single solitary sign of life?"

The people were silent. The wind had died again, so there was no sound at all. Across the corroded wire fence the gray meadows lay strewn with the carcasses of cows and horses and, in one of the fields, sheep. No flies buzzed near the dead animals; there were no maggots burrowing. No vultures; the sky was clean of birds. And in all the untended rolling hills of grass and weeds which had once sung and pulsed with a million voices, in all the land there was only this immense stillness now, still as years, still as the unheard motion of the stars.

Kroner watched the people. The young woman in the gay print dress; the tall African with his bright paint and cultivated scars; the fierce-looking Swede looking not so fierce now in this graying twilight. He watched all the tall and short and old and young people from all over the world, pressed together now, a vast silent polyglot in this country meeting place, this always lonely and long-deserted spot—deserted even before the gas bombs and the disease and the flying pestilences that had covered the earth in three days and three nights. Deserted. Forgotten.

"Talk to us, Jim," the woman who had handed him the notebook said. She was new.

Kroner put the list inside his big overalls pocket.

"Tell us," someone else said. "How shall we be nourished? What will we do?"

"The world's all dead," a child moaned. "Dead as dead, the whole world . . ."

"Todo el mund—"

"Monsieur Kroner, Monsieur Kroner, what will we do?"

Kroner smiled. "Do?" He looked up through the still-hanging poison cloud, the dun blanket, up to where the moon was now risen in full coldness. His voice was steady, but it lacked life. "What some of us have done before," he said. "We'll go back and wait. It ain't the first time. It ain't the last."

A little fat bald man with old eyes sighed and began to waver in the October dusk. The outline of his form wavered and disappeared in the shadows under the trees where the moonlight did not reach. Others followed him as Kroner talked.

"Same thing we'll do again and likely keep on doing. We'll go back and—sleep. And we'll wait. Then it'll start all over again and folks'll build their cities—new folks with new blood—and then we'll wake up. Maybe a long time yet. But it ain't so bad; it's quiet, and time passes." He lifted a small girl of fifteen or sixteen with pale cheeks and red lips. "Come on, now! Why, just think of the appetite you'll have all built up!"

The girl smiled. Kroner faced the crowd and waved his hands, large hands, rough from the stone of midnight pyramids and the feel of muskets, boil-speckled from night hours in packing plants and trucking lines; broken by the impact of a tomahawk and a machine-gun bullet; but white where the dirt was not caked, and bloodless. Old hands, old beyond years.

As he waved, the wind came limping back from the mountains. It blew the heavy iron bell high in the steepled white barn, and set the signboards creaking, and lifted ancient dusts and hissed again through the dead trees.

Kroner watched the air turn black. He listened to it fill with the flappings and the flutterings and the squeakings. He waited; then he stopped waving and sighed and began to walk.

He walked to a place of vines and heavy brush. Here he paused for a moment and looked out at the silent place of high dark grass, of hidden huddled tombs, of scrolls and stone-frozen children stained silver in the night's wet darkness; at the crosses he did not look. The people were gone; the place was empty.

Kroner kicked away the foliage. Then he got into the coffin and closed the lid.

Soon he was asleep.

Afterword
Christopher Beaumont

I had no idea that the Fifties were dull. The current crop of films and literature dealing with the relative calm of the Eisenhower years has been, to a certain extent, news to me.

I was born in 1950, and from the get-go there was a revolution going on. Members of the Revolutionary Council included Bradbury, Matheson, Serling, Nolan, Russell, Tomerlin, Johnson and, of course, Beaumont. The enemy was the mold, and surrender was not an alternative. The Holy Grail was the human spirit, and my father fought with the passion of a man who somewhere knew his time was short.

Revolutions tend to breed excess, and his were legend; expensive race cars, trips to Monaco at a moment's notice, special blends of peanut butter shipped weekly from a shop in the Chicago of his youth. But always there was a gentleness, a tenderness and, most important to a young boy trying to be heard, an ability to listen. He loved to listen. He listened to Beethoven, to Bradbury, to Picasso, to Steinbeck, to Matheson, to family, to friends. And then he would take what he had heard into his study, and the work would begin. And we would wait, and wonder, and sometimes worry. But then the door would open, and it would be our turn to listen.

The stories in this book are windows; windows onto a soul that burned so bright and sang so loud that fourteen years after his death I still see shadows, I still hear echoes. And I always smile whenever I hear someone speak of those terribly dull Fifties.

From *The Seven Faces of Dr. Lao,* by Charles Beaumont

MIKE—CLOSE SHOT

The boy juggles faster and faster without making a mistake. As the CAMERA DRAWS BACK, slowly, Dr. Lao's wisdom filters in:

DR. LAO'S VOICE

Mike . . . the whole world is a circus, if you look at it the right way. Every time you pick up a handful of dust and see not the dust but a mystery, a marvel, there in your hand . . . every time you stop and think "I'm alive, and being alive is faantastic" . . . every time such a thing happens, you are a part of the Circus of Dr. Lao.

Christopher Beaumont
Los Angeles, California
May 1981